DOVER·THRIFT·EDITIONS

Sentimental Education
The Story of a Young Man

Gustave Flaubert

Edited by
DORA KNOWLTON RANOUS

Introduction by
LOUISE BOGAN

DOVER PUBLICATIONS, INC.
Mineola, New York

DOVER THRIFT EDITIONS

GENERAL EDITOR: MARY CAROLYN WALDREP
EDITOR OF THIS VOLUME: T. N. R. ROGERS

Bibliographical Note

This Dover edition, first published in 2006, is an unabridged republication of the uncredited translation, edited by Dora Knowlton Ranous, that was published by Brentano's, New York, in 1922. The Introduction by Louise Bogan is reprinted from the edition of *Sentimental Education* published by New Directions Books, New York, in 1957.

Library of Congress Cataloging-in-Publication Data

Flaubert, Gustave, 1821–1880.
   [Education sentimentale. English]
   Sentimental education : the story of a young man / Gustave Flaubert ; translated by Dora Knowlton Ranous ; introduction by Louise Bogan.
     p. cm.
   "An unabridged republication of the uncredited translation . . . that was published by Brentano's, New York, in 1922. The introduction by Louise Bogan is reprinted from the edition of Sentimental education published by New Directions Books, New York, in 1957"—T.p. verso.
   ISBN 0-486-45233-6 (pbk.)
   1. Young men—Fiction. 2. Married women—Fiction. 3. Unrequited love—Fiction. 4. Paris (France)—Fiction. 5. France—History—February Revolution, 1848—Fiction. 6. Paris (France)—History—June Days, 1848—Fiction. I. Ranous, Dora Knowlton, 1859–1916. II. Title.

PQ2246.E4E5 2006
843'.8—dc22

2006046345

Manufactured in the United States of America
Dover Publications, Inc., 31 East 2nd Street, Mineola, N.Y. 11501

Contents

BOOK II

Introduction

by
Louise Bogan

L'Éducation sentimentale appeared in 1869; it was Flaubert's third published novel. It bore the title of an early work, written between 1840 and 1845, which Flaubert had abandoned and left unpublished, on the advice of his friend, Louis Bouilhet, who then suggested to him the setting and theme of *Madame Bovary.* Both the early and the published versions told the story of Flaubert's youth, but while the first version was filled with a still active Romanticism, the second, coming after *Madame Bovary* (1857) and *Salammbo* (1862) showed Flaubert in full possession of his mature powers. He was forty-eight, and he had come into a settled and large view of the life and social institutions of his time. Viciously attacked by the critics and neglected by the general public at its appearance, *L'Éducation sentimentale* is now generally acknowledged, by modern French critics, as Flaubert's masterpiece. A profound and sardonic comment on Flaubert's own generation and the France of his young manhood, it has remained pertinent to the human and social dilemmas of our own day.

Only a few friends—Banville, the Goncourts, George Sand—understood the book's intentions or appreciated Flaubert's success in putting them through. Sand realized that Flaubert's readers were still too close to the events described, and too involved in the Second Empire point of view, to wish to appreciate the novel's ruthless analysis of social change and human motives. They recognized themselves too easily. And Sand complained that Flaubert gave no overt clue as to where his sympathies lay. She wanted "an expression of blame . . . to condemn the evil. People do not understand that you wanted precisely to depict a deplorable state of society which encourages bad instincts." Flaubert had run into this sort of obtuseness in the French public (and government) before this, on the occasion of the suit brought against the "morality" of *Madame Bovary.* He was incapable of agreeing with Sand's rather sentimental moralistic demands. His idea of the relation between the individual and society was far more complicated than

hers. Society warped the individual, but was it not individuals who had created, and blown up to enormous proportions, the idea of government?
Perhaps the basic evil lay deeper in the constitution of the human heart.

Flaubert was depressed by the book's failure. He wrote in 1874 to
Turgenev that he was still astonished that this work had never been
understood. He finally decided that the book lacked "the falseness of
perspective." "Every work of art," he said, "ought to have a point, a summit, make a pyramid . . . or better, the light should strike some point of
the sphere. Now, there's nothing of that sort in life. But Art is not
nature!" Here Flaubert partially understands that in this novel he has created a new genre—a genre from which modern novelists are still deriv-
ing richness of material and fullness of approach. Critics, including
Henry James, have misunderstood the book's conclusions because they
were in no way dealing, here, with "realism," "naturalism" or "romance,"
but with satire of a high but hidden order.

There is no doubt that *Sentimental Education* is a difficult book to get the
hang of, at first reading. The reader must have a fair working knowledge of
reaction and revolution in nineteenth-century France. To use a figure of
Lowes Dickinson, France was, throughout the century, politically in a state
as though tracked by the Furies. It was a century of nervous unrest and of
new and untried theory. And all the theories, once applied, backfired in the
most appalling way. The revolt against the Bourbon line brought in the July
monarchy (1830) and Louis-Philippe's dead-weight bourgeois rule.
Universal suffrage, granted after 1848 and thought to be the instrument to
establish the kingdom of God on earth, resulted only in Louis Bonaparte,
and, after three years of the Second Republic, in the Second Empire. Paris
fought for freedom; the provinces, fighting for the still unlaid ghosts of the
old régime and of Napoleon, finally voted away the newly granted franchise
itself. Added to the political melee was the social one. The Industrial
Revolution struck France in the thirties, in the factories of Lyons. All political parties were thrown into the rise of money and the new concept of the
right to work. The resulting confusion was severe. It is precisely this confusion, mirrored in the characters of the men and women who are at once its
creators and its victims, that Flaubert here describes.

The book, written under the Second Empire, covers the period from
September 1840 to Louis Napoleon's *coup d'état* of December, 1851—save
for the last two chapters, which form a coda to the whole. The action,
excepting a few short passages, is seen through the eyes of Frederick
Moreau, of the provincial landed class, newly come to Paris as the book
begins to pass his law examinations. A new spirit is in the air. The tradition of Romanticism and of the Bohemian painter, writer and poet had
worn almost completely threadbare. The period of the career based on
money deals of one sort or another (*Enrichissez-vous* was said to be the

counsel of Louis Philippe to his subjects) had begun. Art and industry, art and journalism, stood opposed, in spite of naive efforts to reconcile their purposes. (*Industrial Art* is the name of the magazine run by Arnoux, the husband of the woman Frederick comes to adore; the same paper under the unprincipled Hussonet begins under the name *Art* and ends up entitled *The Man About Town*.) Stock-jobbing, loans, investments and mortgages were the preoccupation of deputies and ministers. Borrowing a little money and making more, getting in with "influential people," occupied the minds of law students, writers, painters and hangers-on. The movement of opportunism elaborates and expands into a mounting frenzy. Notes fall due; debts pile up; the fate of men and women depends upon the worth or worthlessness of shares. Bankruptcies, auctions, bailiffs finish the hopes of guilty and innocent alike. Underneath runs the theme of personal treachery. Friends betray one another; old men revenge themselves in their wills; women take it out on rivals by holding over them old debts and promissory notes.

The revolts of Republicans and the new Socialist against bourgeois rule form the book's secondary theme. The theorists make plans and hold to rigid formulas. Spontaneous outbreaks of the people link up with the planned action of the revolutionaries. Barricades go up; arms are requisitioned from the citizens. The crowd swarms into the Tuilleries; pianos and clocks are flung out of windows. One of the novel's great set-pieces describes the street fighting in 1848. And the book closes with Paris again under arms—the dragoons, aided by the police, galloping against the citizens under the gaslight with drawn sabres—and the Second Empire has begun.

Senecal, the democratic dogmatist who develops by degrees into a tyrant and member of the police, is the character which has astonished modern readers by its deadly accuracy and contemporary pertinence. "Why, then, have you not got the volumes of the working-men poets?" Senecal asks, when shown a library. He wants, in literature, content and not form. He thinks *tableaux vivants* demoralizing for the daughters of the proletariat. As a factory overseer, he extracts fines ruthlessly. "Democracy," he remarks, "is not the unbounded license of individualism. It is the equality of all belonging to the same community before the law, the distribution of work, order." "You are forgetting humanity!" Frederick answers. It is Senecal who kills Dussardier, "the honest fellow," the believer in Socialist virtue, who attributed all the evil in the world to authority.

And Flaubert traces down an insane desire for authority, of whatever kind, in these people who have lost so many natural links to life. "France, no longer feeling herself in command of the situation [after 1848] was beginning to shriek with terror, like a blind man without his stick or an infant that has lost its nurse." And the reader continues to recognize these characters (all of whom, according to Maxime du Camp, had prototypes in reality). There is something startlingly familiar in Hussonet, the journalist, who praises fifth rate, and fears first rate, minds. Arnoux, the intermediate type between Bohemian and businessman, infected with the failings of both—"his intelligence was not high enough to attain to art, nor commonplace enough to desire merely profit, so without satisfying anyone, he had ruined himself"—is closely akin to Frederick, who feels the resemblance. Arnoux is a gourmet and gives little dinners "with ten sorts of mustard." Deslauriers, Frederick's friend, in the words of the Goncourts, is, "with his fond envy, his intermittences of perfidy and friendship, his solicitor's temperament, a perfectly drawn type of the most widespread kind of scurvy humanity." Mlle Vatnatz, the emancipated woman, venomous, the dupe of her passions, a literary hack and go-between with a business head, is still not a complete grotesque.

Then there is the gallery of conservative humbugs, male and female, whom Flaubert does not spare. "The fascination of self-interest equalled the madness of want . . . Property attained in the public regard the level of Religion, and was confounded with God. The attacks made on it appeared sacrilege, almost a species of cannibalism." But Flaubert was out to show up both sides of the picture. He examines with the same detachment the hysterics, terrorists and fakes on the fringes of the Socialist movement, and the conservative money and power jugglers with their "distinguished" circle, ready to grease the palm of any government that came into power. The stupidity of the workers' meeting and the complicated spite of the dinner party are both analyzed. Flaubert wished to clear the reader's mind of all "accepted ideas" concerning the supposed nobility of either group. Suddenly, at the end of the book, we look back and see how each category has received its touch of clearsightedness: these liberals who are at bottom neurotic reactionaries; these members of a new middle class who not only have no intellectual interests, who do not act according to motives of patience, pity, duty, charity or generosity, but actually do not know that such qualities exist. And has Flaubert exempted from his satiric justice of treatment the supposed projection of an actual life-long love, Mme Arnoux? She has been thought to stand in the book as an unclouded exponent of womanly sweetness and virtue. Is she not, rather, a sort of *Madame Bovary* in reverse—a woman who rejects passion because she pietistically fears God's punishment, whose virtue brings her to the pass of offering herself, in age, to a man who suddenly recognizes the true incestuous nature of his devotion to her?

Within the prevalent atmosphere of fiasco, bafflement and fraud, Flaubert releases from time to time effects of tender comedy and moments of delicate and evocative description. He was working, we now realize, at the very beginning of impressionism, when the source was still fresh (Manet and Degas were slightly younger contemporaries). Emotional passages have behind them, over them and *through* them, the full beauty of the natural or man-made scene: architecture, landscape, weather, the seasons and the time of day. Light and shadow fall with varied precision; the slipperiness of the city pavement in the rain becomes part of Frederick's passion as the sight of a kitchen garden in his native town becomes part of his melancholy. Details are often rendered with fantastic sharpness: the whole *décor* of the period, from lamp-lit interiors to the glitter of the equipages in the Champs Elysées—clothes, furniture, jewels, food, flower arrangement, coiffures, silver, china, carpets—become indelibly fixed in the reader's mind. Color, sound and odor rise freshly from page after page—the scent of a meadow or of a woman's perfume; the sound of a well-chain; the pink of a satin chair. It is the method which, although evident in Flaubert's successors, has never been equalled by even the most gifted among them.

The psychological truth of the book's two final chapters is profound. For in these two scenes Flaubert's uncanny knowledge of the pathology of modern life becomes evident. The nostalgic reminiscence of Frederick and Deslauriers casting back over their youthful frightened visit to the prostitutes' house, reveals the continuing infantilism of these two grown-up children who have never been able to lift themselves over the threshold of maturity, who cannot learn, who can only, in spite of some native generosity and decency, repeat. The modern split between emotion and reason stands revealed. Flaubert elsewhere remarks: "You do not possess Christianity any more. What do you possess? Railroads, factories, chemists, mathematicians. Yes, the body fares better, the flesh does not suffer so much, but the heart continues to bleed. Material questions are resolved. Are the others? . . . And as you have not filled that eternal yawning gulf which every man carries in himself, I mock at your efforts, and laugh at your miserable sciences which are not worth a straw." *Sentimental Education* is a handbook to the present because the gulf of which Flaubert speaks, after nearly a century, has not been filled, but only widened and deepened. The thirst for some saving authority is still apparent; the intolerance has assumed new forms. Let us examine our theorists, Flaubert says, and throw out their false premises. Let us enlarge the provable human data. Have these nervous insurrections accomplished anything? Are we following the "advanced notions" of a parcel of "buffoons"? Should "the government of a country be a section of the Institute, and the last section of all?"

Some partial answer lies in this novel, written in the "ivory tower" of Croisset and published one year before the inauspicious events of 1870, which ushered in the Third Republic.

BOOK I

CHAPTER I

A PROMISING EPISODE

IN FRONT of the Quai St. Bernard, the *Ville de Montereau,* which was just about to start, was puffing great whirlwinds of smoke. It was six o'clock on the morning of the 15th of September, 1840.

People rushed on board the vessel in frantic haste. The traffic was obstructed by casks, cables, and baskets of linen. The sailors answered no questions. People jostled one another. Between the two paddle-boxes was a heap of parcels; the clamour was drowned in the loud hissing of the steam, which, making its way through the plates of sheet-iron, encompassed everything in a white mist, while the bell at the prow kept continuously ringing.

At last, the vessel drew away; and the banks of the river, crowded with warehouses, timber-yards, and manufactories, opened out like two huge ribbons being unrolled.

A young man about eighteen, with long hair, holding an album under his arm, stood motionless near the helm. Penetrating the haze, he could see steeples, buildings of which he did not know the names; then, with a farewell glance, he observed the Ile St. Louis, the Cité, and Nôtre Dame. As Paris faded from view he heaved a deep sigh.

Frederick Moreau had just taken his Bachelor's degree, and was returning home to Nogent-sur-Seine, where he would have to lead a monotonous existence for two months, before going back to begin his legal studies. His mother had sent him, with enough money to cover his expenses, to Havre to see an uncle, from whom she had expectations of his receiving an inheritance. He had returned from there only yesterday; and he consoled himself for not having been able to spend a little time in the capital by taking the longest possible though less convenient route to reach his own part of the country.

The uproar had subsided. The passengers were all taking their places. Some of them stood warming themselves around the machinery, and the chimney spat forth with a slow, rhythmic rattle its plume of black smoke. Drops of dew glistened on the copper plates; the deck quivered with the vibration from within; and the two paddle-wheels, rapidly turning, lashed the water. The river edges were covered with sand. The vessel swept past rafts of wood which oscillated under the rippling of the waves, or a boat without sails in which a man sat fishing. Then the drifting haze cleared; the sun appeared; the hill which had been visible on the right of the Seine subsided by degrees, and another rose nearer on the opposite bank.

Frederick was thinking about the apartment which he would occupy over there, on the plan of a drama, on subjects for pictures, on future passions. He was beginning to find that the happiness merited by the excellence of his soul was slow in arriving. He declaimed some melancholy verses as he walked rapidly along the deck till he reached the end at which the bell was. In the centre of a group of passengers and sailors he saw a gentleman talking soft nothings to a country-woman, while fingering the gold cross which she wore over her breast. He was a jovial blade of forty, with frizzled hair. He wore a jacket of black velvet, two emeralds sparkled in his cambric shirt, and his wide, white trousers fell over odd-looking red boots of Russia leather ornamented with blue designs.

The presence of Frederick did not discompose him. He turned round and glanced several times at the young man with winks of inquiry. He next offered cigars to all who were standing near him. But, apparently getting tired of their society, he moved away and took a seat further up. Frederick followed him.

The conversation, at first, was on the various kinds of tobacco, then quite naturally it turned into a discussion about women. The gentleman in the red boots gave the younger man advice; he put forward theories, related anecdotes, referred to himself by way of illustration, and he gave utterance to all these things in a paternal tone, with the ingenuousness of entertaining depravity.

He was republican in his opinions. He had travelled; was familiar with the inner life of theatres, restaurants, and newspapers, and knew all the theatrical celebrities, whom he spoke of by their first names. Frederick told him confidentially about his projects; and the elder man took an encouraging view of them.

He stopped talking a moment to take a look at the funnel, then he mumbled rapidly a long calculation in order to ascertain "how much each stroke of the piston at so many times per minute would come to," etc., and, having found the number, he spoke about the scenery, which he admired immensely. Then he expressed his delight at having got away from business.

Frederick regarded him with a certain amount of respect, and politely intimated a desire to know his name. The stranger, without a moment's hesitation, replied:

"Jacques Arnoux, proprietor of *L'Art Industriel,* Boulevard Montmartre."

A man-servant in a gold-laced cap came up and said:

"Would Monsieur have the kindness to go below? Mademoiselle is crying."

L'Art Industriel was a hybrid establishment, wherein the functions of an art journal and a picture-shop were combined. Frederick remembered seeing this title several times in the bookseller's window in his native place on big prospectuses, on which the name of Jacques Arnoux displayed itself magisterially.

The sun's rays fell perpendicularly, shedding a glittering light on the iron hoops around the masts, the plates of the barricades, and the surface of the water, which, at the prow, was cut into two furrows that spread out as far as the borders of the meadows. At each curve of the river, a screen of pale poplars presented itself with the utmost uniformity. The surrounding country at this point had an empty look. In the sky were little white clouds which remained motionless, and the sense of weariness, which vaguely diffused itself over everything, seemed to retard the progress of the steamboat and to add to the insignificant appearance of the passengers. With the exception of a few persons of good position who were travelling first class, they consisted of artisans or shopmen with their wives and children. It was customary at that time to wear old clothes when travelling, so nearly all had their heads covered with shabby Greek caps or discoloured hats, and wore thin black coats that had become threadbare from constant rubbing against writing-desks, or frock-coats with the casings of their buttons loose from continual service in the shop. Here and there some roll-collar waistcoat afforded a glimpse of a coffee-stained calico shirt. Pinchbeck pins were stuck into torn cravats. List shoes were kept up by stitched straps.

Frederick, in order to get back to his place, pushed against the grating leading into the part of the vessel reserved for first-class passengers, and in so doing disturbed two sportsmen with their dogs.

What he then saw was like a vision. She was seated in the middle of a bench all alone, or, at least it appeared so to him; he could see no one else, dazzled as he was by her eyes. At the moment when he was passing, she raised her head; his shoulders bent involuntarily; and, when he had seated himself, some little distance away, on the same side, he glanced toward her.

She wore a wide straw hat, the red ribbons of which fluttered in the wind behind her. Her black tresses, braided around the top of her large forehead, descended very low near her cheeks, and seemed amorously to press the oval of her face. Her robe of muslin spotted with green spread out in ample folds. She was embroidering something; and her straight nose, her rounded chin, her entire person was outlined on the background of the luminous air and the blue sky.

As she maintained the same attitude, he took several turns to the right and to the left, hiding from her his change of position; then he placed himself close to her parasol, which lay against the bench, and pretended to be looking at a sloop on the river.

Never before had he seen such a lustrous dark skin, such a seductive figure, or more delicately shaped fingers than those through which the sunlight gleamed. He gazed with amazement at her work-basket, as if it were something unusual. What was her name, her place of residence, her life, her past? He longed to become familiar with the furnishings of her apartment, with the dresses that she had worn, with the people whom she visited; and the desire of physical possession yielded to a deeper yearning, a painful and boundless curiosity.

A negress, wearing a silk handkerchief tied round her head, appeared, holding by the hand a little girl already tall for her age. The child, whose eyes were swimming in tears, had just awakened. The lady took the little one on her knees. "Mademoiselle was not good, though she would soon be seven; her mother would not love her any more. She was too often forgiven for being naughty." And Frederick heard those things with delight, as if he had made a discovery, an acquisition.

He concluded that she must be of Andalusian descent, perhaps a creole: had she brought this negress with her from the West Indian Islands?

Meanwhile his attention was directed to a long shawl with violet stripes thrown behind her over the copper support of the bench. She must have, many a time, wrapped it around her, as the vessel sped through the waves; drawn it over her feet, gone to sleep in it!

Frederick suddenly noticed that with the sweep of its fringes it was slipping off, and on the point of falling into the water; with a bound he caught it. She said:

"Thank you, Monsieur."

Their eyes met.

"Are you ready, my dear?" cried my lord Arnoux, presenting himself at the hood of the companion-ladder.

Mademoiselle Marthe ran over to him, and, clinging to his neck, she began pulling at his moustache. The strains of a harp were heard—she wanted to see the music played; and presently the performer on the instrument, at the request of the negress, entered the place reserved for saloon passengers. Arnoux recognised in him a man who had formerly been a model, and "thou'd" him, to the astonishment of the by-standers.

At length the harpist, flinging back his long hair, stretched out his hands and began playing.

It was an Oriental ballad all about poniards, flowers, and stars. The man in rags sang it in a sharp voice; the twanging of the harp-strings broke the harmony of the tune with false notes. He played more vigorously: the chords vibrated, and their metallic sounds seemed to emit sobs, and, as it were, the plaint of a proud and vanquished love. On both sides of the river, woods reached down to the edge of the water. A current of fresh air swept past, and Madame Arnoux gazed vaguely into the distance. When the music stopped, she moved her eyes as if she were starting out of a dream.

The harpist approached them with an air of humility. While Arnoux was searching his pockets for money, Frederick stretched out toward the cap his closed hand, and then, opening it in a shamefaced manner, he deposited in the cap a louis d'or. It was not vanity that had prompted him to bestow this alms in her presence, but the hope of a blessing in which he felt she might share—an almost religious impulse of the heart.

Arnoux, leading the way, cordially invited him to go below. Frederick replied that he had just lunched; on the contrary, he was nearly dying of hunger; but he had not a single centime in his purse.

After that, it seemed to him that he had as much right as anyone else to remain in the cabin.

Ladies and gentlemen were seated before round tables, lunching, while an attendant went about serving coffee. Monsieur and Madame Arnoux were in the extreme right-hand corner. He seated himself on the long bench covered with velvet, picking up a newspaper which he found there.

They would have to take the diligence at Montereau for Châlons. Their tour in Switzerland would last a month. Madame Arnoux blamed her husband for his weakness with the child. He whispered in her ear; it was evidently something agreeable, for she smiled. Then he rose to draw down the window curtain at her back. Under the low, white ceiling, a crude light filled the cabin. Frederick, sitting opposite, could distinguish the shadow made by her eyelashes. She just moistened her lips at her glass and broke a little piece of crust between her fingers. The lapis-lazuli locket fastened by a gold chain to her wrist made a ringing sound, every now and then, as it touched her plate. Those present, however, did not appear to notice it.

At intervals one could see, through the port-holes, the side of a boat which was taking away passengers or putting them on board. Those who sat round the tables looked through the openings, and called out the names of the various places they passed along the river.

Arnoux complained of the cooking. He grumbled particularly at the amount of the bill, and had it reduced. Then he carried off the young man toward the forecastle to drink a glass of grog with him. But Frederick speedily returned to gaze at Madame Arnoux, who had gone back to her seat under the awning. She was reading a thin, grey-covered volume. From time to time the corners of her mouth curled and a gleam of pleasure lighted up her face. He felt jealous of the author of a book which appeared to interest her so much. The more he contemplated her, the more he felt that there were yawning abysses between them. He was reflecting that he should very soon lose sight of her irrevocably, and without having extracted a few words from her, without leaving her even a souvenir!

On the right, a plain was visible. On the left, a strip of pasture-land rose gently to meet a hillock where one could see vineyards, groups of walnut-trees, a mill embedded in the grassy slopes, and, beyond that, little zigzag paths over a white mass of rocks that reached up toward the clouds. What bliss it would have been to ascend side by side with her, his arm around her waist, as her gown swept the yellow leaves, listening to her voice and gazing into her glowing eyes! The steamboat might stop, and all they would have to do would be to step right out; and yet this thing, simple as it seemed, was not less difficult than it would have been to alter the course of the sun.

The little girl kept skipping playfully around the place where he had stationed himself on the deck. Frederick tried to kiss her. She hid herself behind her nurse. Her mother scolded her for not being nice to the gentleman who had rescued her own shawl. Was this an indirect overture?

"Is she going to speak to me?" he asked himself.

Time was flying. How was he to get an invitation to the Arnoux's house? And he could think of nothing better than to draw her attention to the autumnal hues, adding:

"We are approaching winter—the season of balls and dinner-parties."

But Arnoux was entirely occupied with his luggage. They had arrived at the river's bank facing Surville. The two bridges drew nearer. They passed a ropewalk, then a range of low-built houses, inside which there were pots of tar and splinters of wood; and children ran along the sand turning head over heels. Frederick recognised a man with a sleeved waistcoat, and called out to him:

"Make haste."

They were at the landing-place. He looked around anxiously for Arnoux amongst the crowd of passengers, and presently the other came and shook hands with him, saying:

"A pleasant time, Monsieur!"

When he was on the quay, Frederick looked back. She was standing beside the helm. He cast a look toward her into which he tried to put his whole soul. She remained motionless, as if nothing had happened. Then, without paying the slightest attention to the obeisances of his manservant:

"Why is not the trap here?"

The man made excuses.

"Clumsy fellow! Give me some money."

And after that he went off to get something to eat at an inn.

A quarter of an hour later, he felt an inclination to turn into the coachyard, as if by chance. He might see her again.

"What's the use?" he said to himself.

The vehicle carried him off. The two horses did not belong to his mother. She had borrowed one from M. Chambrion, the tax-collector. Isidore, having set forth the day before, had taken a rest at Bray until evening, and had slept at Montereau, so that the animals, with restored vigour, were trotting briskly.

Fields on which the crops had been cut stretched out in apparently endless succession; and by degrees Villeneuve, St. Georges, Ablon, Châtillon, Corbeil, and the other places—his entire journey—came back to his mind with such vividness that he could recall fresh details, more intimate particulars. . . . Under the lowest flounce of her gown, her foot showed itself encased in a dainty silk boot of maroon shade. The awning made of ticking formed a wide canopy over her head, and the little red tassels of the edging kept trembling in the breeze.

She resembled the women of whom he had read in romances. Nothing could be added to the charms of her person, and nothing could be taken from them. The universe had suddenly enlarged. She was the luminous point toward which all things converged; and, lulled by the movement of the vehicle, with half-closed eyes, and his face turned toward the clouds, he abandoned himself to a dreamy, infinite joy.

At Bray, he did not wait till the horses had got their oats; he walked on along the road by himself. Arnoux addressed her as "Marie." He now loudly repeated the name "Marie!" His voice pierced the air and was lost in the distance.

The sky toward the west was one great mass of flaming purple. Huge stacks of wheat, rising up in the midst of the stubble fields, threw giant shadows. A dog barked in a distant farm-house. He shivered, seized with disquietude for which he could assign no cause.

When Isidore came up with him, he jumped into the front seat to drive. His fit of weakness was over. He had thoroughly made up his mind to effect an introduction into the house of the Arnoux, and to become intimate with them. Their house should be entertaining; besides, he liked Arnoux; then—you never can tell! Thereupon a wave of blood rushed up to his face; his temples throbbed; he cracked his whip, shook the reins, and set the horses going at such a pace that the old coachman repeatedly exclaimed:

"Easy! easy now, or they'll get broken-winded!"

Gradually Frederick calmed down, and he attended to what the man was saying. Monsieur's return was impatiently awaited. Mademoiselle Louise had cried to go in the trap to meet him.

"Who, pray, is Mademoiselle Louise?"

"Monsieur Roque's little girl, you know."

"Ah, yes! I had forgotten," rejoined Frederick carelessly.

Meanwhile, the two horses could keep up the furious pace no longer. They were both getting lame; nine o'clock struck at St. Laurent's when he arrived at the parade in front of his mother's house.

This large house, with a garden looking out on the open country, conferred additional social importance on Madame Moreau, who was the most respected lady in the district.

She had descended from an old family of nobles, of which the male line was now extinct. Her husband, a plebeian whom her parents had forced her to marry, met his death by a sword-thrust, during her pregnancy, leaving a much encumbered estate. She received visitors three times a week, and from time to time gave a fashionable dinner. But the number of wax candles was calculated beforehand, and she looked forward with impatience to the payment of her rents. These pecuniary embarrassments, concealed as if there were some guilt attached to them, imparted a certain gravity to her character. Nevertheless, she displayed no prudery, no sourness, in the practice of her particular virtues. Her most trifling charities seemed munificent alms. She was consulted about the selection of servants, the education of young girls, and the art of making preserves, and Monseigneur used to stay at her house on the occasion of his episcopal visitations.

Madame Moreau cherished a lofty ambition for her son. Through a prudence which was grounded on the expectation of favours, she did not care to hear blame cast on the Government. He would require patronage at first; then, with such aid, he might become a councillor of state, an ambassador, a minister. His success at the college of Sens justified this proud anticipation; had he not carried off the prize of honour?

When he entered the drawing-room, all present arose noisily; he was embraced; then the chairs, large and small, were drawn up in a big semicircle around the fireplace. M. Gamblin immediately asked him what his opinion was about Madame Lafarge. This case, the rage of the moment, did not fail to lead to a violent discussion. Madame Moreau stopped it, to the regret, however, of M. Gamblin; he deemed it serviceable to the young man in his character of a future lawyer, and, nettled at what had occurred, he left the drawing-room.

Nothing done by a friend of Père Roque should have caused surprise. The reference to Père Roque led them to speak of M. Dambreuse, who had lately become the owner of the demesne of La Fortelle. But the tax-collector had drawn Frederick aside to ask what he thought of M. Guizot's latest work. They were all anxious to know about his private affairs, and Madame Benoit went cleverly to work, with that end in view, by inquiring about his uncle. How was that worthy relative? They no longer heard from him. Had he not a distant cousin in America?

The cook announced that Monsieur's soup was served. The guests discreetly retired. As soon as they were alone in the dining-room, his mother said to him in a low tone:

"Well?"

The old man had received him in a very cordial manner, but had not disclosed his intentions.

Madame Moreau sighed.

"Where is she now?" was his thought.

The diligence was probably rolling along the road, and, wrapped up in the shawl, doubtless, she was leaning against the cloth of the coupé, her beautiful head nodding as she slept.

He and his mother were about to go up to their apartments when a waiter from the Swan of the Cross brought him a note.

"What is that, pray?"

"It is Deslauriers, who wishes to see me," said he.

"Ha! your chum!" said Madame Moreau, with a contemptuous sneer. "Certainly it is a nice hour to choose!"

Frederick hesitated. But friendship was stronger. He got his hat.

His mother requested him to return quickly.

CHAPTER II

THE WISDOM OF YOUTH

THE FATHER of Charles Deslauriers was an ex-captain in the line. He had retired from the service in 1818 and returned to Nogent, where he had married. With the amount of the dowry he bought up the business of a process-server, which barely maintained him. Made bitter by continuous unjust treatment, suffering still from the effects of old wounds, and always regretting the Emperor, he vented on those around him the fits of rage that seemed to choke him. Few children received so many thrashings as did his son. In spite of blows, however, the child remained obstinate. His mother, when she interposed, was also ill-treated. Finally, the captain placed the boy in his office, and all day long kept him bent over a desk copying documents, with the result that his right shoulder was noticeably higher than his left.

In 1833, on the invitation of the president, the captain sold his office. His wife died of cancer. He then went to live at Dijon and started in business at Troyes, where he was connected with the slave trade. Having obtained a small scholarship for Charles, he placed him at the college of Sens, where Frederick met him. But one of the boys was twelve years old, while the other was fifteen; besides, a thousand differences of character and origin tended to keep them apart.

Frederick had in his chest of drawers all sorts of useful things—choice articles, such as a dressing-case would indicate. He liked to lie in bed in the mornings, to look at the swallows, and to read plays; and, missing the comforts of home, he thought college life rough. To the process-server's son it seemed a pleasant existence. He worked so hard that, at the end of the second year, he got into the third form. However, owing to his poverty or to his quarrelsome disposition, he was intensely disliked. But when on one occasion, in the courtyard where pupils of the middle grade exercised, an attendant openly called him a beggar's child, he sprang at the fellow's throat, and would have killed him if three of the ushers had not intervened. Frederick, moved by admiration, pressed him in his arms. From that day forward they were fast friends. The affection of a *grandee* no doubt flattered the vanity of the youth of meaner rank, and the other accepted as a piece of good fortune the devotion freely offered to him. During the holidays Charles's father left him in the college. A translation of Plato which he chanced on excited his enthusiasm. He became smitten with a love of metaphysical studies; and he made rapid progress, for he came to the subject with all the energy of youth and the self-confidence of an emancipated intellect. Jouffroy, Cousin, Laromiguière, Malebranche, and the Scotch metaphysicians—everything that the library contained dealing with this branch of knowledge passed through his hands. He even stole the key in order to get at the books.

Frederick's intellectual distractions were of a less serious description. He made sketches of the genealogy of Christ as carved on a post in the Rue des Trois Rois, then of the gateway of a cathedral. After a course of mediæval dramas, he turned to memoirs—Froissart, Comines, Pierre de l'Estoile, and Brantôme.

The impressions left on his mind by this kind of reading impressed him to such an extent that he felt a need within him of reproducing those pictures of bygone days. His ambition was to be, one day, the Walter Scott of France. Deslauriers dreamed of formulating an exhaustive system of philosophy, calculated to have the most far-reaching results.

They conversed on all these matters at recreation hours, in the playground, in front of the moral maxim inscribed under the clock. They whispered to each other about them in the chapel, even with St. Louis staring down at them. They dreamed about them in the dormitory, which looked out on a burial-ground. On walking-days they took up a position behind the others, and talked unceasingly.

They spoke of what they would do later, when they had left college. First of all, they would set out on a long voyage with the money which Frederick would take out of his own fortune immediately on reaching his majority. Then they would return to Paris; they would work together, and would never part; and, as a relaxation from their labours, they would have love-affairs with princesses in boudoirs lined with satin, or dazzling orgies with famous courtesans. Their rapturous day-dreams were followed by doubts. After a crisis of verbose gaiety, they would often lapse into a long silence.

On summer evenings, when they had been walking for some time over stony paths which bordered on vineyards, or on the highroad in the open country, and when they saw the wheat waving in the sunlight, while the air was filled with the fragrance of angelica, a sort of suffocating sensation overpowered them, and they stretched themselves on their backs, dizzy, intoxicated.

The proctor maintained that they mutually cried up each other. Nevertheless, if Frederick worked his way up to the higher forms, it was through the persuasions of his friend; and, during the vacation in 1837, he often brought Deslauriers to his mother's house.

Madame Moreau did not like the young man. He had a terrible appetite. He was fond of making republican speeches. To crown all, she got it into her head that he had been the means of leading her son into improper places. Their relations toward each other were watched. This only made their friendship grow stronger, and they bade one another adieu with deep sorrow when, a year later, Deslauriers left the college to study law in Paris.

Frederick anxiously looked forward to the time when they would meet again. For two years they had not seen each other; and, when their embraces were over, they walked across the bridges to talk more at their ease.

The captain, who had set up a billiard-room at Villenauxe, had become very angry when his son demanded an account of the expense of tutelage, and even cut down the cost of food to the lowest figure. As he intended to become a candidate later for a professor's chair at the school, and as he had no money, Deslauriers accepted the post of principal clerk in an attorney's office at Troyes. By dint of sheer privation he spared four thousand francs; and by not drawing upon the sum which came to him through his mother, he would always have enough to enable him to work freely for three years while waiting for a better position. It was necessary, therefore, to abandon their former plan of living together in the capital, at least for the present.

Frederick hung down his head. This was the first of his dreams to crumble into dust.

"Be comforted," said the captain's son. "Life is long. We are both young. We shall meet again. Think no more of it!"

He shook the other's hand warmly, and, to distract his attention, questioned him at length about his journey.

Frederick had little to tell. But, at the recollection of Madame Arnoux, his vexation disappeared. He did not mention her, restrained by a feeling of bashfulness. He made up for this by expatiating on Arnoux, recalling his talk, his agreeable manner, his stories; and Deslauriers urged him strongly to cultivate this new acquaintance.

Frederick had of late written nothing. His literary opinions were changed. Passion was now supreme in his estimation. He was equally enthusiastic over Werther, René, Franck, Lara, Lélia, and other imaginative creations of less merit. Sometimes it seemed to him that music alone was capable of giving expression to his internal agitation; he dreamed of symphonies; or else the surface of things attracted him, and he longed to paint. He had, however, written verses. Deslauriers considered them beautiful, but did not suggest that he should write another poem.

As for himself, he had given up metaphysics. Social economy and the French Revolution absorbed all his attention. He was a tall fellow of twenty-two, thin, with a wide mouth, and a resolute air. On this particular evening, he wore a poor-looking paletôt of lasting; and his shoes were white with dust, for he had come all the way from Villenauxe on foot expressly to see Frederick.

Isidore appeared while they were talking. Madame begged of Monsieur to return home, and, for fear of catching cold, she had sent him his heavy cloak.

"Wait a while!" said Deslauriers. And they continued walking from one end to the other of the two bridges which rest on the narrow islet formed by the canal and the river.

On the side toward Nogent they had immediately in front of them a block of houses which projected a little. At the right was the church, behind the mills, whose sluices had been closed up; and, on the left, were the hedges, covered with shrubs, skirting the wood, and forming a boundary for the gardens, which could scarcely be distinguished. On the side toward Paris the high road formed a sheer descending line, and the meadows lost themselves in the distance amid the vapours of the night. Silence reigned along this road, whose white track gleamed through the surrounding gloom. Odours of damp leaves ascended toward them. The waterfall, where the stream had been diverted from its course a hundred paces farther away, rumbled with that deep harmonious sound which waves make in the night time.

Deslauriers stopped, and said:

"'Tis droll to have all these worthy folks sleeping peacefully! Patience! A new 'eighty-nine is in the air. People are tired of constitutions, charters, subtleties, lies! Ah, if I only had a newspaper, or a platform, how I would wrestle with all these things! But, in order to undertake anything whatever, money is necessary. What a curse it is to be a tavern-keeper's son, and to waste one's youth in quest of bread!"

He hung his head, bit his lips, and shivered beneath his threadbare overcoat.

Frederick flung half his cloak over his friend's shoulders. They both wrapped themselves up in it; and, with their arms around each other, they walked down the road.

"How do you think I can possibly live over there without you?" said Frederick.

His friend's bitterness had revived his own sadness.

"I could have done something, with a woman to love me. Why do you laugh? Love is the inspiration, and, as it were, the atmosphere of genius. Extraordinary emotions produce sublime results. As for seeking after her whom I desire, I will not! Besides, if I should ever find her, she would repel me. I belong to the race of the disinherited, and I shall be swept under by a treasure that will be of paste or of diamond—I know not which."

A shadow fell across the road, and at the same time they heard these words:

"Pardon me, gentlemen!"

The person who had uttered them was a little man attired in an ample brown frock-coat, and with a cap on his head which under its peak afforded a glimpse of a sharp nose.

"Monsieur Roque?" said Frederick.

"The very man!" returned the voice.

He explained his presence by stating that he was inspecting the wolf-traps in his garden near the water-side.

"And so you are back again in the old home? Very good! I heard of it through my little girl. Your health is good, I hope? You are not going away again?"

Then he left them, repelled, probably, by Frederick's coldness.

Madame Moreau, indeed, was not on visiting terms with him. Père Roque lived in peculiar relations with his maidservant, and was held in very poor esteem, although he was the vice-president at elections, and M. Dambreuse's manager.

"The banker who lives in the Rue d'Anjou," observed Deslauriers. "Do you know what you ought to do, my fine fellow?"

Isidore once more interrupted. His orders were positive; he was not to return without Frederick. Madame would be getting uneasy at his absence.

"Well, well, he will go back," said Deslauriers. "He won't stay out all night."

And, as soon as the man-servant had disappeared:

"You ought to get that old fellow to introduce you to the Dambreuses. There's nothing so useful as to be on visiting terms at a rich man's house. Since you have a black coat and white gloves, make use of them. You must mix in that set. You can introduce me later. Just think!—a man worth millions! Do all you can to make him like you, and his wife, too. Become her lover!"

Frederick uttered an exclamation of protest.

"Why, I can quote classical examples for you on that point; I should rather think so! Recall Rastignac in the *Comédie Humaine*. You will succeed, I have no doubt."

Frederick had so much faith in Deslauriers that he felt himself weakening, and forgetting Madame Arnoux, or including her in the prediction made with regard to the other, he could not refrain from smiling.

The clerk added:

"A last piece of advice: pass your examinations. It is always helpful to have a handle to your name: and, without more ado, give up your Catholic and Satanic poets, whose philosophy is as old as the twelfth century! Your despair is absurd. The very greatest men have had more difficult beginnings; for example, Mirabeau. Besides, our separation will not be for long. I will make that pickpocket of a father of mine disgorge. It is time for me to be going back. Farewell! Have you got a hundred sous, that I may pay for my dinner?"

Frederick gave him ten francs, all that was left of what he had got in the morning from Isidore.

Meanwhile, some forty yards away from the bridges, a light shone from the garret-window of a low-built house.

Deslauriers noticed it. Then, removing his hat, he said impressively:

"Your pardon, Venus, Queen of Heaven, but necessity is the parent of wisdom. We have been slandered enough for that—so have mercy."

This allusion to an adventure in which they had both taken part, put them in a merry mood. They laughed loudly as they passed through the streets.

Then, having settled his bill at the inn, Deslauriers walked back with Frederick as far as the crossway near the Hôtel-Dieu. The two friends parted after a fond embrace.

CHAPTER III

THE RULING PASSION

FINDING himself one morning, two months later, in the Rue Coq-Heron, Frederick bethought himself that it was a good opportunity to make his momentous visit.

Chance aided him. Père Roque had given him a roll of papers, requesting him to deliver them up personally to M. Dambreuse; and the worthy man accompanied the package with an open letter of introduction in behalf of his young friend.

Madame Moreau appeared surprised at this proceeding, but Frederick concealed his delight.

M. Dambreuse's real title was the Comte d'Ambreuse; but since 1825, gradually abandoning his title of nobility and his party, he had given his attention to business; and with his ears open in every office, his hand in every enterprise, on the alert for every opportunity, as subtle as a Greek and as industrious as a native of Auvergne, he had amassed a fortune which might be called considerable. Furthermore, he was an officer of the Legion of Honour, a member of the General Council of the Aube, a deputy, and some day would be a peer of France. However, affable as he was in other respects, he wearied the Minister by his continual applications for relief, for crosses, and for licences for tobacconists' shops; and in his complaints against authority he showed inclinations toward the Left Centre.

His wife, the pretty Madame Dambreuse, who figured in the fashion journals, presided at charitable assemblies. By flattering the duchesses, she appeased the rancours of the aristocratic faubourg, and caused the residents to believe that M. Dambreuse might yet repent and render them some services.

The young man was agitated when he made his call.

"It would have been better to take my dress-coat with me. No doubt they will give me an invitation to next week's ball. What will they think of me?"

His self-confidence returned when he reflected that M. Dambreuse was only a person of the middle class, and he sprang out of the cab briskly on reaching the Rue d'Anjou.

When he had pushed open one of the two gateways he crossed the courtyard, mounted the steps in front of the house, and entered a vestibule paved with coloured marble.

A bell rang, upon which a valet made his appearance. He showed Frederick into a little apartment, where there stood two strong-boxes, and numerous pigeon-holes filled with pieces of pasteboard. In the centre of the room M. Dambreuse was writing at a roll-top desk.

He glanced over Père Roque's letter, then opened the canvas in which the papers were wrapped, and examined them.

At some distance M. Dambreuse presented the appearance of being still young, owing to his slight figure. But his thin white hair, his feeble limbs, and, above all, the extraordinary pallor of his face, indicated a shattered constitution. There was an expression of pitiless energy in his sea-green eyes, colder than eyes of glass. His cheek-bones projected, and his finger-joints were knotted.

At length he arose and asked the young man a few questions with regard to mutual acquaintances at Nogent and also with regard to his studies, and then dismissed him with a bow. Frederick went out through another lobby, and found himself at the lower end of the courtyard near the coach-house.

A blue brougham, to which a black horse was yoked, stood before the house. The carriage door opened, a lady stepped in, and the vehicle, with a rumbling noise, went rolling along the gravel. Frederick had reached the courtyard gate from the other side at the same moment. As there was not room enough for him to pass, he waited. The young lady, with her head thrust forward past the carriage blind, spoke to the door-keeper in a very low tone. All he could see was her back, covered with a violet mantle. However, he glanced into the interior of the carriage, lined with blue rep, and ornamented with silk lace and fringes. The lady's robes filled up the space within. He stole away from this little padded box with its perfume of iris, and its vague atmosphere of feminine elegance. The coachman slackened the reins, the horse jerked abruptly past the starting-point, and all disappeared.

Frederick returned on foot, following the track of the boulevard.

He regretted not having been able to get a satisfactory view of Madame Dambreuse. A little higher than the Rue Montmartre a regular jumble of vehicles made him turn his head, and on the opposite side, facing him, he read on a marble plate:

"Jacques Arnoux."

Strange that he had not thought about her sooner! It was Deslauriers' fault; and he approached the shop, which, however, he did not enter. He was waiting for *her* to appear.

The high, transparent plate-glass windows contained statuettes, drawings, engravings, catalogues and numbers of *L'Art Industriel,* arranged in a skilful fashion; and the amounts of the subscriptions were repeated on the door, which was decorated with the publisher's initials.

Frederick pretended to be examining the drawings. After hesitating for a long time, he went in. A clerk lifted the portière, and in reply to a question, said that Monsieur would not be in the shop before five o'clock. But if the message could be conveyed——

"No! I will come back again," Frederick answered blandly.

The following days were occupied in searching for lodgings; and he fixed upon an apartment in the second story of a furnished mansion in the Rue Hyacinthe.

With a fresh blotting-case under his arm, he set out to attend the opening lecture of the course. Three hundred young men, bare-headed, filled an amphitheatre, where an old man in a red gown was delivering a discourse in a monotonous voice. Quill pens could be heard scratching over the paper. In this hall he found once more the dusty odour of the school, a reading-desk of familiar shape, the same wearisome monotony! For a fortnight he regularly attended the law lectures. But he dropped the study of the Civil Code before getting as far as Article 3, and he gave up the Institutes at the *Summa Divisio Personarum*.

The pleasures that he had anticipated did not come to him; and when he had exhausted a circulating library, gone over the collections in the Louvre, and been at the theatre a great many nights in succession, he sank into the lowest depths of idleness.

His depression was augmented by a thousand fresh annoyances. He found it necessary to count his linen and to tolerate the door-keeper, a bore with the figure of a male hospital nurse, who made up his bed in the morning, smelling of alcohol always and grunting. He did not like his apartment, which was ornamented with an alabaster time-piece. The partitions were thin; he could hear the students making punch, laughing and singing.

Tired of this solitude, he sought out one of his old schoolfellows, Baptiste Martinon; he discovered this friend of his boyhood in a middle-class boarding-house in the Rue Saint-Jacques, cramming in legal procedure, seated before a coal fire. A woman in a print dress sat opposite him darning his socks.

Martinon was what people call a very fine man—big, chubby, with regular features, and blue eyes set high up in his face. His father, an extensive landowner, had destined him for the magistracy; and wishing already to present a dignified exterior, he wore his beard cut like a collar round his neck.

As there was no rational foundation for Frederick's complaints, and as he could not give evidence of any real misfortune, Martinon was unable to understand his lamentations about existence. As for him, he went every morning to the school, after that took a walk in the Luxembourg, in the evening swallowed his half-cup of coffee; and with fifteen hundred francs a year, and the love of this work-woman, he felt perfectly happy.

"What happiness!" was Frederick's internal comment.

At the school he had formed another acquaintance, a youth of aristocratic family, who on account of his dainty manners resembled a young lady.

M. de Cisy devoted himself to drawing, and loved the Gothic style. They frequently went together to admire the Sainte-Chapelle and Nôtre Dame. But the young patrician's rank and pretensions covered an intellect of the feeblest order. Everything took him by surprise. He laughed immoderately at the most trifling joke, and displayed such utter simplicity that Frederick at first took him for a wag, and finally regarded him as a booby.

The young man was finding it impossible, therefore, to be cordial with anyone; and he was constantly looking forward to an invitation from the Dambreuses.

On New Year's Day he sent them visiting-cards, but received none in return.

He made his way back to the office of *L'Art Industriel*.

A third time he returned to it, and at last saw Arnoux carrying on an argument with five or six persons around him. He scarcely responded to the young man's bow; and Frederick was hurt by this reception. None the less he cogitated over the best means of finding his way to her side.

His first idea was to come frequently to the shop on the pretext of getting pictures at low prices. Then he conceived the notion of slipping into the letter-box of the journal a few "very strong" articles, which might lead to friendly relations. Perhaps it would be wiser to go straight to the mark at once, and declare his love? Acting on this impulse, he wrote a letter covering a dozen pages, full of lyric lines and apostrophes; but he tore it up, and did nothing, attempted nothing—bereft of motive power by his want of success.

Above Arnoux's shop there were, on the first floor, three windows which were lighted up every evening. Shadows might be seen moving about behind the blinds, especially one; this was hers; and he went far out of his way in order to gaze at the windows, and to contemplate that shadow.

A negress who crossed his path one day in the Tuileries, holding a little girl by the hand, recalled to his mind Madame Arnoux's negress. She was sure to come there, like the others; every time he passed through the Tuileries his heart began to beat with the anticipation of meeting her. On sunny days he continued to walk as far as the end of the Champs-Elysées.

Women seated with careless ease in open carriages, and with their veils floating in the wind, passed close to him, their horses advancing at a steady walking pace, and with an unconscious see-saw movement that made the varnished leather of the harness crackle. His eyes wandered along the rows of female heads, and certain vague resemblances brought back Madame Arnoux to his mind. He pictured her to himself, in the midst of the others, in one of those little broughams like that in which he had seen Madame Dambreuse.

But the sun was setting, the cold wind raised whirling clouds of dust, and all the equipages descended the long sloping avenue at a quick trot, touching, sweeping past one another, getting out of one another's way; then, at the Place de la Concorde, they went off in different directions.

Frederick went to a restaurant in the Rue de la Harpe and got a dinner for forty-three sous. He glanced disdainfully at the old mahogany counter, the soiled napkins, the worn silver-plate, and the hats hanging on the wall.

Those around him were students like himself. They talked about their professors, and about their mistresses. What cared he about professors? And had he a mistress? To avoid being a witness of their enjoyment, he came as late as possible. The tables were all strewn with remnants of food. The two waiters, worn out with attendance on customers, lay asleep, each in a different corner; and an odour of cooking, of an argand lamp, and of tobacco, filled the deserted dining-room. Then he slowly toiled along the streets again.

He was smitten with a vague remorse. He renewed his attendance at lectures. But as he was entirely ignorant of the matters which formed the subject of explanation, things of the simplest description puzzled him. He set about writing a novel, which he entitled *Sylvio, the Fisherman's Son*. The scene of the story was Venice. The hero was himself, and Madame Arnoux was the heroine. She was named Antonia; and, to get possession of her, the hero assassinated a number of noblemen, and burned a portion of the city; after which feats he sang a serenade under her balcony, whereon fluttered in the breeze the red damask curtains of the Boulévard Montmartre.

The numerous reminiscences on which he dwelt produced a disheartening effect on him; he went no farther with the work, and his mental vacuity redoubled.

After this, he begged of Deslauriers to come and share his apartment. They might make arrangements to live together with the aid of his allowance of two thousand francs; anything would be better than this miserable existence. Deslauriers could not yet leave Troyes. He urged his friend to find some means of diverting his thoughts, and, with that end in view, suggested that he should call on Sénécal.

Sénécal was a mathematical tutor, a hard-headed man with republican convictions, a future Saint-Just, according to the clerk. Frederick ascended the five flights, up which he lived, three times in succession, without getting a visit from him in return. He did not go back.

He now determined to amuse himself. He attended the balls at the

Opera House. These exhibitions of riotous gaiety chilled him the moment he had passed the door. Besides, he was embarrassed by the fear of being subjected to insult on the subject of money, his notion being that a supper with a domino entailed considerable expense, and was rather a big adventure.

It seemed to him, nevertheless, that he must needs love her. Sometimes he used to wake up with his heart full of hope, dress himself carefully as if he were going to keep an appointment, and start on interminable excursions all over Paris. Whenever a woman walked in front of him, or came toward him, he would say: "Here she is!" Every time it was only a fresh disappointment. The thought of Madame Arnoux strengthened these desires. Perhaps he might find her on his way; and he conjured up dangerous complications, extraordinary perils from which he might have the opportunity to save her.

So the days slipped by with the same tiresome experiences, and enslavement to contracted habits. Every week he wrote long letters to Deslauriers, dined from time to time with Martinon, and occasionally saw M. de Cisy. Then he hired a piano and composed German waltzes.

One evening at the theatre of the Palais-Royal, he saw, in one of the stage-boxes, Arnoux with a woman by his side. Was it she? The screen of green taffeta, pulled over the side of the box, hid her face. At length, the curtain rose, and the screen was drawn aside. She was a tall woman of about thirty, rather faded, and, when she laughed, her thick lips uncovered a row of shining teeth. She chatted familiarly with Arnoux, tapping him on the fingers from time to time with her fan. Then a fair-haired young girl with eyelids a little red, as if she had just been weeping, seated herself between them. Arnoux, after that, remained stooping over her shoulder, pouring forth a stream of talk to which she listened without replying. Frederick taxed his ingenuity to conceive what the social position of these modestly attired women could be.

At the close of the play, he made a dash for the passages. A crowd of people going out filled them up. Arnoux, just ahead of him, was descending the staircase step by step, with a woman on each arm.

Suddenly a gas-burner shed its light on him. He wore a crape hat-band. She was dead, perhaps? This idea tormented Frederick's mind so much, that he hurried, next day, to the office of *L'Art Industriel,* and paying, without a moment's delay, for one of the engravings exposed in the window for sale, he asked the shop-assistant how Monsieur Arnoux was.

The shop-assistant replied:

"Why, quite well!"

Frederick, growing pale, added:

"And Madame?"

"Madame, also."

Frederick forgot to carry off his engraving.

The winter drew to a close. He was less melancholy in the spring time, and began to study for his examination. After passing it indifferently, he went home.

He refrained from going to Troyes to see his friend, in order to escape his mother's comments. On his return to Paris at the end of the vacation, he moved to two rooms on the Quai Napoléon, which he furnished. He was hopeless now of ever getting an invitation from the Dambreuses. His great passion for Madame Arnoux was also fading away.

CHAPTER IV

THE ETERNAL FEMININE

WHILE ON his way to attend a law lecture one morning in December Frederick noticed more than ordinary excitement in the Rue Saint-Jacques. The students were rushing out of the cafés, and, through the open windows, they were calling from one house to the other. The shopkeepers, standing in the middle of the footpath, were looking about them anxiously; the window-shutters were fastened; and when he reached the Rue Soufflot there was a large assemblage around the Panthéon.

Frederick found himself close to a fair-haired young man of prepossessing appearance, with a moustache and a tuft of beard on his chin, like a dandy of Louis XIII's time. He asked the stranger what the matter was.

"I haven't the least idea," replied the other, "nor have they, for that matter! 'Tis their fashion just now! What a good joke!"

And he burst out laughing. The petitions for Reform, which had been signed at the quarters of the National Guard, together with the property-census of Humann and other events besides, had, for the past six months, led to inexplicable gatherings of riotous crowds in Paris, and so frequently had they broken out that the newspapers had ceased to refer to them.

"This lacks graceful outline and colour," continued Frederick's neighbour. "I am convinced, messire, that we have degenerated. In the good epoch of Louis XI, and even in that of Benjamin Constant, there was more mutiny amongst the students. I find them as pacific as sheep, as stupid as greenhorns, and only fit to be grocers. Ye gods! And these are what we call the youth of the schools!"

He extended his arms after the fashion of Frederick Lemaître in *Robert Macaire*.

"Youth of the schools, I give you my blessing!"

After this, addressing a ragpicker, who was moving a heap of oyster-shells up against the wall of a wine-merchant's house:

"Do you belong to them—the youth of the schools?"

The old man lifted up a hideous countenance in which one could trace, in the midst of a grey beard, a red nose and two dull eyes, blood-shot from drink.

"No, you appear to me rather one of those men with patibulary faces whom we see, on various occasions, liberally scattering gold. Oh, scatter it, my patriarch, scatter it! Corrupt me with the treasures of Albion! Are you English? I do not reject the presents of Artaxerxes! Let us have a little talk about the union of customs!"

Frederick felt a hand on his shoulder. It was Martinon, looking exceedingly pale.

"Well!" said he with a deep sigh, "another riot!"

He was afraid of being compromised, and uttered complaints. Men in blouses especially made him feel uneasy, suggesting a connection with secret societies.

"You mean to say you believe in secret societies," said the young man with the moustaches. "That is a worn-out trick of the Government to frighten the middle-class folk!"

Martinon urged him to speak in a lower tone, for fear of the police.

"You believe also in the police, do you? As a matter of fact, how do you know, Monsieur, that I am not myself a police spy?"

And he looked at him in such a way, that Martinon, much discomposed, was, at first, unable to see the joke. The people pushed them on, and they were all three forced to stand on the little staircase which led, by one of the passages, to the new amphitheatre.

The crowd soon dispersed of its own accord. Many faces could be distinguished. They bowed toward the distinguished Professor Samuel Rondelot, who, wrapped in his big frock-coat, with his silver spectacles up high on his forehead, and breathing hard from his asthma, was advancing at an easy pace, on his way to deliver his lecture. This man was one of the judicial glories of the nineteenth century, the rival of the Zachariæs and the Ruhdorffs. His new dignity as peer of France had in no way altered his external demeanour. He was known to be poor, and was treated with profound respect.

Meanwhile, at the lower end of the square, some persons cried out:

"Down with Guizot!"

"Down with Pritchard!"

"Down with the sold ones!"

"Down with Louis Philippe!"

The crowd swayed to and fro, and, pressing against the gate of the

courtyard, which was shut, the professor was prevented from going farther. He stopped in front of the staircase. He was speedily observed on
he lowest of three steps. He spoke; the loud murmurs of the throng
drowned his voice. Although at another time they might love him, they
hated him now, for he represented authority. He was answered by vocif-
erations from all sides. He shrugged his shoulders disdainfully, and
plunged into the passage. Martinon profited by his situation to disappear
at the same moment.

"What a coward!" said Frederick.

"He was prudent," returned the other.

There was an outburst of applause from the crowd, from whose point
of view this retreat, on the part of the professor, appeared in the light of
a victory. From every window, faces, eager with curiosity, looked out.
Some struck up the "Marseillaise"; others suggested going to Béranger's
house.

"To Laffitte's house!"

"To Chateaubriand's house!"

"To Voltaire's house!" yelled the young man with the fair moustaches.

The police tried to pass around, saying in the mildest tones they could
assume:

"Move on, messieurs! Move on! Take yourselves off!"

Somebody shouted:

"Down with the slaughterers!"

This was a form of insult common since the troubles of September.
Everyone echoed it. The guardians of public order were hooted and
hissed. They began to grow pale. One of them could endure it no longer,
and, seeing a low-sized young man approaching too close, and laughing
in his teeth, he pushed him back so roughly that he tumbled over on his
back some five paces away, in front of a wine-merchant's shop. All made
way; but almost immediately afterward the policeman rolled on the
ground himself, felled by a blow from a species of Hercules, whose hair
hung down like a bundle of tow under an oilskin cap. Having stopped for
a few minutes at the corner of the Rue Saint-Jacques, he had very quickly
laid down a large case, which he had been carrying, in order to make a
spring at the policeman, and, holding down that functionary, punched his
face unmercifully. The other policemen rushed to the rescue of their
comrade. The terrible shop-assistant was so powerfully built that it took
four of them to overcome him. Two shook him, while keeping a grip on
his collar; two others dragged his arms; a fifth gave him digs of the knee
in the ribs; and all of them called him "brigand," "assassin," "rioter." With
his breast bare, and his clothes in rags, he protested that he was innocent;
he could not, in cold blood, look at a child being beaten.

"My name is Dussardier. I'm employed at Messieurs Valincart Brothers' lace and fancy warehouse, in the Rue de Cléry. Where's my case? I want my case!"

He kept repeating:

"Dussardier, Rue de Cléry. My case!"

However, he quieted down, and, with a stoical air, allowed himself to be led toward the guard-house in the Rue Descartes. A flood of people came rushing after him. Frederick and the young man with the moustaches walked immediately behind, full of admiration for the shopman, and indignant at the violence of power.

As they advanced, the crowd thinned.

The policemen from time to time turned round, with threatening looks; and the rowdies, no longer having anything to do, and the spectators not having anything to look at, all drifted away by degrees. The passers-by, who met the procession, stared at Dussardier, and in loud tones made abusive remarks about him. One old woman, at her own door, bawled out that he had stolen a loaf of bread from her. This unjust accusation increased the wrath of the two friends. At length, they reached the guard-house.

Frederick and his companion boldly demanded to have the man under arrest delivered up. The sentinel threatened, if they persisted, to ram them into jail too. They said they desired to see the commander of the guard-house, and stated their names, and the fact that they were law-students, declaring that the prisoner was one also.

They were ushered into a room perfectly bare, in which, amid an atmosphere of smoke, four benches lined the roughly plastered walls. At the lower end there was an open wicket. Then appeared the sturdy face of Dussardier, who, with his hair all tousled, his honest little eyes, and his broad snout, suggested to one's mind in a confused sort of way the physiognomy of a faithful dog.

"Don't you recognise us?" said Hussonnet.

This was the name of the young man with the moustaches.

"Why—" stammered Dussardier.

"Don't play the fool any longer," returned the other. "We know that, like ourselves, you, too, are a law-student."

In spite of their winks, Dussardier failed to understand. He appeared to be collecting his thoughts; then, suddenly:

"Has my case been found?"

Frederick raised his eyes, feeling much discouraged.

Hussonnet, however, said promptly:

"Ha! your case, in which you keep your notes of lectures? Yes, yes, make your mind easy about that!"

They made further pantomimic signs with redoubled energy, till Dussardier at last realised that they had come to help him; and he held his tongue, fearing that he might compromise them. Besides, he experienced a kind of shamefacedness at seeing himself raised to the social rank of student, and to an equality with those young men who had such white hands.

"Do you wish to send any message to anyone?" asked Frederick.

"No, thanks, not to anyone."

"But your family?"

He bent his head without replying; the poor fellow was a bastard. The two friends stood quite astonished at his silence.

"Have you anything to smoke?" was Frederick's next question.

He felt about, then drew forth from the depths of one of his pockets the remains of a pipe—a beautiful pipe, made of white talc with a shank of blackwood, a silver cover, and an amber mouthpiece.

For the last three years he had been engaged in completing this masterpiece. He had carefully kept the bowl of it in a kind of sheath of chamois, smoking it as slowly as possible, without ever letting it lie on any cold stone substance, and hanging it up every evening over the head of his bed. And now he shook out the fragments of it into his hand, the nails of which were covered with blood, and with his chin sunk on his chest, his pupils fixed and dilated, he gazed at this wreck of the thing that had yielded him such delight with unutterable sadness.

"Suppose we give him some cigars, eh?" said Hussonnet in a whisper, making a gesture as if he were handing them out.

Frederick had already laid down a cigar-holder, filled, on the edge of the wicket.

"Pray take this. Good-bye! Cheer up!"

Dussardier flung himself on the two hands that were held out toward him. He pressed them frantically, his voice choked with sobs.

"What? For me!—for me!"

The two friends tore themselves away from this effusive display of gratitude, and went off to lunch together at the Café Tabourey, near the Luxembourg.

While cutting up the beefsteak, Hussonnet informed his companion that he worked for the fashion journals, and manufactured catchwords for L'Art Industriel.

"At Jacques Arnoux's establishment?" said Frederick.

"Do you know him?"

"Yes!—no!—that is to say, I have seen him—I have met him."

He carelessly asked Hussonnet if he ever saw Arnoux's wife.

"Sometimes," the Bohemian replied.

Frederick did not venture to follow up his inquiries. This man hence-forth would occupy a large space in his life. He paid the café bill with-out any protest on the other's part.

There was a bond of mutual sympathy between them; they gave one another their respective addresses, and Hussonnet cordially invited Frederick to accompany him to the Rue de Fleurus.

They had reached the middle of the garden, when Arnoux's clerk, holding his breath, twisted his features into a hideous grimace, and began to crow like a cock. Thereupon all the cocks in the vicinity responded with prolonged "cock-a-doodle-doos."

"It is a signal," explained Hussonnet.

They stopped close to the Théâtre Bobino, in front of a house, which they approached by way of an alley. In the skylight of a garret, between the nasturtiums and the sweet peas, a young woman showed herself, bare-headed, in her stays, her two arms resting on the edge of the roof-gutter.

"Good-morrow, my angel! good-morrow, ducky!" said Hussonnet, sending her kisses.

He made the barrier fly open with a kick, and disappeared.

Frederick waited for him all the week. He did not like to call at Hussonnet's residence, lest it might appear as if he were in a hurry for a luncheon in return for the one he had paid for. But he sought the clerk all over the Latin Quarter. He came across him one evening, and brought him to his apartment on the Quai Napoléon.

They had a long chat, and unbosomed themselves to each other. Hussonnet yearned after the glory and the gains of the theatre. He col-laborated in the writing of vaudevilles which were not accepted, "had heaps of plans," could turn a couplet; he sang for Frederick a few of the verses he had composed. Then, noticing on one of the shelves a volume of Hugo and another of Lamartine, he broke out into sarcastic criticisms of the romantic school. These poets had neither good sense nor cor-rectness, and, above all, did not write French! He plumed himself on his knowledge of the language, and analysed the most beautiful phrases with that snarling severity, that academic taste, which persons of playful dispo-sition exhibit when they are discussing serious art.

Frederick was wounded in his predilections, and felt a desire to shorten the discussion. Why not take the risk at once of uttering the word on which his happiness depended? He asked this literary youth whether it would be possible to get an introduction into the Arnoux's house through him.

The thing was declared to be quite easy, and they fixed upon the fol-lowing day.

Hussonnet failed to keep the appointment, and on three subsequent occasions he did not turn up. One Saturday, about four o'clock, he made his appearance. But, taking advantage of the cab into which they had got, he drew up in front of the Théâtre Français to get a box-ticket, got down at a tailor's shop, then at a dressmaker's, and wrote notes in the doorkeeper's lodge. At last they came to the Boulevard Montmartre. Frederick passed through the shop, and went up the staircase. Arnoux recognised him through the glass-partition in front of his desk, and while continuing to write he stretched out his hand and laid it on Frederick's shoulder.

Five or six persons, standing around, filled the narrow apartment, which was lighted by a single window looking out on the yard; a sofa of brown damask wool filled the interior of an alcove between two door-curtains of similar material. Upon the chimney-piece, covered with old papers, there was a bronze Venus. Two candelabra, garnished with rose-coloured wax-tapers, supported it, one at each side. At the right, near a cardboard chest of drawers, a man, seated in an armchair, and with his hat on, was reading a newspaper. The walls were hidden beneath an array of prints and pictures, precious engravings or sketches by contemporary masters, adorned with dedications testifying the most sincere affection for Jacques Arnoux.

"You're getting on well all this time?" said he, turning round to Frederick.

And, without waiting for an answer, he asked Hussonnet in a low tone:

"What is your friend's name?" Then, raising his voice:

"Take a cigar out of the box on the cardboard stand."

The office of *L'Art Industriel,* situated in a central position in Paris, was a convenient place of resort, a neutral ground wherein rivalries elbowed each other familiarly. On this day might be seen there Anténor Braive, who painted portraits of kings; Jules Burrieu, who by his sketches was popularising the wars in Algeria; the caricaturist Sombary, the sculptor Vourdat, and several others. And not a single one of them corresponded with the student's preconceived ideas. Their manners were simple, their talk free and easy. The mystic Lovarias told an obscene story; and the inventor of Oriental landscape, the famous Dittmer, wore a knitted shirt under his waistcoat, and went home in the omnibus.

The first topic discussed was the case of a girl named Apollonie, formerly a model, whom Burrieu alleged that he had seen on the boulevard in a carriage. Hussonnet explained this metamorphosis through the succession of persons who had loved her.

"How well this sly dog knows the girls of Paris!" said Arnoux.

"After you, if there are any of them left, sire," replied the Bohemian, with a military salute, in imitation of the grenadier offering his flask to Napoléon.

The conversation was interrupted by the entrance of a man of middle stature, whose coat was fastened by a single button, and whose eyes glittered with a rather wild expression.

"What a lot of shopkeepers you are!" said he. "God bless my soul! what does money signify? The old masters did not trouble their heads about the million—Correggio, Murillo——"

"Add Pellerin," said Sombary.

But, without taking the least notice of the epigram, he went on talking with such vehemence that Arnoux was forced to repeat twice to him:

"My wife expects you on Thursday. Don't forget!"

This remark recalled Madame Arnoux to Frederick's thoughts. No doubt, she could be reached through the little room near the sofa. Arnoux had just opened the portière leading into it to get a pocket-handkerchief, and Frederick had seen a wash-stand at the far end of the apartment.

But at this point a kind of muttering sound came from the corner of the chimney-piece; it was caused by the personage who sat in the arm-chair reading the newspaper. He was a man of five feet nine inches in height, with rather heavy eyelashes, a head of grey hair, and an imposing appearance; his name was Regimbart.

"What's the matter now, citizen?" said Arnoux.

"Another piece of rascality on the part of the Government!"

He was referring to the dismissal of a schoolmaster.

Pellerin again took up his parallel between Michael Angelo and Shakespeare. Dittmer was leaving when Arnoux pulled him back in order to put two bank notes into his hand. Thereupon Hussonnet said, considering this an opportune time:

"Couldn't you give me an advance, my dear master——"

But Arnoux had resumed his seat, and was severely reprimanding an old man of mean aspect, who wore a pair of blue spectacles.

"Ha! a nice fellow you are, Père Isaac! Here are three works cried down, destroyed! Everybody is laughing at me! People know what they are now! What can I do with them? I'll have to send them off to California—or to the devil! Hold your tongue!"

The specialty of this old worthy consisted in attaching the signatures of the great masters to pictures. Arnoux refused to pay him, and dismissed him in a brutal fashion. Then, with an entire change of manner, he bowed to a gentleman of affectedly grave demeanour, who wore whiskers and displayed a white tie around his neck and the cross of the Legion of Honour over his breast.

With his elbow resting on the window-fastening, he talked to him for a long time in honeyed tones. At last he exclaimed:

"Ah! well, I am not bothered with brokers, Count."

The nobleman gave way, and Arnoux paid him down twenty-five louis. As soon as he had gone:

"What a plague these big lords are!"

"A lot of scoundrels!" muttered Regimbart.

As it grew later, Arnoux became more busy. He classified articles, tore open letters, set out accounts in a row; at the sound of hammering in the warehouse he went out to look after the packing; then he returned to his ordinary work; and, while he kept his steel pen running over the paper, he indulged in sharp witticisms. He had an invitation to dine with his lawyer that evening, and was starting next day for Belgium.

The door near the sofa flew open, and a tall, thin woman entered with abrupt movements, which made all the trinkets of her watch rattle under her black taffeta gown.

It was the woman of whom Frederick had caught a glimpse last summer at the Palais-Royal. Some of those present, addressing her by name, shook hands with her. Hussonnet had at last managed to extract fifty francs from his employer. The clock struck seven.

All rose to go.

Arnoux told Pellerin to remain, and accompanied Mademoiselle Vatnaz into the dressing-room.

Frederick could not hear what they said; they spoke in whispers. Presently, the woman's voice was raised:

"I have been waiting ever since the job was done, six months ago."

There was a long silence, and then Mademoiselle Vatnaz reappeared. Arnoux had again promised her something.

"Oh! oh! later, we shall see!"

"Good-bye! happy man," said she, as she was going out.

Arnoux quickly reëntered the dressing-room, rubbed some cosmetic over his moustaches, raised his braces, stretched his straps; and said, while he was washing his hands:

"I would require two over the door at two hundred and fifty apiece, in Boucher's style. Is that understood?"

"Very well," said the artist, his face reddening.

"Good! and don't forget my wife!"

Frederick accompanied Pellerin to the end of the Faubourg Poissonnière, and asked his permission to call on him sometimes, a favour which was graciously accorded.

Pellerin read numerous works on æsthetics, in order to find out the true theory of the Beautiful, convinced that, when he had discovered it, he would produce masterpieces. He had surrounded himself with every imaginable auxiliary—drawings, plaster-casts, models, engravings; and he kept searching about, eating his heart out. Tormented by the desire for glory, and wasting his days in discussions, believing in a thousand fool-eries—in systems, in criticisms, in the importance of a regulation or a reform in the domain of Art—he had at fifty as yet produced nothing save mere sketches.

On entering his studio one's attention was directed toward two large pictures, in which the first tones of colour laid on here and there made on the white canvas spots of brown, red, and blue. Overhead was a network of lines in chalk, like stitches of thread repeated twenty times; it was impossible to understand. Pellerin explained the subject of these two compositions by indicating with his thumb the portions that were lacking. The first was intended to represent "The Madness of Nebuchadnezzar," and the second "The Burning of Rome by Nero." Frederick expressed admiration of them.

He admired academies of women with dishevelled hair, landscapes abounding in trunks of trees, twisted by the storm; and, above all, freaks of the pen, imitations from memory of Callot, Rembrandt, or Goya, of which he did not know the models. Pellerin no longer set any value on these works of his youth. He was now all in favour of the grand style; he dogmatised eloquently about Phidias and Winckelmann. The objects around him strengthened the force of his language; a death's head on a prie-dieu, yataghans, a monk's habit. Frederick put on the latter.

Arriving early one day, he surprised the artist in his wretched folding-bed, which was hidden from view by a strip of tapestry; for Pellerin went to bed late, being an assiduous frequenter of the theatres. An old woman in tatters attended on him. He dined at a cookshop, and lived without a mistress.

But why had he never chanced to speak of Madame Arnoux? As for her husband, at one time he called Arnoux a decent fellow, at other times a charlatan. Frederick was waiting for some disclosures on his part.

One day, while looking over one of the portfolios in the studio, he thought he could trace in the portrait of a female Bohemian some resemblance to Mademoiselle Vatnaz; and, as he felt interested in this lady, he desired to know her exact social position.

She had been, at one time, as far as Pellerin could ascertain, a schoolmistress in the provinces. She now gave lessons in Paris, and tried to write for the small journals.

Frederick suggested that one would imagine from her manners with Arnoux that she was his mistress.

"Pshaw! he has others!"

Then, turning away his face, which reddened with shame at the baseness of the suggestion, the young man replied, with a swaggering air:

"Very likely his wife gets even with him?"

"Not at all; she is virtuous."

Frederick again experienced a feeling of compunction, and the result was that his attendance at the office of the art journal became more frequent than before.

The big letters which formed the name of Arnoux on the marble plate above the shop seemed to him quite peculiar and pregnant with significance, like some sacred writing. The wide footpath, by its descent, facilitated his approach; the door almost opened of its own accord; and the handle, smooth to the touch, gave him the sensation of friendly and, as it were, intelligent fingers clasping his. Unconsciously, he became as regular as Regimbart.

Every day Regimbart seated himself in the chimney-corner, in his armchair, got hold of the *National,* and kept possession of it, expressing his thoughts by exclamations or by shrugs of the shoulders.

At eight o'clock in the morning he descended the heights of Montmartre, in order to imbibe white wine in the Rue Nôtre Dame des Victoires. A late breakfast, after several games of billiards, occupied time till three o'clock. He then directed his steps toward the Passage des Panoramas, where he had a glass of absinthe. After the sitting in Arnoux's shop, he entered the Bordelais smoking-divan, where he swallowed some bitters; then, rather than return home to his wife, he preferred to dine alone in a little café in the Rue Gaillon, where he desired them to serve up to him "household dishes, natural things." Finally, he made his way to another billiard-room, and remained there till midnight; in fact, till one o'clock in the morning, up to the last moment, when, the gas being put out and the window-shutters fastened, the master of the establishment, worn out, begged him to leave.

And it was not the love of drinking that attracted Citizen Regimbart to these places, but the inveterate habit of talking politics at such resorts.

Arnoux appeared to have a very great esteem for him. One day he said to Frederick:

"He knows a lot, I can tell you. He is an able man."

On another occasion Regimbart spread over his desk papers relating to the kaolin mines in Brittany. Arnoux referred to his own experience on the subject.

Frederick showed himself more ceremonious toward Regimbart, going so far as to invite him from time to time to join him in a glass of absinthe; and, although he considered him a stupid man, he often remained a full hour in his company solely because he was Jacques Arnoux's friend.

After pushing forward some contemporary masters early in their career, Arnoux, the picture-dealer, a man of progressive ideas, had tried, while clinging to his artistic ways, to extend his pecuniary profits. His object was to emancipate the fine arts, to get the sublime at a cheap price. Over every industry associated with Parisian luxury he exercised an influence which proved advantageous with respect to little things, but fatal with respect to great things. With his mania for pandering to public opinion, he made clever artists swerve from their true path, corrupted the strong, exhausted the weak, and won distinction for those of mediocre talent; he set them up with the assistance of his connections and of his magazine. Tyros in painting were ambitious to see their works in his shop-window, and upholsterers brought specimens of furniture to his house. Frederick regarded him, at the one time, as a millionaire, as a *dilettante,* and as a man of action. However, he noticed many things that filled him with astonishment, for my lord Arnoux was rather sly in his commercial transactions.

He received from the very heart of Germany or of Italy a picture purchased in Paris for fifteen hundred francs, and, exhibiting an invoice that brought the price up to four thousand, he sold it over again for three thousand five hundred. One of his regular tricks with painters was to exact as a drink-allowance an abatement in the purchase-money of their pictures, under the pretence that he would bring out an engraving of it. He always, when selling such pictures, made a profit by the abatement; but the engraving never appeared. To those who complained that he had taken an advantage of them, he would reply by a slap on the stomach. Generous in other ways, however, he squandered money on cigars for his acquaintances, "thee'd" and "thou'd" persons who were unknown, displayed enthusiasm about a work or a man; and, after that, sticking to his opinion, and, regardless of consequences, spared no expense in journeys, correspondence, and advertising. He considered himself very upright, and, yielding to an irresistible impulse to unbosom himself, ingenuously told his friends about certain indelicate acts of which he had been guilty. Once, in order to annoy a member of his own trade who inaugurated another art journal with a big banquet, he asked Frederick to write, under his own eyes, a little before the hour fixed for the entertainment, letters to the guests recalling the invitations.

"This impugns nobody's honour, you understand?"

And the young man did not dare to refuse the service.

Next day, on entering with Hussonnet M. Arnoux's office, Frederick saw through the door (the one opening on the staircase) the hem of a lady's dress disappearing.

"A thousand pardons!" said Hussonnet. "If I had known that there were women—"

"Oh! that one is my own," replied Arnoux. "She just came in to pay me a visit as she was passing."

"You don't say so!" said Frederick.

"Why, yes; she is going back home again."

The charm of the surroundings was suddenly withdrawn. That which had seemed to him to be diffused vaguely through the place had now vanished—or, rather, it had never been there. He felt an infinite amazement, and, as it were, the painful sensation of having been betrayed.

Arnoux, while rummaging about in his drawer, smiled. Was he laughing at him? The clerk laid down a bundle of moist papers on the table.

"Ha! the placards," exclaimed the picture-dealer. "I am not ready to dine this evening."

Regimbart took up his hat.

"What, are you leaving?"

"Seven o'clock," said Regimbart.

Frederick followed him.

At the corner of the Rue Montmartre, he looked back. He glanced toward the windows of the first floor, and he laughed internally with self-pity as he recalled to mind with what love he had so often contemplated them. Where, then, did she reside? How would he ever meet her now? Once more the object of his desire was encompassed by a solitude more immense than ever!

"Are you going to take it?" asked Regimbart.

"To take what?"

"The absinthe."

And, yielding to his importunities, Frederick allowed himself to be led toward the Bordelais smoking-divan. Whilst his companion, leaning on his elbow, was staring at the decanter, he was turning his eyes to the right and to the left. He caught a glimpse of Pellerin's profile on the footpath outside; the painter gave a quick tap at the window-pane, and he had scarcely sat down when Regimbart asked him why they no longer saw him at the office of *L'Art Industriel*.

"May I perish before ever I go back there again. The fellow is a brute, a mere tradesman, a wretch, a downright rogue!"

These insulting words harmonised with Frederick's present angry mood. Nevertheless, he was wounded, for it seemed to him that they hit at Madame Arnoux more or less.

"Why, what has Arnoux done to you?" said Regimbart.

Pellerin stamped with his foot on the ground, and his only response was an energetic puff.

He had been devoting himself to artistic work of a kind that he did not care to connect his name with, such as portraits for two crayons, or pasticcios from the great masters for amateurs of limited knowledge; and, as he felt humiliated by these inferior productions, he preferred usually to hold his tongue on the subject. But "Arnoux's dirty conduct" exasperated him. He had to relieve his feelings.

In accordance with an order, which had been given in Frederick's very presence, he had brought Arnoux two pictures. Thereupon the dealer took the liberty of criticising them. He found fault with the composition, the colouring, and the drawing—above all, the drawing; he would not, in short, take them at any price. But, driven to extremities by a bill falling due, Pellerin had to give them to the Jew Isaac; and, a fortnight later, Arnoux himself sold them to a Spaniard for two thousand francs.

"Not a sou less! What rascality! and, faith, he is always doing things just as bad. One of these mornings we'll see him in the dock!"

"How you exaggerate!" said Frederick, in a timid voice.

"Come, now, that's good; I exaggerate!" exclaimed the artist, giving the table a great blow with his fist.

This violence completely restored the young man's self-command. No doubt he might have acted more generously; still, if Arnoux found these two pictures—

"Bad, say it! Are you then a judge of them? Is that your profession? Now, you know, my boy, I don't allow this sort of thing on the part of mere amateurs."

"Ah, well, it's none of my business," said Frederick.

"Then, what interest have you in defending him?" returned Pellerin, coldly.

The young man faltered:

"Well—since I am his friend—"

"Go, and give him a hug for me. Good evening!"

And the painter rushed away in a rage, and, of course, without paying for his drink.

Frederick, whilst defending Arnoux, had convinced himself. In the heat of his eloquence, he was filled with tenderness toward this man, so intelligent and kind, whom his friends calumniated, and who was now abandoned by them. He could not resist a strange impulse to go at once and see him again. Ten minutes later he pushed open the door of the picture-warehouse.

Arnoux was preparing, with the assistance of his clerks, some huge placards for an exhibition of pictures.

"Halloa! what brings you back again?"

This question, simple though it was, embarrassed Frederick, and, at a loss for an answer, he asked whether they had happened to find a note-book of his—a little notebook with a blue leather cover.

"The one that you put your letters to women in?" said Arnoux.

Frederick, blushing like a young girl, protested against such an assumption.

"Your verses, then?" returned the picture-dealer.

He was handling the pictures that were to be exhibited, examining their form, colouring, and frames; and Frederick felt more and more irritated by his air of abstraction, and particularly by the appearance of his hands—large hands, rather soft, with flat nails. At length, M. Arnoux arose, and saying, "That's disposed of!" he chucked the young man familiarly under the chin. Frederick was offended at this liberty, and recoiled a pace or two; then he made a dash for the shop-door, and passed out through it, as he imagined, for the last time in his life. Madame Arnoux herself had been lowered in his mind by the vulgarity of her husband.

During the same week he got a letter from Deslauriers, informing him that the clerk would be in Paris on the following Thursday. Then he flung himself back violently on this affection as one of a more solid and lofty character. A man of this sort was worth all the women in the world. He would no longer have any need of Regimbart, of Pellerin, of Hussonnet, of anyone! In order to provide his friend with as comfortable quarters as possible, he bought an iron bedstead and a second armchair, stripping off some of his own bed-covering to furnish the new one properly. On Thursday morning he was dressing himself to go to meet Deslauriers when there was a ring at the door.

Arnoux entered.

"Just a word. Yesterday I got a fine trout from Geneva. We expect you to-night—at seven o'clock sharp. The address is the Rue de Choiseul 24 *bis*. Don't forget!"

Frederick was obliged to sit down; his knees were tottering under him. He repeated to himself, "At last! at last!" Then he wrote to his tailor, to his hatter, and to his bootmaker; and he despatched these three notes by three different messengers.

The key turned in the lock, and the door-keeper appeared with a trunk on his shoulder.

Frederick, on seeing Deslauriers, began to tremble like an adulteress before her husband.

"What has happened to you?" said Deslauriers. "Surely you got my letter?"

Frederick had not enough energy left to lie. He flung himself on his friend's breast.

Then the clerk told his story. His father tried to avoid giving an account of the expense of tutelage, thinking that the period limited for rendering such accounts was ten years; but, well versed in legal procedure, Deslauriers had managed to get the share coming to him from his mother into his own possession—seven thousand francs clear—which he had there with him in an old pocket-book.

"'Tis a reserve fund, in case of misfortune. I must think over the best way of investing it, and find quarters for myself to-morrow morning. To-day I'm perfectly free, and am entirely at your service, my old friend."

"Oh, don't put yourself about," said Frederick. "If you had anything of importance to attend to this evening—"

"Come, now! I would be a selfish wretch—"

This epithet, flung out at random, touched Frederick to the quick, like a reproach.

The door-keeper had placed on the table close to the fire some chops, cold meat, a large lobster, some sweets for dessert, and two bottles of Bordeaux.

Deslauriers was touched by these excellent preparations to welcome his arrival.

"Upon my word, you are treating me like a king!"

They talked about the past and about the future; and, from time to time, they grasped each other's hands across the table, gazing at each other tenderly.

But a messenger came with a new hat. Deslauriers, in a loud tone, remarked that it was very showy. Next came the tailor himself to fit on the coat, to which he had given a touch with the smoothing-iron.

"One would imagine you were about to be married," said Deslauriers.

An hour later, a third individual appeared on the scene, and drew forth from a big black bag a pair of shining patent leather boots. While Frederick was trying them on, the bootmaker indirectly drew attention to the shoes of the young man from the country.

"Does Monsieur require anything?"

"No, thanks," replied the clerk, drawing behind his chair his old shoes fastened with strings.

This humiliating incident annoyed Frederick. At length he exclaimed, as if the idea had suddenly taken possession of him:

"Ha! deuce take it! I was forgetting."

"What is it, pray?"

"I have to dine in the city this evening."

"At the Dambreuses'? Why did you never say anything to me about them in your letters?"

"It is not at the Dambreuses', but at the Arnoux's."

"You should have let me know beforehand," said Deslauriers. "I would have come a day later."

"Impossible," returned Frederick, abruptly. "I only received the invitation this morning."

And to redeem his error and distract his friend's mind from the occurrence, he proceeded to unfasten the tangled cords around the trunk, and to arrange the contents in the chest of drawers, expressing his willingness to give him his own bed, and offering to sleep himself in the dressing-room bedstead. Then, at four o'clock, he began the preparations for his toilet.

"You have plenty of time," said the other.

At last he was dressed and off he went.

"That's the way with the rich," thought Deslauriers.

And he went to dine in the Rue Saint-Jacques, at a little restaurant kept by a man he knew.

Frederick stopped several times while going up the stairs, so violently did his heart beat. Arnoux, who was mounting the stairs behind him, took him by the arm and led him in.

Mademoiselle Marthe came to announce that her mamma was dressing. Arnoux raised her in his arms and kissed her; then, as he wished to
select certain bottles of wine from the cellar himself, he left Frederick
with the little girl.

She had grown considerably since the trip in the steamboat. Her dark
hair descended in long ringlets, which curled over her bare arms. Her
dress, more fluffed out than the petticoat of a *danseuse,* disclosed her rosy
calves, and her pretty childlike form had all the fresh odour of a bunch
of flowers. She received the young gentleman's compliments with a
coquettish air, fixed on him her large, dreamy eyes, then slipping on the
carpet, disappeared like a cat.

After this he no longer felt ill at ease. The globes of the lamps, covered with a paper lace-work, sent forth a white light, softening the colour
of the walls, hung with mauve satin. It was altogether a peaceful sight,
suggesting the idea of propriety and innocent family life.

Arnoux returned, and at the same moment Madame Arnoux appeared
at the other doorway. As she was enveloped in shadow, the young man
could at first distinguish only her head. She wore a black velvet gown,
and in her hair she had fastened a long Algerian cap, in a red silk net,
which coiling round her comb, fell over her left shoulder.

Arnoux introduced Frederick.

"Oh! I remember Monsieur perfectly," she responded.

Then the guests arrived, nearly all at the same time—Dittmer, Lovarias,
Burrieu, the composer Rosenwald, the poet Théophile Lorris, two art
critics, colleagues of Hussonnet, a paper manufacturer, and in the rear the
illustrious Pierre Paul Meinsius, the last representative of the grand
school of painting, who blithely carried along with his glory his forty-
five years and his big paunch.

When they were passing into the dining-room, Madame Arnoux took
his arm. A chair had been left vacant for Pellerin. Arnoux, though he
took advantage of him in business, was fond of him. Besides, he was
afraid of his terrible tongue, so much so that, in order to soften him, he
had printed a portrait of him in *L'Art Industriel,* accompanied by exaggerated eulogies; and Pellerin, more sensitive about distinction than
about money, made a breathless appearance about eight o'clock.
Frederick judged that they had been a long time reconciled.

He liked the company, the dishes, everything. He had to make his
choice between ten sorts of mustard. He partook of daspachio, of curry,
of ginger, of Corsican blackbirds, and a species of Roman macaroni
called lasagna; he drank extraordinary wines, lip-fraeli and tokay. Arnoux
indeed prided himself on entertaining people in good style. With an eye
to the procurement of eatables, he paid court to mail-coach drivers, and

was in league with the cooks of great houses, who divulged to him the secrets of rare sauces.

But Frederick was particularly entertained by the conversation. His taste for travelling was tickled by Dittmer, who talked about the East; he gratified his curiosity about theatrical matters by listening to Rosenwald's chat about the opera; and the atrocious existence of Bohemia assumed for him a droll aspect when presented through the gaiety of Hussonnet, who related, in a picturesque fashion, how he had spent an entire winter with no food except Dutch cheese. Then a discussion between Lovarias and Burrieu about the Florentine School gave him new ideas with regard to masterpieces and widened his horizon. He found difficulty in restraining his enthusiasm when Pellerin exclaimed:

"Don't talk to me about your hideous reality! What does it mean— reality? Some see things black, others blue—the multitude sees them brute-fashion. There is nothing less natural than Michael Angelo; there is nothing more powerful! The anxiety about eternal truth is a mark of contemporary baseness; and art will become, if things go on in that way, a sort of poor joke as much below religion as it is below poetry, and as much below politics as it is below business. You will never reach its end—yes, its end!—which is to cause within us an impersonal exaltation, with petty works, in spite of all your finished execution. Look, for instance, at Bassolier's pictures: they are pretty coquettish, spruce, and by no means dull. You might put them into your pocket, carry them with you when you are travelling. Notaries buy them for twenty thousand francs, while pictures of the ideal type bring three sous. But, without ideality, there is no grandeur; without grandeur there is no beauty. Olympus is a mountain. The most effective monument will always be the Pyramids. Exuberance is better than taste; the desert is better than a street-pavement, and a savage is surely better than a hairdresser!"

Frederick, as these words fell upon his ear, glanced towards Madame Arnoux. They sank into his soul like metals falling into a furnace, added to his passion, and supplied the material of love.

His chair was three seats below hers on the same side. From time to time, she bent forward a little, turning aside her head to address a few words to her little daughter; and as she smiled on these occasions, a dimple appeared in her cheek, giving to her face an expression of dainty good-nature.

As soon as the time came for the gentlemen to take their wine, she disappeared. The conversation became more free and easy. M. Arnoux shone in it, and Frederick was amazed at the cynicism of men. However, their preoccupation with women established between them and him, as it were, an equality, which raised him in his own estimation.

When they had returned to the drawing-room, he took up, to keep himself in countenance, one of the albums which lay about on the table. The great artists of the day had illustrated them with drawings, had written in them snatches of verse or prose, or simply their signatures. In the midst of famous names he found many that he had never heard of before, and original thoughts appeared only underneath a flood of nonsense. All these effusions contained a more or less direct expression of homage toward Madame Arnoux. Frederick would have been afraid to write a line beside them.

She went into her boudoir to look at the little chest with silver clasps which he had noticed on the mantel-shelf. It was a present from her husband, a work of the Renaissance. Arnoux's friends complimented him, and his wife thanked him. His tender emotions were aroused, and before all the guests he kissed her.

After this they chatted in groups here and there. The worthy Meinsius was beside Madame Arnoux in an easy chair close by the fire. She was leaning forward toward his ear; their heads were almost touching, and Frederick would have been glad to become deaf, infirm, and ugly if he might thereby gain an illustrious name and white hair—in short, if he only happened to possess something which would justify such intimate association with her. He began once more to eat out his heart, furious at the idea of being so young a man.

But at last she came into the corner of the drawing-room where he was sitting, and asked him whether he was acquainted with any of the guests, whether he was fond of painting, how long he had been a student in Paris. Every word that came out of her mouth seemed to Frederick something entirely new, an exclusive appendage of her personality. He gazed at the fringes of her head-dress, the ends of which caressed her bare shoulder, and he was unable to remove his eyes; he plunged his soul into the whiteness of that feminine flesh, and yet he did not venture to raise his eyes to glance at her higher, face to face.

Rosenwald interrupted them, begging of Madame Arnoux to sing something. He played a prelude, she waited, her lips opened slightly, and a sound, pure, long-continued, silvery, ascended into the air.

Frederick did not understand a single one of the Italian words. The song began with a grave measure, something like church music, then in a more animated strain, with a crescendo movement, it broke into repeated bursts of sound, then suddenly subsided, and the melody came back again in a tender fashion with a wide and rhythmic swing.

She stood beside the keyboard, her arms hanging down and a far-off look on her face. Sometimes, in order to read the music, she advanced her forehead for a moment and her eyelashes moved to and fro. Her contralto voice in the low notes took a mournful intonation which had a chilling effect on the listener, and then her beautiful head, with those great brows of hers, bent over her shoulder; her bosom swelled; her eyes widened; her neck, from which roulades made their escape, fell back as if under aerial kisses. She flung out three sharp notes, came down again, sent forth one higher still, and, after a silence, finished with an organ-point.

Rosenwald did not leave the piano. He continued playing, to amuse himself. From time to time a guest stole away. At eleven o'clock, as the last of them were departing, Arnoux went out along with Pellerin, under the pretext of seeing him home. He was one of those people who claim to be ill when they do not "take a turn" after dinner. Madame Arnoux had made her way toward the anteroom. Dittmer and Hussonnet bowed to her. She stretched out her hand to them. She did the same to Frederick; and he felt, as it were, something penetrating every particle of his skin.

He left his friends. He wished to be alone. His heart was overflowing. Why had she offered him he hand? Was it a thoughtless act, or an encouragement? "Come now! I am mad!" Besides, what did it matter, now that he could visit her entirely at his ease, live in the very atmosphere she breathed?

The streets were deserted. Now and then a heavy waggon would roll past, shaking the pavements. Suddenly he felt himself in the midst of a circle of damp air, and found that he was on the edge of the quays.

He stopped in the middle of the Pont Neuf, and, taking off his hat and exposing his chest, he drank in the air. He felt as if something that was inexhaustible were ascending from the very depths of his being, an afflux of tenderness that enervated him, like the motion of the waves under his eyes. A church-clock slowly struck one, and had the effect of a voice calling out to him.

Then, he was seized with one of those shuddering sensations of the soul in which one seems to be transported into a higher world. He felt, as it were, endowed with some extraordinary faculty, the purpose of which he could not determine. He seriously questioned himself whether he would be a great painter or a great poet; and he decided in favour of painting, for this profession would bring him into closer contact with Madame Arnoux. At last, he had found his vocation! The goal of his life was now perfectly clear, and there could be no mistake about the future.

When he had closed his door, he heard some one snoring in the dark closet near his apartment. It was his friend. He no longer wasted a thought on him.

Looking in the glass he contemplated his own face. It appeared to him handsome. For a whole minute he stood gazing at himself.

CHAPTER V

A CONSUMING LOVE

FREDERICK HAD purchased an easel, a box of paints, and brushes before twelve o'clock the following day. Pellerin agreed to give him lessons, and Frederick brought him to his lodgings to see whether anything more was needed among his painting utensils.

Deslauriers was in, and the second armchair was occupied by a young man. The clerk said, pointing towards him:

"'Tis he! There he is! Sénécal!" Frederick did not like this young man. His forehead was heightened by the manner in which he wore his hair, cut straight like a brush. There was a certain hard, cold look in his grey eyes; and his long black coat, his entire costume, savoured of the pedagogue and the ecclesiastic.

They first discussed topics of the moment, amongst others the *Stabat* of Rossini. Sénécal, in answer to a question, stated that he never went to the theatre.

Pellerin opened the box of colours.

"Are these all yours?" said the clerk.

"Why, certainly!"

"Well, really! What a notion!" And he leaned across the table, at which the mathematical tutor was turning over the leaves of a volume of Louis Blanc. He had brought it with him, and was reading passages from it in low tones, while Pellerin and Frederick examined together the palette, the knife, and the bladders; then the talk came round to the dinner at Arnoux's.

"The picture-dealer, is it?" asked Sénécal. "A nice gentleman, truly!"

"Why, now?" said Pellerin. Sénécal replied:

"A man who makes money by political turpitude!"

And he went on to talk about a well-known lithograph, in which all the Royal Family were represented as being engaged in edifying occupations: Louis Philippe had a copy of the Code in his hand; the Queen had a Catholic prayer-book; the Princesses were embroidering; the Duc de Nemours was girding on a sword; M. de Joinville was showing a map to his young brothers; and at one end of the apartment could be seen a bed with two divisions. This picture, which was entitled "A Good Family," was a source of delight to commonplace middle-class people, but of grief to patriots.

Pellerin, in a tone of annoyance, as if he had been himself the producer of this work, observed by way of answer that every opinion had some value. Sénécal protested: Art should aim exclusively at promoting morality amongst the masses! The only subjects that ought to be reproduced were those which incited to virtuous actions; all others were injurious.

"But that depends on the execution," cried Pellerin. "I might produce masterpieces."

"So much the worse of you, then; you have no right—"

"What?"

"No, Monsieur, you have no right to excite my interest in matters of which I disapprove. What need have we of laborious trifles, from which it is impossible to derive any benefit—those Venuses, for instance, with all your landscapes? They contain no instruction for the people! Show us rather their miseries! arouse enthusiasm in us for their sacrifices! Ah, my God! there is no lack of subjects—the farm, the workshop—"

Pellerin stammered forth his indignation at this, and, imagining that he had found an argument:

"Molière, do you accept him?"

"Certainly!" said Sénécal. "I admire him as the precursor of the French Revolution."

"Ha! the Revolution! What art! Never was there a more pitiable epoch!"

"None greater, Monsieur!"

Pellerin folded his arms, and looking at him straight in the face:

"You have the appearance of a famous member of the National Guard!"

His opponent, accustomed to discussions, responded:

"I am not, and I abhor it just as much as you. But with such principles we corrupt the crowd. This sort of thing, however, is profitable to the Government. It would not be so powerful but for the complicity of rogues of that sort."

The painter commenced to defend the picture-dealer, for Sénécal's opinions exasperated him. He even went so far as to maintain that Arnoux was really a man with a heart of gold, devoted to his friends, deeply attached to his wife.

"Oho! if you offered him a sufficient sum, he would not refuse to let her serve as a model."

Frederick turned pale.

"So then, he has done you some great harm, Monsieur?"

"Me? no! I saw him once at a café with a friend. That's all."

Sénécal had spoken truly. But he had his teeth daily set on edge by the announcements in *L'Art Industriel*. Arnoux to him represented a world which he considered antagonistic to democracy. An austere Republican, he suspected something corrupt in every form of elegance, and the more so as he wanted nothing himself and was inflexible in his integrity.

They found some difficulty in resuming the conversation. The painter soon recalled to mind his appointment, the tutor his pupils; and, when they had gone, after a long silence, Deslauriers asked a number of questions about Arnoux.

"You will introduce me there later, will you not, old fellow?"

"Certainly," said Frederick. Then they talked about settling themselves. Deslauriers had without much trouble obtained the post of second clerk in a solicitor's office; he had also entered his name for the terms at the Law School, and bought the indispensable books. The life of which they had dreamed for so long now began.

It was delightful, owing to their youth, which made everything assume a favourable aspect. As Deslauriers had said nothing relative to any pecuniary arrangement, Frederick did not refer to the subject. He helped to defray all the expenses, kept the cupboard well stocked, and attended to all the household requirements; but if it happened to be necessary to give the doorkeeper a rating, the clerk took that on his own shoulders, still maintaining the part, which he had assumed in their college days, of protector and senior.

Separated all day long, they met in the evenings. Each took his place at the fireside and set about his work. But ere long it would be interrupted. Then would follow endless outpourings, unaccountable bursts of merriment, and occasional disputes about the lamp flaring too much or a book being mislaid, momentary manifestations of anger which subsided in hearty laughter.

While in bed they left open the door of the little room where Deslauriers slept, and kept chattering to each other.

When it was not raining on Sunday they went out together, and, arm in arm, sauntered through the streets. The same ideas nearly always occurred to them simultaneously. Sometimes they would go on chatting without noticing anything around them. Deslauriers longed for riches, as a means for gaining power over men.

Frederick's ideal was to furnish for himself a palace in the Moorish fashion, to spend his life reclining on cashmere divans, listening to the murmur of a jet of water, and attended by negro pages. And these things, of which he had only dreamed, became in time so definite that he felt as dejected as if he had lost them.

"What is the use of talking about all these things," said he, "when we'll never have them?"

"Who knows?" returned Deslauriers.

Despite his democratic views, he urged Frederick to get an introduction into the Dambreuses' house.

The other, by way of objection, pointed to the failure of his previous attempts.

"Bah! go back there. They'll give you an invitation!"

Toward the close of the month of March, they received amongst other bills that of the restaurant-keeper who supplied them with dinners. Frederick, not having the entire amount, borrowed a hundred crowns from Deslauriers. A fortnight afterward, he renewed the same request, and the clerk lectured him on the extravagant habits he was contracting in the Arnoux's society.

As a matter of fact, he put no restraint upon himself in this respect. A view of Venice, a view of Naples, and another of Constantinople occupying the centre of three walls respectively, equestrian subjects by Alfred de Dreux here and there, a group by Pradier over the mantelpiece, numbers of *L'Art Industriel* lying on the piano, and works in boards on the floor in the corners, encumbered the apartment to such an extent that it was difficult to find a place to lay a book on, or to move one's elbows about freely. Frederick maintained that he needed all this for his painting.

He pursued his art-studies under Pellerin. But when he called on the artist, the latter was often out, being accustomed to attend at every funeral and public occurrence of which an account was given in the newspapers, and so it was that Frederick spent hours alone in the studio. His eyes wandering from the task at which he was engaged, roamed over the shell-work on the wall, around the objects of virtù, and, like a traveller who has lost his way in the middle of a wood, and whom every path brings back to the same spot, continually, he found underlying every idea in his mind the recollection of Madame Arnoux.

He selected days for calling on her. When he had reached the second floor, he would pause on the threshold, doubtful as to whether he ought to ring or not. Steps drew nigh, the door opened, and at the announcement "Madame is out," a sense of relief would come upon him, as if a weight had been lifted from his heart. He met her, however. On the first occasion there were three other ladies with her; the next time it was in the afternoon, and Mademoiselle Marthe's writing-master was present. The men whom Madame Arnoux received were not very punctilious about paying visits. For the sake of prudence he deemed it better not to call again.

But he did not fail to appear regularly at the office of *L'Art Industriel* every Wednesday in order to get an invitation to the Thursday dinners, and he remained there later than all the others, even than Regimbart, right up to the last moment, pretending to be looking at an engraving or to be running his eye over a newspaper. At last Arnoux would say to him, "Shall you be disengaged to-morrow evening?" and, before the sentence was finished, he would give an affirmative answer. Arnoux appeared to have taken a fancy to him.

During these dinners he scarcely uttered a word; he kept gazing at her. She had a little mole close to her temple. Her head-bands were darker than the rest of her hair, and were always a little moist at the edges; from time to time she stroked them with only two fingers. He was familiar

with the shape of each of her nails. He took delight in listening to the
rustle of her silk skirt as she swept past doors; he stealthily inhaled the
perfume that came from her handkerchief; her comb, her gloves, her rings
were for him things of special interest, important as works of art, almost
endowed with human life; all took possession of his heart and strengthened his passion.

He had not sufficient self-control to conceal it from Deslauriers. When
he came home from Madame Arnoux's, he would wake up his friend, as
if inadvertently, in order to have an opportunity to talk about her.

Deslauriers, who slept in the little closet-room, close to where they
had their water-supply, would give great yawns. Frederick seated himself
on the side of the bed. At first he spoke about the dinner; then he
referred to a thousand petty details, in which he saw marks of contempt
or of affection. On one occasion, for instance, she had refused his arm, in
order to take Dittmer's; and Frederick gave vent to his humiliation:

"Ah! how stupid!"

Or else she had called him her "dear friend."

"Then go after her gaily!"

"But I dare not," said Frederick.

"Well, then, think no more about her! Good night!"

Deslauriers thereupon turned on his side, and fell asleep. He felt utterly
unable to comprehend this love, which seemed to him the last weakness
of adolescence; and, as his own society was apparently not enough to satisfy Frederick, he conceived the idea of bringing together, once a week,
those whom they both recognised as friends.

They came on Saturday about nine o'clock. The three Algerine curtains were carefully drawn. The lamp and four wax-lights were burning.
In the middle of the table the tobacco-pot, filled with pipes, displayed
itself between the beer-bottles, the tea-pot, a flagon of rum, and some
fancy biscuits.

They discussed the immortality of the soul, and drew comparisons
between the different professors.

One evening Hussonnet introduced a tall young man, wearing a
frock-coat, too short in the wrists, and with a look of embarrassment on
his face. It was the young fellow whom they had tried to release from the
guard-house the year before.

As he had been unable to restore the box of lace lost in the scuffle, his
employer had accused him of theft, and threatened to prosecute him. He
was now a clerk in a wagon-office. Hussonnet had come across him that
morning at the corner of the street, and brought him along, for
Dussardier, in a spirit of gratitude, had expressed a wish to see "the other."

He held out toward Frederick the cigar-holder, which he had religiously preserved, still full, in the hope of being able to give it back. The

young men invited him to pay them a second visit; and he was not slow in doing so.

They all had sympathies in common. Their hatred of the Government reached the height of an unquestionable dogma. Martinon alone attempted to defend Louis Philippe. They overwhelmed him with the commonplaces rampant in the newspapers—the "Bastillization" of Paris, the September laws, Pritchard, Lord Guizot—so that Martinon decided to hold his tongue for fear of giving offence to somebody. During his seven years at college he had never incurred the penalty of an imposition, and at the Law School he knew how to make himself agreeable to the professors. He usually wore a big putty-coloured frock-coat, with india-rubber goloshes; but one evening he presented himself arrayed like a bridegroom, in a velvet roll-collar waistcoat, a white tie, and a gold chain.

The astonishment of the other young men was still greater when they learned that he had just come away from M. Dambreuse's house. In fact, the banker Dambreuse had just bought a portion of an extensive wood from Martinon senior; and, when the worthy man introduced his son, the other had invited them both to dinner.

"Were there plenty of truffles there?" asked Deslauriers. "And did you take his wife by the waist between the two doors, *sicut decet?*"

Hereupon the conversation turned on women. Pellerin would not admit that there were beautiful women (he preferred tigers); besides, the human female was an inferior creature in the æsthetic hierarchy:

"What fascinates you physically is just the very thing that degrades her as an idea; I mean her breasts, her hair—"

"Nevertheless," urged Frederick, "long black hair and large dark eyes—"

"Oh! we know all about that," cried Hussonnet. "Enough of Andalusian beauties on the lawn. Those things are out of date; no, thank you! For the fact is, honour bright! a fast woman is more amusing than the Venus of Milo. Let us be Gallic, in Heaven's name, and after the Regency style, if we can!

'Flow, generous wines; ladies, deign to smile!'

We must pass from the dark to the fair. Do you agree, Father Dussardier?"

Dussardier did not reply. They all pressed him to state what his tastes were.

"Well," said he, colouring, "for my part, I would like to love the same one always!"

This was said in such a way that there was a moment of silence, some of them being surprised at this candour, and others finding in his words, perhaps, the secret yearning of their souls.

Sénécal placed his glass of beer on the mantelpiece, declaring dogmatically that, as prostitution was tyrannical and marriage immoral, it was better to practise abstinence. Deslauriers regarded women as a source of amusement—nothing more. M. de Cisy looked upon them with the utmost dread.

Brought up under the eyes of a grandmother who was a devotee, he found the society of these young fellows as alluring as a place of ill-repute and as instructive as the Sorbonne. Frederick showed him the greatest attention. He admired the shade of his cravat, the fur on his over-coat, and especially his boots, as thin as gloves, and so very neat and fine that they had a look of insolent superiority. His carriage used to wait for him below in the street.

One evening, after his departure, when there was a fall of snow, Sénécal began to complain about his having a coachman. He declaimed against kid-gloved exquisites and against the Jockey Club. He had more respect for a workman than for these fine gentlemen.

"For my part, I work for my livelihood! I am a poor man!"

"That's quite evident," said Frederick, at length, losing patience.

The tutor held a grudge against him for this remark.

But, as Regimbart said he knew Sénécal pretty well, Frederick, wishing to be civil to a friend of the Arnoux, invited him to the Saturday meetings; and the two patriots were glad to be brought together in this way.

However, they took opposite views of most things.

Sénécal—whose skull was of the angular type—fixed his attention entirely on systems, whereas Regimbart, on the contrary, saw in facts nothing more than facts. The thing that chiefly troubled him was the Rhine frontier. He claimed to be an authority on the subject of artillery, and got his clothes made by a tailor of the Polytechnic School.

The first day, when they offered him some cakes, he disdainfully shrugged his shoulders, saying that they might suit women; and on fol-lowing occasions his manner was not much more gracious. Whenever speculative ideas had reached a certain elevation, he would mutter: "Oh! no Utopias, no dreams!" On the subject of Art (though he used to visit the studios, and occasionally, out of complaisance, give a lesson in fenc-ing) his opinions were not remarkable for their excellence. He compared the style of M. Marast to that of Voltaire, and Mademoiselle Vatnaz to Madame de Staël, on account of an Ode on Poland in which "there was some spirit." In short, Regimbart bored everyone, and especially Deslauriers, for the Citizen was a friend of the Arnoux family. Now the clerk was most anxious to visit those people in the hope that he might there make acquaintances who would be of advantage to him.

"When are you going to take me there with you?" he would say. Arnoux was either overburdened with business, or else starting on a jour-ney. Then it was not worth while, as the dinners were soon coming to an end.

If he had been called on to risk his life for his friend, Frederick would have done so. But, as he was desirous of presenting as good a figure as possible, and with this in view was most careful about his language and manners, and so attentive to his costume that he always appeared at the office of *L'Art Industriel* irreproachably gloved, he was afraid that Deslauriers, with his shabby black coat, his attorney-like exterior, and his swaggering kind of talk, might not be agreeable to Madame Arnoux, and thus compromise him and lower him in her estimation. The other results would have been bad enough, but the last one would have annoyed him immeasurably.

The clerk realised that his friend did not wish to keep his promise, and Frederick's silence seemed to him an aggravation of the insult. Moreover, Frederick, with his thoughts full of Madame Arnoux, frequently talked about her husband; and Deslauriers now began an intolerable course of boredom by repeating the name a hundred times a day, at the end of each remark, like the parrot-cry of an idiot.

When there was a knock at the door he would call out, "Come in, Arnoux!" At the restaurant he would order a Brie cheese "*à la* Arnoux," and at night, pretending to wake up from a bad dream, he would rouse his comrade by howling out, "Arnoux! Arnoux!" At last Frederick, worn out, said to him one day, in a piteous voice:

"Oh! don't bother me any more about Arnoux!"

"Never!" replied the clerk:

> "He always, everywhere, burning or icy cold,
>   The pictured form of Arnoux—"

"Hold your tongue, I tell you!" exclaimed Frederick, raising his fist. Then less angrily he added:

"You know very well that this is a painful subject to me."

"Oh! forgive me, old fellow," returned Deslauriers with a very low bow. "From this time forth we will be considerate toward Mademoiselle's nerves. Again, I say, forgive me. A thousand pardons!"

And so this little joke came to an end.

But, three weeks later, one evening, Deslauriers said to him:

"Well, I have just seen Madame Arnoux."

"Where, pray?"

"At the Palais, with Balandard, the solicitor. A dark woman, is she not, of middle height?"

Frederick made a gesture of assent. He waited for Deslauriers to speak further. At the least expression of admiration he would have been most effusive, and would have fairly hugged the other. However, Deslauriers said nothing. At last, unable to contain himself any longer, Frederick, with assumed indifference, asked him what he thought of her.

Deslauriers considered that "she was not so bad, but still nothing extraordinary."

"Ha! you think so," said Frederick.

They soon reached the month of August, the time when he was to present himself for his second examination. According to the prevailing opinion, the subjects could be prepared for in a fortnight. Frederick, having full confidence in his own powers, swallowed up in a trice the first four books of the Code of Procedure, the first three of the Penal Code, fragments of the system of criminal investigation, and a part of the Civil Code, with the annotations of Monsieur Poncelet.

As several examinations were taking place at the same time, there were many persons in the precincts, and among others Hussonnet and Cisy: young men never failed to come and watch these ordeals when the fortunes of their comrades were at stake.

Frederick put on the traditional black gown; then, followed by the throng, with three other students, he entered a spacious apartment, into which the light penetrated through uncurtained windows. There were benches ranged along the walls, and in the centre of the room leather chairs were set round a table adorned with a green cover. This separated the candidates from the examiners in their red gowns and ermine shoulder-knots, the head examiners wearing gold-laced flat caps.

Frederick found himself the last but one in the series—an unfortunate place. In answer to the first question, as to the difference between a convention and a contract, he defined the one as if it were the other; and the professor, who was a fair sort of man, said to him, "Don't be agitated, Monsieur! Compose yourself!" Then, having asked two easy questions, which were answered in a doubtful fashion, he passed on at last to the fourth. This wretched beginning caused Frederick to lose his head. Deslauriers, who was facing him amongst the spectators, made an encouraging sign to him to indicate that it was not a hopeless case yet; and at the second series of questions, dealing with the criminal law, he came out tolerably well. But after the third, with reference to the "mystic will," the examiner having remained impassive the whole time, his mental distress redoubled; for Hussonnet brought his hands together as if to applaud, whilst Deslauriers liberally indulged in shrugs of the shoulders. Finally, the moment was reached for the examination on Procedure. The professor, displeased at listening to theories opposed to his own, presently asked him in a churlish tone:

"And so this is your view, Monsieur? How do you reconcile the principle of Article 1351 of the Civil Code with this application by a third party to set aside a judgment by default?"

Frederick had a bad headache from not having slept the night before. A ray of sunlight, penetrating through one of the slits in a Venetian blind, fell on his face. Standing behind the seat, he kept wriggling about and tugging at his moustache.

"I am still awaiting your answer," the man with the gold-edged cap observed.

And as Frederick's movements, no doubt, irritated him:

"You won't find it in that moustache of yours!"

This sarcasm made the spectators laugh. The professor, feeling flattered, adopted a coaxing tone. He put two more questions with reference to adjournment and summary jurisdiction, then nodded his head by way of approval. The examination was over. Frederick retired into the vestibule.

While an usher was taking off his gown, to put it on some other person immediately afterward, his friends gathered around him and succeeded in fairly worrying him with their conflicting opinions as to the result of his examination. Presently the announcement was made in a sonorous voice at the entrance of the hall: "The third was—put off!"

"Sent packing!" said Hussonnet. "Let us go away!"

In front of the doorkeeper's lodge they met Martinon, flushed, excited, with a smile on his face and the halo of victory around his brow. He had just passed his final examination without any impediment. All he had now to do was the thesis. Before a fortnight was over he would be a licentiate. His family enjoyed the acquaintance of a Minister; "a beautiful career" was opening before him.

"All the same, this puts you into a mess," said Deslauriers.

There is nothing so humiliating as to see blockheads succeed in undertakings in which we ourselves fail. Frederick, filled with vexation, replied that he did not care a straw about the matter. He had higher pretensions; and as Hussonnet made a move to leave, Frederick took him aside, and said to him:

"Not a word about this to them, mind!"

It was easy to keep it secret, since Arnoux was starting the next morning for Germany.

When he returned in the evening the clerk found his friend singularly altered: he was dancing about and whistling; the other was astonished at this capricious change of mood. Frederick declared that he did not intend to go home to his mother, as he meant to spend his holidays working.

At the news of Arnoux's departure, a feeling of joy had taken possession of him. He might present himself at the house whenever he liked without any fear of having his visits interrupted. The consciousness of absolute security would give him confidence. Now he would not stand aloof, he would not be separated from her! Something more powerful than an iron chain attached him to Paris; a voice from the depths of his heart told him to remain.

There were certain obstacles in his path. These he overcame by writing to his mother: first of all he admitted that he had failed to pass, owing to alterations made in the course—a mere mischance—an unfair thing; besides, all the great advocates (he referred to them by name) had been rejected at their examinations. But he planned to present himself again in the month of November. Now, having no time to lose, he would not go home this year; and he asked, in addition to the quarterly allowance, for two hundred and fifty francs, to enable him to get coached in law by a private tutor, which would be of great assistance to him; and he threw around the entire epistle a garland of regrets, condolences, expressions of affection, and protestations of filial love.

Madame Moreau, who had been expecting him the following day, was doubly grieved. She threw a veil over her son's misadventure, and in answer told him to "come all the same." Frederick would not give way, and the result was a falling out between them. However, at the end of the week he received the amount of the quarter's allowance, together with the sum required for the payment of the private tutor. This helped to pay for a pair of pearl-grey trousers, a white felt hat, and a gold-headed switch. When he had procured all these things he thought:

"Perhaps this is only a hairdresser's fancy on my part!"

And a feeling of considerable hesitation took possession of him.

In order to decide as to whether he ought to call on Madame Arnoux, he tossed three coins into the air in succession. On each occasion luck was in his favour. Surely Fate must have ordained it. He hailed a cab and drove to the Rue de Choiseul.

He quickly ascended the staircase and drew the bell-pull, but without effect. He felt as if he were about to faint.

Then, with fierce energy, he pulled the heavy silk tassel. There was a resounding peal which gradually died away till no further sound was heard. Frederick got rather frightened.

He laid his ear to the door—not a breath! He looked in through the key-hole and only saw two reed-points on the wall-paper in the midst of designs of flowers. At last he was on the point of going away when he thought he would try once more. This time he gave a timid little ring. The door flew open, and Arnoux himself appeared on the threshold, with his hair all in disorder, his face crimson, and his features distorted by an expression of sullen embarrassment.

"Hallo! What the deuce brings you here? Come in!"

He led Frederick, not into the boudoir or into the bed-room, but into the dining-room, where on the table was a bottle of champagne and two glasses; and, in an abrupt tone:

"There is something you want to ask me, my dear friend?"

"No! nothing! nothing!" stammered the young man, trying to think of some excuse for his visit. At length he said that he had called to enquire if there were any news from him, as Hussonnet had announced that he had gone to Germany.

"Not at all!" returned Arnoux. "What a feather-headed fellow that is to misunderstand everything!"

In order to conceal his agitation, Frederick kept walking from right to left in the dining-room. Happening to come into contact with a chair, he knocked down a parasol which had been laid across it, and the ivory handle broke.

"Good heavens!" he exclaimed. "How sorry I am for having broken Madame Arnoux's parasol!"

At this remark, the picture-dealer raised his head and smiled in a very peculiar fashion. Frederick, taking advantage of the opportunity thus offered to talk about her, added shyly:

"Could I not see her?"

No. She had gone to the country to see her mother, who was ill.

He did not venture to ask any questions as to the length of time that she would be away. He merely inquired what was Madame Arnoux's native place.

"Chartres. Does this astonish you?"

"Astonish me? Oh, no! Why should it? Not in the least!"

After that they could find absolutely nothing to talk about. Arnoux, having made a cigarette for himself, kept walking round the table, puffing. Frederick, standing near the stove, stared at the walls, the whatnot, and the floor; and the delightful pictures flitted through his memory, or, rather, before his eyes. Then he left the apartment.

A piece of a newspaper, rolled up into a ball, lay on the floor in the anteroom. Arnoux snatched it up, and, raising himself on the tips of his toes, he stuck it into the bell, in order, as he said, that he might be able to go and finish his interrupted siesta. Then, as he grasped Frederick's hand:

"Kindly tell the porter that I am not in."

And he shut the door after him with a bang.

Frederick descended the staircase slowly. The failure of this first attempt discouraged him as to the possible results of those that might follow. Then began three months of absolute boredom.

He went back to his bedchamber; then, throwing himself on the sofa, he abandoned himself to a confused succession of thoughts—plans of work, schemes for the guidance of his conduct, attempts to penetrate the future. At last, in order to shake off broodings which were all about himself, he went out into the open air.

He plunged at random into the Latin Quarter, usually so noisy, but deserted at this particular time, for the students had gone back to their families.

Every day he went to the office of *L'Art Industriel*; and in order to ascertain when Madame Arnoux would be back, he made elaborate enquiries about her mother. Arnoux's answer never varied—"the change for the better was continuing"—his wife, with his little daughter, would be returning the following week. The longer she remained away the more uneasiness Frederick exhibited, so that Arnoux, touched by so much affection, took him five or six times a week to dine at a restaurant.

In the long talks which they had together on these occasions Frederick discovered that the picture-dealer was not a particularly intellectual type of a man. Arnoux might, however, take notice of his chilling manner; and Frederick deemed it advisable to pay back, in a small measure, his polite attentions.

Being anxious to do things on a good scale, the young man sold all his new clothes to a second-hand clothes-dealer for the sum of eighty francs, and having added it to the hundred francs which he still had left, he called at Arnoux's house to bring him out to dine. Regimbart happened to be there, and all three of them set forth for Les Trois Frères Provençaux.

The Citizen began by taking off his surtout, and, knowing that the two others would defer to his gastronomic tastes, he drew up the *menu*. But in vain did he make his way to the kitchen to speak himself to the *chef*, go down to the cellar, with every corner of which he was familiar, and send for the master of the establishment, to whom he gave "a blowing up." He was not pleased with the dishes, the wines, or the attendance. At each new dish, at each fresh bottle, as soon as he had swallowed the first mouthful, the first draught, he threw down his fork or pushed his glass some distance away from him; then, with his elbows on the table-cloth, and stretching out his arms, he declared in a loud tone that it was no longer possible to dine in Paris! Finally, not knowing what to put into his mouth, Regimbart ordered kidney-beans dressed with oil, "quite plain," which, though only a partial success, slightly appeased him. Then he had a talk with the waiter about the latter's predecessors at the "Provençaux":—"What had become of Antoine? And a fellow named Eugène? And Theodore, the little fellow who always used to attend down stairs? There was much better fare in those days, and Burgundy vintages the like of which they would never see again."

They went out to get coffee in the smoking-divan on the ground-floor in the Passage du Saumon. Frederick had to stand around while interminable games of billiards were being played, drenched in innumerable glasses of beer; and he lingered on there till midnight without knowing why, merely through want of energy, through sheer senselessness, in the vague expectation that something might happen which would give a favourable turn to his love.

When, then, would he see her again? Frederick was in a state of despair. But one evening, toward the close of November, Arnoux said to him:

"My wife, you know, came back yesterday!"

Next day, at five o'clock, he made his way to her house. He began by congratulating her on her mother's recovery from such a serious illness.

"Why, no! Who told you that?"

"Arnoux!"

She gave vent to a slight "Ah!" then added that she had grave fears at first, which, however, were now entirely dispelled. She was seated close beside the fire in an upholstered easy-chair. He was on the sofa, with his hat between his knees; and the conversation was difficult to carry on, as it was broken off nearly every minute, so he got no chance of giving utterance to his sentiments. But when he began to complain of having to study legal quibbles, she answered, "Oh! I understand—business!" and she let her face fall, buried suddenly in her own reflections.

He was eager to know what they were, and thought of nothing else. The twilight shadows gathered around them.

She rose, having to do some shopping; then she reappeared in a bonnet trimmed with velvet, and a black mantle edged with minever. He plucked up enough courage to offer to accompany her.

It was now so dark that one could scarcely see anything. The air was cold, and had an unpleasant odour, owing to a heavy fog, which partially blotted out the fronts of the houses. Frederick breathed it with delight; for he could feel through the wadding of his coat the form of her arm; and her hand, cased in a chamois glove with two buttons, her little hand which he would have liked to cover with kisses, leaned on his sleeve. Owing to the slipperiness of the pavement, they lost their balance a little; it seemed to him as if they were both rocked by the wind in the midst of a cloud.

The glitter of the lamps on the boulevard awoke him to the realities of existence. The opportunity was a good one, there was no time to lose. He allowed himself as far as the Rue de Richelieu to declare his love. But almost at that very moment, in front of a china-shop, she stopped abruptly and said to him:

"This is the place. Thanks. On Thursday—is it not?—as usual."

The dinners were now renewed; and the more he visited at Madame Arnoux's the more his love-sickness increased. The contemplation of this woman had an enervating effect upon him, like the use of a perfume that is too strong. It penetrated into the very depths of his nature, and became almost a kind of habitual sensation, a new mode of existence.

The prostitutes whom he brushed past under the gaslight, the female ballad-singers breaking into bursts of melody, the ladies rising on horseback at full gallop, the shopkeepers' wives on foot, the grisettes at their windows, all women brought her before his mental vision, either by their resemblance to her or through the violent contrast they presented.

When he went into the Jardin des Plantes the sight of a palm-tree directed his thoughts to distant countries. They were travelling together on the backs of dromedaries, under the awnings of elephants, in the cabin of a yacht amongst the blue archipelagoes, or side by side on mules with little bells attached to them who went stumbling through the grass against broken columns. Then he saw her descending some wide porphyry staircase in the midst of senators under a daïs of ostriches' feathers, clad in a robe of brocade. At another time he dreamed of her in yellow silk trousers on the cushions of a harem.

As for attempting to make her his mistress, he was sure that it would be futile.

One evening Dittmer, on his arrival, kissed her on the forehead; Lovarias did the same, observing:

"You give me permission—don't you?—as it is a friend's privilege?"

Frederick stammered out:

"It seems to me that we are all friends."

"Not all old friends!" she returned.

This was repulsing him beforehand indirectly.

Besides, what could he do? Tell her that he loved her? No doubt, she would decline to listen to him or else she would feel indignant and order him out of the house. He preferred to submit to even the most painful ordeal rather than run the horrible risk of seeing her no more. He envied pianists for their talents and soldiers for their scars. He longed for a dangerous attack of sickness, hoping in this way to arouse her interest.

One thing caused astonishment to himself, that he felt in no way jealous of Arnoux; and he could not picture her in his imagination undressed, so natural did her modesty appear, and so far did her sex recede into a mysterious background.

Nevertheless, he dreamed of the happiness of living with her, of "theeing" and "thouing" her, of passing his hand lingeringly over her head-bands, or remaining in a kneeling posture on the floor, with both arms clasped round her waist, so as to drink in her soul through his eyes. To accomplish this it would be necessary to overcome Fate; and so, incapable of action, cursing God, and accusing himself of being a coward, he kept moving restlessly within the confines of his passion just as a prisoner keeps moving about in his dungeon. The pangs which he was perpetually enduring were choking him. For hours he would remain quite motionless, or else he would burst into tears; and one day when he had not the strength to control his emotion, Deslauriers said to him:

"Why, goodness gracious! what's the matter with you?"

Frederick's nerves were unstrung. Deslauriers did not believe a word of it. At the sight of so much mental anguish he felt all his old affection reawakening, and he tried to cheer up his friend. A man like him to allow himself to get depressed, what folly! It was all very well whilst one was young; but as one grows older, it is only waste of time.

"You are spoiling my Frederick for me! I want him whom I knew in bygone days. The same boy as ever! I liked him! Come, smoke a pipe, old chap! Shake yourself up a little! You drive me mad!"

"It is true," said Frederick, "I am a fool!"

The clerk replied:

"Ah! old troubadour, I know very well what's troubling you! A little affair of the heart? Confess it! Bah! One lost, four found to replace the one! We console ourselves for virtuous women with the other sort. Would you like me to introduce you to some women? You have only to come to the Alhambra."

(This was a place for public balls recently opened at the top of the Champs-Elysées, which had gone down owing to a display of licentiousness somewhat more extreme than is usual in establishments of the kind.)

"That's a place where there seems to be good fun. You may take your friends, if you like. I can even pass in Regimbart for you."

Frederick did not think fit to ask the Citizen to go. Deslauriers deprived himself of the pleasure of Sénécal's society. They took only Hussonnet and Cisy along with Dussardier; and the same hackney-coach set the group of five down at the entrance of the Alhambra.

Two Moorish galleries extended on the right and on the left, parallel to one another. The wall of a house opposite filled the entire background; and the fourth side (that in which the restaurant was) represented a Gothic cloister with stained-glass windows. A sort of Chinese roof screened the platform reserved for the musicians, and the numerous walks, garnished with sand of a deep yellow, carefully raked, made the garden look much larger than it really was.

Students were escorting their mistresses to and fro; drapers' clerks strutted about with canes in their hands; lads fresh from college were smoking their regalias; old men had dyed beards, carefully combed. There were English, Russians, men from South America, and three Orientals in tarbooshes. Lorettes, grisettes, and girls of the town were there in the hope of finding a protector, a lover, a gold coin, or simply for the pleasure of dancing.

Hussonnet was acquainted with a number of the women through his connection with the fashion-journals and the smaller theatres. He sent them kisses with the tips of his fingers, and from time to time he left his friends to go and chat with them.

Deslauriers felt jealous of these playful familiarities. He accosted in a cynical manner a tall, fair-haired girl in a nankeen costume. After looking him over with a certain air of sullenness, she said:

"No! I wouldn't trust you, my good fellow!" and turned on her heel.

His next attempt was on a stout brunette, who apparently was a little mad; for she gave a bounce at the very first word he spoke to her, threatening, if he went any further, to call the police. Deslauriers pretended to laugh; then, coming across a little woman sitting by herself under a gas-lamp, he asked her to be his partner in a quadrille.

The musicians, perched on the platform in the attitudes of apes, kept scraping and blowing away with desperate energy. The conductor, standing up, kept beating time automatically. The dancers were much crowded and enjoyed themselves thoroughly. The bonnet-strings, getting loose, rubbed against the cravats; the boots sank under the petticoats; and all this bouncing went on to the accompaniment of the music. Deslauriers hugged the little woman, and, seized with the delirium of the cancan, whirled about, like a big marionette, in the midst of the dancers. Cisy and Dussardier were still walking up and down. The young aristocrat kept ogling the girls, but, in spite of the clerk's persuasions, he did not venture to talk to them, having an idea in his head that in the resorts of these women there was always "a man hidden in the cupboard with a pistol who would come out of it and force you to sign a bill of exchange."

They came back and joined Frederick. Deslauriers had stopped dancing; and they were all asking themselves how they were to finish up the evening, when Hussonnet exclaimed:

"Look! Here's the Marquise d'Amaëgui!"

The person referred to was a pale woman with a *retroussé* nose, mittens up to her elbows, and big black earrings hanging down her cheeks, like two dog's ears. Hussonnet said to her:

"We should organise a little fête at your house—a sort of Oriental rout. Try to collect some of your friends here for these French cavaliers. Well, what is the matter? Are you going to wait for your hidalgo?"

The Andalusian hung down her head: being well aware of the by no means generous habits of her friend, she was afraid of having to pay for any refreshments he ordered. When, at length, she let the word "money" slip from her, Cisy offered five napoleons—all he had in his purse; and so it was settled that the thing should come off.

But Frederick was absent. He fancied that he had recognised the voice of Arnoux, and suddenly got a glimpse of a woman's hat; he hastened toward an arbour which was not far off.

Mademoiselle Vatnaz was alone there with Arnoux.

"Excuse me! I am in the way?"

"Not in the least!" returned the picture-merchant.

Frederick, from the concluding words of their conversation, understood that Arnoux had come to the Alhambra to talk over an important matter of business with Mademoiselle Vatnaz; and it was evident that he was not completely reassured, for he said to her, with some uneasiness in his manner:

"You are quite sure?"

"Perfectly certain! You are loved. Ah! what a man you are!"

And she assumed a pouting look, putting out her big lips, so red that they seemed tinged with blood. But she had wonderful eyes, of a tawny hue, with specks of gold in the pupils, full of vivacity, amorousness, and sensuality. They lit up, like lamps, the rather yellow tint of her thin face. Arnoux seemed to relish her exhibition of pique. He stooped over her, saying:

"You are nice—give me a kiss!"

She caught hold of his two ears, and pressed her lips against his forehead.

At that moment the dancing stopped; and in the conductor's place appeared a handsome young man, rather fat, with a waxen complexion. He had long black hair, which he wore in the same fashion as Christ, and a blue velvet waistcoat embroidered with large gold palm-branches. He looked as proud as a peacock, and as stupid as a turkey-cock; and, having bowed to the audience, he began a ditty. A villager was supposed to be giving an account of his journey to the capital. The singer used the dialect of Lower Normandy, and played the part of a drunken man. The refrain—

> "Ah! I laughed at you there, I laughed at you there,
> In that rascally city of Paris!"

was greeted with prolonged applause. Delmas, "a vocalist who sang with expression," was too clever to let the excitement of his listeners cool. A guitar was quickly handed to him and he moaned forth a ballad entitled "The Albanian Girl's Brother."

The words recalled to Frederick those which had been sung by the man in rags between the paddle-boxes of the steamboat. His eyes involuntarily rested on the hem of the dress spread out before him.

After each couplet there was a long pause, and the blowing of the wind through the trees resembled the sound of waves.

Mademoiselle Vatnaz blushed the moment she saw Dussardier. She soon rose, and stretching out her hand toward him:

"You do not remember me, Monsieur Auguste?"

"How do you know her?" asked Frederick.

"We have been in the same house," he replied.

Cisy pulled him by the sleeve; they went out; and, scarcely had they disappeared, when Madame Vatnaz began to pronounce a eulogy on his character. She even went so far as to say that he possessed "the genius of the heart."

Then they chatted about Delmas, admitting that as a mimic he might be a success on the stage; and a discussion followed in which Shakespeare, the Censorship, Style, the People, the receipts of the Porte Saint-Martin, Alexandre Dumas, Victor Hugo, and Dumersan were all mixed up together.

Arnoux had known many celebrated actresses; the young men listened eagerly to what he had to say about these ladies. But his words were lost in the noise of the music; and, as soon as the quadrille or the polka was over, they all sat round the tables, called the waiter, and laughed. Behind the mediæval cloister could be heard crackling sounds; squibs went off; artificial suns began revolving; the gleam of the Bengal fires, like emeralds in colour, lighted up for the space of a minute the entire garden; and, with the last rocket, a great sigh escaped from the assembled throng.

It slowly died away. A cloud of gunpowder floated into the air. Frederick and Deslauriers were walking side by side through the midst of the crowd, when they happened to see something that made them suddenly stop: Martinon was in the act of paying some money at the place where umbrellas were left; and he had with him a woman of fifty, plain-looking, magnificently dressed, and of problematic social rank.

"That sly dog," said Deslauriers, "is not so simple as we imagine. But where in the world is Cisy?"

Dussardier pointed toward the smoking-divan, where they perceived the knightly youth, with a bowl of punch before him, and a pink hat by his side, to keep him company. Hussonnet, who had been away for the past few minutes, reappeared at the same moment with a young girl leaning on his arm, who addressed him in a loud voice as "My little cat."

"Oh, no!" said he to her—"not in public! Call me rather 'Vicomte.' That gives you a cavalier style—Louis XIII and dainty boots—the sort of thing I like! Yes, my good friends, one of the old *régime!*—nice, isn't she?"—and he chucked her under the chin—"Salute these gentlemen! they are all the sons of peers of France. I associate with them in order that they may get an appointment for me as an ambassador."

"How insane you are!" sighed Mademoiselle Vatnaz. She asked Dussardier to see her as far as her own door.

Arnoux watched them going off; then, turning toward Frederick:

"Did you like the Vatnaz? At any rate, you're not quite frank about these affairs. I believe you keep your amours secret."

Frederick, turning pale, swore that he kept nothing hidden.

"Can it be possible you don't know what it is to have a mistress?" said Arnoux.

Frederick felt a longing to mention some woman's name at random. But the story might be repeated to her. So he replied that as a matter of fact he had no mistress.

The picture-dealer reproached him for this.

"This evening you had a good opportunity! Why didn't you do like the others, each of whom went off with a woman?"

"Well, and what about yourself?" said Frederick, irritated by his persistency.

"Oh! myself—that's quite another matter, my lad! I go home to my own one!"

Then he called a cab, and disappeared.

The two friends walked homeward. An east wind was blowing. They did not exchange a word. Deslauriers was regretting that he had not succeeded in making a *shine* before a certain newspaper-manager, and Frederick was lost once more in his melancholy broodings. At length, breaking the silence, he remarked that this public-house ball appeared to him a stupid affair.

"Whose fault is that? If you had not left us, to join that Arnoux of yours—"

"Bah! anything I could have done would have been utterly useless!"

But the clerk had theories of his own. All that was necessary in order to get a thing was to desire it strongly.

"Nevertheless, you yourself, a little while ago—"

"I don't care a straw about that sort of thing!" returned Deslauriers, cutting short Frederick's allusion. "Am I going to get entangled with women?"

And he declaimed against their affectations, their silly ways—in short, he disliked them.

"Don't be acting, then!" said Frederick.

Deslauriers was silent. Then, all at once:

"Will you bet me a hundred francs that I won't catch the first woman that passes?"

"Yes—it's a bet!"

The first who passed was a hideous-looking beggar-woman, and they were giving up all hope of a chance presenting itself when, in the middle of the Rue de Rivoli, they saw a tall girl with a little bandbox in her hand.

Deslauriers accosted her under the arcades. She turned up abruptly by the Tuileries, and soon diverged into the Place du Carrousel. She looked to the right and to the left. She ran after a hackney-coach; Deslauriers overtook her. He walked by her side, talking to her with expressive gestures. At length, she accepted his arm, and they walked on together along the quays. Then, when they reached the rising ground in front of the Châtelet, they kept tramping up and down for at least twenty minutes, like two sailors keeping watch. But, all of a sudden, they passed over the Pont-au-Change, through the Flower Market, and along the Quai Napoléon. Frederick came up behind them. Deslauriers gave him to understand that he would be in their way, and had better follow his example.

"How much have you got left?"

"Two hundred sous pieces."

"That's enough—good night to you!"

Frederick was seized with the astonishment one feels at seeing a piece of foolery coming to a successful issue.

"He has the laugh at me," was his reflection. "Suppose I went back again?"

Perhaps Deslauriers imagined that he was envious of this paltry love! "As if I had not one a hundred times more satisfying, more noble, more absorbing." He felt a sort of angry feeling impelling him onward. He arrived in front of Madame Arnoux's door.

None of the outer windows belonged to her apartment. Nevertheless, he remained with his eyes fixed on the front of the house—as if he fancied he could, by his contemplation, penetrate the walls. No doubt, she was now sunk in repose, tranquil as a sleeping flower, with her beautiful black hair resting on the lace of the pillow, her lips slightly parted, and one arm under her head. Then Arnoux's face rose before him, and he rushed away to escape from this vision.

The advice which Deslauriers had given to him came back to his memory. It only filled him with horror. Then he walked about the streets in a vagabond fashion. He found himself on the Pont de la Concorde.

Then he recalled that evening in the previous winter, when, as he left her house for the first time, he was forced to stand still, so rapidly did his heart beat with the hopes that filled him. And now they had all withered!

He resumed his walk. But, as he was exceedingly hungry, and none of the restaurants were open, he went to get a "snack" at a tavern by the fish-markets; after which, thinking it too soon to return home, he kept wandering about the Hôtel de Ville till a quarter past eight.

Deslauriers had long since got rid of his wench; and he was writing at the table in the middle of his room. About four o'clock that afternoon, Monsieur de Cisy came in.

Thanks to Dussardier, he had enjoyed the society of a lady the night before; and he had even accompanied her home in the carriage with her husband to the very threshold of their house, where she had given him an assignation. He parted with her without even finding out her name.

"And what do you propose that I should do in that way?" said Frederick.

Thereupon the young gentleman began to cudgel his brains to think of a suitable woman; he mentioned Mademoiselle Vatnaz, the Andalusian, and all the others. At length, with much circumlocution, he came to the object of his visit. Relying on the discretion of his friend, he came to aid him in taking an important step, after which he might definitely regard himself as a man; and Frederick showed no reluctance. He told the story to Deslauriers without relating the facts with reference to himself personally.

The clerk was of opinion that he was now progressing very well. This respect for his advice increased his good humour. He owed to that quality his success, on the very first night he met her, with Mademoiselle Clémence

Daviou, embroideress in gold for military outfits, the sweetest creature that ever lived, as slender as a reed, with large blue eyes, perpetually staring with wonder. The clerk had taken advantage of her credulity to such an extent as to make her believe that he had been decorated. At their private meetings he had his frock-coat adorned with a red ribbon, but divested himself of it on public occasions in order, as he put it, not to humiliate his master. However, he kept her at a distance, allowed himself to be fawned upon, like a pasha, and, in a laughing sort of way, called her "daughter of the people." Every time they met, she brought him little bunches of violets. Frederick would not have enjoyed a love affair of this sort.

Meanwhile, whenever they set forth arm-in-arm to visit Pinson's or Barillot's circulating library, he experienced a feeling of singular depression. Frederick did not realise how much pain he had caused Deslauriers for the past year, while brushing his nails preparatory to dining in the Rue de Choiseul!

One evening, when from the commanding position in which his balcony stood, he had just been watching them as they went out together, he saw Hussonnet, some distance off, on the Pont d'Arcole. The Bohemian made signals to him, and, when Frederick had descended the five flights of stairs:

"Here is the thing—it is next Saturday, the 24th, Madame Arnoux's feast-day."

"How is that, when her name is Marie?"

"And Angèle also—no matter! They will entertain their guests at their country-house at Saint-Cloud. I was told to give you due notice about it. You'll find a vehicle waiting at the magazine-office at three o'clock. So that makes matters all right! Excuse me for having disturbed you! But I have such a number of calls to make!"

Frederick had scarcely turned round when his doorkeeper placed a letter in his hand:

"Monsieur and Madame Dambreuse beg of Monsieur F. Moreau to do them the honour to come and dine with them on Saturday the 24th inst.—R.S.V.P."

"Too late!" he said to himself. Nevertheless, he showed the letter to Deslauriers, who exclaimed:

"Ha! at last! But you don't look as if you were pleased. Why?"

After some little hesitation, Frederick said that he had another invitation for the same day.

"Be kind enough to let me run across to the Rue de Choiseul. I'm not joking! I'll answer this for you if it disturbs you."

And the clerk wrote an acceptance of the invitation in the third person.

Having seen nothing of the social world save through the fever of his desires, he pictured it to himself as an artificial creation discharging its functions by virtue of mathematical laws. A dinner in the city, an accidental meeting with a man in office, a smile from a pretty woman, might, by a series of actions deducing themselves from one another, have gigantic results. Certain Parisian drawing-rooms were similar to those machines which take a material in the rough and render it a hundred times more valuable. He believed in courtesans advising diplomatists, in wealthy marriages brought about by intrigues, in the cleverness of convicts, in the capacity of strong men for getting the better of fortune. In short, he considered it so important to visit the Dambreuses, and talked about it so plausibly, that Frederick was at a loss to know what to do.

The least attention he could show, as it was Madame Arnoux's feast-day, was to make her a present. He naturally thought of a parasol, in order to replace the one he had broken. He came across a shot-silk parasol with a little carved ivory handle, which had come all the way from China. But the price of it was a hundred and seventy-five francs, and he had not a sou, having in fact to live on the credit of his next quarter's allowance. However, he wished to get it; he was determined to have it; and in spite of his repugnance to doing so, he had recourse to Deslauriers.

Deslauriers answered Frederick's first question by saying that he had no money.

"I need some," said Frederick—"I need some very badly!"

As the other made the same excuse again, he flew into a passion.

"You might find it to your advantage some time—"

"What do you mean by that?"

"Oh! nothing."

The clerk understood. He took the sum required out of his reserve-fund, and when he had counted out the money, coin by coin:

"I am not asking you for a receipt, as I see you have a lot of expense!"

Frederick threw himself on his friend's neck with a thousand affectionate protestations. Deslauriers received this display of emotion frigidly. Then, next morning, noticing the parasol on the top of the piano:

"Ah! it was for that!"

"I may send it, perhaps," said Frederick, with an air of carelessness.

Good fortune was on his side, for that evening he received a note with a black border from Madame Dambreuse announcing that she had lost an uncle, and excusing herself for having to defer till a later period the pleasure of making his acquaintance.

At two o'clock, he reached the office of the art journal. Instead of waiting to drive him in his carriage, Arnoux had left the city the night before, unable to resist the opportunity of getting some fresh air.

Every year it had been his custom, as soon as the leaves were budding forth, to start early in the morning and to remain away several days, making long journeys across the fields, drinking milk at the farm-houses, romping with the village girls, asking questions about the harvest, and carrying back home with him stalks of salad in his pocket-handkerchief. At length, he realised a long-cherished dream of his, by buying a country-house.

While Frederick was talking to the picture-dealer's clerk, Mademoiselle Vatnaz suddenly made her appearance, and expressed herself disappointed at not seeing Arnoux. He would, perhaps, be remaining away two days longer. The clerk advised her "to go there"—she could not; to write a letter—she was afraid that it might get lost. Frederick offered to be the bearer of it himself. She rapidly scribbled off a letter, and implored him to let nobody see him delivering it.

Forty minutes later, he found himself at Saint-Cloud. The house, which was about a hundred paces farther away than the bridge, stood half-way up the hill. The garden-walls were hidden by two rows of linden-trees, and a wide lawn sloped to the bank of the river. The railed entrance before the door was open, and Frederick went in.

Arnoux, stretched on the grass, was playing with a litter of kittens. This amusement appeared to absorb him completely. Mademoiselle Vatnaz's letter aroused him out of his sleepy idleness.

"The deuce! the deuce!—this is a bore! She is right, though; I must go."

Then, having stuck the missive into his pocket, he showed the young man through the grounds with evident delight. Presently a few harmonious notes burst forth above their heads: Madame Arnoux, fancying that there was nobody near, was singing to amuse herself. She ceased all at once, when M. and Madame Oudry, two neighbours, presented themselves.

Then she appeared herself at the top of the steps in front of the house; and, as she descended, he caught a glimpse of her foot. She wore little open shoes of reddish-brown leather, with three straps crossing each other so as to draw just above her stockings a wire-work of gold.

Those who had been invited arrived. With the exception of Maître Lefaucheur, an advocate, they were the same guests who came to the Thursday dinners. Each had brought some present—Dittmer a Syrian scarf, Rosenwald a scrap-book of ballads, Burrieu a water-colour painting, Sombary one of his own caricatures, and Pellerin a charcoal-drawing, representing a kind of dance of death, a hideous fantasy, poorly executed. Hussonnet dispensed with the formality of making a present.

Frederick was waiting to offer his gift.

She thanked him very much for it. Thereupon, he said:

"Why, 'tis nothing more than a debt. I have been so much annoyed—"

"At what, pray?" she returned. "I don't understand."

"Come! dinner is waiting!" said Arnoux, catching hold of his arm; then in a whisper: "You are not very knowing, certainly!"

Nothing could well be prettier than the dining-room, decorated in water-green. Through the open windows the entire garden could be seen with the long lawn flanked by an old Scotch fir.

They chatted first about the view before them, then about scenery in general; and they were beginning to plunge into discussions when Arnoux, at half-past nine o'clock, ordered the carriage to be brought round.

"Would you like me to go back with you?" said Madame Arnoux.

"Why, certainly!" and, making her a graceful bow: "You know well, Madame, that it is impossible to live without you!"

Everyone congratulated her on having so good a husband.

"Ah! it is because I am not the only one," she replied quietly, pointing toward her little daughter.

Then, the conversation having turned once more on painting, there was some talk about a Ruysdaël, for which Arnoux expected a big sum, and Pellerin asked him if it were true that the celebrated Saul Mathias from London had come over during the past month to make him an offer of twenty-three thousand francs for it.

"'Tis an absolute fact!" and turning toward Frederick: "That was the very same gentleman I brought with me a few days ago to the Alhambra, much against my will, I assure you, for these English are by no means congenial companions."

Frederick, who suspected that Mademoiselle Vatnaz's letter contained some reference to an intrigue, was amazed at the facility with which my lord Arnoux found a way of passing it off as a perfectly honourable transaction; but this new lie, which was quite unnecessary, made the young man open his eyes in speechless astonishment.

The picture-dealer added, with an air of simplicity:

"What's the name, by-the-by, of that young fellow, your friend?"

"Deslauriers," said Frederick quickly.

And, in order to repair the injustice which he felt he had done to his comrade, he praised him as one who possessed exceptional ability.

"Ah! indeed? But he doesn't look such a fine fellow as the other—the clerk in the waggon office."

Frederick bestowed a mental imprecation on Dussardier. She would now be thinking that he associated with the common herd.

Then they began to talk about the decorating of the capital—the new districts of the city—and the worthy Oudry happened to refer to M. Dambreuse as one of the big speculators.

Frederick, taking advantage of the opportunity to make a good figure, remarked that he was acquainted with that gentleman. But Pellerin launched into a harangue against shopkeepers—he saw no difference between them, whether they were sellers of candles or of money.

When they had taken their coffee, while they smoked, under the linden-trees, and strolled about the garden for some time, they went for a walk along the river.

The party stopped before a fishmonger's shop, where a man was washing eels. Mademoiselle Marthe wished to look at them. He emptied the box out on the grass; and the little girl threw herself on her knees in order to catch them, laughed with delight, and then began to scream with terror. They all got spoiled, and Arnoux paid for them.

He next took it into his head to go out for a sail in the cutter.

One side of the horizon was beginning to assume a pale aspect, while on the other side a wide strip of orange colour appeared, deepening into purple at the summits of the hills, which were steeped in shadow. Madame Arnoux seated herself on a big stone, this glittering splendour forming a background. The other ladies sauntered about. Hussonnet, at the lower end of the river's bank, made ducks and drakes over the water.

Arnoux presently returned, followed by a weather-beaten long boat, into which, in spite of the most prudent remonstrances, he packed his guests. The boat got upset, and they had to go ashore again.

By this time wax tapers were burning in the drawing-room, all hung with chintz, and with branched candlesticks of crystal fixed close to the walls. Mère Oudry was sleeping comfortably in an armchair, and the others were listening to M. Lefaucheux expatiating on the glories of the Bar. Madame Arnoux was seated by herself near the window. Frederick went over to her.

They chatted about the remarks which were being made in their vicinity. She admired oratory; he preferred the renown gained by writing. But, she ventured to suggest, it must give a man greater pleasure to move crowds directly by addressing them in person, face to face, than it does to infuse into their souls by his pen all the sentiments that animate his own. Such triumphs as these did not tempt Frederick much, as he lacked ambition.

Then he broached the subject of sentimental adventures. She spoke pityingly of the havoc wrought by passion, but expressed indignation at hypocritical vileness, and this rectitude of spirit harmonised so well with the regular beauty of her face that it seemed indeed as if her physical beauty were the outcome of her moral nature.

She smiled, every now and then, letting her eyes rest on him for a moment. Then he felt her glances penetrating his soul like those great rays of sunlight which descend into the depths of the water. He loved her without a single mental reservation, without any hope of his love being reciprocated, unconditionally; and in those silent transports, which were like outbursts of gratitude, he would fain have covered her forehead with a rain of kisses. An inspiration from within carried him beyond himself—he felt moved by a longing for self-sacrifice, an imperative impulse toward immediate self-devotion, and it was all the stronger because he could not gratify it.

He did not leave with the others. Neither did Hussonnet. They were to go back in the carriage; and the vehicle was waiting just in front of the steps when Arnoux rushed into the garden to gather some flowers. Then the bouquet having been tied round with a thread, as the stems were uneven, he searched in his pocket, which was full of papers, took out a piece at random, wrapped them up, completed his handiwork with the aid of a strong pin, and then offered the flowers to his wife with a certain amount of gallant tenderness.

"Look here, my darling! Forgive me for having forgotten you!"

But she uttered a little scream: the pin, having been awkwardly fixed, had scratched her, and she hastened up to her room. They waited nearly a quarter of an hour for her. At last, she reappeared, picked up Marthe, and threw herself into the carriage.

"And your bouquet?" said Arnoux.

"No! no—it is not worth while!" Frederick was running off to fetch it for her; she called out to him:

"I don't want it!"

But he speedily brought it to her, saying that he had just put it into an envelope again, as he had found the flowers lying on the floor. She thrust them behind the leathern apron of the carriage close to the seat, and off they started.

Frederick, seated by her side, noticed that she was trembling frightfully. Then, when they had passed the bridge, as Arnoux was turning to the left:

"Why, no! you are making a mistake!—the other way, to the right!"

She seemed irritated; everything annoyed her. At length, Marthe having closed her eyes, Madame Arnoux drew forth the bouquet, and flung it out through the carriage-door, then caught Frederick's arm, making a sign to him with the other hand to say nothing.

After this, she pressed her handkerchief to her lips, and sat quite motionless.

The two others, on the dickey, kept talking about printing and about subscribers. Arnoux, who was driving recklessly, lost his way in the middle of the Bois de Boulogne. Then they plunged into narrow paths. The horse proceeded along at a walking pace; the branches of the trees grazed the hood. Frederick could see nothing of Madame Arnoux save her two eyes. Marthe lay stretched across her lap while he supported the child's head.

"She is tiring you!" said her mother.

He replied:

"No! Oh, no!"

Whirlwinds of dust rose up slowly. They passed through Auteuil. All the houses were closed; a gas-lamp here and there lighted up the angle of a wall; then again they were surrounded by darkness. At one time he noticed that she was shedding tears.

Was this from remorse or passion? What in the world was it? This grief, of whose exact cause he was ignorant, interested him like a personal matter. There was now a new bond between them, as if, in a sense, they were accomplices; and he said to her in the most caressing voice he could assume:

"You are ill?"

"Yes, a little," she returned.

The carriage rolled on, and the honeysuckles and the syringas trailed over the garden fences, sending forth an enervating odour into the night air. He bent over the little girl, and spreading out her pretty brown tresses, kissed her softly on the forehead.

"You are good!" said Madame Arnoux.

"Why?"

"Because you are fond of children."

"Not of all children!"

He said no more, but he let his left hand hang down by her side wide open, fancying that she might do likewise, and that he would find her palm touching his. Then he felt ashamed and withdrew it. They soon reached the paved street. The carriage advanced more quickly; the number of gaslights increased—it was Paris.

Next morning he began working as hard as ever he could.

He fancied himself in an Assize Court, on a winter's evening, at the close of the advocates' speeches, when the jurymen are looking pale, and when the panting audience make the partitions of the prætorium creak; and after having been four hours speaking, he was recapitulating all his proofs, feeling with every phrase, with every word, with every gesture, the chopper of the guillotine, which was suspended behind him, ready to fall; then in the tribune of the Chamber, an orator who bears on his lips the safety of an entire people, drowning his opponents under his figures of rhetoric, crushing them under a repartee, with thunders and musical intonations in his voice, ironical, pathetic, fiery, sublime. She would be there somewhere amidst the others, hiding beneath her veil her enthusiastic tears.

Deslauriers, who had found it so troublesome to coach him once more for the second examination at the close of December, and for the third in February, was astonished at his enthusiasm. Then the great expectations of former days returned. In ten years Frederick might be deputy; in fifteen a minister. Why not? With his patrimony, which would soon be in his own hands, he might at first start a newspaper; this would be the first step in his career; after that they would see what the future would bring. As for himself, he was still ambitious of obtaining a chair in the Law School; and he sustained his thesis for the degree of Doctor with such remarkable ability that it won for him the compliments of the professors.

Three days afterward, Frederick took his own degree. Before leaving for his holidays, he conceived the idea of getting up a picnic to bring to a close their Saturday reunions.

He displayed the utmost gaiety on the occasion. Madame Arnoux was at the time with her mother at Chartres. But he would soon see her again, and would end by being her lover.

Deslauriers, admitted the same day to the young advocates' pleading rehearsals at Orsay, had made a speech which was greatly applauded. Although he was sober, he drank a little more wine than was good for him, and said to Dussardier at dessert:

"You are an honest fellow!—and when I'm a rich man I'll make you my manager."

All were delighted. Cisy did not intend to finish his law-course. Martinon planned to remain during the period before his admission to the Bar, in the provinces, where he would be nominated a deputy-magistrate. Pellerin was devoting himself to the production of a large picture representing "The Genius of the Revolution." Hussonnet was, in the following week, to submit to the Director of Public Amusements the scheme of a play, and had no doubt as to its success:

"As for the framework of the drama, they may rely on me! As for the passions, I have knocked about enough to comprehend them thoroughly; and as for witticisms, they're entirely in my line!"

He gave a spring, fell on his two hands, and thus moved for some time around the table with his legs in the air. This performance, worthy of a street-urchin, did not banish Sénécal's frowns. He had just been dismissed from the boarding-school, in which he had been a teacher, for having given a whipping to an aristocrat's son. His straitened circumstances had got worse in consequence: he laid the blame of this on the inequalities of society, and cursed the wealthy. He poured out his grievances into the sympathetic ears of Regimbart, who every day became more and more disillusioned, saddened, and disgusted. The Citizen had now turned his attention toward questions arising out of the Budget, and blamed the Court party for the loss of millions in Algeria.

As he could not sleep without first paying a visit to the Alexandre smoking-divan, he disappeared at eleven o'clock. The rest went away some time afterward; and Frederick, as he was parting with Hussonnet, learned that Madame Arnoux had been due the night before.

He accordingly went to the coach-office to change his time for starting to the next day and at about six o'clock in the evening presented himself at her house. Her return, the doorkeeper said, had been postponed for a week. Frederick dined alone, and then lounged about the boulevards.

He stopped in front of the theatre of the Porte Saint-Martin to look at the bill; and, for want of something to occupy him, paid for a seat and went in.

An old-fashioned dramatic version of a fairy-tale was being played. There was a very small audience; and through the skylights of the top gallery the vault of heaven seemed cut up into little blue squares, whilst the stage lamps above the orchestra formed a single line of yellow illuminations.

He had just got to his seat when, glancing at the balcony, he saw a lady and a gentleman enter the first box in front of the stage. The husband had a pale face with a narrow strip of grey beard round it, the rosette of a Government official, and that frigid look which is supposed to characterise diplomatists.

His wife, who was at least twenty years younger, and who was neither tall nor under-sized, neither ugly nor pretty, wore her fair hair in corkscrew curls in the English fashion, and displayed a long-bodiced dress and a large black lace fan. Frederick could not recall to mind where he had seen that face.

In the next interval between the acts, while passing through one of the lobbies, he came face to face with both of them. As he bowed in an undecided manner, M. Dambreuse, at once recognising him, came up and apologised for having treated him with unpardonable neglect. This was an allusion to the numerous visiting-cards he had sent in accordance with the clerk's advice. However, he confused the periods, supposing that Frederick was in the second year of his law-course. Then he said he envied the young man the opportunity of going into the country. He sadly needed a little rest himself, but business kept him in Paris.

Madame Dambreuse, leaning on his arm, nodded her head slightly, and the agreeable sprightliness of her face contrasted with its gloomy expression of a short time before.

"One finds charming diversions in it, nevertheless," she said, after her husband's last remark. "What a stupid play that was—was it not, Monsieur?" And all three of them remained there chatting about theatres and new pieces.

Frederick, accustomed to the grimaces of provincial dames, had not seen in any woman such ease of manner combined with that simplicity which is the essence of refinement, and in which ingenuous souls imagine the expression of instantaneous sympathy.

They would anticipate seeing him as soon as he returned. M. Dambreuse asked him to give his kind remembrances to Père Roque.

Frederick, when he reached his lodgings, did not fail to inform his friend Deslauriers of their hospitable invitation.

"Splendid!" was the clerk's reply; "and don't let your mamma get round you! Come back without delay!"

On the day after his arrival, when breakfast was over, Madame Moreau brought her son out into the garden.

She said she was happy to see him in a profession, for they were not as rich as people thought. The land brought in little; the people who farmed it paid badly. She had even been compelled to part with her carriage. Finally, she placed their situation in its true colours before him.

During the first embarrassments which followed the death of her late husband, M. Roque, a man of great cunning, had made her loans of money which had been renewed, and left long unpaid, in spite of her desire to clear them off. He had suddenly made a demand for immediate payment, and she had gone beyond the strict terms of the agreement by giving up to him, at an unreasonable figure, the farm of Presles. Ten years later her capital was lost through the failure of a banker at Melun. Because of a horror which she had of mortgages, and to keep up appearances, which might be necessary in view of her son's future, she had, when Père Roque presented himself again, listened to him once more. But now she was free from debt. In short, there was left them an income of only about ten thousand francs, of which two thousand three hundred belonged to him—his entire patrimony.

"It isn't possible!" exclaimed Frederick.

She nodded her head, as if to declare that it was perfectly possible.

But he would inherit something from his uncle?

That was by no means positive!

And they took a turn around the garden without exchanging a word. At last she pressed him to her heart, and in a voice choked with rising tears:

"Ah! my poor boy! I have had to relinquish all my dreams!"

He seated himself on a bench beneath a large acacia.

Her advice was that he should become a clerk to M. Prouharam, solicitor, who would assign over his office to him; if he increased its value, he might sell it again and find a better practice.

Frederick was no longer listening to her. He was gazing automatically across the hedge into the other garden opposite.

A little girl of about twelve with red hair was there all alone. She had made earrings for herself with the berries of the service-tree. Her bodice, made of grey linen, allowed her shoulders, slightly burned by the hot sun, to be seen. Her short white petticoat was spotted with berry stains; and there was, so to speak, the grace of a young wild animal about her entire person, which was at the same time nervous and thin. Apparently, the presence of a stranger astonished her, for she had stopped abruptly with her watering-pot in her hand darting glances at him with her large bright eyes, which were of a limpid greenish-blue colour.

"That is Monsieur Roque's little girl," said Madame Moreau. "He has married his servant after all and legitimised their child."

CHAPTER VI

HOPES DEFERRED

STILL SEATED on the bench, as if stunned, he cursed Fate—stripped of everything, ruined. He would have liked to beat somebody; and, to increase his despair, he felt a kind of outrage, a sense of disgrace, oppressing him; for Frederick had been under the impression that the fortune coming to him through his father would mount up one day to an income of fifteen thousand livres, and he had so informed the Arnoux' in an indirect sort of way. So now he would be looked upon as a braggart, a rogue, an obscure blackguard, who had forced himself upon them in the expectation of making some profit out of them! And as for her— Madame Arnoux—how could he ever see her again?

Moreover, all that he had hoped was completely impossible when he had only a yearly income of three thousand francs. He could not always lodge on the fourth floor, have the doorkeeper as a servant, and make his appearance with wretched black gloves turning blue at the ends, a greasy hat, and the same frock-coat for a whole year. No, no! never! And yet without her existence was intolerable. Some people were able to live without any fortune, Deslauriers amongst the rest; and he thought himself a coward to attach so much importance to matters of trifling consequence. Necessity would perhaps multiply his faculties a hundredfold. He tried to inspire himself by thinking of the great men who had worked in garrets. A soul like that of Madame Arnoux ought to be touched at such a spectacle, and moved by it to sympathetic tenderness. So, after all, this catastrophe was a piece of good fortune; like those earthquakes which unveil treasures, it had revealed to him the hidden wealth of his nature. But there was only one place in the world where this could be utilised— Paris; for to his mind, art, science, and love (those three faces of God, as Pellerin would have said) were associated exclusively with the capital. That evening, he informed his mother of his intention to go back there. Madame Moreau was surprised and indignant. She regarded it as a foolish and absurd course. It would be far better to follow her advice, namely, to remain near her in an office. Frederick shrugged his shoulders, "Come now"—looking on this proposal as an insult to himself.

Thereupon, the good lady followed another course. In a tender voice broken by sobs she began to speak of her solitude, her old age, and the sacrifices she had made for him. Now that she was more unhappy than ever, he was abandoning her. Then, alluding to the anticipated close of her life:

"A little patience—good heavens! you will soon be free!"

These lamentations were renewed twenty times a day for three months; and at the same time the luxuries of a home made him effeminate. He found it enjoyable to have a softer bed and napkins that were not torn; so that, weary, enervated, overcome by the insinuating force of comfort, Frederick allowed himself to be brought to Maître Prouharam's office.

He displayed neither knowledge nor aptitude. Up to this time, he had been regarded as a young man of great means who would probably be the shining light of the Department. The public would now come to the conclusion that he was an impostor.

At first, he said to himself:

"It is necessary to inform Madame Arnoux about it;" and for a whole week he kept formulating in his own mind dithyrambic letters and short notes in an eloquent and sublime style. The fear of avowing his actual position restrained him. Then he thought that it might be better to write to the husband. Arnoux knew life and could appreciate the true state of the case. At length, after a fortnight's hesitation:

"Bah! I ought not to see them any more: let them forget me! At any rate, I shall be cherished in her memory without having grown less in her estimation! She will believe that I am dead, and will regret me—perhaps."

As extravagant resolutions cost him little, he swore in his own mind that he would never return to Paris, and that he would not even make inquiries about Madame Arnoux.

He arose very late, and looked through the window at the passing teams of waggoners. The first six months especially were hateful.

On certain days, however, he was possessed by a feeling of indignation even against her. Then he would wander through the meadows, half covered in winter time by the inundations of the Seine. They were divided up by rows of poplar-trees. Here and there was a little bridge. He tramped about till evening, rolling the yellow leaves under his feet, inhaling the fog, and jumping over the ditches. As his arteries began to throb more vigorously, he felt himself carried away by a desire to do something wild; he longed to become a trapper in America, to attend on a pasha in the East, to take ship as a sailor; and he gave vent to his melancholy in long letters to Deslauriers.

The latter was struggling to get on. The idleness of his friend and his eternal jeremiads appeared to him simply stupid. Their correspondence soon became a mere form. Frederick had left all his furniture with Deslauriers, who stayed on in the same lodgings. From time to time his mother mentioned it. One day he told her about the present he had made, and she was giving him a rating for it, when a letter was placed in his hands.

"What is the matter now?" she said, "you are trembling."

"There is nothing the matter with me," replied Frederick.

Deslauriers informed him that he had taken Sénécal under his protection, and that for the past fortnight they had been living together. So now Sénécal was settled in the midst of things that had come from the

Arnoux's shop. He might sell them, criticise, make jokes about them. Frederick was wounded in the depths of his soul. He went up to his own apartment. He felt a yearning for death.

His mother called him to consult him about some plants in the garden.

This garden was, after the fashion of an English park, divided in the middle by a stick fence; and the half of it belonged to Père Roque, who had another garden for vegetables on the bank of the river. The two neighbours, having disagreed, abstained from making their appearance there at the same hour. But since Frederick's return the old gentleman used to walk about them more frequently, and was not stinted in his courtesies towards Madame Moreau's son. He sympathised with the young man for having to live in a country town. One day he told him that Madame Dambreuse had been anxious to hear from him. On another occasion he expatiated on the custom of Champagne, where the stomach conferred nobility.

"At that time you would have been a lord, since your mother's name was De Fouvens. And 'tis all very well to talk—never mind! there's something in a name. After all," he added, with a sly glance at Frederick, "that depends on the Keeper of the Seals."

This pretension to aristocracy contrasted strangely with his personal appearance. As he was small, his big chestnut-coloured frock-coat exaggerated the length of his bust. When he removed his hat, a face almost like that of a woman with an extremely sharp nose could be seen; his hair, which was of a yellow colour, resembled a wig. He saluted people with a very low bow, brushing against the wall.

Up to his fiftieth year he had been content with the domestic services of Catherine, a native of Lorraine, of the same age as himself and strongly marked with smallpox. But in the year 1834, he brought back with him from Paris a handsome blonde with a sheep-like type of countenance and a "queenly carriage." Ere long, she was noticed strutting about with large earrings; and everything was explained by the birth of a daughter who was introduced to the world under the name of Elisabeth Olympe Louise Roque.

Catherine, in her first ebullition of jealousy, expected that she would hate this child. On the contrary, she became fond of the little girl, and treated her with the utmost care, consideration, and tenderness, in order to win her affections from her mother and render her odious—an easy task, inasmuch as Madame Eléonore entirely neglected the little one, preferring to gossip at the tradesmen's shops. On the day after her marriage, she paid a visit at the Subprefecture, no longer "thee'd" and "thou'd" the servants, and took it into her head that, as a matter of good form, she ought to exhibit a certain severity toward the child. She was present while the little one was at her lessons. The teacher, an old clerk who had been employed at the Mayor's office, did not know how to set about instructing the girl. The pupil rebelled, got her ears boxed, and rushed away to shed tears on the lap of Catherine, who always took her part. After this the two women wrangled, and M. Roque ordered them to hold their tongues. He had married only out of tender regard for his little daughter, and did not wish to be annoyed by them.

Louise wore a white dress with ribbons, and pantalettes trimmed with lace; and on great festival-days she would leave the house attired like a princess, in order to mortify the matrons of the town, who forbade their children to associate with her on account of her illegitimate birth.

She passed her life mostly by herself in the garden, went see-sawing in the swing, chased butterflies, then suddenly stopped to watch the floral beetles swooping down on the rose-trees. It was, no doubt, these habits which imparted to her face an expression at the same time of audacity and dreaminess. She had, moreover, a figure like Marthe, so that at their second interview Frederick said to her:

"Will you permit me to kiss you, Mademoiselle?"

The little girl lifted up her head and replied:

"I will!"

But the stick-hedge separated them.

"We must climb over," said Frederick.

"No, lift me up!"

He stooped over the hedge, and raising her off the ground, kissed her on both cheeks; then he put her back on her own side; and this performance was repeated on the next occasions when they met.

With less reserve than a child of four, as soon as she heard her friend coming, she sprang forward to meet him, or else, hiding behind a tree, she began yelping like a dog to frighten him.

One day, when Madame Moreau was out, he brought her up to his own room. She opened all the scent-bottles, and pomaded her hair plentifully; then, without the slightest embarrassment, she lay down on the bed, where she remained stretched out at full length, wide awake.

"I fancy myself your wife," she said to him.

Next day he found her in tears. She confessed that she had been "weeping for her sins;" and, when he wished to know what they were, she hung down her head, and answered:

"Ask me no more!"

The time for first communion was at hand. She had been taken to confession in the morning. The sacrament scarcely made her wiser. Occasionally, she flew into a real passion; and Frederick was sent for to appease her.

He often took her with him in his walks. While he indulged in daydreams as he walked along, she would gather wild poppies at the edges of the cornfields; and, when she saw him more melancholy than usual, she tried to cheer him with her pretty childish prattle. His heart, bereft of love, fell back on this friendship inspired by a little girl. He gave her sketches of old fogies, told her stories, and read books to her.

He began with the *Annales Romantiques,* a collection of prose and verse popular at the period. Then, forgetting her age, so much was he charmed by her intelligence, he read for her in succession, *Atala, Cinq-Mars,* and *Les Feuilles d'Automne.* One night (she had that very evening heard *Macbeth* in Letourneur's simple translation) she woke up, exclaiming:

"The spot! the spot!" Her teeth chattered, she shivered, and, fixing terrified glances on her right hand, she kept rubbing it, saying:

"Always a spot!"

At last a doctor was brought, who ordered that she should be kept free from violent emotions.

The townsfolk saw in all this only an unfavourable prognostic for her morals. It was said that "young Moreau" wished to make an actress of her later.

Soon another event became the subject of discussion—namely, the arrival of Uncle Barthélemy. Madame Moreau gave up her sleeping-apartment to him, and was so gracious as to serve up meat to him on fast-days.

The old man was not very amiable. He was perpetually making comparisons between Havre and Nogent, the air of which he considered heavy, the bread bad, the streets ill-paved, the footed indifferent, and the inhabitants very lazy. "How miserable trade is with you in this place!" He blamed his deceased brother for his extravagance, pointing out by way of contrast how he had himself accumulated an income of twenty-seven thousand livres a year. He left at the end of the week, and on the footboard of the carriage gave utterance to these by no means reassuring words:

"I am always very glad to feel that you are in a comfortable position."

"You will get nothing," said Madame Moreau as they reëntered the dining-room.

He had come only at her urgent request, and for eight days she had been seeking for an opening—only too obviously perhaps. She repented now of having done so, and remained seated in her armchair with her head bent and her lips tightly pressed together. Frederick sat opposite, staring at her; and they were both silent, as they had been five years before on his return home by the Montereau steamboat. This coincidence, which presented itself even to her mind, recalled Madame Arnoux to his recollection.

At that moment the crack of a whip outside the window reached their ears, while a voice was heard calling out to him.

It was Père Roque, who was alone in his tilted cart. He was going to spend the whole day at La Fortelle with M. Dambreuse, and cordially offered to take Frederick with him.

"You have no need of an invitation as long as you are with me. Don't be afraid!"

Frederick felt inclined to accept this offer. But how would he explain his fixed sojourn at Nogent? He had no proper summer suit. Finally, what would his mother say? He accordingly decided not to go.

From that time, their neighbour exhibited less friendliness. Louise was growing tall; Madame Eléonore fell dangerously ill; and the intimacy was broken, to the great delight of Madame Moreau, who feared lest her son's prospects of being settled in life might be affected by association with such people.

She was thinking of purchasing for him the registrarship of the Court of Justice. Frederick raised no particular objection to this scheme. He now accompanied her to mass; in the evening he took a hand in a game of "all fours." He had become accustomed to provincial habits of life, and allowed himself to slide into them; and even his love had assumed a character of mournful sweetness, a kind of soporific charm.

One day, the 12th of December, 1845, about nine o'clock in the morning, the cook brought up a letter to his room. The address, which was in big characters, was written in a hand he was not familiar with; and Frederick, feeling sleepy, was in no great haste to break the seal. At length, when he did so, he read:

> "Justice of the Peace at Havre,
> 111th Arrondissement.

"MONSIEUR,—Monsieur Moreau, your uncle, having died intestate—"

He had fallen in for the inheritance! As if a conflagration had burst out behind the wall, he jumped out of bed, and flung the window wide open.

He read the letter over three times in succession. Could there be anything more certain? His uncle's entire fortune! A yearly income more than a thousand pounds! And he was overwhelmed with frantic joy at the thought of seeing Madame Arnoux once more. Then he thought of his mother; and he descended the stairs with the letter in his hand.

Madame Moreau made an effort to control her emotion, but could not keep herself from swooning. Frederick caught her in his arms and kissed her on the forehead.

"Dear mother, you can now buy back your carriage—laugh then! shed no more tears! be happy!"

Ten minutes later the news had travelled as far as the faubourgs. Then M. Benoist, M. Gamblin, M. Chambion, and other friends hurried toward the house. Frederick left them a minute in order to write to Deslauriers. Then other visitors arrived. The afternoon passed in congratulations. They had forgotten all about "Roque's wife," who was declared to be "very low."

When they were alone, the same evening, Madame Moreau advised her son to set up as an advocate at Troyes. As he was better known in his own part of the country than in any other, he would more easily find there a profitable connection.

"Ah, it is too hard!" exclaimed Frederick. He had scarcely grasped his good fortune in his hands when he yearned to carry it to Madame Arnoux. He announced his express determination to live in Paris.

"And what are you going to do there?"

"Nothing!"

Madame Moreau, astonished at his manner, asked what he intended to become.

"A minister," was Frederick's reply. And he declared that he was not joking, that he meant to plunge at once into diplomacy, and that his studies and his instincts impelled him in that direction. He would first enter the Council of State under M. Dambreuse's patronage.

"So then, you are acquainted with him?"

"Oh, yes—through M. Roque."

"That is singular," said Madame Moreau. He had stirred in her heart her former ambitious dreams. She internally abandoned herself to them, and said no more about other matters.

If he had yielded to his impatience, Frederick would have left that very instant. Next morning every seat in the diligence had been engaged; and so he kept eating out his heart till seven o'clock in the evening.

They were seated at dinner when three prolonged tolls of the church-bell fell on their ears; and the housemaid, coming in, informed them that Madame Eléonore had just died.

This death, after all, was not a misfortune for anyone, not even for her child. The young girl would only find it advantageous for herself afterward.

As the two houses were close to each other, a great coming and going and a clatter of tongues could be heard; and the idea of this corpse being so near threw a certain funereal gloom over their parting. Madame Moreau wiped her eyes two or three times. Frederick felt his heart oppressed.

When the meal was over, Catherine stopped him between two doors. Mademoiselle had expressed a wish to see him. She was waiting for him in the garden. He went out there, strode over the hedge, and knocking more or less against the trees, directed his steps toward M. Roque's house. Lights glittered through a window in the second story, then a form appeared in the midst of the darkness and a voice whispered:

"'Tis I!"

She seemed to him taller than usual, probably owing to her black dress.

Not knowing what to say to her, he contented himself with catching her hands, and sighing:

"Ah! my poor Louise!"

She did not reply. She gazed at him for a long time with an expression of sad, deep earnestness.

Frederick was afraid of missing the coach; he fancied that he could hear the rolling of wheels some distance away, and, in order to put an end to the interview:

"Catherine told me that you had something—"

"Yes—'tis true! I wanted to tell you—"

He was astonished to find that she addressed him in the plural; and, as she again stopped:

"Well, what?"

"I don't know. I cannot remember! Is it true that you're going away?"

"Yes, I'm starting now."

She repeated: "Ah, now?—for good?—we'll never meet again?"

She was choking with sobs.

"Good-bye! good-bye! embrace me then!"

And passionately she threw her arms about him.

CHAPTER VII

PARIS AGAIN

FREDERICK plunged into an intoxicating dream of the future, after he had seated himself behind the other passengers in the front of the diligence and the five horses had started off at a brisk trot. As an architect draws up the plan of a palace, so he mapped out his future life. He filled it with dainties and with splendours; it rose up to the sky; there was a profuse display of allurements; and so deeply was he buried in the contemplation of these things that he became oblivious to all external objects.

At the foot of the hill of Sourdun his attentions were directed to the stage which they had reached in their journey. They had not travelled more than five kilometres at the most. He was annoyed at this tardy rate of travelling. He pulled down the coach-window in order to get a view of the road. He asked the conductor several times at what hour they were due at their destination. However, he eventually regained his composure, and remained seated in his corner of the vehicle with wide-open eyes.

At Mormans, the clocks struck a quarter past one.

"So then we are in another day," he thought, "we have been in it for some time!"

Gradually his hopes and his recollections, Nogent, the Rue de Choiseul, Madame Arnoux, and his mother, were all confused together.

He was awakened by the dull sound of wheels passing over planks: they were crossing the Pont de Charenton—it was Paris. Then his two travelling companions, the first taking off his cap, and the second his silk handkerchief, put on their hats, and began to chat.

The first, a big, red-faced man in a velvet frock-coat, was a merchant; the second was coming up to the capital to consult a physician; and, fearing that he had disturbed this gentleman during the night, Frederick spontaneously apologised to him, so much had the young man's heart been softened by the happiness that possessed it. They turned into Ivry, then drove up a street: all at once, he saw before him the dome of the Panthéon.

They were kept waiting a long time at the barrier, for vendors of poultry, waggoners, and a flock of sheep caused an obstruction there. The conductor uttered his sonorous shout:

"Look alive! look alive! oho!" and the scavengers drew out of the way, the pedestrians sprang back, the mud gushed against the coach-windows; they passed dung-carts, cabs, and omnibuses. At length, the iron gate of the Jardin des Plantes came into sight.

They once more crossed the Seine over the Pont-Neuf, descended in the direction of the Louvre; and, having traversed the Rues Saint-Honoré, Croix des Petits-Champs, and Du Bouloi, reached the Rue Coq-Héron, and entered the courtyard of the hotel.

So that his enjoyment might last the longer, Frederick dressed himself as slowly as possible, and even walked as far as the Boulevard Montmarte. He smiled at the thought of presently beholding once more the beloved name on the marble plate.

He hastened to the Rue de Choiseul. M. and Madame Arnoux no longer lived there, and a woman next door was keeping an eye on the porter's lodge. Frederick waited to see the porter himself. After some time he made his appearance—it was no longer the same man. He did not know their address.

Frederick went into a café, and, while at breakfast, consulted the Commercial Directory. There were three hundred Arnoux in it, but not one Jacques Arnoux. Where, then, could they be living? Pellerin ought to know.

He made his way to the top of the Faubourg Poissonnière, to the artist's studio. As the door had neither a bell nor a knocker, he rapped loudly on it with his knuckles, and then called out—shouted. But the only response was the echo of his voice from the empty house.

Then he thought of Hussonnet; but where could one discover a man

of that sort? On one occasion he had waited on Hussonnet when the latter was paying a visit at his mistress's house in the Rue de Fleurus.
Frederick had just reached the Rue de Fleurus when he realised that he
did not even know the young woman's name.

He had recourse to the Prefecture of Police. He wandered from staircase to staircase, from office to office. He found that the Intelligence
Department was closed for the day, and was told to come back again next
morning.

Then he called at all the picture-dealers' shops that he could find, and
inquired whether they could give him any information as to Arnoux's
whereabouts. The only answer he got was that M. Arnoux was no longer
in the trade.

At last, discouraged, weary, sickened, he returned to his hotel, and went
to bed. Just as he was stretching himself between the sheets, an idea
flashed upon him which made him leap up with delight:

"Regimbart! what a stupid I was not to think of him before!"

Next morning, at seven o'clock, he arrived in the Rue Notre Dame
des Victoires, in front of a dramshop, where Regimbart habitually drank
white wine. It was not yet open. He walked about the neighbourhood,
and at the end of about half-an-hour, presented himself at the place
again. Regimbart had left.

Frederick rushed out into the street. He fancied that he could see
Regimbart's hat some distance away. A hearse and some mourning
coaches intercepted his progress. When they had got out of the way, the
vision had disappeared.

Fortunately, he recalled to mind that the Citizen breakfasted every day
at eleven o'clock sharp, at a little restaurant in the Place Gaillon. All he
had to do was to wait patiently till then; and, after wandering about from
the Bourse to the Madeleine, and from the Madeleine to the Gymnase,
so long that it seemed unending, Frederick, just as the clocks were striking eleven, entered the restaurant in the Rue Gaillon, convinced that he
would find Regimbart there.

"Don't know!" said the restaurant-keeper, in an unceremonious tone.

Frederick persisted: the man replied:

"I have no longer any acquaintance with him, Monsieur"—and, as he
spoke, he raised his eyebrows majestically and shook his head in a mysterious fashion.

But in their last interview, the Citizen had mentioned the Alexandre
smoking-divan. Frederick swallowed a cake, jumped into a cab, and asked
the driver whether there happened to be anywhere on the heights of
Sainte-Geneviève a certain Café Alexandre. The cabman drove him to
the Rue des Francs Bourgeois Saint-Michel, where there was an establishment of that name, and in answer to his question:

"Monsieur Regimbart, if you please?" the keeper of the café said with an unusually gracious smile:

"He has not arrived as yet, Monsieur," while he directed toward his wife, who sat behind the counter, a look of intelligence. And the next moment, turning toward the clock:

"But he'll be here, I hope, in ten minutes, or at most a quarter of an hour. Celestin, hurry with the newspapers! What would Monsieur like to take?"

Though he did not desire anything, Frederick swallowed a glass of rum, then a glass of kirsch, then a glass of curaçoa, then several glasses of grog, both cold and hot. He read through that day's *Siècle,* and then re-read it; he examined the caricatures in the *Charivari* down to the very tissue of the paper. When he had finished, he knew the advertisements by heart.

What in the world could Regimbart be doing? Frederick waited in an exceedingly miserable frame of mind.

At length when it was half-past four, Frederick, who had been there since about twelve, sprang to his feet, and declared that he would not wait any longer.

"I can't understand it at all myself," replied the café-keeper, in a straight-forward tone. "This is the first time that M. Ledoux has failed to come!"

"What! Monsieur Ledoux?"

"Why, yes, Monsieur!"

"I said Regimbart," exclaimed Frederick, exasperated.

"Ah! a thousand pardons! You are making a mistake! Madame Alexandre, did not Monsieur say Monsieur Ledoux?"

And, questioning the waiter: "You heard him yourself, just as I did?"

No doubt, to pay his master off for old scores, the waiter contented himself with smiling.

Frederick drove back to the boulevards, furious at having his time wasted, raging against the Citizen, but longing for his presence as if for that of a god, and firmly resolved to drag him forth, if necessary, from the depths of the most remote cellars. In one café he was told that Regimbart had just gone out; in another, that he might perhaps call at a later hour; in a third, that they had not seen him for six months; and, in another place, that he had the day before ordered a leg of mutton for Saturday. Finally, at Vautier's dining-rooms, Frederick, on opening the door, knocked against the waiter.

"Do you know Monsieur Regimbart?"

"What, Monsieur! do I know him? 'Tis I who have the honour of attending on him. He's upstairs—he is just finishing his dinner!"

And, with a napkin under his arm, the master of the establishment himself accosted him:

"You're asking for Monsieur Regimbart, Monsieur? He was here a moment ago."

Frederick gave vent to an oath, but the proprietor of the dining-rooms stated that he would certainly find the gentleman at Bouttevilain's.

"I assure you, on my honour, he left a little earlier than usual, for he had a business appointment with some gentlemen. But you'll find him, I tell you again, at Bouttevilain's, Rue Saint-Martin, Number Ninety-two, the second row of steps at the left at the end of the courtyard—first floor—door to the right!"

At last; he saw Regimbart, in a cloud of tobacco-smoke, at the lower end of the refreshment-room.

"Ah! I have been a long time trying to find you!"

Without rising, Regimbart extended toward him only two fingers, and, as if he had seen Frederick the day before, he gave utterance to a number of commonplace remarks about the opening of the session.

Frederick interrupted him, saying in the least concerned tone he could assume:

"Is Arnoux going on well?"

The reply was a long time coming, as Regimbart was gargling the liquor in his throat:

"Yes, not badly."

"Where is he living now?"

"Why, in the Rue Paradis Poissonnière," the Citizen returned with astonishment.

"What number?"

"Thirty-seven—confound it! what an odd fellow you are!"

Frederick rose.

"What! are you going?"

"Yes, yes! I have to make a call—some business matter I had forgotten! Good-bye!"

Frederick covered the distance from the smoking-divan to the Arnoux's residence, as if carried along by a tepid wind, with the sensation of extreme ease that people experience in dreams.

He soon found himself on the second floor in front of a door, at the ringing of whose bell a servant appeared. A second door was flung open. Madame Arnoux was seated near the fire. Arnoux jumped up, and rushed across to embrace Frederick. She had on her lap a little boy not quite three years old. Her daughter, now as tall as herself, was standing at the opposite side of the mantelpiece.

"Allow me to present this gentleman to you," said Arnoux, taking his son up in his arms. And he amused himself for some minutes by throwing the child high up in the air, and then catching him with both hands as he came down.

"You'll kill him!—ah! good heavens, have done!" exclaimed Madame Arnoux.

But Arnoux, declaring that there was not the slightest danger, still kept tossing up the child, and even addressed him in words of endearment such as nurses use in the Marseillaise dialect, his natal tongue: "Ah! my fine picheoun! my ducksy of a little nightingale!"

Then, he asked Frederick why he had been so long without writing to them, what he had been doing down in the country, and why he had returned.

"As for me, I am at present, my dear friend, a dealer in faïence. But let us talk about yourself!"

Frederick gave as reasons for his absence a protracted lawsuit and the condition of his mother's health. He laid special stress on the latter subject in order to make himself interesting. He ended by saying that this time he was to settle in Paris for good; but he did not mention the inheritance, lest it might be prejudicial to his past.

Madame Arnoux wore a large blue merino dressing-gown. With her face turned toward the fire and one hand on the shoulder of the little boy, she unfastened with the other his bodice. The youngster in his shirt began to cry, while scratching his head, like the son of M. Alexandre.

Frederick expected to experience spasms of joy; but the passions grow pale when we find ourselves in an altered situation; and, as he no longer saw Madame Arnoux in the environment wherein he had known her, she seemed to him to have lost some of her fascination; to have degenerated in some way that he could not comprehend—in fact, not to be the same. He was surprised at the serenity of his own heart. He made enquiries about some old friends, Pellerin, amongst others.

"I don't see him often," said Arnoux. She added:

"We no longer entertain as we used to do formerly!"

Was the object of this remark to let him know that he would get no invitation from them? But Arnoux, continuing to exhibit the same cordiality, reproached him for not having come to dine with them uninvited; and he explained the reason why he had changed his business.

"What can be done in an age of decadence like ours? Great painting is gone out of fashion! Besides, we may import art into everything. You know that, for my part, I am a lover of the beautiful. I must bring you one of these days to see my earthenware works."

And he wanted to show Frederick at once some of his productions in the store which he had between the ground-floor and the first floor. Frederick, who was cold and hungry, was bored with Arnoux's display of his wares. He hurried off to the Café Anglais, where he ordered a sumptuous supper, and while eating, said to himself:

"I was well off enough below there with all my troubles! She scarcely noticed me! How like a shopkeeper's wife!"

And in an abrupt expansion of healthfulness, he formed egoistic resolutions. He felt his heart as hard as the table on which his elbows rested. So then he could this time plunge fearlessly into the vortex of society. The thought of the Dambreuses recurred to his mind. He would make use of them. Then he recalled Deslauriers. "Ah! faith, so much the worse!" Nevertheless, he sent him a note by a messenger, making a breakfast appointment with him for the following day.

Fortune had not been so kind to the other.

He had presented himself at the examination for a fellowship with a thesis on the law of wills, in which he held that the powers of testators ought to be restricted as much as possible; and, as his adversary provoked him in such a way as to cause him to say foolish things, he gave utterance to many of these absurdities without in any way inducing the examiners to falter in deciding that he was wrong. Then fate so willed it that he should choose by lot, as a subject for a lecture, Prescription. Thereupon, Deslauriers gave vent to some lamentable theories: the questions in dispute in former times ought to be brought forward as well as those which had recently arisen; why should the proprietor be deprived of his estate because he could furnish his title-deeds only after the lapse of thirty-one years? This was giving the security of the honest man to the inheritor of the enriched thief. Every injustice was consecrated by extending this law, which was a form of tyranny, the abuse of force! He had even exclaimed: "Abolish it; and the Franks will no longer oppress the Gauls, the English oppress the Irish, the Yankee oppress the Redskins, the Turks oppress the Arabs, the whites oppress the blacks, Poland—"

The President interrupted him: "Well! well! Monsieur, we have no interest in your political opinions—you will have them represented in your behalf by-and-by!"

Deslauriers did not desire to have his opinions represented; but this unfortunate Title XX. of the Third Book of the Civil Code had become a sort of mountain over which he stumbled. He was elaborating a great work on "Prescription considered as the Basis of the Civil Law and of the Law of Nature amongst Peoples"; and he got lost in Dunod, Rogerius, Balbus, Merlin, Vazeille, Savigny, Traplong, and other weighty authorities on the subject. In order to have more time for devoting himself to this task, he had resigned his post of head-clerk. He lived by giving private tuitions and preparing theses.

He came to keep the appointment in a big paletôt, lined with red flannel, like the one Sénécal used to wear in former days.

Only respect for the passers-by prevented them from straining one another in an embrace of friendship; and they made their way to Véfour's arm-in-arm, laughing happily, though with tear-drops lingering in the depths of their eyes. Then, as soon as they were free from observation, Deslauriers exclaimed:

"Ah! damn it! we'll have a jolly time now!"

Frederick was not quite pleased to find Deslauriers all at once associ-
ating himself in this way with his own newly-acquired inheritance. His
friend manifested too much pleasure on account of them both, and not
enough on his account alone.

After this, Deslauriers gave details about the reverses he had met with,
and gradually told Frederick all about his occupations and his daily existence, speaking of himself in a stoical fashion, and of others in tones of
intense bitterness. He found fault with everything; every man in office
was an idiot or a rascal. He flew into a passion against the waiter because
a glass was badly rinsed, and when Frederick uttered a reproach with a
view to mitigating his wrath: "As if I were going to annoy myself with
such numbskulls, who, you must know, can earn as much as six and even
eight thousand francs a year, who are electors, perhaps eligible as candidates. Ah! no, no!"

Then, with a sprightly air, "But I've forgotten that I'm talking to a
capitalist, to a Mondor,★ for you are a Mondor now!"

And, returning to the question of the inheritance, he gave expression
to this view—that collateral successorship (a thing unjust in itself, though
in the present case he was glad it was possible) would be abolished one
of these days during the approaching revolution.

"Do you believe in that?" said Frederick.

"I am sure of it!" he replied. "This sort of thing cannot last. There is
too much suffering. When I see into the wretchedness of men like
Sénécal—"

"Always Sénécal!" thought Frederick.

"But at all events, tell me the news? Are you still in love with Madame
Arnoux? Or is it all over—eh?"

Frederick, not knowing what to answer, closed his eyes and hung
down his head.

With regard to Arnoux, Deslauriers told him that the journal was now
the property of Hussonnet, who had transformed it. It was called "*L'Art*,
a literary institution—a company with shares of one hundred francs
each; capital of the firm, forty thousand francs," each shareholder having
the privilege of putting into it his own contributions; for "the company
has for its object to publish the works of beginners, to spare talent, perchance genius, the sad crises which drench," etc.

"You see the trick!" There was, however, something to be effected by
the change—the tone of the journal could be elevated; then, without any

---

★A notorious Italian charlatan, who, in the seventeenth century, settled in Paris and made
  a large fortune.

delay, while retaining the same writers, and promising a continuation of the feuilleton, to supply the subscribers with a political organ: the amount to be advanced would not be very great.

"What do you think of it? Come! would you like to have an interest in it?"

Frederick did not reject the proposal; but he pointed out that it was necessary for him to attend to the regulation of his affairs.

"After that, if you require anything—"

"Thanks, my boy!" said Deslauriers.

Then they smoked puros, leaning with their elbows on the shelf covered with velvet beside the window. Deslauriers, with half-closed eyes, was staring vacantly into the distance. His breast heaved, and he broke out:

"Ah! those were better days when Camille Desmoulins, standing below there on a table, drove the people on to the Bastille. Men really lived in those times; they could assert themselves, and prove their power! Simple advocates commanded generals. Kings were beaten by beggars; whilst now—"

He stopped, then added all of a sudden:

"Pooh! the future is big with great things!"

And, drumming a battle-march on the window-panes, he declaimed some verses of Barthélemy, which ran thus:

> "'That dread Assembly shall again appear,
>   Which, after forty years, fills you with fear
>   Marching with giant stride and dauntless soul,'

—I don't know any more of it! But 'tis late; suppose we go?"

And he continued setting forth his theories in the street.

Frederick, without heeding him, was looking at certain materials and articles of furniture in the shop-windows which would be suitable for his new residence in Paris; and it was, perhaps, the thought of Madame Arnoux that made him stop before a second-hand dealer's window, where three plates made of fine ware were exposed to view. They were decorated with yellow arabesques with metallic reflections, and were worth a hundred crowns apiece. He ordered them put aside for him.

"For my part, if I were in your place," said Deslauriers, "I would rather buy silver plate," revealing by this love of substantial things the man of mean extraction.

As soon as he was alone, Frederick went to the establishment of the celebrated Pomadère, where he ordered three pairs of trousers, two coats, a pelisse trimmed with fur, and five waistcoats. Then he visited a boot-maker's, shirtmaker's, and hatter's, giving them directions in each shop to be as speedy as possible. Three days later, on the evening of his return from Havre, he found his complete wardrobe awaiting him in his Parisian abode; and impatient to make use of it, he resolved to pay an immediate visit to the Dambreuses. But it was too early yet—scarcely eight o'clock.

"Suppose I go to see the others?" said he to himself.

He found Arnoux, all alone, in the act of shaving in front of his glass. The latter proposed to drive him to a place where they could amuse themselves, and when M. Dambreuse was mentioned, "Ah, that's just lucky! You'll see some of his friends there. Come on! It will be good fun!"

Frederick asked to be excused. Madame Arnoux recognised his voice, and wished him good-day, through the partition, for her daughter was indisposed, and she was not feeling well herself. The noise of a soup-ladle against a glass could be heard from within, and all those sounds made by things being lightly moved about, which are usual in a sick-room. Then Arnoux left his dressing-room to say good-bye to his wife. He brought forward many reasons for going out:

"You know well that it is a serious matter! I really must go there; 'tis a case of necessity. They'll be waiting for me!"

"Go, go, my dear! Amuse yourself!"

Arnoux hailed a hackney-coach:

"Palais Royal. Number Seven Montpensier Gallery."

And, as he let himself sink back in the cushions:

"Ah! how tired I am, my dear fellow! It will be the death of me! However, I can tell it to you—to you!"

He whispered in Frederick's ear in a mysterious fashion:

"I am trying to re-discover the red of Chinese copper!"

And he explained the nature of the glaze and the little fire.

On their arrival at Chevet's shop, a large hamper was brought to him, which he stowed away in the hackney-coach. Then he ordered for his "poor wife" pine-apples and various dainties, and directed that they should be sent early next morning.

After this, they called at a costumer's establishment; it was to a ball they were going.

Arnoux selected blue velvet breeches, a vest of the same material, and a red wig; Frederick a domino, after which they went down the Rue de Laval toward a house the second floor of which was illuminated by coloured lanterns.

At the foot of the stairs they heard the sound of violins from above.

"Where the deuce are you bringing me to?" said Frederick.

"To see a pretty girl! don't be afraid!"

The door was opened for them by a groom; and they entered the ante-room, where paletôts, mantles, and shawls were thrown together in a heap on some chairs. A young woman in the costume of a dragoon in the reign of Louis XIV was passing at that moment. It was Mademoiselle Rosanette Bron, the mistress of the place.

"Well?" said Arnoux.

"'Tis done!" she replied.

"Ah! thanks, my angel!"

And he tried to kiss her.

"Take care, now, you foolish man! You'll spoil the paint on my face!"

Arnoux introduced Frederick.

"Step in there, Monsieur; you are very welcome!"

She drew aside a door-curtain, and cried out with a certain emphasis:

"Here's my lord Arnoux, girls, and a princely friend of his!"

Frederick was at first dazzled by the lights. He could distinguish nothing save some silk and velvet dresses, naked shoulders, a mass of colours swaying to and fro to the accompaniment of an orchestra hidden behind green foliage, between walls hung with yellow silk, with pastel portraits here and there and crystal chandeliers in Louis XVI style.

The dancing stopped, and there were bursts of applause, a general hubbub of delight, as Arnoux advanced with his hamper on his head; the eatables contained in it made a lump in the centre.

"Make way for the lustre!"

Frederick raised his eyes: it was the lustre of old Saxe that had adorned the shop attached to the office of *L'Art Industriel*. The memory of former days came back to his mind. But a foot-soldier of the line in undress, with that silly expression of countenance ascribed by tradition to conscripts, planted himself right in front of him. Frederick recognised his old friend Hussonnet. In a half-Alsatina, half-negro kind of gibberish, the Bohemian loaded him with congratulations, addressing him as "colonel." Frederick, embarrassed by the crowd of personages assembled around him, was at a loss for an answer. At a tap on the desk from a fiddlestick, the partners in the dance fell into place.

They numbered about sixty, the women being for the most part dressed either as village-girls or marchionesses, and the men, who were nearly all of mature age, appeared as waggoners, 'longshoremen, or sailors.

Frederick having placed himself close to the wall, stared at those who were going through the quadrille.

An old beau, dressed like a Venetian Doge in a long gown of purple silk, was dancing with Mademoiselle Rosanette, who wore a green coat, laced breeches, and boots of soft leather with gold spurs. In front of them were an Albanian laden with yataghans and a Swiss girl with blue eyes and skin white as milk, who looked as plump as a quail with her chemisesleeves and red corset exposed to view. In order to display her hair, which fell down to her hips, a tall blonde, a walking lady in the opera, had assumed the part of a female savage; and over her brown swaddling-cloth she wore nothing save leathern breeches, glass bracelets, and a tinsel diadem, from which rose a large sheaf of peacock's feathers. In front of her, a gentleman intended to represent Pritchard, muffled up in a grotesquely big black coat, was beating time with his elbow on his snuff-box. A little Watteau shepherd in blue-and-silver, like moonlight, dashed his crook against the thyrsus of a Bacchante crowned with grapes, who wore a leopard's skin over her left side, and buskins with gold ribbons. On the other side, a Polish lady, in a spencer of nacarat-coloured velvet, wore a gauze petticoat, which fluttered over her pearl-grey stockings and fashionable pink boots bordered with white fur. She was smiling on a big-paunched man of forty, robed as a choir-boy, who was skipping very high, raising his surplice with one hand, and with the other his red clerical cap. But the queen, the star, was Mademoiselle Loulou, a celebrated dancer at public halls. As she had lately become wealthy, she wore a large lace collar over her vest of smooth black velvet; and her gay trousers of poppy-coloured silk, clinging closely to her figure, and drawn tight round her waist by a cashmere scarf, had all over their seams little natural white camellias. Her pale face, a little puffed, and with the nose some-what *retroussé*, looked all the more pert from the disordered appearance of her wig, over which she had clapped a man's grey felt hat, so that it covered her right ear; and, with every kick she gave, her pumps, adorned with diamond buckles, nearly reached the nose of her neighbour, a big mediæval baron, who was continually getting entangled in his steel armour. There was also an angel, with a gold sword in her hand, and two swan's wings over her back, who kept running up and down, every minute losing her partner, who appeared as Louis XIV, and who was in utter ignorance of the figures and confused the quadrille.

Frederick, as he gazed at these people, experienced a sense of forlorn-ness, a feeling of uneasiness. He was still thinking of Madame Arnoux, and it seemed to him as if he were furthering some plot that was being hatched against her.

When the quadrille was over, Mademoiselle Rosanette accosted him. She was slightly out of breath, and her gorget, polished like a mirror, swelled up softly under her chin.

"And you, Monsieur," said she, "don't you dance?"

Frederick excused himself; he did not know how to dance.

"Really! but with me? Are you quite sure?" And, poising herself on one hip, with her other knee a little drawn back, while she stroked with her left hand the mother-of-pearl pommel of her sword, she kept look-ing up at him for a minute with a half-beseeching, half-teasing air. At last she said, "Good-night, then!" made a pirouette, and disappeared.

Frederick, dissatisfied with himself, and not well knowing what to do, wandered through the rooms.

He entered the boudoir padded with pale blue silk, with bouquets of flowers from the fields, whilst on the ceiling, in a circle of gilt wood, Cupids, emerging out of an azure sky, played over the clouds. This display of luxuries, which would now-a-days be only trifles to persons like Rosanette, dazzled him, and he admired everything—the artificial convolvuli decorating the surface of the mirror, the curtains on the mantel-piece, the Turkish divan, and a sort of tent in a recess in the wall, with pink silk hangings and a covering of white muslin. Furniture made of dark wood with inlaid work of copper filled the sleeping apartment, where, on a platform covered with swan's-down, stood a large canopied bedstead trimmed with ostrich-feathers.

Here were surroundings specially calculated to fascinate him. In a sudden revolt of his youthful blood he swore that he would enjoy such things; he grew bold; then, coming back to the place opening into the drawing-room, where there was now a larger gathering—it kept moving about in a kind of luminous pulverulence—he stood to watch the quadrilles, blinking his eyes to see better, and inhaling the soft perfumes of the women, which floated through the atmosphere like an all-pervading kiss.

But, close to him, on the other side of the door, was Pellerin—Pellerin, in full dress, his left hand over his breast, his hat and a torn white glove in his right.

"Halloa! 'Tis a long time since we saw you! Where the deuce have you been? Travelling in Italy? 'Tis a commonplace country enough—Italy, eh? not so unique as people say it is? No matter! Will you bring me your sketches one of these days?"

And, without allowing him time to answer, the artist began talking about himself. He had made considerable progress, having definitely satisfied himself as to the stupidity of studying the line. We ought not to look so much for beauty and unity in a work as for character and diversity of subject.

"For everything exists in nature; therefore, everything is legitimate; everything is plastic. It is only a question of catching the mood, mind you! I have discovered the secret," and giving him a nudge, he repeated several times, "I have discovered the secret, you see! Just look at that little woman with the head-dress of a sphinx who is dancing with a Russian postilion—that's neat, dry, fixed, all in flats and in stiff tones—indigo under the eyes, a patch of vermilion on the cheek, and bistre on the temples—pif! paf!" And with his thumb he drew, as it were, pencil-strokes in the air. "Whilst the big one over there," he continued, pointing toward a fishwife in a cherry gown with a gold cross hanging from her neck, and a lawn fichu fastened round her shoulders, "is nothing but curves. The nostrils are spread out just like the borders of her cap; the corners of the mouth are rising up; the chin sinks: all is fleshy, melting, abundant, tranquil, and sunshiny—a true Rubens! Nevertheless, both are perfect! Where, then, is the type?" He grew warm with the subject. "What is this but a beautiful woman? What is it but the beautiful? Ah! the beautiful—tell me what that is—"

Frederick interrupted him to inquire who was the merry-andrew with the face of a he-goat, who was in the act of blessing all the dancers in the middle of a pastourelle.

"Oh! he's not anybody!—a widower, the father of three boys. He leaves them without breeches, spends all his time at the club, and lives with the servant!"

"And who is that dressed like a bailiff talking in the recess of the window to a Marquise de Pompadour?"

"The Marquise is Mademoiselle Vandael, at one time an actress at the Gymnase, the mistress of the Doge, the Comte de Palazot. They have now been twenty years living together—nobody can tell why. Had she fine eyes at one time, that woman? As for the citizen beside her, his name is Captain d'Herbigny, an old man of the hurdy-gurdy sort that you can play on, with nothing in the world except his Cross of the Legion of Honour and his pension. He passes for the uncle of the grisettes at festival times, arranges duels, and dines in the city."

"A rascal?" said Frederick.

"No! an honest man!"

"Ha!"

The artist was about to mention the names of others, when, perceiving a gentleman who, like Molière's physician, wore a big black serge gown opening very wide as it descended in order to display all his trinkets:

"The person there is Doctor Des Rogis, who, full of bitterness at not having become famous, has written a book of medical pornography, and willingly blacks people's boots in society, while he is at the same time discreet. These ladies adore him. He and his wife (that lean châtelaine in the grey dress) are seen together at every public place—aye, and at other places too. In spite of domestic embarrassments, they have *a day*—artistic teas, at which verses are recited. Attention!"

Between two quadrilles, Rosanette went toward the mantelpiece, where an obese little old man, in a maroon coat with gold buttons, was seated in an armchair. In spite of his withered cheeks, which hung over his white cravat, his hair, still fair, and curling naturally like that of a poodle, gave him a frivolous appearance.

She was listening to him with her face bent close to his. Presently, she handed him a little glass of syrup; and nothing could be more dainty than her hands under their laced sleeves, which passed over the facings of her green coat. When the old man had swallowed it, he kissed them.

"Why, that's Monsieur Oudry, a neighbour of Arnoux!"

"He has lost her!" said Pellerin, smiling.

A Longjumeau postilion caught her by the waist. A waltz was beginning. Then all the women, seated round the drawing-room on benches, rose up quickly; and their petticoats, their scarfs, and their head-dresses went whirling round.

They whirled so close to him that Frederick could see the beads of perspiration on their foreheads; and this gyral movement, more and more lively, regular, provocative of dizzy sensations, communicated to his mind a sort of intoxication, which made other images surge up within it, while each woman passed with the same dazzling effect, and with a special kind of exciting influence, according to her style of beauty.

The Polish lady, surrendering herself in a languorous fashion, inspired him with a longing to clasp her to his heart while they were both spinning forward on a sledge along a plain covered with snow. Horizons of tranquil voluptuousness in a châlet at the side of a lake opened out under the footsteps of the Swiss girl, who waltzed with her bust erect and her eyelashes drooping. Then, suddenly, the Bacchante, bending back her head with its dark locks, made him dream of devouring caresses in a wood of oleanders, in the midst of a storm, to the confused accompaniment of tabours. The fishwife, who was panting from the rapidity of the music, which was far too great for her, gave vent to bursts of laughter; and he would have liked, while drinking with her in some tavern in the "Porcherons," to rumple her fichu with both hands, as in the good old times. But the 'longshore-woman, whose light toes barely skimmed the floor, seemed to conceal under the suppleness of her limbs and the seriousness of her face all the refinements of modern love, which possesses the exactitude of a science and the mobility of a bird. Rosanette was whirling with arms akimbo; her wig, in an awkward position, bobbed over her collar, and flung iris-powder around her; and, at every turn, she was near catching hold of Frederick by the ends of her gold spurs.

During the closing bar of the waltz, Mademoiselle Vatnaz made her appearance.

Behind her came a tall fellow in the classical costume of Dante, who happened to be—she now made no concealment of it—the ex-singer of the Alhambra, and who, though his name was Auguste Delamare, had first called himself Anténor Delamarre, then Delmas, then Belmar, and at last Delmar, thus modifying and perfecting his name, as his celebrity increased, for he had forsaken the public-house concert for the theatre, and had just made his *début* in a noisy fashion at the Ambigu in *Gaspardo le Pêcheur.*

Hussonnet, on noticing him, knitted his brows. Since his play had been rejected, he hated actors. It was impossible to conceive the vanity of individuals of this sort, and above all of this fellow. "What a prig! Just look at him!"

After a slight bow toward Rosanette, Delmar leaned against the mantelpiece; and there he remained, motionless, with one hand over his heart, his left foot thrust forward, his eyes raised toward heaven, with his wreath of gilt laurels above his cowl, while he strove to put a poetical expression on his face in order to fascinate the ladies. They made, at some distance, a circle around him.

The Vatnaz, having given Rosanette a prolonged embrace, came to beg of Hussonnet to revise, with a view to the improvement of the style, an educational work which she intended to publish, under the title of *The Young Ladies' Garland,* a collection of literary and moral philosophy.

The man of letters agreed to assist her in the preparation of the work. Then she asked him whether he could not in one of the publications to which he had access give her friend a slight puff, and even assign to him some employment. Hussonnet in his interest had forgotten to take a glass of punch.

It was Arnoux who had brewed the beverage; and, followed by the Comte's groom carrying an empty tray, he offered it to the ladies with a self-satisfied air.

When he was passing in front of M. Oudry, Rosanette stopped him.

"Well—and this little business?"

He coloured slightly; finally, addressing the old man:

"Our fair friend tells me that you would have the kindness—"

"What of that, neighbour? I am quite at your service!"

And M. Dambreuse's name was pronounced. As they were talking in low tones, Frederick could only hear indistinctly; and he made his way to the other side of the mantelpiece, where Rosanette and Delmar were chatting.

The mummer had a vulgar countenance, made, like the scenery of the stage, to be viewed from a distance—coarse hands, big feet, and a heavy jaw; and he spoke slightingly of the most distinguished actors, and of poets with patronising contempt, making use of the expressions "my organ," "my physique," "my powers," enamelling his conversation with words that were scarcely intelligible even to himself, and for which he had quite an affection, such as *"morbidezza,"* "analogue," and "homogeneity."

Rosanette listened to him with little nods of approval. One could see her enthusiasm burning under the paint on her cheeks, and a touch of moisture appeared like a veil over her bright eyes of an indefinable colour. How could such a man as this fascinate her? Frederick internally excited himself to still greater contempt for him, in order to banish, perhaps, a species of envy which he felt with regard to him.

Mademoiselle Vatnaz was now with Arnoux, and, while laughing from time to time very loudly, she cast glances toward Rosanette, whom Monsieur Oudry kept in sight.

Then Arnoux and the Vatnaz disappeared. The old man began talking in a subdued voice to Rosanette.

"Well, yes, 'tis settled then! Leave me alone!"

And she asked Frederick to give a glance into the kitchen to see whether Arnoux happened to be there.

A battalion of half-full glasses covered the floor; and the saucepans, the pots, the turbot-kettle, and the frying-stove were all in a state of confusion. Arnoux was giving directions to the servants, whom he "thee'd" and "thou'd," beating up the mustard, tasting the sauces, and flirting with the housemaid.

"All right," he said; "tell them 'tis ready! I'm going to have it served up."

The dancing had ceased. The women sat down; the men were walking about.

Where could Rosanette be? Frederick went on further to find her, even into her boudoir and her bedroom. Some, in order to be alone, or in pairs, had retreated into the corners. Whisperings intermingled with the shade. There were little laughs stifled under handkerchiefs, and at the sides of women's corsages one could catch glimpses of fans quivering with slow, gentle movements, like the beating of a wounded bird's wings.

As he entered the conservatory, he saw under the large leaves of a caladium near the fountain, Delmar lying at length on the linen-covered sofa. Rosanette, seated beside him, was passing her fingers through his hair; and they were gazing into each other's faces. At the same moment, Arnoux came in at the opposite side—that which was near the aviary. Delmar sprang to his feet; then he went out at a rapid pace, without turning round; but he paused close to the door to gather a hibiscus flower, with which he adorned his button-hole. Rosanette hung her head; Frederick, who caught sight of her profile, saw that she was in tears.

"I say! What's the matter with you?" exclaimed Arnoux.

She shrugged her shoulders without replying.

"Is it on his account?" he went on.

She threw her arms round his neck, and kissing him on the forehead, slowly:

"You should know that I will always love you, my big fellow! Think no more about it! Let us go to supper!"

A copper chandelier with forty wax tapers lighted up the dining-room, the walls of which were hidden from view under some fine old earthenware that was hung up there. With a rustle of garments, the women took their seats beside one another; the men, standing up, posted themselves at the corners. Pellerin and M. Oudry were placed near

Rosanette, Arnoux was facing her. Palazot and his female companion had just gone out.

"Good-bye to them!" said she. "Now let us begin the attack!"

And the choir-boy, a facetious man, with a big sign of the cross, said grace.

The ladies were scandalised, and especially the fishwife, who was the mother of a young girl of whom she wished to make an honest woman. Neither did Arnoux care for "that sort of thing," as he considered that religion ought to be respected.

A German clock with a cock attached to it happening to chime out the hour of two, gave rise to a number of jokes about the cuckoo. All kinds of talk followed—puns, anecdotes, bragging remarks, bets, lies taken for truth, improbable assertions, a tumult of words, which soon became dispersed in the form of conversation between particular individuals. The wines went round; the dishes succeeded one another; the doctor carved. The angel poised on the piano-stool—the only place on which her wings permitted her to sit—was placidly masticating without stopping.

"What an appetite!" the choir-boy kept repeating in amazement, "what an appetite!"

And a sphinx drank brandy, screamed out with her mouth full, and wriggled like a demon. Suddenly her jaws swelled, and no longer being able to keep down the blood which rushed to her head and nearly choked her, she pressed her napkin against her lips and threw herself under the table.

Frederick had seen her falling: "'Tis nothing!" And at his request to be allowed to go and look after her, she replied slowly:

"Pooh! what's the use? That's just as pleasant as anything else. Life is not so amusing!"

Then, he shivered, a feeling of icy sadness taking possession of him, as if he had caught a glimpse of whole worlds of wretchedness and despair—a chafing-dish of charcoal beside a folding-bed, the corpses of the Morgue in leathern aprons, with the stream of cold water flowing over their heads.

Meanwhile Hussonnet, seated at the feet of the female savage, was howling in a hoarse voice in imitation of the actor Grassot:

"Be not cruel, O Celuta! this little family fête is charming! Intoxicate me with delight, my loves! Let us be gay! let us be gay!"

And he began kissing the women on the shoulders. They quivered under the tickling of his moustaches. Then he conceived the idea of breaking a plate over his head. Others followed his example. The broken earthenware flew about in bits like slates in a storm; and the 'longshore-woman exclaimed:

"Don't bother yourselves about that; they cost nothing. We get a present of them from the merchant who makes them!"

Every eye was riveted on Arnoux. He replied:

"Ha! about the invoice—allow me!" desiring, no doubt, to pass for not being, or for no longer being, Rosanette's lover.

But two angry voices here interrupted:

"Idiot!"

"Rascal!"

"I am at your command!"

"So am I at yours!"

It was the mediæval knight and the Russian postilion who were disputing, the latter having stated that armour dispensed with bravery, while the other regarded this view as an insult. He desired to fight; all interposed to prevent him, and in the midst of the uproar the captain tried to make himself heard.

"Listen to me, Messieurs! One word! I have some experience, Messieurs!"

Rosanette, by tapping with her knife on a glass, succeeded eventually in restoring silence, and, addressing the knight, who had his helmet on, and then the postilion, whose head was covered with a large hairy cap:

"Take off that saucepan of yours! and you, there, your wolf's head! Are you going to obey me, damn you? Show respect to my epaulets! I am your commanding officer!"

They complied, and everyone applauded, exclaiming, "Long live the Maréchale! long live the Maréchale!" Then she took a bottle of champagne off the stove, and poured its contents into the cups which they successively stretched out to her.

The little birds of the aviary, the door of which had been left open, flew into the apartment, quite scared; they flew round the chandelier, knocking against the window-panes and against the furniture, and some of them, alighting on the heads of the guests, looked like large flowers.

The musicians had gone. The piano had been drawn out of the anteroom. The Vatnaz seated herself before it, and, accompanied by the choir-boy, who thumped his tambourine, she wildly dashed into a quadrille, striking the keys like a horse pawing the ground, and wriggling her waist, the better to mark the time. The Maréchale dragged out Frederick; Hussonnet took the windmill; the 'longshore-woman worked her joints like a circus-clown; the merry-andrew acted after the manner of an orang-outang; the female savage, with outspread arms, imitated the swaying motion of a boat. At last, unable to keep it up any longer, they all stopped; and a window was flung open.

The broad daylight penetrated the apartment with the cool breath of morning. There was an exclamation of astonishment, followed by silence. The hangings were soiled, the dresses rumpled and dusty. The plaits of the women's hair hung loose over their shoulders, and the paint, trickling down with the perspiration, revealed pallid faces and red, blinking eyelids.

The Maréchale, fresh as if she had just stepped out of a bath, had rosy cheeks and sparkling eyes. She flung her wig away, and her hair fell around her like fleece, allowing none of her uniform to be seen except her breeches, the effect thus produced being at the same time comical and pretty.

The Sphinx, whose teeth chattered as if she had the ague, asked for a shawl.

Rosanette rushed up to her own room to look for one, and, as the other came after her, she quickly shut the door in her face.

The Turk remarked, in a loud tone, that M. Oudry had not been seen going out. Nobody paid any attention to the maliciousness of this observation, so worn out were they all.

Then, while waiting for vehicles, they managed to get on their broad-brimmed hats and cloaks. It struck seven. The angel was still in the dining-room, with a plate of sardines and fruit stewed in melted butter in front of her, and close beside her was the fishwife, smoking cigarettes, while giving her advice as to the right way to live.

At last, the cabs having arrived, the guests took their departure. But the angel, attacked by the preliminary symptoms of indigestion, was unable to rise. A mediæval baron carried her to a cab.

"Take care of her wings!" cried the 'longshore-woman through the window.

At the head of the stairs, Mademoiselle Vatnaz said to Rosanette:

"Good-bye, darling! It has been a very nice party."

Then, bending close to her ear: "Take care of him!"

"Till better times come," returned the Maréchale, in drawling tones, as she turned her back.

Arnoux and Frederick returned together, just as they had come. The dealer in faïence looked so gloomy that his companion asked if he were ill.

"I? Not at all!"

He bit his moustache, knitted his brows; and Frederick inquired if it were his business that annoyed him.

"By no means!"

Then all of a sudden:

"You know him—Père Oudry—don't you?"

And, with a spiteful expression on his countenance:

"He's rich, the old scoundrel!"

After this, Arnoux spoke about an important piece of ware-making, which had to be finished that day at his works. He wished to see it; the train was starting in an hour.

"Meantime, I must go and embrace my wife."

"Ha! his wife!" thought Frederick. Then he made his way home to go to bed, with his head aching terribly; and, to appease his thirst, he swallowed a whole carafe of water.

Another thirst had come to him—the thirst for women, for licentious pleasure, for all that Parisian life permitted him to enjoy. Then, two large black eyes, which had not been at the ball, appeared; and, light as butterflies, burning as torches, they came and went, ascended to the cornice and descended to his very mouth.

Frederick strove desperately to recognise those eyes, but could not do so. Already the dream had taken hold of him. It seemed to him that he was yoked beside Arnoux to the pole of a hackney-coach, and that the Maréchale sat astride of him, and disembowelled him with her gold spurs.

CHAPTER VIII

FREDERICK ENTERTAINS
AND IS ENTERTAINED

AT the corner of the Rue Rumfort was a small mansion which was just what Frederick needed. He purchased it, along with the horse, the brougham, the furniture, and a couple of flower stands which were taken from the Arnoux's house to be placed on each side of his drawing-room door. In the rear of the apartment were a bedroom and a closet. The idea occurred to his mind to take in Deslauriers with him. But how could he receive her—her, his future mistress? The presence of a friend would be inconvenient. He knocked down the partition-wall in order to enlarge the drawing-room, and converted the closet into a smoking-room.

He bought the works of the poets whom he loved, books of travel, atlases, and dictionaries, for he had innumerable plans of study. He hurried on the workmen, rushed about to the different shops, and in his impatience to enjoy, carried off everything without even bargaining beforehand.

From the tradesmen's bills, Frederick calculated that he would have to expend very soon forty thousand francs, not including the succession duties, which would exceed thirty-seven thousand. As his fortune was in landed property, he wrote to the notary at Havre to sell a portion of it that he might pay off his debts and have some money at his disposal. Then, anxious to become acquainted at last with that vague entity, glittering and indefinable, which is known as "society," he sent a note to the Dambreuses to know whether he might call upon them. Madame, in reply, said she would expect a visit from him the following day.

This happened to be their reception-day. Carriages were standing in the courtyard. Two footmen rushed forward under the marquée, and a third at the head of the stairs walked before him.

Frederick smiled with pleasure in spite of himself.

At last he reached an oval apartment wainscoted in cypress-wood, full of dainty furniture, and letting in the light through a single sheet of plate-glass, which looked out on a garden. Madame Dambreuse was seated at the fireside, with a dozen persons gathered round her in a circle. With a polite greeting, she signed to him to take a seat, without, however, exhibiting any surprise at not having seen him for so long a time.

Just at the moment he was entering the room, they had been praising the eloquence of the Abbé Cœur. Then they deplored the immorality of servants, a topic suggested by a theft which a *valet-de-chambre* had committed, and they began to indulge in tittle-tattle. Old Madame de Sommery had a cold; Mademoiselle de Turvisot had married; the Montcharrons were not expected before the end of January; neither would the Bretancourts return for some time, now that people remained in the country till late in the year.

Madame Dambreuse received all of them graciously. When it was mentioned that anyone was ill, she knitted her brows with a pained expression, and when balls or evening parties were discussed, assumed a joyous air. She would ere long be compelled to deprive herself of these pleasures, for she was going to take away from a boarding-school a niece of her husband, an orphan. The guests extolled her devotedness: this was behaving like a true mother of a family.

Frederick gazed at her attentively. The dull skin of her face looked as if it had been stretched out, and had a bloom in which there was no brilliancy, like that of preserved fruit. But her hair, which she wore in corkscrew curls, after the English fashion, was finer than silk; her eyes were of a sparkling blue; and all her movements were dainty. Seated at the lower end of the apartment, on a small sofa, she kept brushing off the red flock from a Japanese screen, probably to let her hands be seen to greater advantage—long narrow hands, a trifle thin, with fingers tilting up at the points. She wore a grey moiré gown with a high-necked body, like a Puritan lady.

Frederick inquired whether she intended to go to La Fortelle this year. Madame Dambreuse was unable to say. He was sure, however, of one thing, that one would be bored to death in Nogent.

Then the visitors thronged in more quickly. It soon became impossible to follow the conversation; as Frederick withdrew Madame Dambreuse said to him:

"Every Wednesday, is it not, Monsieur Moreau?" making up for her previous apparent indifference by these simple words.

He was satisfied. Nevertheless, he took a deep breath when he got out into the open air; and, craving a less artificial environment, Frederick recalled to mind that he owed the Maréchale a visit.

The door of the anteroom was open. Two Havanese lapdogs rushed forward. A voice exclaimed:

"Delphine! Delphine! Is that you, Félix?"

He stood there without advancing a step. The two little dogs kept up a continuous yelping. At length Rosanette appeared, wrapped up in a sort of dressing-gown of white muslin trimmed with lace, and with her stockingless feet in Turkish slippers.

"Ah! excuse me, Monsieur! I thought it was the hairdresser. One minute; I am coming back!"

And he was left alone in the dining-room. The Venetian blinds were closed. Frederick, as he glanced round, was beginning to recall the hub-bub of the other night, when he noticed on the table, in the middle of the room, a man's hat, an old felt hat, bruised, greasy, dirty. To whom did this hat belong? Impudently displaying its torn lining, it seemed to say:

"I have the laugh, after all! I am the master!"

The Maréchale suddenly reappeared on the scene. She picked up the hat, opened the conservatory, flung it in there, shut the door again (other doors flew open and closed again at the same moment), and, having brought Frederick through the kitchen, she introduced him into her dressing-room.

It was evident that this was the most frequented room in the house, and, so to speak, its true moral centre. The walls, the armchairs, and a big divan with a spring were adorned with a chintz pattern on which was traced a great deal of foliage. On a white marble table stood two large washhand-basins of fine blue earthenware. Crystal shelves, forming a what-not, were laden with phials, brushes, combs, sticks of cosmetic, and powder-boxes. The fire was reflected in a high cheval-glass. A sheet was hanging outside a bath, and odours of almond-paste and of benzoin were exhaled.

"You'll excuse the disorder. I'm dining out this evening."

As she turned on her heel, she nearly crushed one of the little dogs. Frederick declared that they were charming. She lifted up the pair of them, and raising their black snouts up to her face:

"Come! do a laugh—kiss the gentleman!"

A man dressed in a dirty overcoat with a fur collar entered abruptly.

"Félix, my worthy fellow," said she, "you'll have that business of yours attended to next Sunday without fail."

The man proceeded to dress her hair. Frederick told her he had heard news of her friends, Madame de Rochegune, Madame de Saint-Florentin, and Madame Lombard, every woman being noble, just as it might be at the mansion of the Dambreuses. Then he talked about the theatres. An extraordinary performance was to be given that evening at the Ambigu.

"Shall you be there?"

"Faith, no! I'm staying at home."

Delphine appeared. Her mistress scolded her for having gone out without permission.

The other vowed that she was "just returning from market."

"Well, bring me your book. You have no objection, isn't that so?"

And, reading the pass-book in a low tone, Rosanette made remarks on every item. The different sums were not added up correctly.

"Hand me four sous!"

Delphine handed the amount over to her, and, when she had sent the maid away:

"Ah! Holy Virgin! could I be more unfortunate than I am with these creatures?"

Frederick was shocked at this grumbling about servants. It recalled the others too vividly to his mind, and established between the two houses a kind of irritating equality.

When Delphine came back again, she drew close to the Maréchale's side in order to whisper something in her ear.

"Ah, no! I don't want her!"

Delphine presented herself once more.

"Madame, she insists."

"Ah, what a nuisance! Throw her out!"

At the same moment, an old lady, dressed in black, pushed open the door. Frederick heard nothing, saw nothing. Rosanette rushed into the other room to meet her.

When she reappeared her cheeks were flushed, and she dropped into one of the armchairs without saying a word. A tear fell down her face; then, turning toward the young man softly:

"What is your first name?"

"Frederick."

"Ha! Frederico! It doesn't annoy you when I address you in that way?"

And she gazed at him coaxingly, almost amorously.

All of a sudden she uttered an exclamation of delight at the entrance of Mademoiselle Vatnaz.

The lady-artist had no time to spare before presiding at her *table d'hôte* at six o'clock sharp; and she was panting for breath, being completely exhausted. She first took out of her pocket a gold chain in a paper, then various objects that she had bought.

"You should know that there are in the Rue Joubert splendid Suède gloves at thirty-six sous. Your dyer requires eight days more. As for the guipure, I told you that they would dye it again. Bugneaux has received the instalment you paid. That's all, I think. You owe me a hundred and eighty-five francs."

Rosanette went to a drawer to get ten napoleons. Neither of the pair had any money. Frederick offered some.

"I'll pay you back," said the Vatnaz, as she stuffed the fifteen francs into her handbag. "But you are a naughty boy! I don't love you any longer—you didn't ask me to dance with you even once the other evening! Ah! my dear, I came across a case of stuffed humming-birds which are perfect loves at a shop in the Quai Voltaire. If I were in your place, I would make myself a present of them. Look here! What do you think of it?"

And she exhibited an old remnant of pink silk which she had purchased at the Temple to make a mediæval doublet for Delmar.

"He was here to-day, wasn't he?"

"No."

"That's strange."

And, after a minute's silence:

"Where are you going this evening?"

"To Alphonsine's," said Rosanette, this being the third version given by her as to the way in which she was going to pass the evening.

Mademoiselle Vatnaz went on: "And what news about the old man of the mountain?"

But, with an abrupt wink, the Maréchale bade her hold her tongue; and she accompanied Frederick out as far as the anteroom to find out how soon he would see Arnoux.

"Pray ask him to come—not before his wife, mind!"

At the top of the stairs an umbrella was standing against the wall near a pair of goloshes.

"Vatnaz's goloshes," said Rosanette. "What a foot, eh? My little friend is rather strongly built!"

And, in a melodramatic tone, making the final letter of the word roll:

"Don't tru-us-st her!"

Frederick, emboldened by this confidence, tried to kiss her on the neck.

"Oh, do it! It costs nothing!"

He felt light-hearted as he left her, having no doubt but that ere long the Maréchale would be his mistress. This desire awakened another, and, in spite of the species of grudge that he owed her, he felt a longing to see Madame Arnoux.

Besides, he would have to call at her house in order to execute the commission with which he had been entrusted by Rosanette.

"But now," thought he (it had just struck six), "Arnoux is probably at home."

So he postponed his visit till the following day.

She was seated in the same attitude as on the former day, and was sewing a little boy's shirt.

The child, at her feet, was playing with a wooden toy menagerie. Marthe, a short distance away, was writing.

He began by complimenting her on her children. She replied without any exaggeration of maternal silliness.

The room had a peaceful aspect. A glow of sunshine crept in through the window-panes, lighting up the angles of the furniture, and, as Madame Arnoux sat close beside the window, a large ray, falling on the curls over the nape of her neck, penetrated with liquid gold her skin, which appeared like amber.

Then he said:

"This young lady has grown very tall during the past three years! Do you remember, Mademoiselle, when you slept on my knees in the carriage?"

Marthe did not remember.

"One evening, returning from Saint-Cloud?"

There was a look of peculiar sadness in Madame Arnoux's face. Did she wish to prevent any allusion on his part to the memories they possessed in common?

Her beautiful black eyes glistened as they moved gently under their somewhat drooping lids, and her pupils revealed in their depths an inexpressible kindness of heart. He was seized with a love stronger than ever, a passion that knew no bounds. It enervated him to contemplate the object of his attachment; with an effort, he shook off this feeling. How was he to make the most of himself? by what means? And, having turned the matter over thoroughly in his mind, Frederick could think of none more effectual than money.

He began talking about the weather, which was less cold than it had been at Havre.

"You have been there?"

"Yes; about a family matter—an inheritance."

"Ah! I am very glad," she said, with an air of such genuine pleasure that he felt as touched as if she had rendered him a great service.

She asked him what he intended to do, as it was necessary for a man to occupy himself with something.

He recalled to mind his false position, and said that he hoped to reach the Council of State with the help of M. Dambreuse, the secretary.

"You are acquainted with him, then?"

"Merely by name."

Then, in a low tone:

"*He* brought you to the ball the other night, did he not?"

Frederick remained silent.

"That was all I wanted to know; thanks!"

After that she put two or three discreet questions to him about his family and the part of the country in which he lived. It was very kind of him not to have forgotten them after having lived so long away from Paris.

"But could that be possible?" he rejoined. "Have you any doubt about it?"

Madame Arnoux arose: "I believe that you entertain toward us a true and steadfast affection. *Au revoir!*"

And she extended her hand toward him in a sincere and virile fashion.

Was this not an engagement, a promise? Frederick felt a sense of delight at merely living; he had to restrain himself to keep from singing. He wanted to do generous deeds, to give alms.

Then he remembered his friends. The first of whom he thought was Hussonnet, the second Pellerin. The humble position of Dussardier naturally claimed consideration. As for Cisy, he was not unwilling to let that young aristocrat get a slight glimpse of the extent of his fortune. He wrote accordingly to all four to come to a housewarming the following Sunday at eleven o'clock sharp; and he invited Deslauriers to bring Sénécal.

The tutor had been dismissed from the third boarding-school in which he had been employed for not having given his consent to the distribution of prizes—a custom which he looked upon as dangerous to equality. He was now with an engine-builder, and for the past six months had not lived with Deslauriers. There had been nothing unpleasant about their parting.

Sénécal had been visited by men in blouses—all patriots, all workmen, honest fellows no doubt, but at the same time men whose society was distasteful to the advocate. Besides, he disliked certain ideas of his friend, excellent though they might be as weapons of warfare. He held his tongue through motives of ambition, deeming it prudent to pay deference to him in order to exercise control over him, for he looked forward impatiently to a revolutionary movement, in which he calculated on making an opening for himself and occupying a prominent position.

Sénécal's convictions were more disinterested. Every evening, when his work was finished, he returned to his garret and sought in books for something that might justify his dreams. He had annotated the *Contrat Social*; he had crammed himself with the *Revue Indépendante*; he was acquainted with Mably, Morelly, Fourier, Saint-Simon, Comte, Cabet, Louis Blanc—the heavy cartload of Socialistic writers—those who claim for humanity the dead level of barracks, who would like to amuse it in a brothel or to bend it over a counter; and from a medley of all these things he constructed an ideal of virtuous democracy, with the double aspect of a farm in which the landlord was to receive a share of the produce, and a spinning-mill, a sort of American Lacedæmon, in which the individual would only exist for the benefit of the community, which was to be more omnipotent, absolute, infallible, and divine than the Grand Lamas and the Nebuchadnezzars. He had no doubt as to the early realisation of this ideal; and Sénécal raged against everything that he considered hostile to it with the logic of a geometrician and the zeal of an Inquisitor. Titles of nobility, crosses, plumes, liveries especially, and even reputations that were too loud-sounding, scandalised him, his studies as well as his sufferings intensifying day by day, his essential hatred of every kind of distinction and every form of social superiority.

"What do I owe to this gentleman that I should be polite to him? If he wants me, he can come to me."

Deslauriers, however, induced him to go to Frederick's reunion.

They found their friend in his bedroom. Spring-roller blinds and double curtains, Venetian mirrors—nothing was wanting there. Frederick, in a velvet vest, was lying back on an easy-chair, smoking cigarettes of Turkish tobacco.

Sénécal wore the stern look of a bigot arriving in the midst of a pleasure-party.

Deslauriers gave him a single comprehensive glance; then, with a very low bow:

"Monseigneur, permit me to pay my respects to you!"

Dussardier leaped on his neck. "So you are a rich man now. Ah! upon my soul, so much the better!"

Cisy appeared with crape on his hat. Since the death of his grandmother, he was in the enjoyment of a considerable fortune, and was less bent on amusing himself than on being distinguished from others—not being the same as everyone else—in short, on "having the proper stamp." This was his favourite phrase.

However, it was now midday, and they were all yawning.

Frederick was waiting for some one.

At the mention of Arnoux's name, Pellerin made a wry face. He considered him a renegade since he had abandoned the fine arts.

"Suppose we pass over him—what do you all say to that?"

They all approved of this suggestion.

The door was opened by a man-servant in long gaiters; and the dining-room could be seen with its lofty oak plinths relieved with gold, and its two side-boards laden with plate.

These luxuries were lost on Sénécal. He began by asking for household bread (the hardest that could be got), and in connection with this subject, spoke of the murders of Buzançais and the crisis arising from lack of the means of subsistence.

Nothing of this sort could have happened if agriculture had been better protected, if everything had not been given up to competition, to anarchy, and to the deplorable system of "Let things alone! let things go their own way!" It was in this manner that the feudalism of money was established—the worst form of feudalism. But let them beware! The people in the end will get tired of it, and may make the capitalist pay for their sufferings either by bloody proscriptions or by the plunder of their houses.

Frederick saw, as if by a lightning-flash, a mob of men with bare arms invading Madame Dambreuse's drawing-room, and smashing the mirrors with blows of pikes.

Sénécal went on to say that the workman, owing to the insufficiency of wages, was more unfortunate than the helot, the negro, and the pariah, especially if he has children.

"Ought he to get rid of them by asphyxia, as some English doctor, whose name I don't remember—a disciple of Malthus—advises?"

And, turning towards Cisy: "Are we to be forced to follow the advice of the infamous Malthus?"

Cisy, who was ignorant of the infamy and even of the existence of Malthus, said by way of reply, that after all, much human misery was relieved, and that the higher classes—

"Ha! the higher classes!" said the Socialist, with a sneer. "To commence with, there are no higher classes. 'Tis the heart alone that makes anyone higher than another. We want no alms, understand! but equality, the fair division of what is produced."

What he required was that the workman might become a capitalist, just as the soldier might become a colonel. The trade-wardenships, at least, in limiting the number of apprentices, prevented workmen from growing inconveniently numerous, and the sentiment of fraternity was kept up by means of the fêtes and the banners.

Hussonnet, as a poet, regretted the banners; so did Pellerin, too—a predilection which had taken possession of him at the Café Dagneaux, while listening to the Phalansterians talking. He expressed the opinion that Fourier was a great man.

"Come now!" said Deslauriers. "An old fool who sees in the overthrow of governments the effects of Divine vengeance. He is just like my lord Saint-Simon and his church, with his hatred of the French Revolution—a set of buffoons who would fain reestablish Catholicism."

M. de Cisy, no doubt in order to get information or to make a good impression, broke in with this remark, which he uttered in a mild tone:

"These two men of science are not, then, of the same way of thinking as Voltaire?"

"That fellow! I make you a present of him!"

"How is that? Why, I thought—"

"Oh! no, he did not love the people!"

Then the conversation came down to contemporary events: the

Spanish marriages, the dilapidations of Rochefort, the new chapter-house of Saint-Denis, which had led to the taxes being doubled. But, according to Sénécal, they were not high enough!

"And why are they paid? My God! to erect the palace for apes at the Museum, to allow showy staff-officers to parade along our squares, or to maintain a Gothic etiquette among the flunkeys of the Château!"

"I read in the *Mode,*" said Cisy, "that at the Tuileries ball on the feast of Saint-Ferdinand, everyone was disguised as a miser."

"How pitiable!" said the Socialist, with a shrug of his shoulders, as if to indicate his disgust.

"And the Museum of Versailles!" exclaimed Pellerin. "Let us talk about that! These idiots have foreshortened a Delacroix and lengthened a Gros! At the Louvre they have so well restored, scratched, and made a jumble of all the canvases, that in ten years probably not one will be left. As for the mistakes in the catalogue, a German has written a whole volume on the subject. Upon my word, the foreigners are laughing at us."

"Yes, we are the laughing-stock of Europe," said Sénécal.

"'Tis because Art is conveyed in fee-simple to the Crown."

"As long as we haven't universal suffrage—"

"Allow me!"—for the artist, having been rejected at every *salon* for the last twenty years, was filled with bitterness against Power.

"Ah! why let them bother us? As for me, I ask for nothing. Only the Chambers ought to pass enactments in the interests of Art. A chair of æsthetics should be established with a professor who, being a practical man as well as a philosopher, would succeed, I hope, in grouping the multitude. You would do well, Hussonnet, to touch on this matter with a word or two in your newspaper!"

"Are newspapers free? are we ourselves free?" said Deslauriers in an angry tone. "When one reflects that there might be as many as twenty-eight different formalities to set up a boat on the river, it makes me feel a longing to go and live amongst the cannibals! The Government is eating us up. Everything belongs to it—philosophy, law, the arts, the very air of heaven; and France, bereft of all energy, lies under the boot of the gendarme and the cassock of the devil-dodger with the death-rattle in her throat!"

The future Mirabeau thus poured out his bile in abundance. Finally he raised his glass in his right hand, and with his other arm akimbo, and his eyes flashing:

"I drink to the utter destruction of the existing order of things—that is to say, of everything included in the words Privilege, Monopoly, Regulation, Hierarchy, Authority, State!"—and in a louder voice—"which I would like to smash as I do this!" dashing on the table the beautiful wine-glass, which broke into a thousand pieces.

They all applauded, and especially Dussardier.

Frederick was a little surprised at these views. They probably bored Cisy, for he changed the conversation to the *tableaux vivants* at the Gymnase, which at that time were very popular.

Sénécal regarded them with disfavour. Such exhibitions demoralised the daughters of the proletariat. Then, it was noticeable that they went in for a display of shameless luxury. He approved of the conduct of the Bavarian students who insulted Lola Montès. In imitation of Rousseau, he expressed more esteem for the wife of a coal-porter than for the mistress of a king.

"You don't appreciate dainties," retorted Hussonnet in a majestic tone. And he took up the championship of ladies of this class in order to praise Rosanette. Then, as he happened to make an allusion to the ball at her house and to Arnoux's costume, Pellerin remarked:

"It is rumoured that he is becoming shaky."

The picture-dealer had just been engaged in a lawsuit with reference to his grounds at Belleville, and he was actually in a kaolin company in Lower Brittany with other rogues of the same sort.

Dussardier knew still more about him, for his own master, M. Moussinot, having made inquiries about Arnoux from the banker, Oscar Lefébvre, the latter had said that he considered him by no means solvent, as he knew that bills of his had been renewed.

Dessert was over; they passed into the drawing-room, which was hung, like that of the Maréchale, in yellow damask in the style of Louis XVI.

Pellerin criticised Frederick for not having chosen in preference the Neo-Greek style; Sénécal rubbed matches against the hangings; Deslauriers said nothing.

There was a bookcase set up there, which he referred to as "a little girl's library." The principal contemporary writers were to be found there. It was impossible to speak about their works, for Hussonnet immediately began relating anecdotes with reference to their personal characteristics, criticising their faces, their habits, their dress, glorifying fifth-rate intellects and disparaging the greater ones; and all the while making it clear that he deplored and despised modern decadence.

He instanced some village ditty as containing in itself alone more poetry than all the lyrics of the nineteenth century. He maintained that Balzac was overrated, that Byron was effaced, and that Hugo knew nothing about the stage.

"Why, then," said Sénécal, "have you not got the volumes of the working-men poets?"

And M. de Cisy, who devoted his attention to literature, was astonished at not seeing on Frederick's table some of those new physiological studies—the physiology of the smoker, of the angler, of the man employed at the barrier.

They irritated him to such an extent that he would have liked to shove them out by the shoulders.

"They are making me appear quite stupid!" And he drew Dussardier aside, and wished to know whether he could do him any service.

The honest fellow was moved. He answered that his post of cashier entirely sufficed for his wants.

After that, Frederick led Deslauriers into his own apartment, and, taking out of his escritoire two thousand francs:

"Look here, old boy, put this money in your pocket. 'Tis the balance of my old debts to you."

"But—what about the journal?" said the advocate. "You know, of course, that I spoke about it to Hussonnet."

And, when Frederick replied that he was "a little short of cash just now," the other smiled in a sinister fashion.

After the liqueurs they drank beer, and after the beer, grog; then they lighted their pipes once more. At last they left, at five o'clock in the evening. They were walking along at each other's side without speaking, when Dussardier broke the silence by saying that Frederick had entertained them in excellent style. They all agreed with him on that point.

Then Hussonnet remarked that his luncheon was too heavy. Sénécal complained of the trivial character of his household arrangements. Cisy took the same view. It was absolutely devoid of the "proper stamp."

"For my part, I think," said Pellerin, "he might have had the grace to give me an order for a picture."

Deslauriers held his tongue, as he had the banknotes that had been given to him in his breeches' pocket.

Frederick was left by himself. He thought about his friends, and it seemed to him as if a huge, dark ditch separated him from them. He had held out his hand to them, and they had not responded to the sincerity of his heart.

He recalled what Pellerin and Dussardier had said about Arnoux. Surely it must be an invention, a calumny? But why? And he had a vision of Madame Arnoux, ruined, weeping, selling her furniture. This idea tormented him all night long. Next day he presented himself at her house.

At a loss to find any way of telling her what he had heard, he asked, as if in casual conversation, whether Arnoux still held possession of his building grounds at Belleville.

"Yes, he has them still."

"He is now, I believe, a shareholder in a kaolin company in Brittany."

"That is so."

"His earthenware-works are going on very well, are they not?"

"Well—I suppose so—"

And, as he hesitated:

"What is the matter? You alarm me!"

He told her the story about the renewals. She hung down her head, and said:

"I thought so!"

In fact, Arnoux, thinking them a good speculation, had refused to sell his grounds, had borrowed money extensively on them, and finding no purchasers, had thought of rehabilitating himself by establishing the earthenware manufactory. The expense of this had exceeded his calculations. She knew nothing more. He evaded all her questions, and declared repeatedly that everything was going on very well.

Frederick tried to reassure her. These in all probability were mere temporary embarrassments. However, if he got any information, he would impart it to her.

"Oh! yes, will you not?" said she, clasping her two hands with an air of charming supplication.

So thus he had it in his power to be useful to her. He was now entering into her existence—occupying a place in her heart.

Arnoux appeared.

"Ha! how nice of you to come to take me out to dine!"

Frederick was silent.

Arnoux spoke about general topics, then informed his wife that he would be home very late, as he had an appointment with Monsieur Oudry.

"At his house?"

"Why, certainly, at his house."

As they went down the stairs, he confessed that, as the Maréchale had no engagement at home, they were going on a secret pleasure-party to the Moulin Rouge; and, as he always needed somebody to be the recipient of his outpourings, he got Frederick to drive him to the door.

Instead of entering, he walked about on the footpath, looking up at the windows on the second floor. Suddenly the curtains parted.

"Ha! bravo! Oudry is gone! Good evening!"

Frederick did not know what to think.

From this day forth, Arnoux was still more cordial than before; he invited the young man to dine with his mistress; and ere long Frederick frequented both houses.

Rosanette's residence furnished him with amusement. He used to call there of an evening on his way back from the club or the play. He would take a cup of tea, or play a game of loto. On Sundays they played charades; Rosanette, more noisy than the rest, made herself conspicuous by funny tricks, such as running on all-fours or muffling her head in a cotton cap, so that she might watch the passers-by through the window, she had a hat of waxed leather; she smoked chibouks and sang Tyrolese airs.

In the afternoon, to kill time, she cut out flowers in a piece of chintz and pasted them against the window-panes, smeared her two little dogs with varnish, burned pastilles, or drew cards to tell her fortune. Incapable of resisting a desire, she became infatuated about some trinket which she happened to see, and could not sleep till she had bought it, then bartered it for another, sold costly dresses for little or nothing, lost her jewellery, wasted money, and would have sold her chemise for a stage-box at the theatre. Often she asked Frederick to explain to her some word she came across when reading a book, but paid no attention to his answer; she jumped quickly to another idea, while heaping questions on top of each other. After periods of gaiety came childish outbursts of rage, or sometimes she sat on the ground dreaming before the fire with her head bent and her hands clasping her knees, more inert than a torpid adder. Quite indifferently, she made her toilet in his presence, drew on her silk stockings, then washed her face with great splashes of water, throwing back her figure as if she were a shivering naïad; her laughing white teeth, her sparkling eyes, her beauty, her gaiety, dazzled Frederick, and made his nerves tingle under the lash of desire.

Usually he found Madame Arnoux teaching her little boy to read, or standing behind Marthe's chair while she played her scales on the piano. When she was sewing, it was a great source of delight to him to pick up her scissors now and then. In all her movements there was a tranquil majesty. Her little hands seemed made to scatter alms and to wipe away tears, and her voice, naturally rather hollow, had caressing intonations and a sort of breezy lightness.

She was not very enthusiastic about literature; but her intelligence exercised a charm by the use of a few simple and penetrating words. She loved travelling, the sound of the wind in the woods, and to walk with uncovered head under the rain.

Frederick listened to these confidences with rapture, fancying that he saw in them the beginning of a certain self-abandonment on her part.

His association with these two women made, as it were, two different strains of music in his life, the one playful, passionate, diverting, the other grave and almost religious, and vibrating both at the same time, they increased in volume and gradually blended with one another; for if Madame Arnoux happened merely to touch him with her finger, the image of the other immediately presented itself to him as an object of desire, because from that quarter a better opportunity was thrown in his way, and when his heart happened to be touched by Rosanette, he was immediately reminded of the woman for whom he felt such a consuming passion.

This confusion was occasioned, in some measure, by a similarity which existed between the interiors of the two houses. One of the cabinets which was formerly in the Boulevard Montmartre now adorned Rosanette's dining-room. The same courses were served up for dinner in both places, and even the same velvet cap was to be found trailing over the easy-chairs; then, a heap of little presents—screens, boxes, fans—went to the mistress's house from the wife's and returned again, for Arnoux, without the slightest embarrassment, often took from the one some thing he had given her in order to make a present of it to the other.

The Maréchale laughed with Frederick at the utter lack of propriety which his habits exhibited. One Sunday, after dinner, she led him behind the door, and showed him in Arnoux's overcoat a bag of cakes which he had just pilfered from the table, in order, no doubt, to regale his little family at home. Monsieur Arnoux lent himself to some rogueries which bordered on vileness. It seemed to him a duty to practise fraud with regard to the city dues; he never paid when he went to the theatre, or if he took a ticket for the second seats always tried to make his way into the first; and he used to tell, as an excellent joke, that it was his custom at the cold baths to put into the waiters' collection-box a breeches' button instead of a ten-sous piece—and this did not prevent the Maréchale from loving him.

One day, however, she said, while talking about him:

"Ah! he's becoming a nuisance to me, at last! I've had enough of him! Faith, so much the better—I'll find some one else instead!"

Frederick believed that the other had already been found, and that his name was Monsieur Oudry.

"Well," said Rosanette, "what does that signify?"

Then, in a voice choked with rising tears:

"I ask him for very little, however, and he won't give me that."

He had even promised a fourth of his profits in the famous kaolin mines. No profit made its appearance any more than the cashmere with which he had been luring her on for the last six months.

Frederick thought of making her a present himself. Arnoux might regard it as a reproof, and be annoyed at it.

For all that, he was good-natured, his wife herself said so, but so foolish! Instead of bringing people to dine every day at his house, he now entertained at a restaurant. He bought things that were utterly useless, such as gold chains, timepieces, and household articles. Madame Arnoux even pointed out to Frederick in the lobby an enormous number of tea-kettles, foot-warmers, and samovars. Finally, she one day confessed that a certain matter caused her much anxiety. Arnoux had made her sign a promissory note payable to Monsieur Dambreuse.

Meanwhile Frederick still cherished his literary projects as if it were a point of honour with himself to do so. He wished to write a history of æsthetics, a result of his conversations with Pellerin; next, to write dramas dealing with different epochs of the French Revolution, and to compose a great comedy, an idea resulting from the indirect influence of Deslauriers and Hussonnet. In the midst of his work her face or that of the other passed before his mental vision. He combatted the longing to see her, but always yielded to it; and he felt sadder as he returned from Madame Arnoux's house.

One morning, while he was brooding over his melancholy thoughts by the fireside, Deslauriers came in. The incendiary speeches of Sénécal had filled his master with uneasiness, and once more he was without resources.

"What do you want me to do?" said Frederick.

"Nothing! I know you have no money. But it will be no trouble for you to get him a post either through Monsieur Dambreuse or else through Arnoux. The latter is sure to have need of engineers in his establishment."

Frederick had an inspiration. Sénécal would let him know when the husband was away, carry letters for him and assist him on a thousand occasions when opportunities presented themselves. Services of this sort are always rendered between man and man. Besides, he would find means of using him without arousing any suspicion on his part. Chance offered him an auxiliary; it was a circumstance that omened well for the future, and he hastened to take advantage of it; with an affectation of indifference, he replied that the thing was feasible perhaps, and that he would attend to it.

And he did so at once. Arnoux devoted a great deal of time to his earthenware works. He was endeavouring to discover the copper-red of the Chinese, but his colours evaporated in the process of baking. In order to prevent cracks in his ware, he mixed lime with his potter's clay; but the articles got broken for the most part; the enamel of his paintings on the raw material boiled away; his large plates became bulged; and, attributing these mischances to the inferior plant of his manufactory, he was anxious to start other grinding-mills and other drying-rooms. Frederick recalled some of these things to mind, and, when he met Arnoux, said that he knew a very able man, who would be capable of finding his famous red. Arnoux gave a jump; then, having listened to what the young man had to tell him, replied that he wanted assistance from nobody.

Frederick spoke in a very laudatory style about Sénécal's prodigious attainments, pointing out that he was at the same time an engineer, a chemist, and an accountant, being a mathematician of the first rank.

The earthenware-dealer agreed to see him.

But they squabbled over the emoluments. Frederick interposed, and, at the end of a week, succeeded in getting them to come to terms.

But as the works were situated at Creil, Sénécal could not assist him in any way. This thought alone was enough to make his courage flag, as if he had met with some misfortune. His idea was that the more Arnoux could be kept apart from his wife the better would be his own chance with her. Then he proceeded to make repeated apologies for Rosanette. He referred to all the wrongs she had sustained at the other's hands, referred to the vague threats which she had uttered a few days before, and even mentioned the cashmere without concealing the fact that she had accused Arnoux of avarice.

Arnoux, nettled at the word (and, furthermore, feeling some uneasiness), brought Rosanette the cashmere, but scolded her for having complained to Frederick. When she told him that she had reminded him a hundred times of his promise, he pretended that, owing to pressure of business, he had forgotten all about it.

The next day Frederick presented himself at her abode, and found the Maréchale still in bed, though it was two o'clock, with Delmar beside her finishing a *pâté de foie gras* at a little round table. She broke out into a cry of delight, saying: "I have him! I have him!" Then she seized him by the ears, kissed him on the forehead, thanked him effusively, "thee'd" and "thou'd" him, and even wanted him to sit down on the bed. Her fine eyes, full of tender emotion, were sparkling with pleasure. There was a smile on her humid mouth. Her two round arms emerged through the sleeveless opening of her night-dress, and, from time to time, he could feel through the cambric the well-rounded outlines of her form.

All this time Delmar kept rolling his eyeballs.

"But really, my dear, my own pet . . ."

It was the same way on the occasion when he saw her next. As soon as Frederick entered, she sat up on a cushion in order to embrace him with more ease, called him a darling, a "dearie," put a flower in his button-hole, and settled his cravat. These attentions were redoubled when Delmar happened to be there. Were they advances on her part? So it seemed to Frederick.

As for deceiving a friend, Arnoux, in his place, would have had no scruples on that score, and he could not be expected to adhere to rigidly virtuous principles with regard to this man's mistress, seeing that his relations with the wife had been strictly honourable, for so he thought—or rather he would have liked Arnoux to think so, in any event, as a sort of justification of his own prodigious cowardice. Nevertheless he felt somewhat bewildered; presently he made up his mind to lay siege boldly to the Maréchale.

So one afternoon, just as she was stooping down in front of her chest of drawers, he went across to her, and repeated his overtures without a pause.

Thereupon she began to cry, saying that she was very unfortunate, but that she should not be despised on that account.

He only made fresh advances. She now adopted a different plan, namely, to laugh at his attempts without stopping. He thought it a clever thing to answer her sarcasms with repartees in the same strain, in which there was even a touch of exaggeration. But he made too great a display of gaiety to convince her that he was in earnest; and their comradeship was an impediment to any expression of serious feeling. At last, when she said one day, in reply to his amorous whispers, that she would not take another woman's leavings, he answered.

"What other woman?"

"Ah! yes, go and meet Madame Arnoux again!"

For Frederick used to talk about her continually. Arnoux, on his side, had the same mania. At last she lost patience at always hearing this woman's praises sung, and her insinuation was a kind of revenge.

Frederick resented it. However, Rosanette was beginning to excite his love to an unusual degree. Sometimes, pretending to be a woman of experience, she spoke lightly of love with a sceptical smile that made him feel inclined to box her ears. A quarter of an hour afterward, it was the only thing that mattered in the world, and, with her arms crossed over her breast, as if she were clasping some one close to her: "Oh, yes, 'tis good! 'tis good!" and her eyelids would quiver in a kind of rapturous swoon. It was impossible to understand her, to know, for instance, whether she loved Arnoux, for she ridiculed him, and yet seemed jealous of him. So likewise with the Vatnaz, whom she would sometimes call a wretch, and at other times her best friend. In short, there was about her entire person, even to the arrangement of her chignon upon her head an inexpressible something which seemed like a challenge; and he desired her for the satisfaction, above all, of conquering her and being her master.

How was he to accomplish this? for she often dismissed him unceremoniously, appearing only for a moment between two doors in order to say in a subdued voice, "I'm engaged—for the evening;" or else he found her surrounded by a dozen persons; and when they were alone, so many impediments presented themselves one after the other, that one would have sworn there was a bet to keep matters from going any further. He invited her to dinner; as a rule, she declined the invitation. On one occasion, she accepted it, but did not come.

A Machiavellian idea arose in his mind.

Having heard from Dussardier about Pellerin's complaints against himself, he thought of giving the artist an order to paint the Maréchale's portrait, a life-sized portrait, which would necessitate a number of sittings. He would be present at all of them. The habitual incorrectness of the painter would facilitate their private conversations. So then he would urge Rosanette to get the picture executed in order to make a present of her face to her dear Arnoux. She consented, for she saw herself in the midst of the Grand Salon in the most prominent position with a crowd of people staring at her picture, and the newspapers would all talk about it, which at once would set her afloat.

As for Pellerin, he eagerly snatched at the offer. This portrait might be the making of him; it ought to be a masterpiece. He reviewed in his memory all the portraits by great masters with which he was acquainted, and decided finally in favour of a Titian, which would be set off with ornaments in the style of Veronese. Therefore, he would carry out his design without artificial backgrounds in a bold light, which would illuminate the flesh-tints with a single tone, and make the accessories glitter.

"Suppose I were to put on her," he thought, "a pink silk dress with an Oriental bournous? Oh, no! the bournous is only a cheap thing! Or suppose, rather, I were to make her wear blue velvet with a grey background, richly coloured? We might likewise give her a white guipure collar with a black fan and a scarlet curtain behind." And thus, seeking for ideas, his conception grew, and he regarded it with great admiration.

He felt his heart beating when Rosanette, accompanied by Frederick, arrived at his house for the first sitting. He placed her standing up on a sort of platform in the centre of the apartment, and, finding fault with the light and expressing regret at the loss of his former studio, he first made her lean on her elbow against a pedestal, then sit down in an armchair, and, drawing away from her and coming near her again by turns in order to adjust with a fillip the folds of her dress, he observed her with eyes half-closed, and appealed to Frederick's taste with a passing word.

"Well, no," he exclaimed; "I return to my own idea. I will paint you in the Venetian style."

She would have a poppy-coloured velvet gown with a jewelled girdle; and her wide sleeve lined with ermine would afford a glimpse of her bare arm, which was to touch the balustrade of a staircase rising behind her. At her left, a large column would rise to the top of the canvas to meet certain structures so as to form an arch. Underneath would vaguely be distinguishable groups of orange-trees almost black, through which the blue sky, with its streaks of white cloud, would seem cut into fragments. On the baluster, covered with a carpet, there would be, on a silver dish, a bouquet of flowers, a chaplet of amber, a poniard, and a little chest of antique ivory, rather yellow with age, which would appear to be disgorging gold sequins. Some of them, falling on the ground here and there, would form brilliant splashes, as it were, in such a way as to direct one's glance toward the tip of her foot, for she would be standing on the last step but one in a natural position, as if in the act of moving under the glow of the broad sunlight.

He went to look for a picture-case, which he had laid on the platform to represent the step. Then he arranged as accessories, on a stool by way of balustrade, his pea-jacket, a buckler, a sardine-box, a bundle of pens, and a knife; and when he had flung in front of Rosanette a dozen big sous, he got her to assume the attitude he required.

"Just imagine that these things are riches, magnificent presents. The head a little on one side! Perfect! and don't stir! This majestic pose exactly suits your style of beauty."

She wore a plaid dress and carried a big muff, and only kept from laughing outright by an effort.

"As regards the headdress, we will mingle with it a circle of pearls. It always produces a striking effect with red hair."

The Maréchale burst out into an exclamation, denying that she had red hair.

"Nonsense! The red of painters is not that of ordinary people."

He began to sketch the position of the masses; and he was so much preoccupied with the great artists of the Renaissance that he kept talking about them persistently.

"You were made to live in those days. A creature of your calibre would have deserved a monseigneur."

Rosanette thought the compliments he paid her very pretty. The day was fixed for the next sitting. Frederick took it on himself to bring the accessories.

As the heat of the stove had stupefied her a little, they returned home on foot through the Rue du Bac, and reached the Pont Royal.

It was fine weather, piercingly bright and warm. The windows of some houses in the city shone in the distance, like plates of gold, whilst behind them at the right the turrets of Nôtre Dame showed their outlines in black against the blue sky, softly bathed at the horizon in grey vapours.

The wind began to swell; and Rosanette, having declared that she felt hungry, they entered the "Patisserie Anglaise."

Young women with their children stood eating in front of the marble buffet, where plates of little cakes were under glass covers. Rosanette ate two cream-tarts. The powdered sugar formed moustaches at the sides of her mouth. From time to time she drew out her handkerchief from her muff, and her face, under her green silk hood, looked like a full-blown rose in the midst of its leaves.

They resumed their walk. In the Rue de la Paix she paused before a goldsmith's shop to look at a bracelet. Frederick immediately wished to make her a present of it.

"No!" said she; "keep your money!"

He was hurt by these words.

"What's the matter now with the ducky? We are melancholy?"

And, the conversation having been renewed, he repeated the same protestations of love to her as usual.

"You know well 'tis impossible!"

"Why?"

"Ah! because—"

They went on, she leaning on his arm, and the flounces of her gown kept flapping against his legs. Then, he recalled to mind one winter twilight when on the same footpath Madame Arnoux walked thus by his side, and he became so much absorbed in this recollection that he no longer noticed Rosanette, and did not bestow a thought upon her.

She looked straight before her in a careless fashion, lagging a little, like a lazy child. It was the hour when people were returning from their promenade, and equipages were making their way at a quick trot over the hard pavement.

Pellerin's flatteries having probably recurred to her mind, she heaved a sigh.

"Ah! there are some lucky women in the world. Decidedly, I was made for a rich man!"

He replied, with a certain brutality in his tone:

"Well, you have one!" for Monsieur Oudry was looked upon as a man that could count a million three times over.

She wished nothing better than to get free from him.

"What prevents you from doing so?" And he gave utterance to bitter jests about this old bewigged citizen, pointing out to her that such an intrigue was unworthy of her, and that she ought to break it off.

"Yes," replied the Maréchale, as if talking to herself. "'Tis what I shall end by doing, no doubt!"

Frederick was charmed by this disinterestedness. She slackened her pace, and he suggested that she was fatigued. She obstinately refused to let him take a cab, and she parted with him at her door, sending him a kiss with her finger-tips.

"Ah! what a pity! and to think that imbeciles take me for a man of wealth!"

He reached home in a gloomy frame of mind.

Hussonnet and Deslauriers were awaiting him. The Bohemian, seated before the table, made sketches of Turks' heads; and the advocate, in dirty boots, lay asleep on the sofa.

"Ha! at last," he exclaimed. "But how solemn you look! Listen to me!"

His vogue as a tutor had fallen off, for he crammed his pupils with theories unfavourable for their examinations. He had appeared in two or three unsuccessful cases, and each new disappointment flung him back with greater force on the dream of his earlier days—a journal in which he could display himself, avenge himself, and spit forth his bile and his opinions. Fortune and reputation, moreover, would follow as a necessary consequence. It was in this hope that he had won over the Bohemian, Hussonnet happening to be the possessor of a press.

At present, he printed it on pink paper. He invented hoaxes, composed rebuses, tried to engage in polemics, and even intended, in spite of the location of the premises, to get up concerts. A year's subscription was to include admittance to a place in the orchestra in one of the principal theatres of Paris. Besides, the board of management took on itself to furnish foreigners with all necessary ability, artistic and otherwise. But the printer gave vent to threats; there were three quarters' rent due to the landlord. All sorts of embarrassments arose; and Hussonnet would have allowed *L'Art* to perish, were it not for the exhortations of the advocate, who kept every day exciting his mind. He had brought the other with him, in order to give more weight to the proposition he was now making.

"We've come about the journal," said he.

"What! are you still thinking about that?" said Frederick, in an absent tone.

"Certainly, I am thinking about it!"

And he explained his plan anew. By means of the Bourse returns, they would get into communication with financiers, and would thus obtain the hundred thousand francs indispensable as security. But, in order that the print might be transformed into a political journal, it was necessary beforehand to have a large *clientèle,* and for that purpose to make up their minds to go to some expense—so much for the cost of paper and printing, and for outlay at the office; in short, a sum of about fifteen thousand francs.

"I have no funds," said Frederick.

"Then what are we to do?" said Deslauriers, folding his arms.

Frederick, hurt by the attitude which Deslauriers was assuming, replied:

"Is it my fault?"

"Ah! very fine. A man has wood in his fire, truffles on his table, a good bed, a library, a carriage, every kind of comfort. But let another man shiver under the slates, dine at twenty sous, work like a convict, and sprawl through want in the mire—is it the rich man's fault?"

And he repeated, "Is it the rich man's fault?" with a Ciceronian irony which smacked of the law-courts.

Frederick tried to speak.

"Certainly, I understand one has certain wants—aristocratic wants; for, no doubt, some woman—"

"Well, even if that were so? Am I not free—?"

"Oh! quite free!"

And, after a minute's silence:

"Promises are so convenient!"

"Good God! I don't deny that I gave them!" said Frederick.

The advocate went on:

"At college we take oaths; we are going to set up a phalanx; we are going to be as Balzac's Thirteen. Then, on meeting a friend after a separation: 'Good night, old fellow! go about your business!' For the one who might help the other carefully keeps everything for himself alone."

"How is that?"

"Yes, you have not even given one an introduction to the Dambreuses."

Frederick cast a scrutinising glance at him. With his shabby frockcoat, his spectacles of rough glass, and his sallow face, the advocate seemed to him such a typical specimen of the penniless pedant that he could not prevent his lips from curling with a disdainful smile.

Deslauriers saw this, and reddened.

He had already taken his hat to leave. Hussonnet, filled with uneasiness, tried to mollify him with appealing looks, and, as Frederick was turning his back on him:

"Look here, my boy, become my Mæcenas! Protect the arts!"

Frederick, with an abrupt movement of resignation, took a sheet of paper, and, having scrawled some lines on it, handed it to him. The Bohemian's face lighted up.

Then, handing the sheet of paper to Deslauriers:

"Apologise, my fine fellow!"

Their friend requested his notary to send him fifteen thousand francs as quickly as possible.

"Ah! I recognise you in that," said Deslauriers.

"On the faith of a gentleman," added the Bohemian, "you are a noble fellow, you deserve a place in the gallery of useful men!"

The advocate remarked:

"You'll lose nothing by it, 'tis an excellent speculation."

"Faith," exclaimed Hussonnet, "I'd stake my head at the scaffold on its success!"

And he talked so foolishly, and promised so many extravagant things, in which perhaps he believed, that Frederick did not know whether he did this in order to laugh at others or at him.

The same evening he received a letter from his mother. She expressed astonishment at not seeing him yet a minister, while indulging in a little banter at his expense. Then she spoke of her health, and informed him that Monsieur Roque had now become one of her visitors.

"Since he is a widower, I thought there would be no objection to inviting him to the house. Louise is greatly changed for the better." And in a postscript: "You have written me nothing about your fine acquaintance, Monsieur Dambreuse; if I were you, I would make use of him."

Why not? His intellectual ambitions had left him, and his fortune (he saw it clearly) was insufficient, for when his debts had been paid, and the sum agreed on remitted to the others, his income would be diminished by four thousand at least! Moreover, he felt that he must give up this sort of life, and attach himself to some pursuit. So next day, when dining at Madame Arnoux's, he said that his mother was tormenting him to take up a profession.

"But I understood," she said, "that Monsieur Dambreuse was going to get you into the Council of State? That would suit you very well."

So, then, she desired him to take this course. He regarded her wish as a command.

The banker, as on the first occasion, was seated at his desk, and, with a gesture, intimated that Frederick was to wait a few minutes; for a gentleman who was standing at the door with his back turned had been discussing some serious topic with him.

The subject of their conversation was the proposed amalgamation of the different coal-mining companies.

Frederick noticed particularly two chests of prodigious size which stood in the corners. He wondered how many millions they might contain. The banker unlocked one of them, and as the iron plate swung back, it disclosed to view nothing inside but blue paper books full of entries.

At last, the person who had been talking to Monsieur Dambreuse passed in front of Frederick. It was Père Oudry. They saluted each other, their faces colouring—a circumstance which surprised Monsieur Dambreuse. However, he exhibited the utmost affability, observing that nothing would be easier than to recommend the young man to the Keeper of the Seals. They would be delighted to have him, he added, concluding his polite attentions by inviting him to an evening party which he would be giving in a few days.

Frederick was stepping into a brougham on his way to this party when a note from the Maréchale reached him. By the light of the carriage-lamps he read:

"Darling, I have followed your advice: I have just expelled my savage. After to-morrow evening, liberty! Say whether I have not courage!"

Nothing more. But it was clearly an invitation to him to take the vacant place. He uttered an exclamation, squeezed the note into his pocket, and set forth at once.

Two municipal guards on horseback were stationed in the street. A row of lamps burned on the two front gates, and servants were calling out in the courtyard for the carriages to come up to the end of the steps before the house under the marquée.

Then suddenly the noise in the handsome vestibule ceased.

Large trees filled up the space in front of the staircase. The porcelain globes shed a light which waved like white moiré satin on the walls.

Frederick ascended the steps in a joyous frame of mind. An usher announced his name. Monsieur Dambreuse extended his hand. Almost at the very same moment, Madame Dambreuse appeared. She wore a mauve dress trimmed with lace. The ringlets of her hair were more abundant than usual, and she wore not a single jewel.

She complained of his coming so seldom to visit them, and seized the opportunity to exchange a few confidential words with him.

The guests began to arrive. When they bowed they twisted their bodies on one side or bent in two, or merely lowered their heads a little.

The crowd of men who were standing with their hats in their hands seemed, at some distance, like one black mass, into which the ribbons in the button-holes introduced red points here and there, and rendered all the duller the monotonous whiteness of their cravats. With the exception of the very young men with the down on their faces, all appeared to be bored.

A large number of men-servants, with fine gold-laced livery, kept moving about on every side. The large branched candlesticks, like bouquets of flame, threw a glow over the hangings. They were reflected in the mirrors; and at the bottom of the dining-room, which was adorned with trailing jessamine, the side-board resembled the high altar of a cathedral or an exhibition of jewellery, there were so many dishes, bells, knives and forks, silver and silver-gilt spoons.

The three other reception-rooms overflowed with artistic objects— landscapes by great masters on the walls, ivory and porcelain at the sides of the tables, and Chinese ornaments on the brackets. Lacquered screens were displayed in front of the windows, clusters of camelias rose above the mantel-shelves, and music could be heard in the distance, like the humming of bees.

There were few quadrilles, and the dancers, judging by the indifferent fashion in which they dragged their pumps after them, seemed to be going through the performance of a duty.

Behind Frederick, three greybeards, who had placed themselves in the recess of a window, were whispering some *risqué* remarks. A sportsman told a hunting story, while a Legitimist carried on an argument with an Orléanist. And, wandering about from one group to another, he reached the card-room, where, in the midst of grave-looking men gathered in a circle, he recognised Martinon, now attached to the Bar of the capital.

His big face with its waxen complexion, filled up the space encircled by his collar-like beard, which was a marvel with its even surface of black hair; and, observing the golden mean between the elegance which his age might yearn for and the dignity which his profession exacted from him, he kept his thumbs stuck under the armpits, according to the custom of beaux, and then put his hands into his waistcoat pockets after the manner of learned personages. Though his boots were polished to excess, he kept his temples shaved in order to have the forehead of a thinker.

After he had addressed a few chilling words to Frederick, he turned once more toward those who were chatting around him. A landowner was saying: "This is a class of men that dreams of upsetting society."

"They are calling for the organisation of labour," said another: "Can this be conceived?"

"What could you expect," said a third, "when we see M. de Genoude giving his assistance to the *Siècle?*"

"And even Conservatives style themselves Progressives. To lead us to what? To the Republic! as if such a thing were possible in France!"

Everyone declared that the Republic was impossible in France.

"No matter!" remarked one gentleman in a loud tone. "People take too much interest in the Revolution. A heap of histories, of different kinds of works, are published concerning it!"

"Without taking into account," said Martinon, "that there are probably subjects of far more importance which might be studied."

A gentleman occupying a ministerial office laid the blame on the scandals associated with the stage:

"Thus, for instance, this new drama of *La Reine Margot* really goes beyond the proper limits. What need was there for telling us about the Valois? All this exhibits loyalty in an unfavourable light. 'Tis just like your press! There is no use in talking, the September laws are altogether too mild. For my part, I would like to have court-martials, to gag the journalists! At the slightest display of insolence, drag them before a council of war, and then make an end of the business!"

"Oh, take care, Monsieur! take care!" said a professor. "Don't attack the precious boons we gained in 1830! Respect our liberties!" It would be better, he contended, to adopt a policy of decentralisation, and to distribute the surplus populations of the towns through the country districts.

"But they are gangrened!" exclaimed a Catholic. "Let religion be more firmly established!"

Martinon hastened to observe:

"As a matter of fact, it is a restraining force."

All the evil lay in this modern longing to rise above one's class and to possess luxuries.

"However," urged a manufacturer, "luxury aids commerce. Therefore, I approve of the Duc de Nemours' action in insisting on having short breeches at his evening parties."

"M. Thiers came to one of them in a pair of trousers. You know his joke on the subject?"

"Yes; charming! But he turned round to the demagogues, and his speech on the question of incompatibilities was not without its influence in bringing about the attempt of the twelfth of May."

"Oh, pooh!"

"Ay, ay!"

The circle had to make a little opening to give a passage to a man-servant carrying a tray, who was trying to make his way into the card-room.

Under the green shades of the wax-lights the tables were covered with two rows of cards and gold coins. Frederick stopped at one corner of the table, lost the fifteen napoleons which he had in his pocket, whirled lightly about, and found himself on the threshold of the boudoir in which Madame Dambreuse happened to be at the moment.

It was filled with women sitting close to one another in little groups on seats without backs. Their long skirts, swelling round them, seemed like waves, from which their waists emerged; and their breasts were clearly outlined by the slope of their corsages. Nearly every one had a bouquet of violets in her hand. The dull shades of their gloves showed off the whiteness of their arms, which formed a contrast with the human flesh tints. Over the shoulders of some of them hung fringe or mourning-weeds, and, every now and then, as they quivered with emotion, it seemed as if their bodices were about to fall down.

But the decorum of their countenances tempered the exciting effect of their costumes. Several had a placidity almost like that of animals; and this resemblance to the brute creation in these half-nude women made him think of the interior of a harem—indeed, a grosser comparison suggested itself to the young man's mind.

Every variety of beauty was to be found there—some English ladies with the profile familiar in "keepsakes"; an Italian, whose black eyes shot forth lava-like flashes, like a Vesuvius; three sisters, dressed in blue; three Normans, fresh as April apples; a tall red-haired girl, with a set of amethysts. And the bright scintillation of diamonds, which trembled in aigrettes worn over their hair, the luminous spots of precious stones laid over their breasts, and the delightful radiance of pearls which adorned their foreheads, mingled with the glitter of gold rings, as well as with the lace, powder, feathers, the vermilion of dainty mouths, and the mother-of-pearl hue of teeth. The ceiling, rounded like a cupola, gave to the boudoir the form of a flower-basket, and a current of perfumed air circulated under the flapping of fans.

Frederick, standing behind them, put up his eyeglass and scanned their shoulders, not all of which did he consider irreproachable. He thought about the Maréchale, and this dispelled the temptations that beset him or consoled him for not yielding to them.

He gazed long, however, at Madame Dambreuse, and he considered her charming, in spite of her mouth being rather large and her nostrils too dilated. But she was remarkably graceful in appearance. There was, as it were, an expression of passionate languor in the ringlets of her hair, and her forehead, which was like agate, seemed to cover a great deal, and to indicate a masterful intelligence.

She had placed beside her her husband's niece, a rather plain-looking young person. From time to time she left her seat to receive those who had just arrived; and the murmur of feminine voices, made, as it were, a cackling like that of birds.

They were talking about the Tunisian ambassadors and their costumes. One lady had been present at the last reception of the Academy. Another referred to the *Don Juan* of Molière, which had recently been performed at the Théâtre Français.

But with a significant glance toward her niece, Madame Dambreuse laid a finger on her lips, while her smile contradicted this display of austerity.

Suddenly, Martinon, who was now attached to the Bar of the Capital, appeared at the door directly in front of her. She arose at once. He offered her his arm. Frederick, in order to watch the progress of these gallantries on Martinon's part, walked past the card-table, and came up with them in the large drawing-room. Madame Dambreuse very soon left her cavalier, and began chatting with Frederick himself in a very familiar tone.

She understood that he did not play cards, and did not dance.

"Young people are apt to be melancholy!" Then, with a single comprehensive glance around:

"Besides, this sort of thing is not amusing—at least to certain natures!"

And she drew up in front of the row of armchairs, uttering a few polite remarks here and there, while some old men with double eyeglasses came to pay court to her. She introduced Frederick to some of them. M. Dambreuse touched him lightly on the elbow, and led him out on the terrace.

He had seen the Minister. The thing was not easy to manage. Before he could be qualified for the post of auditor to the Council of State, he would have to pass an examination. Frederick, seized with an unaccountable self-confidence, replied that he had a knowledge of the subjects prescribed for it.

The financier was not surprised at this, after all the eulogies M. Roque had pronounced on his abilities.

At the mention of this name, a vision of little Louise, her house and her room, passed through his mind, and he remembered how he had on nights like this stood at her window listening to the waggoners driving past. This recollection of his griefs brought back the thought of Madame Arnoux, and he relapsed into silence as he paced up and down the terrace. The windows blazed amid the darkness like slabs of flame. The buzz of the ball gradually grew fainter; the carriages were beginning to leave.

"Why in the world," M. Dambreuse went on, "are you so extremely anxious to be attached to the Council of State?"

And he declared in the tone of a man of broad views, that the public functions led nowhere—he could speak with some authority on that point—business was much preferable.

Frederick urged as an objection the difficulty of grappling with all the details of business.

"Pooh! I could post you up well in them in a very short time."

Would he care to be a partner in any of his own undertakings?

The young man saw, as by a lightning-flash, an enormous fortune coming into his hands.

"Let us go in again," said the banker. "You are remaining for supper with us, are you not?"

It was three o'clock. They left the terrace.

In the dining-room, a table at which supper was served up awaited the guests.

M. Dambreuse perceived Martinon, and, drawing near his wife, in a low tone:

"Did you invite him?"

She answered dryly:

"Yes, of course."

The niece was not present.

The guests drank a quantity of wine, and laughed very loudly; risky jokes did not give any offence, all present experiencing that sense of relief which follows a somewhat prolonged period of constraint.

Martinon alone displayed anything like gravity. Thinking it good form, he refused to drink champagne, and, moreover, assumed an air of tact and politeness, for when M. Dambreuse, who had a contracted chest, complained of an oppression, he made repeated enquiries about that gentleman's health, and then let his blue eyes wander in the direction of Madame Dambreuse.

She questioned Frederick in order to find out which of the young ladies he liked best. He had noticed none of them in particular, and besides, he preferred the women of thirty.

"There, perhaps, you show good sense," she returned.

Then, as they were putting on their pelisses and paletots, M. Dambreuse said to him:

"Come and see me one of these mornings and we'll have a chat."

Martinon, at the foot of the stairs, was lighting a cigar, and, as he puffed it, he presented such a heavy profile that his companion could not help remarking:

"Upon my word, you have a fine head!"

"It has turned a few other heads," replied the young magistrate, with an air of mingled self-complacency and annoyance.

As soon as Frederick was in bed, he summed up the main features of the evening party. In the first place, his own toilet (he had looked at himself several times in the mirrors), from the cut of his coat to the knot of his pumps left nothing to be desired. He had spoken to influential men, and seen wealthy ladies at close quarters. M. Dambreuse had proved himself to be an admirable type of man, and Madame Dambreuse an almost bewitching type of woman. He weighed one by one her slightest words, her looks, a thousand things incapable of being analysed. It would be a splendid thing to have such a mistress. And, after all, why not? He would have as good a chance with her as any other man. Perhaps she was not so difficult to win? Then Martinon came back to his recollection; and, as he fell asleep, he smiled with pity for this worthy fellow.

He woke up with the thought of the Maréchale in his mind. Those words of her note, "After to-morrow evening," were without doubt an appointment for the very same day.

He waited until nine o'clock, and then hurried to her house.

Some one, going up the stairs before him, shut the door. He rang the bell; Delphine came and told him that "Madame" was not there.

Frederick persisted, begging of her to admit him. He had something of a very serious nature to communicate to her; only a word would suffice. At length, the hundred-sous-piece argument proved successful, and the maid let him into the anteroom.

Rosanette appeared. She was in a négligée, with her hair loose, and, shaking her head, she waved her arms when she was some paces away from him to indicate that she could not receive him then.

Frederick descended the stairs slowly. This caprice was worse than any of the others she had indulged in. He could not understand the situation at all.

In front of the porter's lodge Mademoiselle Vatnaz stopped him.

"Has she received you?"

"No."

"You've been put out?"

"How do you know that?"

"'Tis quite plain. But come; let us go away. I am suffocating!"

She made him accompany her along the street; she panted for breath; he could feel her thin arm trembling on his own. Suddenly, she broke out:

"Ah! the wretch!"

"Who, pray?"

"Why, he—he—Delmar!"

This revelation humiliated Frederick. He next asked:

"Are you quite sure of it?"

"Why, I tell you I followed him!" exclaimed the Vatnaz. "I saw him enter! Now do you understand? I ought to have expected it for that matter—'twas I, in my stupidity, that introduced him to her. And if you only knew all—my God! Why, I picked him up, supported him, clothed

him! And then all the paragraphs I got into the newspapers about him!
I loved him like a mother!"

Then, with a sneer:

"Ha! Monsieur craves velvet robes! You may be sure 'tis a speculation
on his part. And as for her!—to think that I knew her when she earned
her living as a seamstress! If it were not for me, she would have fallen into
the mire twenty times over? But I will plunge her into it yet! I'll see her
dying in a hospital—and everything about her will be known!"

And, like a torrent of dirty water from a vessel full of refuse, her rage
poured out in a tumultuous fashion into Frederick's ear the recital of her
rival's disgraceful acts.

"She lived with Jumillac, with Flacourt, with little Allard, with
Bertinaux, with Saint-Valéry, the pock-marked fellow! No, 'twas the
other! They are two brothers—it makes no difference. And when she
was in difficulties, I settled everything. She is avaricious! And then, you
will agree with me, 'twas generous of me to visit her, for we are not persons of the same grade! Am I a fast woman—I? Do I sell myself? She is
as stupid as a head of cabbage. She writes 'category' with a 'th.' After all,
they are well met. They make a precious couple, though he styles himself an artist and thinks himself a man of genius. But, my God! if he had
only intelligence, he would not have done such an infamous thing! Men
don't, as a rule, leave a superior woman for a hussy! What do I care about
him after all? He is becoming ugly. I hate him! If I met him, mind you,
I'd spit in his face." She spat out as she uttered the words. "Yes, that is
what I think about him now. And Arnoux, eh? Isn't it abominable? He
has forgiven her again and again. You can't conceive the sacrifices he has
made for her. She ought to kiss his feet! He is so generous, so good!"

Frederick was delighted at hearing Delmar disparaged. He had taken
sides with Arnoux. This perfidy on Rosanette's part seemed to him an
abnormal and inexcusable thing; and, infected with this elderly spinster's
emotion, he felt a sort of tenderness toward her. Suddenly he found himself in front of Arnoux's door. Mademoiselle Vatnaz, without his having
noticed it, had led him down toward the Rue Poissonnière.

"Here we are!" said she. "As for me, I can't go up; but you, surely there
is nothing to prevent you?"

"From doing what?"

"From telling him everything, of course!"

Frederick, as if waking up with a start, saw the baseness towards which
she was urging him.

"Well?" she said after a pause.

He raised his eyes towards the second floor. Madame Arnoux's lamp was
burning. There was, certainly, nothing to prevent him from going up.

"I shall wait for you here. Go on, then!"

This direction had the effect of chilling him, and he said:

"I shall be a long time; you would do better to return home. I will call on you to-morrow."

"No, no!" replied the Vatnaz, stamping with her foot. "Take him with you! Bring him there! Let him catch them together!"

"But Delmar will no longer be there."

She hung down her head.

"Yes; that's true, perhaps."

And she stood without speaking, in the middle of the street, with vehicles all around her; then, fixing on him her wild-cat's eyes:

"I may rely on you, may I not? There is now a sacred bond between us. Do what you say, then; we'll talk about it to-morrow."

Frederick in passing through the lobby heard two voices responding to one another.

Madame Arnoux's voice was saying:

"Don't lie! don't lie, pray!"

He entered. The voices suddenly ceased.

Arnoux was walking from one end of the apartment to the other, and Madame was seated on the little chair near the fire, extremely pale and staring straight before her. Frederick stepped back, and was about to retire, when Arnoux grasped his hand, glad that some one had come to his rescue.

"But I fear—" said Frederick.

"Stay, I beg of you!" he whispered in his ear.

Madame remarked:

"You must make some allowance for this scene, Monsieur Moreau. Such things sometimes unfortunately occur in households."

"They do when we introduce them there ourselves," said Arnoux in a jolly tone. "Women have crotchets, I assure you. This, for instance, is not a bad one—see! No; quite the contrary. Well, she has been amusing herself for the last hour by teasing me with a lot of idle stories."

"They are true," retorted Madame Arnoux, losing patience; "for, in fact, you bought it yourself."

"I?"

"Yes, you yourself, at the Persian House."

"The cashmere," thought Frederick.

He was filled with a consciousness of guilt, and got quite alarmed.

She quickly added:

"It was on Saturday, the fourteenth."

"The fourteenth," said Arnoux, looking up, as if he were searching his mind for a date.

"And, furthermore, the clerk who sold it to you was a fair-haired young man."

"How could you expect me to remember what sort of man the clerk was?"

"And yet it was at your dictation he wrote the address, 18 Rue de Laval."

"How do you know?" said Arnoux in amazement.

She shrugged her shoulders.

"Oh! 'tis very simple: I went to get my cashmere altered, and the superintendent of the millinery department told me that they had just sent another of the same sort to Madame Arnoux."

"Is it my fault if there is a Madame Arnoux in the same street?"

"Yes; but not Jacques Arnoux," she returned.

Thereupon he began to talk incoherently, protesting that he was innocent. It was some misapprehension, some accident, one of those things that happen in an utterly unaccountable way. Men should not be condemned on mere suspicion, vague probabilities; and he referred to the case of the unfortunate Lesurques.

"In short, I say you are wrong. Do you want me to take my oath on it?"

"'Tis not worth while."

"Why?"

She looked him straight in the face without speaking, then stretched out her hand, took down the little silver chest from the mantelpiece, and handed him a bill which was spread open.

Arnoux coloured up to his ears, and his swollen and distorted features betrayed his confusion.

"But," he said in faltering tones, "what does this prove?"

"Ah!" she said, with a peculiar ring in her voice, in which sorrow and irony were blended. "Ah!"

Arnoux turned the bill round in his hands without removing his eyes from it, as if he were going to find in it the solution of a great problem.

"Ah! yes, yes; I remember," said he at length. "'Twas a commission. You ought to know about that matter, Frederick." Frederick remained silent. "A commission that Père Oudry entrusted to me."

"And for whom?"

"For his mistress."

"For your own!" exclaimed Madame Arnoux, springing to her feet and standing erect before him.

"I swear to you!"

"Don't begin again. I know all."

"Ha! quite right. So you're spying on me!"

She returned coldly:

"Perhaps that wounds your delicacy?"

"Since you are in a passion," said Arnoux, looking for his hat, "and can't be reasoned with—"

Then, with a big sigh:

"Don't marry, my poor friend, don't, if you take my advice!"

And he took himself off, finding it absolutely necessary to get into the open air.

Then there was a deep silence, and it seemed as if everything in the room had become stiller than before.

Madame Arnoux had just seated herself in the armchair at the opposite side of the chimney-piece. She bit her lip and shivered. Putting her hands up to her face, a sob broke from her, and she began to weep.

He sat down on the little couch, and in the soothing tone in which one addresses a sick person:

"You don't suspect me of having anything to do with—?"

She made no reply. But, continuing presently to give utterance to her own thoughts:

"I leave him perfectly free! There was no necessity for lying!"

"That is quite true," said Frederick. "No doubt," he added, "it was the result of Arnoux's habits; he had acted thoughtlessly, but perhaps in matters of a graver character—"

"What do you know of, then, that can be graver?"

"Oh, nothing!"

Frederick bent his head with a smile of acquiescence. Nevertheless, he urged, Arnoux possessed certain good qualities; he was fond of his children.

"Ay, and he does all he can to ruin them!"

Frederick urged that this was caused by an excessively easy-going disposition, for indeed he was a good fellow?

She exclaimed:

"But what does that mean—a good fellow!"

And he proceeded to defend Arnoux in the vaguest kind of language he could think of, and, while expressing his sympathy with her, he rejoiced, he was delighted, at the bottom of his heart. Through desire for retaliation or need of affection she would fly to him for refuge. His love was intensified by the hope which had now grown immeasurably stronger in his breast.

Never had she appeared to him so captivating, so absolutely, perfectly beautiful. From time to time a deep breath made her bosom swell. Her eyes, gazing fixedly into space, seemed dilated by a vision in the depths of her consciousness, and her lips were slightly parted, as if to let her soul escape through them. Sometimes she pressed her handkerchief to them tightly. He would have liked to be this dainty little piece of cambric moistened with her tears. In spite of himself, he cast a glance at the bed at the end of the alcove, picturing to himself her head lying on the pillow, and so vividly did this present itself to his imagination that he had to restrain himself from clasping her in his arms. She closed her eyelids, and became quiescent and languid. Then he drew closer, and, bending over her, he eagerly scanned her face. At that moment, he heard the noise of boots in the lobby outside—it was the other. They heard him shutting the door of his own room. Frederick made a sign to Madame Arnoux to ascertain from her whether he ought to go to him.

She signified "Yes," in the same voiceless fashion, and this mute exchange of thoughts between them was, as it were, an assent—the preliminary step in adultery.

Arnoux was just removing his coat to go to bed.

"Well, how is she now?"

"Oh! better," said Frederick; "this will pass off."

But Arnoux was in an anxious state of mind.

"You don't know her; she has got hysterical now! Idiot of a clerk! This is what comes of being too good. If I had not given that cursed shawl to Rosanette!"

"Don't regret having done so. Nobody could be more grateful to you than she is."

"Do you really think so?"

Frederick had not a doubt of it. The best proof of it was her dismissal of Père Oudry.

"Ah! poor little thing!"

And in the excess of his emotion, Arnoux wanted to rush off to her at once.

"'Tisn't worth while. I am calling to see her. She is not well."

"All the more reason for my going."

He quickly put on his coat again, and took up his candlestick. Frederick cursed his own stupidity, and insisted that for decency's sake he ought to remain this night with his wife. He could not leave her; it would be very unjust.

"I tell you frankly you would be doing wrong. There is no hurry over there. You will go to-morrow. Come; do this for my sake."

Arnoux put back his candlestick, and, embracing him, said:

"You are a fine fellow!"

CHAPTER IX

THE FAMILY FRIEND

FREDERICK became the parasite of the house of Arnoux, and a miserable existence stretched out before him.

If anyone were ill, he called several times a day to know how the patient was, went to the piano-tuner's, contrived to do a thousand acts of kindness; and he suffered with an air of contentment Mademoiselle Marthe's poutings and the caresses of little Eugène, who was always running his dirty hands over the young man's face. He was present at dinners at which Monsieur and Madame, facing each other, did not exchange a word, unless it happened that Arnoux provoked his wife with the ridiculous remarks he made. When the meal was finished, he would play about the room with his son, conceal himself behind the furniture, or carry the little boy on his back, walking about on all fours. At last, he would go out, and she would at once plunge into the eternal subject of complaint—Arnoux.

It was not that his misconduct excited her indignation, but her pride appeared to be wounded, and she made no effort to hide her repugnance toward this man, who showed neither delicacy, dignity, nor honour.

"It must be that he is mad!" she said.

Frederick artfully induced her to confide in him. Ere long he knew all the details of her life. Her parents were people of humble rank at Chartres. One day, Arnoux, while sketching on the bank of the river (at this period he believed himself to be a painter), saw her leaving the church, and made her an offer of marriage. On account of his wealth, he was immediately accepted. Besides, he was desperately in love with her. She added:

"Good heavens! he loves me still, after his fashion!"

They spent the few months immediately after their marriage in travelling through Italy.

Arnoux, in spite of his enthusiasm over the scenery and the masterpieces, did nothing but groan over the wine, and, to find some kind of amusement, organised picnics along with some English people. The profit which he had made by reselling some pictures tempted him to take up the fine arts as a commercial speculation. Then, he became infatuated about pottery. Just now other branches of commerce attracted him; and as he became more and more vulgarised, he contracted coarse and extravagant habits. It was not so much for his vices she reproached him as for his entire conduct. No change could be expected in him, and her unhappiness was irreparable.

Frederick declared that his own life in the same way was a failure.

He was still a young man, however. Why should he be melancholy? And she gave him good advice: "Work and marry!" He answered her with bitter smiles; for instead of telling the real cause of his grief, he pretended that it was of a different character, a sublime feeling, and he assumed the part of an Antony, the man accursed by fate—language which did not, however, change very materially the complexion of his thoughts.

For certain men action becomes more difficult as desire becomes stronger. They are embarrassed by self-distrust, and terrified by the fear of making themselves disliked. Besides, deep attachments resemble virtuous women: they are afraid of being discovered, and pass through life with downcast eyes.

Though he was now better acquainted with Madame Arnoux (for that very reason perhaps), he was still more faint-hearted than before. Each morning he swore to himself that he would take a bold course. He was prevented from doing so by an unconquerable feeling of bashfulness; and he had no example to guide him, inasmuch as she was different from other women. From the force of his imaginings, he had placed her outside the ordinary pale of humanity. When beside her he felt himself of less importance in the world than the sprigs of silk that escaped from her scissors.

Then he thought of monstrous and absurd devices, such as surprises at night, with narcotics and false keys—anything appearing easier to him than to face her disdain.

Besides, the children, the two servant-maids, and the relative position of the rooms were insurmountable obstacles. Then he made up his mind to possess her himself alone, and to bring her to live with him far away in the depths of some solitude. He even questioned himself what lake would be blue enough, what seashore would be delightful enough for her, whether it would be in Spain, Switzerland, or the East; and expressly fixing on days when she seemed more irritated than usual, he told her that it would be necessary for her to leave the house, to find some justification for such a step, and that he saw no way out of it but a separation. However, for the sake of the children whom she loved, she would never resort to such an extreme course. So much virtue served to increase his respect for her.

He spent each afternoon in thinking over the visit he had paid the night before, and in longing for the evening to come in order that he might call again. When he did not dine with them, he posted himself about nine o'clock at the corner of the street, and, as soon as Arnoux had slammed the hall-door behind him, Frederick quickly went up the two flights of stairs, and asked the servant-girl in an ingenuous fashion:

"Is Monsieur in?"

Then he would exhibit surprise at finding that Arnoux was out.

The latter frequently came back unexpectedly. Then Frederick had to accompany him to the little café in the Rue Sainte-Anne, which Regimbart now frequented.

The Citizen would give vent to some fresh grievance which he had against the Crown. Then they would chat, pouring out friendly abuse on each other, for the earthenware manufacturer took Regimbart for a thinker of a high order, and, vexed at seeing him neglecting so many chances of winning distinction, chaffed the Citizen about his laziness. It seemed to Regimbart that Arnoux was a man full of heart and imagination, but of decidedly lax morals; therefore he was quite unceremonious toward a personage he respected so little, refusing even to dine at his house on the ground that "such formality was a bore."

Sometimes, at the moment of parting, Arnoux would be seized with hunger. He would order an omelet or some roasted apples; and, as there was never anything to eat in the establishment, he sent out for something. They would wait. Regimbart did not leave, and usually ended by consenting in a grumbling fashion to have something himself. He was nevertheless gloomy, for he remained for hours seated before a half-filled glass. As Providence did not regulate things in harmony with his ideas, he was becoming a hypochondriac, no longer cared even to read the newspapers, and at the mere mention of England began to bellow with rage. On one occasion, referring to a waiter who attended on him carelessly, he exclaimed:

"Have we not enough insults from the foreigner?"

Except at these critical periods he remained taciturn, contemplating "an infallible stroke of business that would burst up the whole shop."

Whilst he was lost in these reflections, Arnoux in a monotonous voice and with a mild look of intoxication, related incredible anecdotes of which he was always the hero; and Frederick (this was, no doubt, due to some deep-rooted resemblances) felt more or less attracted toward him. He blamed himself for this weakness, believing that he ought to hate this man.

Arnoux, in Frederick's presence, complained of his wife's ill-temper, her obstinacy, her unjust accusations. She had never been like this in former days.

"If I were you," said Frederick, "I would make her an allowance and live alone."

Arnoux made no reply; but the next moment he began to sound her praises. She was good, devoted, intelligent, and virtuous; and, passing to her personal beauty, he made some revelations on the subject with the thoughtlessness of people who display their treasures at taverns.

His equilibrium was much disturbed by a catastrophe.

He had been appointed one of the Board of Superintendence in a kaolin company. But placing reliance on all that he was told, he had signed inaccurate reports and approved, without verification, of the annual inventories fraudulently prepared by the manager. The company had now failed, and Arnoux, being legally responsible, was, along with the others who were liable under the guaranty, condemned to pay damages, meaning a loss to him of thirty thousand francs, not to speak of the costs of the judgment.

Frederick saw the report of the case in a newspaper, and at once hurried off to the Rue de Paradis.

He was ushered into Madame's apartment. It was breakfast-time. A round table close to the fire was laden with bowls of *café au lait*. Slippers trailed over the carpet, and clothes over the armchairs. Arnoux was attired in trousers and a knitted vest, with his eyes bloodshot and his hair in disorder. Little Eugène was crying at the pain caused by an attack of mumps, while nibbling at a slice of bread and butter. His sister was eating quietly. Madame Arnoux, a little paler than usual, was attending on all three of them.

"Well," said Arnoux, heaving a deep sigh, "you know all about it?"

And, as Frederick gave him a sympathetic look: "There, you see, I have been the victim of my own trustfulness!"

Then he relapsed into silence, and so great was his distress, that he pushed his breakfast away from him. Madame Arnoux raised her eyes as she shrugged her shoulders. He passed his hand across his forehead.

"After all, I am not guilty. I have nothing to reproach myself with. 'Tis a misfortune. It will be overcome—ay, and so much the worse, faith!"

He took a piece of cake, however, in obedience to his wife's entreaties.

That evening he invited her to dine with him alone in a private room at the Maison d'Or. Madame Arnoux did not understand this emotional impulse, taking offence, in fact, at being treated as if she were a light woman. Arnoux, on the contrary, meant it as a proof of affection. Then, as he was beginning to feel dull, he paid the Maréchale a visit in order to amuse himself.

Up to this time, he had been pardoned for many things owing to his reputation for good-fellowship. His lawsuit placed him amongst men of bad repute. No one visited his house.

Frederick, however, considered that he was bound in honour to go there more frequently than ever. He hired a box at the Italian opera, and took them with him every week. Meanwhile, the pair had reached that stage in unsuitable unions when an invincible lassitude springs from concessions which people get into the habit of making, and which render existence intolerable. Madame Arnoux restrained her pent-up feelings; Arnoux became gloomy; and Frederick grew sad at witnessing the unhappiness of these two ill-fated beings.

She had imposed on him the obligation, since she had given him her confidence, of making inquiries into her husband's affairs. But shame prevented him from doing so. It was painful to him to reflect that he coveted the wife of this man, at whose dinner-table he constantly sat. Nevertheless, he continued his visits, excusing himself on the ground that he was bound to protect her, and that an occasion might present itself for being of service to her.

Eight days after the ball, he had paid a visit to M. Dambreuse. The financier had offered him twenty shares in a coal-mining speculation;

Frederick did not return there again. Deslauriers had written letters to him, which he left unanswered. Pellerin had invited him to go and see the portrait; he always excused himself. He gave way, however, to Cisy's persistent appeals to be introduced to Rosanette.

She received him very kindly, but without springing on his neck as she used to do formerly. His comrade was delighted at being received by a woman of easy virtue, and above all at having a chat with an actor. Delmar was there when he called. A drama in which he appeared as a peasant lecturing Louis XIV and prophesying the events of '89 had made him so conspicuous that similar parts were continually assigned to him; and now his function consisted of attacks on the monarchs of all nations. As an English brewer, he inveighed against Charles I; as a student at Salamanca, he cursed Philip II; or, as a sensitive father, he expressed indignation against the Pompadour—this was the most beautiful bit of acting!

All this had fascinated Rosanette; and she had got rid of Père Oudry, without caring one jot about consequences, as she was not covetous.

Arnoux, who knew her disposition, had taken advantage of the state of affairs for some time past to spend very little money on her. M. Roque appeared occasionally, and all three of them carefully avoided anything like a candid explanation. Then, fancying that she had got rid of the other solely on his account, Arnoux increased her allowance, for she was living very expensively. She had even sold her cashmere in her anxiety to pay off her old debts, as she said; and he was continually giving her money, whilst she bewitched him and imposed upon him pitilessly. Therefore, bills and stamped paper rained all over the house. Frederick felt that a crisis was approaching.

One day he called to see Madame Arnoux. She was out. Monsieur was at work below stairs in the shop. In fact, Arnoux, in the midst of his Japanese vases, was trying to impress a newly-married pair who happened to be well-to-do people from the provinces.

When the customers had gone, he told Frederick that he had that very morning been engaged in a little altercation with his wife. In order to obviate any remarks about expense, he had declared that the Maréchale was no longer his mistress. "I even told her that she was yours."

Frederick was annoyed at this; but to utter reproaches might only betray him. He faltered: "Ah! you were in the wrong—greatly in the wrong!"

"What does that matter?" said Arnoux. "Where is the disgrace of passing for her lover? I am really so myself. Would you not be flattered at being in such a position?"

Had she spoken? Was this a hint? Frederick hastened to reply:

"No! not at all! on the contrary!"

"Well, what then?"

"Yes, 'tis true; it makes no difference so far as that's concerned."

Arnoux next asked: "And why don't you call there oftener?"

Frederick promised that he would do so.

"Ah! I forgot! you ought, when talking about Rosanette, to admit in some way to my wife that you are her lover. I can't suggest how you can best do this, but you'll find that out. I ask this of you as a special favour—eh?"

The young man's only answer was an equivocal grimace. This calumny had undone him. He called on her that evening, and swore that Arnoux's accusation was false.

"Is that really so?"

He appeared to be speaking sincerely, and, when she had taken a long breath of relief, she said to him:

"I believe you," with a beautiful smile. Then, with bent head, and, without looking at him:

"Besides, nobody has any claim on you!"

So then she had divined nothing; and she despised him, seeing that she did not think he could love her well enough to remain faithful to her! Frederick, forgetting his overtures while with the other, looked on the permission accorded to him as an insult.

After this she suggested that he ought now and then to visit Rosanette, to get a little glimpse of what she was like.

Arnoux presently made his appearance, and, five minutes later, wished to carry him off to Rosanette's.

The situation was becoming intolerable.

His attention was diverted by a letter from the notary, announcing that he would send him fifteen thousand francs the following day; and, in order to make up for his neglect of Deslauriers, he went forthwith to tell him this good news.

The advocate was lodging in the Rue des Trois-Maries, on the fifth floor, over a courtyard. His study, a little tiled apartment, chilly, and with a grey paper on the walls, had as its principal decoration a gold medal, the prize awarded him when he took his degree as a Doctor of Laws. It was his consultation-hour, and the advocate had on a white cravat.

The news as to the fifteen thousand francs (he had, no doubt, given up all hope of getting the amount) made him chuckle with delight.

"That's right, old fellow, that's right—that's quite right!"

He threw some wood into the fire, sat down again, and immediately began talking about the journal. The first thing to do was to get rid of Hussonnet.

"I'm tired of that idiot! As for officially professing opinions, my own idea is that the most equitable and forcible position is to have no opinions at all."

Frederick appeared astonished.

"Why, the thing is perfectly plain. It is time that politics should be dealt with scientifically. The old men of the eighteenth century began it when Rousseau and the men of letters introduced into the political sphere philanthropy, poetry, and other fudge, to the great delight of the Catholics—a natural alliance, however, since the modern reformers (I can prove it) all believe in Revelations. But, if you sing high masses for Poland, if, in place of the God of the Dominicans, who was an executioner, you take the God of the Romanticists, who is an upholsterer, if, in fact, you have not a wider conception of the Absolute than your ancestors, Monarchy will penetrate underneath your Republican forms, and your red cap will never be other than the headpiece of a priest. The only difference will be that the cell system will take the place of torture, the outrageous treatment of Religion that of sacrilege, and the European Concert that of the Holy Alliance; and in this beautiful order which we admire, composed of the wreckage of the followers of Louis XIV, the remnants of the Voltaireans, with some Imperial whitewash on top, and some fragments of the British Constitution, you will see the municipal councils trying to give trouble to the Mayor, the general councils to their Prefect, the Chambers to the King, the Press to Power, and the Administration to everybody. But simple-minded people get enthusiastic about the Civil Code, a work fabricated—let them say what they like—in a mean and tyrannical spirit, for the legislator, instead of doing his duty to the State, which simply means to observe customs in a regular fashion, claims to model society like another Lycurgus. Why does the law impede fathers of families with regard to the making of wills? Why does it place shackles on the compulsory sale of real estate? Why does it punish as a misdemeanour vagrancy, which ought not even to be regarded as a technical contravention of the Code. And there are other things! I know all about them! and so I am going to write a little novel, entitled *The History of the Idea of Justice,* which will be amusing. But I am infernally thirsty! And you?"

He leaned out of the window, and called to the porter to bring them two glasses of grog from the public-house over the way.

"To sum up, I see three parties—no! three groups—in none of which do I take the slightest interest: those who have, those who have nothing, and those who are trying to have. All agree in their idiotic worship of Authority! For example, Mably recommends that philosophers should be prevented from publishing their doctrines; M. Wronsky, the geometrician, describes the censorship as the 'critical expression of speculative spontaneity'; Père Enfantin gives his blessing to the Hapsburgs for having passed a hand across the Alps to keep Italy down; Pierre Leroux wishes people to be compelled to listen to an orator; and Louis Blanc inclines toward a State religion—so much rage for government have these vassals whom we call the people! Nevertheless, there is not a single legitimate government, in spite of their sempiternal principles. 'Principle' signifies 'origin.' It is always necessary to go back to a revolution, to an act of violence, to a transitory fact. Thus, our principle is the national sovereignty embodied in the Parliamentary form, though the Parliament does not agree to this! But in what way could the sovereignty of the people be more sacred than the Divine Right? They are both fictions. Enough of metaphysics; no more phantoms! Dogmas are not required in order to get the streets swept! It may be said that I am turning society upside down. Well, after all, where would be the harm of that? It is, indeed, a nice thing—this society of yours."

Frederick could have said much. But, seeing that his theories were far less advanced than those of Sénécal, he was full of indulgence toward Deslauriers. He contented himself with arguing that such a system would make them generally hated.

"On the contrary, as we should have given to each party a pledge of hatred against his neighbour, all will reckon on us. You are about to come into it yourself, and to furnish us with some transcendent criticism!"

It was necessary to attack accepted ideas—the Academy, the Normal School, the Conservatoire, the Comédie Francaise, everything that resembled an institution. It was in that way that they would give consistency to the doctrines taught in their review. Then, as soon as it had been thoroughly well-established, it would suddenly be converted into a daily publication. Upon which they could find fault with individuals.

"And they will respect us, you may be sure!"

Deslauriers referred to that old dream of his—the position of editor-in-chief, so that he might have the unutterable happiness of directing others, of cutting down their articles, of ordering them to be written or declining them. His eyes twinkled under his goggles; he worked himself into a state of excitement, and drank a few glasses of brandy, one after the other, in an automatic fashion.

"You'll have to stand me a dinner once a week. That's indispensable, even though you should have to squander half your income on it. People would feel pleasure in going to it; it would be a centre for the others, a lever for yourself; and by manipulating public opinion at its two ends—literature and politics—you will see how, before six months have passed, we shall occupy the first rank in Paris."

Frederick, as he listened to Deslauriers, experienced a sensation of rejuvenescence, like a man who, after having been confined in a room for a long time, is suddenly taken into the open air. The enthusiasm of his friend was contagious.

"Yes, I have been an idler, an idiot—you are right!"

"All in good time," said Deslauriers. "I have found my Frederick again!"

And, holding up his jaw with closed fingers:

"Ah! you have made me suffer! Never mind, I love you all the same."

They stood gazing into each other's faces, both deeply affected, and were on the point of embracing each other.

A woman's cap appeared on the threshold of the anteroom.

"What do you want?" said Deslauriers.

It was Mademoiselle Clémence, his mistress.

She replied that, as she happened to be passing, she could not resist the desire to come in to see him, and in order that they might have a little repast together, she had brought some cakes, which she laid on the table.

"Take care of my papers!" said the advocate, sharply. "Besides, this is the third time that I have forbidden you to come at my consultation-hours."

She wished to embrace him.

"Very well! Now be off!"

He repelled her; she sighed heavily.

"Ah! you are plaguing me again!"

"'Tis because I love you!"

"I don't want you to love me, but to oblige me!"

This harsh remark stopped Clémence's tears. She went over to the window, and remained there motionless, with her forehead against the pane.

Her attitude and her silence irritated Deslauriers.

"When you have quite finished, you will order your carriage, will you not?"

She turned round with a start.

"You are sending me away?"

"Exactly."

She fixed on him her large blue eyes, no doubt as a last appeal, then drew the two ends of her tartan across each other, lingered for a minute, then went away.

"You ought to call her back," said Frederick.

"Come, now!"

And, as he wished to go out, Deslauriers went into the kitchen, which also served as his dressing-room. On the stone floor, beside a pair of boots, were to be seen the remains of a meagre breakfast, and a mattress with a coverlid was rolled up on the floor in a corner.

"This will show you," said he, "that I receive few marchionesses. 'Tis easy to get enough of them, ay, faith! and others, too! Those who cost nothing take up your time—'tis money under another form. Now, I'm not rich! And then they are all so silly, so silly! Can you converse with a woman yourself?"

As they parted, at the corner of the Pont Neuf, Deslauriers said: "It's settled, then; you'll bring the thing to me to-morrow as soon as you have it!"

"Agreed!" said Frederick.

When he awoke next morning, he received through the post a cheque on the bank for fifteen thousand francs.

This scrap of paper represented to him fifteen large bags of money; and he thought to himself that, with such a sum he could, first of all, keep his carriage for three years instead of selling it, as he would soon be forced to do, or buy for himself two beautiful damaskeened pieces of armour, which he had seen on the Quai Voltaire, then a quantity of other things, pictures, books and what numerous bouquets of flowers, presents for Madame Arnoux! anything, in short, was preferable to risking losing all in that journal! Deslauriers seemed to him presumptuous, his insensibility on the night before had chilled Frederick's affection for him; the young man was indulging in these feelings of regret, when he was surprised by the sudden appearance of Arnoux, who sat down heavily on the side of the bed, like a man overwhelmed with trouble.

"What is the matter now?"

"I am ruined!"

He had to deposit that very day at the office of Maître Beaumont, notary, in the Rue Saint-Anne, eighteen thousand francs lent him by one Vanneroy.

"'Tis an unaccountable disaster. I have given him a mortgage, which ought to keep him quiet. But he threatens me with a writ if it is not paid this afternoon promptly."

"And what next?"

"Oh! the next step is easy enough; he will take possession of my real estate. Once the thing is publicly announced, it means ruin to me—that's all! Ah! if I could find anyone to advance me this cursed sum, he might take Vanneroy's place, and I should be saved! You don't happen to have it yourself?"

The cheque was still on the night-table near a book. Frederick picked up a volume, and placed it on the cheque, while he replied:

"Good heavens, my dear friend, no!"

But it was painful to him to say "no" to Arnoux.

"Don't you know anyone who would—?"

"Nobody! and to think that in eight days I should be getting in money! There is owing to me probably fifty thousand francs at the end of the month!"

"Couldn't you ask some of the persons in your debt to make you an advance?"

"Ah! well, so I did!"

"But have you any bills or promissory notes?"

"Not one!"

"What is to be done?" said Frederick.

"That's what I'm asking myself," said Arnoux. "'Tisn't for myself, my God! but for my children and my poor wife!"

Then, each phrase falling from his lips in a broken fashion:

"In fact—I could rough it—I could pack off all I have—and go and seek my fortune—I don't know where!"

"Impossible!" exclaimed Frederick.

Arnoux replied with an air of calmness:

"How do you think I could remain in Paris now?"

There was a long silence. Frederick broke it by saying:

"When could you pay back this money?"

Not that he himself had it; quite the contrary! But there was nothing to prevent him from seeing some friends, and making an application to them.

And he rang for his servant to get himself dressed.

Arnoux thanked him.

"The amount you need is eighteen thousand francs—isn't it?"

"Oh! I could manage with sixteen thousand! For I could make two thousand five hundred out of it, or get three thousand on my silver plate, if Vanneroy meanwhile would give me till to-morrow; and, I repeat to you, you may inform the lender, give him a solemn promise, that in eight days, perhaps even in five or six, the money will be returned. Besides, the mortgage will be security for it. So there is no risk, you understand?"

Frederick assured him that he thoroughly understood the state of affairs, and added that he was going out immediately.

He would be sure on his return to bestow hearty maledictions on Deslauriers, for he wished to keep his word, and in the meantime, to oblige Arnoux.

"Suppose I applied to Monsieur Dambreuse? But on what pretext could I ask for money? 'Tis I, on the contrary, that owe him some for the shares I took in his coal-mining company. Ah! let him go hang himself—his shares! After all, I am not actually liable for them!"

And Frederick approved himself for his own independence, as if he had refused to do some service for M. Dambreuse.

"Ah, well," said he to himself afterward, "since I'm going to meet with a loss in this way—for with fifteen thousand francs I might gain a hundred thousand! such things happen on the Bourse—well, then, since I am breaking my promise to one of them, am I not free? Besides, Deslauriers might wait? No, no; that's wrong; let us go there."

He looked at his watch.

"Ah! there's no hurry. The bank does not close till five o'clock."

And, at half-past four, when he had cashed the cheque:

"'Tis useless now; he would not be in. I'll go this evening." Thus giving himself the opportunity of changing his mind, for there always remain in the conscience some of those sophistries which we pour into it ourselves. It preserves the after-taste of them, like unwholesome liquor.

He walked along the boulevards, and dined alone at a restaurant. Then he listened to one act of a play at the Vaudeville, in order to divert his thoughts. But his bank-notes caused him as much uneasiness as if he had stolen them. He would not have been very sorry if he had lost them.

When he reached home he found a letter containing these words: "What news? My wife joins me, dear friend, in the hope, etc.—Yours." And then there was a flourish after his signature.

"His wife! She appeals to me!"

At the same moment Arnoux appeared, anxious to know whether he had been able to obtain the sum so sorely needed.

"Wait a moment; here it is," said Frederick.

And, twenty-four hours later, he gave this reply to Deslauriers: "I have no money."

The advocate called three days, one after the other, and urged Frederick to write to the notary. He even offered to take a trip to Havre himself in connection with the matter.

At the end of the week, Frederick nervously asked the worthy Arnoux for his fifteen thousand francs. Arnoux put it off till the following day, and then till the day after. Frederick ventured out late at night, fearing lest Deslauriers might come on him by surprise.

One evening, somebody ran against him at the corner of the Madeleine. It was he.

And Deslauriers accompanied Frederick as far as the door of a house in the Faubourg Poissonnière.

"Wait for me!"

He waited. At last, after three quarters of an hour, Frederick came out, accompanied by Arnoux, and made signs to him to have patience a little longer. The two men went up the Rue de Hauteville arm-in-arm, and presently they turned down the Rue de Chabrol.

The night was dark, with gusts of tepid wind. Arnoux walked on slowly, talking about the Galleries of Commerce—a succession of covered passages leading from the Boulevard Saint-Denis to the Châtelet, a marvellous speculation, into which he was very anxious to enter.

Frederick could hear Deslauriers' steps behind him like reproachful blows falling on his conscience. But he did not venture to claim his money, through a feeling of bashfulness, and also through a fear that it would be useless. The other was drawing nearer. He made up his mind to ask.

Arnoux, in a very flippant tone, said that, as he had not got in his outstanding debts, he was really unable to pay back the fifteen thousand francs.

"You have no need of money, I fancy?"

At that moment Deslauriers came up to Frederick, and, taking him aside:

"Be honest. Have you got the amount? Yes or no?"

"Well, then, no," said Frederick; "I've lost it."

"Ah! and in what way?"

"At play."

Deslauriers, without saying another word, made a very low bow, and went away. Arnoux had taken advantage of the opportunity to light a cigar in a tobacconist's shop. When he came back, he inquired, "Who was that young man?"

"Oh! nobody—a friend."

Then, three minutes later, in front of Rosanette's door:

"Come on up," said Arnoux; "she'll be pleased to see you. What a savage you are just now!"

A gas-lamp, which was directly opposite, threw its light on him; and, with his cigar between his white teeth and his air of contentment, there was something intolerable about him.

"Ha! now that I think of it, my notary has been at your place this morning about that mortgage-registry matter. My wife reminded me about it."

"A wife with brains!" returned Frederick automatically.

"I believe you."

And once more Arnoux began to sing his wife's praises. There was no one like her for spirit, tenderness, and thrift; he added in a low tone, rolling his eyes about: "And a woman with so many charms, too!"

"Good-bye!" said Frederick.

Arnoux made a step closer to him.

"Hold on! Why are you going?" And, with his hand half-stretched out toward Frederick, he stared at the young man, quite abashed by the look of anger in his face.

Frederick repeated in a dry tone, "Good-bye!"

He hurried down the Rue de Bréda like a stone rolling headlong, raging against Arnoux, swearing in his own mind that he would never see him again, nor her either, so broken-hearted and desolate did he feel.

Deslauriers descended the Rue des Martyrs, swearing aloud in his indignation; for his project, like an obelisk that has fallen, now assumed extraordinary proportions. He considered himself robbed, and felt as if he had suffered a great loss. His affection for Frederick was dead, and he experienced a feeling of joy at it—it was a sort of compensation to him! A hatred of all rich people took possession of him. He leaned toward Sénécal's opinions, and resolved to make every effort to propagate them.

All this time, Arnoux was comfortably seated in an easy-chair near the fire, sipping his cup of tea, with the Maréchale on his knee.

Frederick did not go back there; and, in order to distract his attention from his unhappy passion, he determined to write a *History of the Renaissance*. He piled up confusedly on his table the humanists, the philosophers, and the poets, and he went to inspect some engravings of Mark Antony, and tried to study Machiavelli. Gradually, the serenity of intellectual work had a soothing effect upon him. While his mind was steeped in the personality of others, he lost sight of his own—which is the only way, perhaps, to get rid of suffering.

One day, while he was quietly taking notes, the door opened, and the man-servant announced Madame Arnoux.

It was she, indeed! and alone? But, no! for she was holding little Eugène by the hand, followed by a nurse in a white apron. She sat down, and after a preliminary cough:

"It is a long time since you came to see us."

As Frederick could think of no excuse at the moment, she added:

"It was delicacy on your part!"

He asked in return:

"Delicacy about what?"

"About all you have done for Arnoux!" said she.

Frederick made a significant gesture. "What do I care about him, indeed! It was for your sake I did it!"

She sent off the child to play with his nurse in the drawing-room. Two or three words passed between them as to their state of health; then the conversation hung fire.

She wore a brown silk gown, the colour of Spanish wine, with a paletot of black velvet bordered with sable. He yearned to pass his hand over the fur; and her headbands, so long and so exquisitely smooth, seemed to draw his lips toward them. But he was agitated by emotion, and, turning his eyes toward the door:

"It is rather warm here!"

Frederick understood what her discreet glance meant.

"Ah! excuse me! the two leaves of the door are merely drawn together."

"Yes, that's true!"

And she smiled, as much as to say:

"I'm not the least afraid!"

He asked her presently what was the object of her visit.

"My husband," she replied with an effort, "has urged me to call on you, not venturing to do so himself!"

"And why?"

"You know Monsieur Dambreuse, don't you?"

"Yes, slightly."

"Ah! slightly."

She relapsed into silence.

"No matter! finish what you were about to say."

Thereupon she told him that, two days before, Arnoux had found himself unable to meet four bills of a thousand francs, made payable at the banker's order and with his signature attached to them. She felt sorry for having compromised her children's fortune. But anything was preferable to dishonour; and, if Monsieur Dambreuse stopped the proceedings, they would certainly pay him soon, for she was going to sell a little house which she had at Chartres.

"Poor woman!" murmured Frederick. "I will surely go. Rely on me!"

"Thanks!"

And she arose to leave.

"Oh! do not hurry away."

She remained standing, examining the trophy of Mongolian arrows suspended from the ceiling, the bookcase, the bindings, all the utensils for writing. She lifted up the bronze bowl which held his pens. Her feet rested on different portions of the carpet. She had visited Frederick several times, but always accompanied by Arnoux. They were now alone together—alone in his own house. It was a wonderful event—almost a successful issue of his love.

She wished to see his little garden. He offered her his arm to show her his property—thirty feet of ground enclosed by some houses, adorned with shrubs at the corners and flower-borders in the middle. The early days of April had arrived. The leaves of the lilacs were already showing their borders of green. A breath of pure air was diffused around, and the little birds chirped, their song alternating with the distant sounds that came from a coachmaker's forge.

Frederick procured a fire-shovel; and, while they walked on side by side, the child made sand-pies on the walk.

Madame Arnoux did not think that, as he grew older, he would have a great imagination; but he had a winning disposition. His sister, on the other hand, possessed a caustic humour that sometimes wounded her.

"That will change," said Frederick. "We must never despair."

She returned:

"We must never despair!"

This automatic repetition of the phrase he had used appeared to him a sort of encouragement; he plucked a rose, the only one in the garden.

"Do you remember a certain bouquet of roses one evening, in a carriage?"

She coloured a little; and, with an air of bantering pity:

"Ah, but I was very young then!"

"And this one," continued Frederick, in a low tone, "will it be treated the same way?"

She replied, while turning about the stem between her fingers, like the thread of a spindle:

"No, I will preserve it."

She called the nurse, who took the child in her arms; then, on the threshold of the door in the street, Madame Arnoux inhaled the odour of the rose, leaning her head on her shoulder with a look as sweet as a kiss.

When he returned to his study, he gazed at the arm-chair in which she had sat, and every object which she had touched. Some portion of her was diffused around him. The sweet caress of her presence lingered there still.

"So, then, she has been here," said he to himself.

And his soul was bathed in waves of infinite tenderness.

Next morning, at eleven o'clock, he presented himself at M. Dambreuse's house. He was received in the dining-room. The banker was seated opposite his wife at breakfast. Beside her sat his niece, and at the other side of the table was the governess, an English woman, strongly pitted with smallpox.

M. Dambreuse invited Frederick to take his place amongst them, and when he declined:

"What can I do for you? I am all attention."

Frederick confessed, while affecting indifference, that he had come to make a request in behalf of one Arnoux.

"Ha! ha! the ex-picture-dealer," said the banker, with a noiseless laugh which exposed his gums. "Oudry formerly gave security for him; he has given a lot of trouble."

And he proceeded to read the letters and newspapers which lay beside him on the table.

Madame noticed that Frederick was embarrassed.

"Do you sometimes see our friend Martinon?"

"He will be here this evening," said the young girl in a lively tone.

"Ha! so you know him?" said her aunt, turning on her a freezing look.

At that moment one of the men-servants, bending forward, whispered in her ear.

"Your dressmaker, Mademoiselle—Miss John!"

And the governess, in obedience to this summons, left the room with her pupil.

M. Dambreuse, annoyed at the disarrangement of the chairs by this movement, asked what was the matter.

"It is Madame Regimbart."

"Wait a moment! Regimbart! I know that name. I have seen his signature."

Frederick at length broached the question. Arnoux deserved some consideration; he was even going, for the sole purpose of fulfilling his engagements, to sell a house belonging to his wife.

"She is thought very pretty," said Madame Dambreuse.

The banker added, with a display of good-nature:

"Are you on friendly terms with them—on intimate terms?"

Frederick, without giving an explicit reply, said that he would appreciate it if he would consider the matter.

"Well, since it pleases you, be it so; we will wait. I have some time to spare yet; suppose we go down to my office. Would you mind?"

They had finished breakfast. Madame Dambreuse bowed slightly toward Frederick, smiling in a singular fashion, with a mingling of politeness and irony. Frederick had no time to reflect about it, for M. Dambreuse, as soon as they were alone:

"You did not come for your shares?"

And, without permitting him to make any excuses:

"Well! well! 'tis right that you should know a little more about the business."

He offered Frederick a cigarette, and began his statement.

The General Union of French Coal Mines had been constituted. All that they were waiting for was the order for its incorporation. The mere fact of the amalgamation had lessened the cost of superintendence, and of manual labour, and increased the profits. Besides, the company had conceived a new idea, which was to interest the workmen in its undertaking. It would erect houses for them, healthful dwellings; finally, it would constitute itself the purveyor of its *employés,* and would have everything supplied to them at net prices.

"And they will be the gainers by it, Monsieur: that's true progress! that's the way to answer effectively certain Republican brawlings. We have on our Board"—he showed the prospectus—"a peer of France, a scholar who is a member of the Institute, a retired field-officer of genius. Such elements reassure the timid, and appeal to intelligent capitalists!"

The company would have in its favour the sanction of the State, then the railways, the steam service, the metallurgical establishments, the gas companies, and ordinary households.

"Thus we heat, we light, we penetrate to the very hearth of the humblest home. But how, you will ask, can we be sure of selling? By the aid of protective laws, dear Monsieur, and we shall get them!—that is a matter that concerns us! For my part, however, I am a downright prohibitionist! The country before anything!"

He had been appointed a director; but he had not the time to occupy himself with certain details, amongst other things with the editing of their publications.

"I find myself rather muddled with my authors. I have forgotten my Greek. I should need some one to put my ideas into shape."

And suddenly: "Will you be the man to perform those duties, with the title of general secretary?"

Frederick did not know what to say.

"Well, what is there to prevent you?"

His functions would be confined to writing a report every year for the shareholders. He would be day by day in communication with the most notable men in Paris. Representing the company with the workmen, he would ere long be worshipped by them as a natural consequence, and by this means he would be able, later, to push his way into the General Council, and into the position of a deputy.

Frederick's ears tingled. Whence came this goodwill? He became confused in returning thanks. It was not necessary, the banker said, that he should be dependent on anyone. The best course was to take some shares, "a splendid investment besides, for your capital guarantees your position, as your position does your capital."

"About how much should it amount to?" said Frederick.

"Oh, well! whatever you please—from forty to sixty thousand francs, I suppose."

This sum was so trifling in M. Dambreuse's eyes, and his authority was so great, that the young man determined immediately to sell a farm.

He accepted the offer. M. Dambreuse was to select one of his disengaged days for an appointment when they might finish their arrangements.

"So I can say to Jacques Arnoux—?"

"Anything you like—the poor chap—anything you like!"

Frederick wrote to the Arnoux to make their minds easy, and he despatched the letter by a man-servant, who brought back the answer: "All right!" His action in the matter deserved fuller recognition. He expected a visit, or, at least, a letter. He did not receive either.

Was it thoughtlessness on their part, or was it intentional? Since Madame Arnoux had come once, what was to prevent her from coming again? The species of confidence, of avowal, of which she had made him the recipient on that occasion, was nothing better, then, than a manœuvre, executed through interested motives.

"Are they playing on me? and is she an accomplice of her husband?" A sort of shame, in spite of his desire, prevented him from going to their house.

One morning (three weeks after their interview), M. Dambreuse wrote to him, saying that he would expect him the same day in an hour's time.

On the way, the thought of Arnoux oppressed him once more, and, not having been able to discover any reason for his conduct, he was seized with a feeling of wretchedness, a melancholy presentiment. In order to get rid of it, he hailed a cab, and drove to the Rue de Paradis.

Arnoux was away travelling.

"And Madame?"

"In the country, at the works."

"When is Monsieur expected back?"

"To-morrow, without fail."

He would find her alone; this was the opportune moment. Something imperious seemed to cry out in the depths of his consciousness: "Go, then, and see her!"

But M. Dambreuse? "Ah! well, so much the worse. I'll say that I was ill."

He rushed to the railway-station, and, as soon as he was in the carriage:

"Perhaps I have done wrong. Pshaw! what does it matter?"

Frederick, through sheer weariness, was lost in that languor which is produced by the very excess of impatience. Cranes and warehouses presently appeared. They had reached Creil.

After crossing the bridge, he found himself in an avenue, on his right the ruins of an abbey. A mill with its wheels revolving barred up the entire width of the second arm of the Oise, over which the factory projected. Frederick was greatly surprised by the imposing character of this structure. He felt more respect for Arnoux on account of it. Three paces further on, he turned up an alley, which had a grating at its lower end.

He went in. The doorkeeper called him back, asking:

"Have you a permit?"

"For what purpose?"

"For the purpose of visiting the establishment."

Frederick said in a rather curt tone that he had come to see M. Arnoux.

"Who is Monsieur Arnoux?"

"Why, the chief, the master, the proprietor, in fact!"

"No, Monsieur! These are Messieurs Lebœuf and Milliet's works!"

Frederick left the premises, staggering like a drunken man; and he had such a look of perplexity, that on the Pont de la Boucherie an inhabitant of the town, who was smoking his pipe, asked whether he was looking for anything. This man knew where Arnoux's factory was. It was situated at Montataire.

Frederick asked whether a vehicle was to be got. He was told that the only place where he could find one was at the station. He went back there. A shaky-looking calash, to which was yoked an old horse, with torn harness hanging over the shafts, stood in front of the luggage office. An

urchin who was looking on offered to go and find Père Pilon. In ten minutes' time he came back, and announced that Père Pilon was at his breakfast. Frederick, unable to bear this any longer, walked away. But the gates
of the thoroughfare across the line were closed. He would have to wait till
two trains had passed. At last, he made a dash into the open country.

The monotonous greenery made it look like the cover of an immense
billiard-table. A little further on, some factory chimneys were smoking
close beside each other. Long walls formed irregular lines past the trees;
and, further down, the houses of the village could be seen.

They had only a single story, with staircases consisting of three steps
made of uncemented blocks.

Frederick pursued his way along the middle of the street. Then, he
saw on his left, at the opening of a pathway, a large wooden arch,
whereon was traced, in letters of gold, the word, "Faïences."

It was not without an object that Jacques Arnoux had selected the
vicinity of Creil. By locating his works as close as possible to the other
works (which had long borne a high reputation), he had created a certain confusion in the public mind, with a favourable result so far as his
own interests were concerned.

Heaps of white clay were drying under sheds. There were others in
the open air; and in the midst of the yard stood Sénécal with his ever-
lasting blue paletot lined with red.

The ex-tutor extended toward Frederick his cold hand.

"You've come to see the master? He's not here."

Frederick, nonplussed, replied in a stupefied fashion:

"I know it." But the next moment correcting himself:

"It is about a matter that concerns Madame Arnoux. Can she see me?"

"Ha! I have not seen her for the last three days," said Sénécal.

And he broke into a long string of complaints. When he accepted the
post of manager, he understood that he would have been able to reside
in Paris, and not be forced to bury himself in this country district, far
from his friends, deprived of newspapers. No matter! he had overlooked
all that. But Arnoux did not recognise his merits. He was, moreover, shal-
low and retrograde—no one could be more ignorant. Instead of seeking
for artistic improvements, it would have been better to introduce fire-
wood instead of coal and gas. The shopkeeping spirit *thrust itself in*—
Sénécal laid stress on the last words. In short, he disliked his present occupation, and he all but appealed to Frederick to say a word in his behalf
that he might get an increase of salary.

"Make your mind easy," said the other.

He met nobody on the staircase. On the first floor, he pushed his way
into an empty room. It was the drawing-room. He called out at the top
of his voice. There was no reply. No doubt, the cook had gone out, and

so had the housemaid. At length, having reached the second floor, he pushed another door open. Madame Arnoux was alone in this room, before a press with a mirror attached. The belt of her dressing-gown hung down her hips; one entire half of her hair fell in a dark wave over her right shoulder; and she had raised both arms in order to hold up her chignon with one hand and to put a pin through it with the other. She gave an exclamation and disappeared.

Then she came back again properly dressed. Her waist, her eyes, the rustle of her dress, her entire appearance, charmed him. Frederick had to restrain himself to keep from covering her with kisses.

"I beg your pardon," said she, "but I could not—"

He had the boldness to interrupt her with these words:

"Nevertheless—you looked very nice—just now."

She probably thought this compliment a little coarse, for her cheeks reddened. He was afraid that he might have offended her. She went on:

"What lucky chance has brought you here?"

He did not know what reply to make; and, after a slight chuckle, which gave him time for reflection:

"If I told you, would you believe me?"

"Why not?"

Frederick said to her that he had had a frightful dream a few nights before.

"I dreamt that you were seriously ill—almost dying."

"Oh! my husband and I are never ill."

"I dreamt only of you," said he.

She gazed at him calmly: "Dreams are not always realised."

Frederick stammered, sought to find appropriate words to express himself in, and then plunged into a flowing period about the affinity of souls.

She listened to him with downcast face, while she smiled that beautiful smile of hers. He watched her out of the corner of his eye with delight, and poured out his love all the more freely through the easy channel of a commonplace remark.

She offered to show him the works; and, as she persisted, he made no objection.

To divert his attention with something of an amusing nature, she drew his attention to the species of museum that decorated the staircase. The specimens, hung up against the wall or laid on shelves, bore witness to the efforts and the successive fads of Arnoux. After seeking vainly for the red of Chinese copper, he had wished to manufacture majolicas, faïence, Etruscan and Oriental ware, and had, in fact, attempted all the improvements which were realised at a later period.

So it was that one could observe in the series big vases covered with figures of mandarins, porringers of shot reddish-brown, pots adorned with

Arabian inscriptions, drinking-vessels in the style of the Renaissance, and large plates on which two personages were outlined as it were on blood-stone, in a delicate, aërial fashion. He now made letters for sign-boards and wine-labels; but his intelligence was not high enough to attain to art, nor commonplace enough to desire merely profit; so without satisfying anyone, he had ruined himself.

They were both looking at these things when Mademoiselle Marthe passed.

"So, then, you do not recognise our friend?" said her mother to her.

"Yes, indeed," she replied, bowing to him, while her clear and sceptical glance—the glance of a virgin—seemed to say in a whisper: "What are you coming here for?" and she ran up the steps with her head slightly bent over her shoulder.

Madame Arnoux led Frederick into the yard attached to the works, and then explained to him in a grave tone how different clays were ground, cleaned, and sifted.

"The most important item is the preparation of pastes."

And she brought him into a hall filled with vats, in which a vertical axis with horizontal arms kept turning. Frederick regretted that he had not flatly declined her offer a little while before.

"These things are merely the slobberings," said she.

He thought the word grotesque, and, in a measure, unbecoming on her lips.

They left the spot, and passed close to a ruined hut, which had formerly been used as a repository for gardening implements.

"It is no longer of any use," said Madame Arnoux.

He replied in a tremulous voice:

"Happiness may have once been associated with it!"

The clacking of the fire-pump drowned his words, and they entered the workshop where rough drafts were made.

Men, seated at a narrow table, placed, each in front of himself on a revolving disc, a piece of paste. Then each man with his left hand scooped out the insides of his own piece while smoothing its surface with the right; and vases could be seen bursting into shape like blossoming flowers.

Madame Arnoux had the moulds for more difficult works shown to him.

In another portion of the building, the threads, the necks, and the projecting lines were being formed. On the floor above, they removed the seams, and stopped up with plaster the little holes that had been left by the preceding operations.

At every opening in the walls, in corners, in the middle of the corridor, everywhere, earthenware vessels stood side by side.

Frederick began to feel bored.

"Perhaps these things are wearisome to you?" said she.

Fearing lest this might mean the termination of his visit, he affected, on the contrary, a tone of great enthusiasm. He even expressed regret at not having devoted himself to this branch of industry.

She appeared surprised.

"Certainly! I should have been able to live near you."

And as he endeavoured to catch her eye, Madame Arnoux, in order to avoid him, removed off a bracket little balls of paste, which had come from abortive readjustments, flattened them out into a thin cake, and pressed her hand over them.

"Might I take these away with me?" said Frederick.

"Good heavens! are you so childish?"

He was about to reply when Sénécal came in.

Frederick, annoyed by his presence, asked Madame Arnoux in a low tone whether they would have an opportunity of seeing the kilns. They descended to the ground-floor; and she was just explaining the use of caskets, when Sénécal, who had followed close behind, placed himself between them.

He continued the explanation of his own motion, expatiated on the various kinds of combustibles, the process of placing in the kiln, the pyroscopes, the cylindrical furnaces; the instruments for rounding, the lustres, and the metals, making a prodigious display of chemical terms, such as "chloride," "sulphuret," "borax," and "carbonate." Frederick did not understand a single word, and kept turning round every minute toward Madame Arnoux.

"You are not listening," said she. "Monsieur Sénécal, however, is very clear. He understands all these things much better than I."

The mathematician, flattered by this eulogy, proposed to show the way in which colours were laid on. Frederick gave Madame Arnoux an anxious, questioning look. She remained impassive, not caring to be alone with him, very probably, and yet unwilling to leave him.

He offered her his arm.

"No—many thanks! the staircase is too narrow!"

And, when they had reached the top, Sénécal opened the door of an apartment filled with women.

They were handling brushes, phials, shells, and plates of glass. Along the cornice, close to the wall, extended boards with figures engraved on them; scraps of thin paper floated about, and a melting-stove emitted fumes that made the temperature oppressive, while there mingled with it the odour of turpentine.

The workwomen were nearly all poorly dressed. It was noticeable, however, that one of them wore a Madras handkerchief and long earrings. Of slight frame, and yet plump, she had large black eyes and the fleshy lips of a negress. Her ample bosom projected from under her chemise, which was fastened round her waist by the string of her petticoat; and, with one elbow on the board of the work-table and the other arm hanging down, she gazed vaguely at the open country, a long distance away. Beside her were a bottle of wine and some pork chops.

The regulations forbade eating in the work-shops, a rule intended to secure cleanliness at work and to keep the hands in a healthy condition.

Sénécal, through a sense of duty or a desire to exercise despotic authority, shouted out to her, while pointing toward a framed placard:

"I say, you girl from Bordeaux over there! read out for me Article Nine!"

"Well, what then?"

"What then, Mademoiselle? You'll have to pay a fine of three francs."

She looked him straight in the face in an impudent way.

"What does that matter to me? The master will take off your fine when he comes back! I laugh at you, my good man!"

Sénécal, who was walking with his hands behind his back, like an usher in the study-room, contented himself with smiling.

"Article Thirteen, insubordination, ten francs!"

The girl from Bordeaux resumed her work. Madame Arnoux, through a sense of propriety, said nothing; but her brows contracted. Frederick murmured:

"Ha! you are very severe for a democrat!"

The other replied in a magisterial tone:

"Democracy is not the unbounded license of individualism. It is the equality of all belonging to the same community before the law, the distribution of work, order."

"You are forgetting humanity!" said Frederick.

Madame Arnoux took his arm. Sénécal, perhaps offended by this token of silent approbation, went away.

Frederick felt an immense relief. Since morning he had been looking for the opportunity to declare itself; now it had arrived. Besides, Madame Arnoux's spontaneous movements seemed to him to contain promises; and he asked her, as if on the pretext of warming their feet, to come up to her room. But, when he was seated close beside her, he began once more to feel embarrassed. He was at a loss for a starting-point. Sénécal, luckily, suggested an idea to his mind.

"Nothing could be more stupid," said he, "than this punishment!"

Madame Arnoux replied: "There are certain severe measures which are unavoidable!"

"What! you who are so good! Oh! I am mistaken, for you sometimes take pleasure in making other people suffer!"

"I don't understand riddles, my friend!"

And her stern look, still more than the words she used, checked him. Frederick was determined to go on. A volume of De Musset chanced to be on the chest of drawers; he turned over some pages, then began to talk about love, about his hopes and his transports.

All this, according to Madame Arnoux, was criminal or factitious. The young man felt wounded by this negative attitude with regard to his passion, and, in order to combat it, he cited, by way of proof, the suicides which they read about every day in the newspapers, extolled the great literary types, Phèdre, Dido, Romeo, Desgrieux. He talked as if he meant to do away with himself.

He wanted to cast himself at her feet. There was a creaking sound in the lobby, and he did not dare to carry out his intention.

He was, moreover, restrained by a kind of religious awe. That robe, mingling with the surrounding shadows, appeared to him boundless, infinite, impossible to touch; and for this very reason his desire became intensified. But the fear of doing too much, and, again, of not doing enough, deprived him of all judgment.

"If she dislikes me," he thought, "let her drive me away; if she cares for me, let her encourage me."

He said, with a sigh:

"So, then, you don't admit that a man may love—a woman?"

Madame Arnoux replied:

"Assuming that she is at liberty to marry, he may marry her; when she belongs to another, he should keep away from her."

"So happiness is impossible?"

"No! But it is never to be found in falsehood, mental anxiety, and remorse."

"What does it matter, if one is compensated by the enjoyment of supreme bliss?"

"The experience is too costly."

Then he sought to assail her with satire.

"Would not virtue in that case be merely cowardice?"

"Say rather, clear-sightedness. Even for those women who might forget duty or religion, simple good sense is sufficient. A solid foundation for wisdom may be found in self-love."

"Ah, what shopkeeping maxims these are of yours!"

"But I don't pretend to be a fine lady."

At that moment the little boy rushed in.

"Mamma, are you coming to dinner?"

"Yes, in a moment."

Frederick arose. At the same instant, Marthe made her appearance.

He could not make up his mind to go away, and, with a look of entreaty:

"These women you speak of are very unfeeling, then?"

"No, but deaf when it is necessary to be so."

And she stood on the threshold of her room with her two children beside her. He bowed without saying a word. She mutely returned his salutation.

His first feeling was an unspeakable astonishment. He felt crushed by this mode of impressing on him the emptiness of his hopes. It seemed to him as if he were lost, like a man who has fallen to the bottom of an abyss and knows that no help will come, and that he must die. He walked on, however, but at random, without looking before him.

The railway lamps traced on the horizon a line of flames. He arrived just as the train was starting, let himself be pushed into a carriage, and very soon fell asleep.

An hour later on the boulevards, the gaiety of Paris by night made his journey all at once recede into an already far-distant past. He resolved to be strong, and relieved his heart by vilifying Madame Arnoux with insulting epithets.

"She is an idiot, a goose, a mere animal; let us not waste another thought on her!"

When he got home, he found in his study a letter of eight pages on blue glazed paper, with the initials "R. A."

It began with friendly reproaches.

"What has become of you, my dear? I am getting quite bored."

But the handwriting was so illegible that Frederick was about to fling away the entire bundle of sheets, when he noticed in the postscript the following words:

"I count on you to come to-morrow and drive me to the races."

What was the meaning of this invitation? Was it another trick of the Maréchale? But a woman does not make a fool of the same man twice without some object; and, seized with curiosity, he read the letter over again attentively.

Frederick was able to distinguish "Misunderstanding—to have taken a wrong path—disillusions—poor children that we are!—like two rivers that join each other!" etc.

He held the sheets for a long time between his fingers. They had the odour of orris; and there was in the form of the characters and the irregular spaces between the lines something suggestive, as it were, of a disorderly toilet, that fired his blood.

"What reason have I for not going?" he said to himself at length. "But if Madame Arnoux were to know about it? Well! let her know! So much the better! and let her feel jealous over it! I shall thus be avenged!"

CHAPTER X

A PLEASANT LITTLE DINNER

ROSANETTE was eagerly waiting for him.

"This is nice of you!" she said, fixing her fine eyes on his face, with an expression at once tender and mirthful.

When she had fastened her bonnet-strings, she sat down on the divan, and remained silent.

"Shall we go?" said Frederick. She looked at the clock on the mantelpiece.

"Not yet! not before half-past one!" as if she had imposed this limit to her indecision.

At last, when the hour had struck:

"Ah! well, *andiamo, caro mio!*" And she gave a final touch to her head-bands, and left directions for Delphine.

"Will Madame be home to dinner?"

"Why should we, indeed? Let us dine together somewhere—at the Café Anglais, wherever you wish."

"Be it so!"

Her little dogs began yelping around her.

"We can take them with us, can't we?"

Frederick carried them himself to the vehicle. It was a hired berlin with two post-horses and a postilion. His man-servant was in the back seat. The Maréchale appeared satisfied with his attentions. Then, as soon as she had seated herself, she asked him whether he had been recently at the Arnoux'.

"Not for the past month," said Frederick.

"As for me, I met him the day before yesterday. He would have even come to-day, but he has all sorts of troubles—another lawsuit—I don't know what. He is a queer man!"

Frederick inquired with an air of indifference:

"Now that I think of it, do you still see—what's that his name is?—that ex-vocalist—Delmar?"

She replied dryly:

"No; that's all over."

So it was evident that there had been a rupture between them. Frederick derived some hope from this circumstance.

They descended the Quartier Bréda at an easy pace. Frederick let himself jog up and down with the rocking of the carriage-straps. The Maréchale turned her head to the right and to the left with a smile on her face.

Her straw hat of mother-of-pearl colour was trimmed with black lace.

The hood of her bournous floated in the wind, and she sheltered herself from the rays of the sun under a parasol of lilac satin pointed at the top like a pagoda.

"What dear little fingers!" said Frederick, softly taking her other hand, her left being adorned with a gold bracelet in the form of a curb-chain.

"I say! that's pretty! Where did it come from?"

"Oh! I have had that a very long time," said the Maréchale.

The young man did not challenge this hypocritical answer in any way. He preferred to profit by the circumstance. And still holding the wrist, he pressed his lips on it between the glove and the cuff.

"Stop! People will see us!"

"Pooh! What does that signify?"

After passing by the Place de la Concorde, they drove along the Quai de la Conférence and the Quai de Billy, where they noticed a cedar of Lebanon in a garden. Rosanette believed that Lebanon was situated in China; she laughed herself at her own ignorance, and asked Frederick to give her lessons in geography. Then, leaving the Trocadéro at the right, they crossed the Pont de Jéna, and drew up in the middle of the Champ de Mars, near some other vehicles already in the Hippodrome.

The grass hillocks were covered with working people. Some spectators might be seen on the balcony of the Military School; and the two pavilions outside the weighing-room, the two galleries contained within its enclosure, and another in front of that of the king, were filled with a fashionably dressed crowd whose deportment showed their regard for this as yet novel form of amusement.

The public around the course, more select at this period, had a less vulgar aspect. It was the era of trouser-straps, velvet collars, and white gloves. The ladies, attired in brilliant colours, displayed long-waisted gowns; and seated on the tiers of the stands, they formed, so to speak, immense groups of flowers, spotted here and there with the black of the men's costumes. But every glance was directed toward the celebrated Algerian Bou-Maza, who sat, impassive, between two staff officers in one of the private galleries. That of the Jockey Club contained none but gravelooking gentlemen.

On every side was a great murmur. The municipal guards passed to and fro. A bell, hung from a post covered with figures, began ringing. Five horses appeared, and the spectators in the galleries resumed their seats.

Meanwhile, big clouds descended with their winding outlines on the tops of the elms opposite. Rosanette was afraid that it would rain.

"I have umbrellas," said Frederick, "and everything that we need for our diversion," he added, lifting up the chest, in which there was a stock of provisions in a basket.

"Bravo! we understand each other!"

"And we'll understand each other still better, shall we not?"

"That may be," she said, colouring.

A red flag was lowered. Then five jockeys bent over the bristling manes, and off they went. At first they pressed close to one another in a single mass; this presently stretched out and became cut up. The jockey in the yellow jacket came near falling in the middle of the first round; for a long time it was uncertain whether Filly or Tibi should take the lead; then Tom Thumb shot in front. But Clubstick, who had been in the rear since the start, came up with the others and outstripped them, reaching the winning-post first, and beating Sir Charles by two lengths. It was a surprise. There was a shout of applause; the planks shook with the stamping of feet.

"This is amusing," said the Maréchale. "I love you, darling!"

Frederick no longer doubted that his happiness was secure. Rosanette's words were a confirmation of it.

A hundred paces away from him, in a four-wheeled cabriolet, a lady could be seen. She stretched her head out of the carriage-door, and then quickly drew it in again. This movement was repeated several times. Frederick could not distinguish her face. He had a strong suspicion, however, that it was Madame Arnoux. And yet this seemed impossible! Why should she be there?

He stepped out of his own vehicle on the pretence of strolling into the weighing-room.

"You are not very gallant!" said Rosanette.

He paid no heed to her, and went on. The four-wheeled cabriolet, turning back, broke into a trot.

Frederick at the same moment found himself button-holed by Cisy.

"Good-morrow, my dear boy! how are you getting on? Hussonnet is over there! Don't you hear me?"

Frederick tried to shake him off in order to get up with the four-wheeled cabriolet. The Maréchale beckoned to him to come to her. Cisy saw her, and obstinately persisted in wishing her good-day.

Since the termination of the regular period of mourning for his grandmother, he had realised his ideal, succeeded in "getting the proper stamp." A Scotch plaid waistcoat, a short coat, large bows over the pumps, and an entrance-card stuck in the ribbon of his hat; nothing, in fact, was wanting to produce what he described as *chic*—a *chic* characterised by Anglomania and the swagger of the musketeer. Leaning against the Maréchale's carriage-door on one elbow, he kept talking nonsense, with the handle of his walking-stick in his mouth, his legs wide apart, and his back stretched out. Frederick, standing beside him, smoked, while endeavouring to make out what had become of the cabriolet.

The bell having rung, Cisy took himself off, to the great delight of Rosanette, who said he bored her to death.

The second race had nothing special about it; neither had the third, save that a man was thrown over the shaft of a cart while it was taking place. The fourth, in which eight horses contested the City Stakes, was more interesting.

The spectators in the gallery had clambered to the top of their seats. The others, standing up in the vehicles, followed with opera-glasses in their hands the movements of the jockeys. They started out like red, yellow, white, or blue spots across the entire space occupied by the crowd that had gathered around the ring of the hippodrome. At a distance, their speed did not appear to be very great; at the opposite side of the Champ de Mars, they seemed even to be slackening their pace, and to be merely slipping along in such a way that the horses' bellies touched the ground without their outstretched legs bending at all. But, coming back at a more rapid stride, they looked bigger; they cut the air in their wild gallop. The sun's rays quivered; pebbles went flying about under their hoofs. The wind, blowing out the jockeys' jackets, made them flutter like veils. Each of them lashed the animal he rode with great blows of his whip to spur him on to the goal. One swept away the figures, another was hoisted off his saddle, and, in the midst of a burst of applause, the victorious horse dragged his feet to the weighing-room, all covered with sweat, his knees stiffened, his neck and shoulders bent down, while his rider, looking as if he were expiring in his saddle, clung to the animal's flanks.

The final start was retarded by a dispute which had arisen. The crowd, getting tired, began to scatter. Groups of men were chatting at the lower end of each gallery. The talk was of a free-and-easy description. Some fashionable ladies left, scandalised by seeing fast women in their immediate vicinity.

There were also some ladies who appeared at public balls, some light-comedy actresses of the boulevards, and it was not the best-looking that got the most appreciation. Madame de Remoussat, who had become fashionable by means of a notorious trial in which she figured, sat enthroned on the seat of a brake in company with some Americans; and Thérèse Bachelu, with her look of a Gothic virgin, filled with her dozen fur-belows the interior of a trap which had, in place of an apron, a flower-stand filled with roses. The Maréchale was jealous of these magnificent displays. In order to attract attention, she began to make vehement gestures and speak in a very loud voice.

Gentlemen, recognising her, bowed. She returned their salutations while telling Frederick their names. They were all counts, viscounts, dukes, and marquises, and he carried a high head, for in all eyes he could read a certain respect for his good fortune.

Cisy had a no less happy air in the midst of the circle of mature men that surrounded him. Their faces wore cynical smiles above their cravats, as if they were laughing at him. At length he gave a tap to the hand of the oldest of them, and made his way toward the Maréchale.

She was eating, with an affectation of gluttony, a slice of *pâté de foie gras*. Frederick, in order to please her, followed her example, with a bottle of wine on his knees.

The four-wheeled cabriolet reappeared. It *was* Madame Arnoux! Her face was startlingly pale.

"Give me some champagne," said Rosanette.

And, lifting up her glass, full to the brim, as high as possible, she exclaimed: "Look over there! See my protector's wife, one of the virtuous women!"

There was a great burst of laughter all round her; and the cabriolet disappeared from view. Frederick tugged impatiently at her dress, and was on the point of flying into a passion. But Cisy was there, in the same attitude as before, and, with increased assurance, he invited Rosanette to dine with him that very evening.

"Impossible!" she replied; "we're going together to the Café Anglais."

Frederick, as if he had heard nothing, kept silent; and Cisy quitted the Maréchale with a look of disappointment on his face.

While he had been talking to her at the right-hand door of the carriage, Hussonnet appeared at the opposite side, and, catching the words "Café Anglais":

"It's a nice establishment; suppose we have a bite there, eh?"

"Just as you like," said Frederick, who, sunk in the corner of the berlin, was gazing at the horizon as the four-wheeled cabriolet vanished from his sight, feeling that an irreparable thing had happened, and his great love ended. And the other woman was there beside him, the gay and easy love! But, worn out, full of conflicting desires, and no longer even knowing what he wanted, he was possessed by a feeling of infinite sadness, a longing to die.

The crush of vehicles increased, and Hussonnet got lost in it.

"Well! so much the better!" said Frederick.

"We like to be alone better—don't we?" said the Maréchale, as she placed her hand in his.

Then there swept past him with a glitter of copper and steel a magnificent landau to which were yoked four horses driven in the Daumont style by two jockeys in velvet vests with gold fringes. Madame Dambreuse was by her husband's side, and Martinon was on the seat facing them. All three gazed at Frederick in astonishment.

"They have recognised me!" said he to himself.

Rosanette wished to stop in order to get a better view of the people driving away from the course. Madame Arnoux might again make her appearance! He called out to the postilion:

"Go on! go on! forward!" And the berlin dashed toward the Champs-Elysées in the midst of the other vehicles—calashes, britzkas, wurths, tandems, tilburies, dog-carts, tilted carts with leather curtains, in which workmen in a jovial mood were singing, or one-horse chaises driven by fathers of families.

Frederick and Rosanette did not say a word to each other, feeling a sort of dizziness at seeing all these wheels continually revolving close to them.

At times, the rows of carriages, too closely pressed together, stopped all at the same time in several lines. Then they remained side by side, and their occupants scanned one another. Over the sides of panels adorned with coat-of-arms indifferent glances were cast on the crowd. Eyes full of envy gleamed from the interiors of hackney-coaches. Depreciatory smiles responded to the haughty manner in the carriage of a head. Mouths gaping wide expressed idiotic admiration; and, here and there, some lounger, in the middle of the road, jumped back with a bound, in order to avoid a rider who had been galloping through the midst of the vehicles, and had succeeded in getting away from them. Then, everything set itself in motion once more; the coachmen let go the reins, and lowered their long whips; the horses, excited, shook their curb-chains, and flung foam around them; and the cruppers and the harness getting moist, were smoking with the watery evaporation, through which struggled the rays of the sinking sun. Passing under the Arc de Triomphe, there stretched out at the height of a man a reddish light, which shed a glittering lustre on the naves of the wheels, the handles of the carriage-doors, the ends of the shafts, and the rings of the carriage-beds; and on the two sides of the great avenue—like a river in which manes, garments, and human heads were undulating—the trees, all glittering with rain, rose up like two green walls. The blue of the sky overhead, reappearing in certain places, had the soft hue of satin.

Then Frederick recalled the days, already far distant, when he yearned for the inexpressible happiness of finding himself in one of these carriages by the side of one of these women. He had attained to this bliss, and yet he was not thereby one jot the happier.

When they reached the Chinese Baths, as there were holes in the pavement, the berlin slackened its pace. A man in a hazel-coloured paletot was walking on the edge of the footpath. A splash, spurting out from under the springs, showed itself on his back. The man turned round in a rage. Frederick grew pale; it was Deslauriers.

At the door of the Café Anglais he dismissed the carriage. Rosanette had gone in before him while he was paying the postilion.

He found her subsequently on the stairs chatting with a gentleman. Frederick took her arm; but in the lobby a second gentleman stopped her.

"Go on," said she; "I am at your service."

And he entered the private room alone. Through the two open windows people could be seen at the casements of the other houses opposite. Large watery masses were glistening on the pavement as it began to dry, and a magnolia, on the side of a balcony, shed a perfume through the apartment. This fragrance and freshness had a relaxing effect on his nerves. He sank down on the red divan underneath the glass.

The Maréchale entered the room, and, kissing him on the forehead:

"Poor pet! something is annoying you!"

"Perhaps so," was his reply.

"You are not alone; take heart!"—which was as much as to say: "Let us each forget our own troubles in a bliss which we shall enjoy in common."

Then she placed the petal of a flower between her lips and extended it toward him so that he might peck at it. This movement, full of grace and of almost voluptuous gentleness, had a softening effect on Frederick.

"Why do you give me pain?" said he, thinking of Madame Arnoux.

"I give you pain?"

And, standing before him, she gazed at him with her lashes drawn close together and her two hands resting on his shoulders.

All his virtue, all his rancour gave way before the utter weakness of his will.

He continued:

"Because you won't love me," and he took her on his knees.

She yielded to him. He pressed his two hands round her waist. The crackling sound of her silk dress inflamed him.

"Where are they?" said Hussonnet's voice in the lobby outside.

The Maréchale rose abruptly, and walked across to the other side of the room, where she sat down with her back to the door.

She ordered oysters, and they seated themselves at table.

Hussonnet was not amusing. By dint of writing every day on all sorts of subjects, reading many newspapers, listening to a great number of discussions, and uttering paradoxes for the purpose of dazzling people, he had in the end lost the exact idea of things, deluding himself with his own feeble fireworks. The embarrassments of a life which had formerly been frivolous, but which was now full of difficulty, kept him in a state of perpetual agitation; and his impotency, which he did not wish to avow, rendered him snappish and sarcastic. Referring to a new ballet entitled *Ozaï,* he gave a thorough blowing-up to the dancing, and then, when the opera was in question, he attacked the Italians, now replaced by a company of Spanish actors.

Frederick was quite bored. In an outburst of impatience he pushed his foot under the table, and pressed it on one of the little dogs.

Thereupon both animals began barking in a horrible fashion.

"You ought to have them sent home!" said he, abruptly.

Rosanette did not know anyone to whom she could intrust them.

Then, he turned round to the Bohemian:

"Look here, Hussonnet; sacrifice yourself!"

"Certainly, my boy!"

Hussonnet set off, without even requiring to have an appeal made to him.

How could they repay him for his kindness? Frederick did not bestow a thought on it. He was beginning to rejoice at finding himself alone with her, when a waiter entered.

"Madame, somebody is asking for you!"

"What! again?"

"However, I must see who it is," said Rosanette.

He was thirsting for her; he wanted her. This disappearance seemed to him an act of prevarication, almost a piece of rudeness. What, then, did she mean? Was it not enough to have insulted Madame Arnoux? So much for the latter, all the same! Now he hated all women; and he felt the tears choking him, for his love had been misunderstood and his desire eluded.

The Maréchale returned, and presented Cisy.

"I have invited Monsieur. I have done right, have I not?"

"Oh! certainly."

Frederick, with the smile of a criminal about to be executed, requested the gentleman to take a seat.

The Maréchale began to run her eye over the bill of fare, stopping at every fantastic name.

"Suppose we eat a turban of rabbits *à la Richelieu* and a pudding *à la d'Orléans?*"

"Oh! not Orléans, pray!" exclaimed Cisy, who was a Legitimist, and thought of making a pun.

"Would you prefer a turbot *à la Chambord?*" she next inquired.

Frederick was disgusted with this display of politeness.

The Maréchale finally decided to order a simple *filet* of beef cut up into steaks, some crayfishes, truffles, a pine-apple salad, and vanilla ices.

"We'll see what next. That will do for the present! Ah! I was forgetting! Bring me a sausage!—not with garlic!"

And she called the waiter "young man," struck her glass with her knife, and flung up the crumbs of her bread to the ceiling. She wished to have some Burgundy immediately.

"It is not taken in the beginning," said Frederick.

It was sometimes done, according to the Vicomte.

"Oh! no. Never!"

"Yes, indeed; I assure you!"

"Ha! you see!"

The look with which she accompanied these words meant: "This is a rich man—pay attention to what he says!"

Meantime, the door was opening every moment; the waiters kept shouting; and on an infernal piano in the adjoining room some one was strumming a waltz. The races led to a discussion about horsemanship and the two rival systems. Cisy was upholding Baucher and Frederick the Comte d'Aure when Rosanette shrugged her shoulders:

"Enough—my God!—he is a better judge of these things than you are—come now!"

She kept nibbling at a pomegranate, with her elbow resting on the table. The wax-candles of the candelabrum in front of her flickered in the wind. This white light penetrated her skin with mother-of-pearl tones, gave a pink hue to her lids, and made her eyeballs glitter. The red colour of the fruit blended with the purple of her lips; her thin nostrils dilated; and there was about her entire person an air of insolence, intoxication, and recklessness that exasperated Frederick, and yet filled his heart with wild desires.

She asked, in a calm voice, who owned that big landau with chestnut-coloured livery.

Cisy replied that it was "the Comtesse Dambreuse."

"They're very rich—aren't they?"

"Oh! very rich! although Madame Dambreuse, who was merely a Mademoiselle Boutron and the daughter of a prefect, had a very modest fortune."

Her husband, on the other hand, must have inherited several estates—Cisy enumerated them: as he visited the Dambreuses, he knew their family history.

Frederick, in order to make himself disagreeable to the other, took a pleasure in contradicting him. He maintained that Madame Dambreuse's maiden name was De Boutron, which proved that she was of noble family.

"No matter! I'd like to have her equipage!" said the Maréchale, throwing herself back on the armchair.

And the sleeve of her dress, slipping up a little, discovered on her left wrist a bracelet adorned with three opals.

Frederick noticed it.

"Look here! why—"

All three looked into one another's faces, and reddened.

The door was cautiously half-opened; the brim of a hat could be seen, and then Hussonnet's profile appeared.

"Pray excuse me if I disturb the lovers!"

Then he stopped, astonished at seeing Cisy, who had taken his seat.

Another cover was brought; and, as he was very hungry, he snatched up at random from what remained of the dinner, some meat which was in a dish, fruit out of a basket, and drank with one hand while he helped himself with the other, all the time telling them the result of his mission. The two bow-wows had been taken home. Nothing fresh at the house. He had found the cook in the company of a soldier—a fictitious story which he had invented on the way for the sake of effect.

The Maréchale took down her cloak from the window-screw. Frederick rushed toward the bell, calling out to the waiter, who was some distance away:

"A carriage!"

"I have one of my own," said Cisy.

"But, Monsieur!"

"Nevertheless, Monsieur!"

And they looked into each other's eyes, both pale and their hands trembling.

At last, the Maréchale took Cisy's arm, and pointing toward the Bohemian seated at the table:

"Pray mind him! He's choking himself. I wouldn't like his devotion to my pugs to be the cause of his death."

The door closed behind them.

"Well?" said Hussonnet.

"Well, what?"

"I thought—"

"What did you think?"

"Were you not—?"

He completed the sentence with a gesture.

"Oh! no—never in all my life!"

Hussonnet did not press the matter further.

He had a motive in inviting himself to dinner. His journal—which was no longer called *L'Art,* but *Le Flambart,* with this epigraph, "Gunners, to your cannons!"—not being at all in a flourishing condition, he had a mind to change it into a weekly review, conducted by himself, without any assistance from Deslauriers. He again referred to the old project and explained his latest plan.

Frederick, probably not understanding what he was talking about, replied with some vague words. Hussonnet snatched up several cigars from the tables, said "Good-bye, old chap," and disappeared.

Frederick called for the bill. It had a long list of items; and the waiter, with his napkin under his arm, was waiting to be paid, when another, a sallow-faced individual, who resembled Martinon, came and said to him:

"Excuse me; they forgot at the bar to add in the charge for the cab."

"What cab?"

"The cab the gentleman took a short time ago for the little dogs."

The waiter looked grave, as if he pitied the poor young man. Frederick would have liked to box the fellow's ears. He gave the waiter the twenty francs' change as a *pour-boire*.

The man bowed low, murmuring, "Thanks, Monseigneur!"

CHAPTER XI

A DUEL

THE WHOLE of the next day Frederick brooded over his humiliation. He blamed himself for not having slapped Cisy in the face. As for the Maréchale, he swore never to see her again. Others as good-looking could be easily found; and, as money was necessary in order to possess these women, he would speculate on the Bourse with the purchase-money of his farm. He would get rich; he would crush the Maréchale and everyone else with his wealth. When the evening had come, he was surprised at not having thought of Madame Arnoux.

"So much the better. What's the use of it?"

Two days later, at eight o'clock, Pellerin came to pay him a visit. He began by expressing his admiration of the furniture and talked in a wheedling tone. Then, abruptly:

"You were at the races on Sunday?"

"Yes, alas!"

Thereupon the painter criticised the anatomy of the English horses, and praised the horses of Gericourt and the Parthenon.

"Rosanette was with you?"

And he artfully proceeded to speak in flattering terms about her.

Frederick's icy manner put him a little out of countenance.

He did not know how to introduce the question of her portrait. His first idea had been to do it in the style of Titian. But gradually the varied colouring of his model had bewitched him; he had gone on boldly with the work, heaping up paste on paste and light on light. Rosanette, at first, was enchanted. Her appointments with Delmar interrupted the sittings, and left Pellerin all the time to get bedazzled. Then, as his admiration began to subside, he asked himself whether the picture might not be on a larger scale. He had gone to have another look at the Titians, realised how the great artist had filled in his portraits with such finish, and saw wherein his own deficiencies lay; and then he began to go over the outlines again in the most simple fashion. After that, he sought, by scraping them off, to lose, or to mingle, all the tones of the head and those of the background; the face assumed consistency and the shades vigour—the whole work had a look of greater firmness. At length the Maréchale came back again. She indulged in some hostile criticisms. The painter naturally persevered in his own course. After getting into a violent passion at her silliness, he thought to himself that, after all, perhaps she was right. Then began an era of doubts, twinges of reflection which brought about cramps in the stomach, insomnia, feverishness and disgust with himself. He had the courage to make some retouchings, but without much heart, and with a feeling that his work was bad.

He complained merely of having been refused a place in the Salon; then he reproached Frederick for not having come to see the Maréchale's portrait.

"What do I care about the Maréchale?"

Such an expression of indifference emboldened the artist.

"Would you believe that this brute has no interest in the thing any longer?"

What he did not mention was that he had asked her for a thousand crowns. Now the Maréchale did not bother herself about ascertaining who was going to pay, and, preferring to screw money out of Arnoux for more urgent requirements, she had not even spoken to him on the subject.

"Well, and Arnoux?"

She had thrown it on him. The ex-picture-dealer wished to have nothing to do with the portrait.

"He maintains that it belongs to Rosanette."

"In fact, it is hers."

"How is that? 'Tis she that sent me to you," was Pellerin's answer.

If he had been thinking of the excellence of his work, he would not have dreamed perhaps of making capital out of it. But a sum—and a big sum—would be an effective reply to the critics, and would strengthen his own position. Finally, to get rid of his importunities, Frederick courteously inquired his terms.

The extravagant figure named by Pellerin quite took away his breath, and he replied:

"Oh! no—no!"

"You, however, are her lover—you gave me the order!"

"Excuse me, I was only an agent."

"But I can't remain with this on my hands!"

The artist lost his temper.

"Ha! I didn't know you were so covetous!"

"Nor I that you were so stingy! I wish you good morning!"

He had just gone when Sénécal made his appearance.

Frederick was in a state of great agitation.

"What's the matter?"

Sénécal told this story:

"On Saturday, at nine o'clock, Madame Arnoux received a letter which summoned her back to Paris. As there happened to be nobody in the place at the time to go to Creil for a vehicle, she asked me to attend to it. I refused, for this was no part of my duties. She left, and came back on Sunday evening. Yesterday morning, Arnoux came down to the works. The girl from Bordeaux made a complaint to him. I don't know what passed between them; but he took off, before everyone, the fine I had imposed on her. Some sharp words passed between us. In short, he closed accounts with me, and here I am!"

Then, with a pause between every word:

"Furthermore, I am not sorry. I have done my duty. No matter—you were the cause of it."

"In what way?" exclaimed Frederick, alarmed lest Sénécal might have guessed his secret.

Sénécal had not, however, guessed anything about it, for he replied:

"I mean that but for you I might have done better."

Frederick was seized with a kind of remorse.

"In what way can I help you now?"

Sénécal wanted some employment, a situation.

"That is an easy thing for you to manage. You know many people of good position, Monsieur Dambreuse amongst others; at least, so Deslauriers told me."

This allusion to Deslauriers was by no means agreeable to his friend. He scarcely cared to call on the Dambreuses again after his unfortunate meeting with them in the Champ de Mars.

"I am not on sufficiently intimate terms with them to recommend anyone."

The democrat bore this refusal stoically, and after a minute's silence:

"All this, I am sure, is due to the girl from Bordeaux, and to your Madame Arnoux."

This "your" had the effect of killing the slight modicum of regard he entertained for Sénécal. Nevertheless, he stretched out his hand toward the key of his escritoire through delicacy.

Sénécal anticipated him:

"Thanks!"

Then, forgetting his own troubles, he talked about the affairs of the nation, the crosses of the Legion of Honour wasted at the Royal Fête, the rumour of a change of ministry, the Drouillard case and the Bénier case—scandals of the day—declaimed against the middle class, and predicted a revolution.

His eyes were attracted by a Japanese dagger hanging on the wall. He took hold of it; then he flung it on the sofa with an air of disgust.

"Well, then! good-bye! I must go to Nôtre Dame de Lorette."

"Hold on! Why?"

"The anniversary service for Godefroy Cavaignac is taking place there to-day. He died at work—that man! But all is not over. Who knows?"

And Sénécal, with a show of fortitude, put out his hand:

"Perhaps we shall never meet again! Good-bye!"

This "good-bye," repeated several times, his knitted brows as he gazed at the dagger, his resignation, and the solemnity of his manner, above all, plunged Frederick into a thoughtful mood, but very soon he forgot about Sénécal.

During the same week, his notary at Havre sent him the sum realised by the sale of his farm—one hundred and seventy-four thousand francs. He divided it into two portions, invested half in the Funds, and brought the second half to a stock-broker to take his chance of making money by it on the Bourse.

He dined at fashionable taverns, went to the theatres, and was trying to amuse himself as best he could, when Hussonnet addressed a letter to him announcing in a gay fashion that the Maréchale had got rid of Cisy the very day after the races. Frederick was delighted at this intelligence, without troubling to ascertain what the Bohemian's motive was in giving him the information.

It so happened that he met Cisy, three days later. That aristocratic young gentleman kept his countenance, and even invited Frederick to dine on the following Wednesday.

On the morning of that day, the latter received a notification from a process-server, in which M. Charles Jean Baptiste Oudry informed him that by the terms of a legal judgment he had become the purchaser of a property situated at Belleville, belonging to M. Jacques Arnoux, and that he was ready to pay the two hundred and twenty-three thousand for which it had been sold. But, as it appeared by the same decree that the amount of the mortgages with which the estate was encumbered exceeded the purchase-money, Frederick's claim would in consequence be completely forfeited.

The entire mischief arose from not having renewed the registration of the mortgage within the proper time. Arnoux had undertaken to attend to this matter himself, and had then forgotten all about it. Frederick was furious, and when the young man's anger had passed off, he said to himself:

"Well, afterward—what? If this can save him, so much the better. It won't kill me! Let us think no more about it!"

But, while moving about his papers on the table, he came across Hussonnet's letter, and saw the postscript, which he had not at first noticed. The Bohemian wanted just five thousand francs to give the journal a start.

"Ah! this fellow is worrying me to death!"

And he sent a curt answer, unceremoniously refusing the application. After that, he dressed himself and went to the Maison d'Or.

Cisy introduced his guests, beginning with the most important of them, a big, white-haired gentleman.

"The Marquis Gilbert des Aulnays, my godfather. Monsieur Anselme de Forchambeaux," he said next—(a thin, fair-haired young man, already bald); then, pointing toward a simple-mannered man of forty: "Joseph Boffreu, my cousin; and here is my old tutor, Monsieur Vezou"—a person who seemed a mixture of a ploughman and a seminarist, with large whiskers and a long frock-coat fastened at the end by a single button, so that it fell over his chest like a shawl.

Cisy was awaiting some one else—the Baron de Comaing, who "might perhaps come, but it was not certain." He left the room every minute, and appeared to be in a restless frame of mind. Finally, at eight o'clock, they proceeded toward an apartment splendidly lighted up and much more spacious than the number of guests required. Cisy had selected it so as to make a display.

A vermilion épergne laden with flowers and fruit occupied the centre of the table, which was covered with silver dishes, after the old French fashion; glass bowls full of salt meats and spices formed a border all around. Jars of iced red wine stood at regular distances from one another. Five glasses of different sizes were before each plate, with other things of which the use could not be divined—a thousand dinner utensils of an ingenious description. For the first course alone, there was a sturgeon's jowl moistened with champagne, a Yorkshire ham with tokay, thrushes with sauce, roast quail, a béchamel vol-au-vent, a stew of red-legged partridges; at both ends of all this were fringes of potatoes mingled with truffles. The apartment was illuminated by a lustre and some girandoles, and it was hung with red damask curtains.

Four men-servants in black coats stood behind the armchairs, which were upholstered in morocco. At this sight the guests uttered an exclamation—the tutor more emphatically than the rest.

"Upon my word, our host has indulged in a foolishly lavish display of luxury. It is altogether too beautiful!"

"Is that so?" said the Vicomte de Cisy; "Come on, then!"

And, as they were swallowing the first spoonful:

"Well, my dear old friend Aulnays, have you been to the Palais-Royal to see *Père et Portier?*"

"You know well that I have no time to go!" replied the Marquis.

His mornings were occupied with a course of arboriculture, his evenings were spent at the Agricultural Club, and all his afternoons were engaged by a study of the implements of husbandry in manufactories. As he resided at Saintonge for three fourths of the year, he took advantage of his visits to the capital to get new information; and his large-brimmed hat, which lay on a side-table, was crammed with pamphlets.

But Cisy, observing that M. de Forchambeaux refused wine:

"Go on, damn it, drink! You're not in good form for your last bachelor's meal!"

At this remark all bowed and congratulated him.

"And the young lady," said the tutor, "is doubtless charming?"

"Faith, she is!" exclaimed Cisy. "No matter, he is making a great mistake; marriage is such a stupid thing!"

"You talk in a thoughtless fashion, my friend!" returned Monsieur des Aulnays, while tears gathered in his eyes at the recollection of his own dead wife.

And Forchambeaux repeated several times in succession:

"It will sometimes be your own case—it will be your own case!"

Cisy protested. He preferred to enjoy himself—to "live in the free-and-easy style of the Regency days." He hoped to learn the shoe-trick, in order to visit the thieves' taverns of the city, like Rodolphe in the *Mysteries of Paris*; he drew out of his pocket a dirty clay pipe, abused the servants, and drank freely; then, in order to create a good impression, he disparaged all the dishes. He even sent away the truffles; and the tutor, who was exceedingly fond of them, said through servility:

"These are not as good as your grandmother's snow-white eggs."

Then he began to chat with the person sitting next to him, the agriculturist, who found many advantages from his sojourn in the country, if it were only to be able to bring up his daughters with simple tastes. The tutor approved of his ideas and toadied to him, supposing that this gentleman possessed influence over his former pupil, whose man of business he was anxious to become.

Frederick had come filled with hostility to Cisy; but the young aristocrat's idiocy disarmed him. However, as the other's gestures, face, and entire person brought back to his mind the dinner at the Café Anglais, he got more and more irritated; and he lent his ears to the complimentary remarks made in a low tone by Joseph, the cousin, a fine young fellow without any money, who was a lover of the chase and a University prizeman. Cisy, for the sake of a laugh, called him a "catcher"* several times; then suddenly:

"Ha! here comes the Baron!"

Voleur. May be translated as "hunter" or "thief," hence the joke.—TRANSLATOR.

At that moment, there entered a jovial blade of thirty, with somewhat rough-looking features and active limbs, wearing his hat over his ear and displaying a flower in his button-hole. He was the Vicomte's ideal. The young aristocrat was delighted to see him; and stimulated by his presence, he even attempted a pun; for he said, as they passed a fine, roasted heath-cock:

"There's the best of La Bruyère's characters!"*

After that, he put a number of questions to M. de Comaing about persons unknown to society; then, as if an idea had suddenly seized him:

"Tell me, pray! have you thought about me?"

The other shrugged his shoulders:

"You are not old enough, my little man. It is impossible!"

Cisy had begged of the Baron to get him admitted into his club. But the other having, no doubt, taken pity on his vanity:

"Ha! I was forgetting! A thousand congratulations on having won your bet, my dear fellow!"

"What bet?"

"The bet you made at the races to effect an entrance the same evening into that lady's house."

Frederick felt as if he had had a lash with a whip. He was speedily appeased by the expression of utter confusion in Cisy's face.

In fact, the Maréchale, next morning, was filled with regret when Arnoux, her first lover, her good friend, presented himself that very day. Both gave the Vicomte to understand that he was in the way, and kicked him out without much ceremony.

He pretended not to have heard the remark.

The Baron went on:

"What has become of her, this fine Rose? Is she as charming as ever?" showing by his manner that he had been on terms of intimacy with her.

Frederick was chagrined by the discovery.

"There's nothing to blush at," said the Baron, pursuing the topic, "'tis a good thing!"

Cisy smacked his tongue.

"Whew! not so good!"

"Ha!"

"Oh, dear, yes! In the first place, I found her nothing extraordinary, and then, you pick up that sort as often as you please; in fact, she is for sale!"

"Not for everyone!" remarked Frederick, with some bitterness.

"He thinks that he is different from the others," was Cisy's comment. "What a good joke!"

And a laugh ran round the table.

**Coq de bruyère means a heath-cock or grouse; hence the pun on the name of La Bruyère, author of *Caractères*.—EDITOR.

Frederick felt as if the palpitations of his heart would suffocate him. He swallowed two glasses of water one after the other.

But the Baron had preserved a lively recollection of Rosanette.

"Is she still interested in a fellow in trade named Arnoux?"

"I haven't the faintest idea," said Cisy, "I don't know the gentleman!"

Nevertheless, he suggested that he believed Arnoux was a sort of swindler.

"A moment!" exclaimed Frederick.

"Oh, there is no doubt about it! Legal proceedings have been taken against him."

"That is not true!"

Frederick began to defend Arnoux, vouched for his honesty, ended by convincing himself of it, and concocted figures and proofs. The Vicomte, full of spite, and tipsy in addition, persisted in his assertions, so that Frederick said to him gravely:

"Is the object of this to give offence to me, Monsieur?"

And he looked Cisy full in the face, with eyeballs as red as his cigar.

"Oh! not at all. I acknowledge that he possesses something very nice—his wife."

"Do you know her?"

"Faith, I do! Sophie Arnoux; everyone knows her."

"You mean to tell me that?"

Cisy, who had staggered to his feet, hiccoughed:

"Everyone—knows—her."

"Hold your tongue. It is not with women of her class you keep company!"

"I—flatter myself—it is."

Frederick flung a plate at his face. It passed like a flash of lightning over the table, knocked down two bottles, demolished a fruit-dish, and breaking into three pieces, by knocking against the épergne, hit the Vicomte in the stomach.

All the other guests arose to hold him back. He struggled and shrieked, possessed by a kind of frenzy.

M. des Aulnays kept repeating:

"Come, be calm, my dear boy!"

"Why, this is awful!" shouted the tutor.

Forchambeaux, livid as a plum, was trembling. Joseph indulged in repeated outbursts of laughter. The attendants sponged out the traces of the wine, and gathered up the remains of the dinner from the floor; and the Baron shut the window, for the uproar, in spite of the noise of carriage-wheels, could be heard on the boulevard.

As all present at the moment the plate had been flung had been talking at the same time, it was impossible to discover the cause of the attack—whether it was on account of Arnoux, Madame Arnoux, Rosanette, or somebody else. One thing only they were certain of, that Frederick had acted with indescribable brutality. On his part, he refused positively to express the slightest regret for what he had done.

M. des Aulnays tried to soften him. Cousin Joseph, the tutor, and Forchambeaux himself joined in the effort. The Baron, all this time, was encouraging Cisy, who, yielding to nervous weakness, began to shed tears.

Frederick, on the contrary, was getting more and more angry, and they would have remained there till daybreak if the Baron had not said:

"The Vicomte, Monsieur, will send his seconds to call on you to-morrow."

"Your hour?"

"Twelve, if it suits you."

"Perfectly, Monsieur."

Frederick, as soon as he was in the open air, drew a deep breath. He had been keeping his feelings too long under restraint; he had satisfied them at last. He felt, so to speak, the pride of virility, a superabundance of energy within him which intoxicated him. He required two seconds. The first person he thought of for the purpose was Regimbart, and he immediately directed his steps toward the Rue Saint-Denis. The shop-front was closed, but a light shone through a pane of glass over the door. It opened and he went in, stooping very low as he passed under the penthouse.

A candle at the side of the bar lighted up the deserted smoking-room. All the stools, with their feet in the air, were piled on the table. The master and mistress, with their waiter, were at supper in a corner near the kitchen; and Regimbart, with his hat on his head, was sharing their meal, and even disturbed the waiter, who was compelled every moment to turn aside a little. Frederick, having briefly explained the matter, asked Regimbart to assist him. The Citizen at first made no reply. He rolled his eyes about, looked as if he were plunged in reflection, took several strides around the room, and at last said:

"Yes, by all means!" and a homicidal smile smoothed his brow when he learned that the adversary was a nobleman.

"Make your mind easy; we'll rout him with flying colours! In the first place, with the sword—"

"But perhaps," broke in Frederick, "I have not the right."

"I tell you 'tis necessary to take the sword," the Citizen replied roughly. "Do you know how to make passes?"

"A little."

"Oh! a little. That is the way with you all; and yet you have a mania for committing assaults. What does the fencing-school teach? Listen to me: keep a good distance off, always confining yourself in circles, and parry—parry as you retire; that is permitted. Tire him out. Then boldly make a lunge on him! and, above all, no malice, no strokes of the La Fougère kind. No! a simple one-two, and some disengagements. Look here! do you see? while you turn your wrist as if opening a lock. Père Vauthier, give me your cane. Ha! that will do. Now, my friends, observe me carefully."

He grasped the rod which was used for lighting the gas, rounded his left arm, bent his right, and began to make thrusts against the partition. He stamped with his foot, got animated, and pretended to be encountering difficulties, while he exclaimed: "Are you there? Is that it? Are you there?" and his enormous silhouette projected itself on the wall while his hat apparently touched the ceiling. The owner of the café shouted from time to time: "Bravo! very good!" His wife, though a little unnerved, was likewise filled with admiration; and Théodore, who had been in the army, remained riveted to the spot with amazement, the fact being that he regarded M. Regimbart with an enthusiastic degree of hero-worship.

Next morning, at an early hour, Frederick hurried to the establishment in which Dussardier was employed. After having passed through a succession of departments all full of clothing-materials, either piled on the shelves or lying on tables, while here and there shawls were fixed on wooden racks shaped like toadstools, he saw the young man, in a sort of railed cage, surrounded by account-books, and standing in front of a desk at which he was writing. The honest fellow left his work.

The seconds arrived before twelve o'clock.

Frederick, as a matter of good taste, was absent at the conference.

The Baron and M. Joseph declared that they would be satisfied with the simplest apology. But Regimbart's principle being never to yield, and his contention being that Arnoux's honour should be vindicated (Frederick had not spoken to him about anything else), he asked that the Vicomte should apologise. M. de Comaing was indignant at this presumption. The Citizen would not give way an inch. As all conciliation proved impracticable, there was nothing for it but to fight.

Other difficulties arose, for the choice of weapons lay with Cisy, as the person to whom the insult had been offered. But Regimbart maintained that by sending the challenge he had constituted himself the offending party. His seconds loudly protested that a buffet was the most cruel of offences. The Citizen carped at the words, pointing out that a buffet was not a blow. Finally, they decided to take the advice of a military man; and the four seconds went off to consult the officers in some of the barracks.

They drew up at the barracks on the Quai d'Orsay. M. de Comaing, having accosted two captains, explained to them the question in dispute.

The captains did not understand a word of what he was saying, owing to the confusion caused by the Citizen's incidental remarks. In short, they advised the gentlemen who consulted them to draw up a minute of the proceedings; after which they would give their decision. Thereupon,

they repaired to a café; where they, in order to do things with more cir-
cumspection, referred to Cisy as H, and to Frederick as K.

Then they returned to the barracks. The officers were out. They reappeared, and declared that the choice of arms manifestly belonged to H.

They all returned to Cisy's abode. Regimbart and Dussardier remained
on the footpath outside.

The Vicomte, when he was informed of the solution of the case, was
seized with such extreme agitation that they had to repeat for him several times the decision of the officers; and, when M. de Comaing came
to deal with Regimbart's contention, he murmured "Nevertheless," not
being very reluctant himself to yield to it. Then he sank into an armchair, and declared that he would not fight.

"Eh? What?" said the Baron. Then Cisy indulged in a confused flood
of mouthings. He wished to fight with firearms—to discharge a single
pistol at close quarters.

"Or else we will put arsenic into a glass, and draw lots to see who must
drink it. That's sometimes done."

The Baron, naturally rather impatient, addressed him harshly:

"These gentlemen are waiting for your answer. This is indecent, to put
it shortly. What weapons do you prefer? Come! is it the sword?"

The Vicomte gave an affirmative reply by merely nodding his head;
and it was arranged that the meeting should take place next morning at
seven o'clock sharp at the Maillot gate.

Dussardier, having to go back to his business, Regimbart went to
inform Frederick of the arrangement. He had been left all day without
any news, and his impatience was becoming intolerable.

"So much the better!" he exclaimed.

The Citizen was satisfied with his courageous deportment.

"Would you believe it? They wanted an apology from us. It was nothing—a mere word! But I knocked them off their beam-ends nicely. The
right thing to do, wasn't it?"

"Undoubtedly," said Frederick, thinking that it might have been better to choose another second.

Then, when he was alone, he repeated several times in a very loud tone:

"I am going to fight! Hold on, I am going to fight! 'Tis funny!"

And, as he walked up and down his room, while passing in front of the
mirror, he noticed that he was pale.

"Have I any reason to be afraid?"

He was seized with a feeling of intolerable misery at the prospect of
exhibiting fear on the ground.

"And yet, suppose I am killed? My father met his death thus. Yes, I
shall probably be killed!"

And, suddenly, his mother rose up before him in a black dress; incoherent images floated before his mind. His own cowardice exasperated him. A paroxysm of courage, a thirst for human blood, took possession of him. A battalion could not have made him retreat. When this feverish excitement had cooled down, he was overjoyed to feel that his nerves were perfectly steady. To divert his thoughts, he went to the opera, where a ballet was being performed. He listened to the music, looked at the *danseuses* through his opera-glass, and drank a glass of punch between the acts. But when he got home again, the sight of his study, of his furniture, in the midst of which he found himself for the last time, made him feel ready to swoon.

He went down to the garden. The stars were shining; he gazed up at them. The idea of fighting about a woman gave him a greater importance in his own eyes, and surrounded him with a halo of nobility. He retired in a tranquil frame of mind.

It was otherwise with Cisy. After the Baron's departure, Joseph had tried to revive his drooping spirits, and, as the Vicomte remained in the same dull mood:

"However, old boy, if you prefer to remain at home, I'll go and say so."

Cisy durst not answer "Certainly;" but he would have liked his cousin to do him this service without speaking to him about it.

He wished that Frederick would die during the night of an attack of apoplexy, or that a riot would break out so that next morning all the approaches to the Bois de Boulogne would be barricaded, or that some emergency might prevent one of the seconds from being present, for in the absence of seconds the duel would fall through. He felt a longing to save himself by taking an express train—no matter where. He regretted that he did not understand medicine so as to be able to take something which, without endangering his life, would cause it to be believed that he was dead. He finally wished to be ill in earnest.

In order to get advice and assistance from someone, he sent for M. des Aulnays. That worthy man had gone back to Saintonge on receiving a letter advising him of the illness of one of his daughters. This appeared an ominous circumstance to Cisy. Luckily, M. Vezou, his tutor, came to see him. Then he unbosomed himself.

"What am I to do? my God! what am I to do?" he wailed.

"If I were in your place, Monsieur, I should pay some strapping fellow from the market-place to go and give him a drubbing."

"He would still know who was responsible for it," replied Cisy.

And from time to time he uttered a groan; then:

"But is a man bound to fight a duel?"

"'Tis a relic of barbarism! What is a gentleman to do?"

Out of complaisance the pedagogue invited himself to dinner. His pupil did not eat anything, but, after the meal, took a short walk.

As they were passing a church, he said:

"Suppose we go in for a little while—to look?"

M. Vezou asked nothing better, and even offered him holy water.

It was the month of May. The altar was a mass of flowers; voices were chanting; the organ was resounding through the church. But he found it impossible to pray, as the pomps of religion inspired him merely with thoughts of funerals. He fancied that he could hear the murmurs of the *De Profundis*.

"Let us go away. I don't feel well."

They passed the whole night playing cards. The Vicomte endeavoured to lose in order to exorcise ill-luck, a thing which M. Vezou turned to his own advantage. At last, at the first streak of dawn, Cisy, who could bear up no longer, sank down on the green cloth, and was soon plunged in a sleep which was disturbed by unpleasant dreams.

If courage, however, consists in wishing to get the better of one's own weakness, the Vicomte was courageous, for in the presence of his seconds, who came to seek him, he stiffened himself up with all the strength he could command, vanity making him realise that to attempt to draw back now would ruin him. M. de Comaing congratulated him on his good appearance.

But the jolting of the cab and the heat of the morning sun made him languish. His energy weakened again. He could not even distinguish any longer where they were. The Baron amused himself by increasing his terror, talking about the "corpse," and of the way they intended to get back clandestinely to the city. Joseph gave the rejoinder; both, considering the affair ridiculous, were certain that it would be settled.

Cisy kept his head on his breast; he lifted it up slowly, and drew attention to the fact that they had not taken a doctor with them.

"'Tis unnecessary," said the Baron.

"Then there's no danger?"

Joseph answered in a grave tone:

"Let us hope so!"

And nobody in the carriage made any further remark.

At ten minutes past seven they arrived in front of the Maillot gate. Frederick and his seconds were there, the entire group being dressed in black. Regimbart, instead of a cravat, wore a stiff horse-hair collar, like a trooper; and he carried a long violin-case adapted for adventures of this kind. They exchanged frigid bows. Then they all plunged into the Bois de Boulogne, taking the Madrid road, in order to find a suitable place.

Regimbart said to Frederick, who was walking between him and Dussardier:

"Well, and this scare—what does that matter? If you want anything, don't annoy yourself about it; I know what to do. Fear is natural to man!"

Then, in a low tone:

"Don't smoke any more; it has a weakening effect."

Frederick threw away his cigar, which was only disturbing his brain, and went on with a firm step. The Vicomte advanced behind, leaning on the arms of his two seconds. Occasional wayfarers crossed their path. The sky was blue, and from time to time they heard rabbits skipping about. At the turn of a path, a woman in a Madras handkerchief was chatting with a man in a blouse; and in the large avenue under the chestnut-trees some grooms in vests of linen-cloth were walking horses up and down.

Cisy recalled the happy days when, mounted on his own chestnut horse, and with his glass stuck in his eye, he rode up to carriage-doors. These recollections intensified his wretchedness. An intolerable thirst parched his throat. The buzzing of flies mingled with the throbbing of his arteries. His feet sank into the sand. It seemed to him as if he had been walking during a period which had neither beginning nor end.

The seconds examined with keen glances each side of the path they were traversing. They hesitated as to whether they would go to the Catelan Cross or under the walls of the Bagatelle. At last they took a turn to the right, drawing up in a kind of quincunx in the midst of the pine-trees.

The spot was chosen in such a way that the level ground was cut equally into two divisions. The places at which the principals in the duel were to take their stand were marked out. Then Regimbart opened his case. It was lined with red sheep's leather, and contained four charming swords hollowed in the centre, with highly ornamented handles, which were adorned with filigree. A ray of light, passing through the leaves, fell on them, and they appeared to Cisy to glitter like silver vipers on a sea of blood.

The Citizen showed that they were of equal length. He took one himself, in order to separate the combatants in case of necessity. M. de Comaing held a walking-stick. There was an interval of silence. They looked at each other. All the faces appeared either fierce or cruel.

Frederick had taken off his coat and his waistcoat. Joseph aided Cisy to do the same. When his cravat was removed a blessed medal could be seen on his neck. This made Regimbart smile contemptuously.

Then M. de Comaing (in order to allow Frederick another moment for reflection) tried to raise some quibbles. He demanded the right to put on a glove, and to catch hold of his adversary's sword with the left hand. Regimbart, who was in a hurry, made no objection to this. At last the Baron, addressing Frederick:

"Everything depends on you, Monsieur! There is never any dishonour in acknowledging one's mistakes."

Dussardier made a gesture of approval. The Citizen gave vent to his indignation:

"Do you think we came here as a mere sham, damn it! Be on your guard, each of you!"

The combatants were facing each other, with their seconds by their sides.

He uttered the single word: "Come!"

Cisy became dreadfully pale. The end of his blade was quivering like a horsewhip. His head fell back, his hands dropped helplessly, and he sank unconscious on the ground. Joseph raised him up and while holding a scent-bottle to his nose, gave him a good shaking.

The Vicomte reopened his eyes, then suddenly grasped at his sword like a madman. Frederick had held his in readiness, and now awaited him with steady eye and uplifted hand.

"Stop! stop!" cried a voice, which came from the road simultaneously with the sound of a horse at full gallop, and the hood of a cab broke the branches. A man bending out his head waved a handkerchief, still shouting:

"Stop! stop!"

M. de Comaing, believing that this meant the intervention of the police, lifted up his walking-stick.

"Make an end of it. The Vicomte is bleeding!"

"I?" said Cisy.

In fact, he had in his fall taken the skin off his left thumb.

"But this was done by falling," observed the Citizen.

The Baron pretended not to understand.

Arnoux jumped out of the cab.

"I have arrived too late? No! Thanks be to God!"

He threw his arms around Frederick, felt him, and covered his face with kisses.

"I am the cause of it. You were defending your old friend! That's right—that's right! Never shall I forget it! How good you are! Ah! my own dear boy!"

He gazed at Frederick and shed tears, while he chuckled with delight. The Baron turned toward Joseph:

"I believe we are in the way at this little family party. It is over, Messieurs, is it not? Vicomte, put your arm into a sling. Hold on! here is my silk handkerchief."

Then, with an imperious gesture: "Come! no spite! This is as it should be!"

The two adversaries shook hands in a very lukewarm fashion. The Vicomte, M. de Comaing, and Joseph went off in one direction, and Frederick left with his friends in the opposite direction.

As the Madrid Restaurant was not far off, Arnoux proposed that they should go and drink a glass of beer there.

"We might even have breakfast."

But, as Dussardier had no time to lose, they confined themselves to taking some refreshment in the garden.

They all felt that sense of satisfaction which follows happy *dénouements*. The Citizen, nevertheless, was annoyed at the duel having been interrupted at the most critical stage.

Arnoux had been apprised of it by a person named Compain, a friend of Regimbart; and with an irrepressible outburst of emotion he had rushed to the spot to prevent it, under the impression that he was the occasion of it. He begged Frederick to furnish him with the details. Frederick, touched by these proofs of affection, felt some scruples at the idea of increasing his misapprehension of the facts.

"For mercy's sake, don't say any more about it!"

Arnoux thought that this reserve showed great delicacy. Then, with his habitual levity, he passed on to another subject.

"What news, Citizen?"

And they began talking about banking transactions, and the number of bills that were falling due. In order to be more private, they went to another table, where they exchanged whispered confidences.

Frederick could overhear the following words: "You are going to back me up with your signature." "Yes, but you, mind!" "I have negotiated it for three hundred!" "A nice commission, faith!"

In short, it was evident that Arnoux was mixed up in a great many shady transactions with the Citizen.

Frederick thought of mentioning the fifteen thousand francs. But his last step forbade the utterance of any reproachful words even of the mildest description. Besides, he felt tired himself, and this was not a convenient place for talking about such a thing. He put it off till some future day.

Arnoux, seated in the shade of an evergreen, was smoking, and with a look of joviality in his face. He raised his eyes toward the doors of private rooms that looked out on the garden, remarking that he had often paid visits to the house in former days.

"Probably not alone?" returned the Citizen.

"Faith, you're right there!"

"What blackguardism you do indulge in! you, a married man!"

"Well, and what about yourself?" retorted Arnoux; and, with an indulgent smile: "I am sure that even this rascal here has a room of his own somewhere into which he takes his friends."

The Citizen acknowledged this by simply shrugging his shoulders. Then these two gentlemen compared their respective tastes with regard to the sex: Arnoux now preferred youth, work-girls; Regimbart hated affected women, and went in for the genuine article before anything else.

The opinion which the earthenware-dealer expressed at the close of this discussion was that women were not to be taken seriously.

"Nevertheless, he is fond of his own wife," thought Frederick, as he made his way home; and he looked on Arnoux as a coarse-grained man. He had a grudge against him on account of the duel, as if it had been for his sake that he had risked his life a little while before.

But he felt grateful to Dussardier for his devotion. Ere long the book-keeper came at his invitation to pay him a visit every day.

Frederick lent him books—Thiers, Dulaure, Barante, and Lamartine's *Girondins*.

The honest fellow listened to everything the other said with a thoughtful air, and accepted his opinions as those of a master.

One evening he arrived looking quite alarmed.

That morning, on the boulevard, a man who was running so quickly that he was almost breathless, had jostled against him, and having recognised him as a friend of Sénécal, had said to him:

"He has just been arrested! I am making my escape!"

There was no doubt about it. Dussardier had spent the day making inquiries. Sénécal was in jail charged with an attempted crime of a political nature.

The son of an overseer, he was born at Lyons, and having had as his teacher a former disciple of Chalier, he had, on his arrival in Paris, obtained admission into the "Society of Families." His ways were known, and the police kept a watch on him. He was one of those who fought in the outbreak of May, 1839, and since then he had remained in the background; but, his self-importance increasing, he became a fanatical follower of Alibaud, mixing up his own grievances against society with those of the people against monarchy, and waking up every morning in the hope of a revolution which in a fortnight or a month would turn the world upside down. At last, discouraged at the inactivity of his brethren, enraged at the obstacles that retarded the realisation of his dreams, and despairing of the country, he entered in his capacity of chemist into a conspiracy for the use of incendiary bombs; and he had been caught carrying gunpowder, of which he was going to make a trial at Montmartre—a supreme effort to establish the Republic.

Dussardier was no less attached to the Republican idea, for, from his point of view, it meant enfranchisement and universal happiness. One day—at the age of fifteen—in the Rue Transonain, in front of a grocer's shop, he had seen soldiers' bayonets reddened with blood and they showed human hairs pasted to the butt-ends of their guns. Since that time, the Government had filled him with rage as the very incarnation of injustice. He frequently confused the assassins with the gendarmes; and in his eyes a police-spy was just as bad as a parricide. All the evil scattered over the earth he ingeniously attributed to Power; and he hated it with a deep-rooted, undying hatred that held possession of his heart and made his sensibility all the more acute. He had been dazzled by Sénécal's declamations. It was irrelevant whether he happened to be guilty or not, or whether the attempt with which he was charged could be characterised as an odious proceeding! Since he was the victim of Authority, it was only right to support him.

"The Peers will condemn him, certainly! Then he will be conveyed in a prison-van, like a convict, to Mont Saint-Michel, where the Government lets people die! Austen went mad! Steuben killed himself! In order to transfer Barbès to a dungeon, soldiers had dragged him by the legs and by the hair. They trampled on his body, and his head rebounded along the staircase at every step they took. How abominable!"

He was choking with angry sobs, and he walked about the apartment excitedly.

"In the meantime, something must be done! For my part, I don't know what to do! Suppose we tried to rescue him, eh? While they are bringing him to the Luxembourg, we could throw ourselves on the escort in the passage! A dozen resolute men—that sometimes is enough to accomplish it!"

There was so much fire in his eyes that Frederick was startled. He recalled Sénécal's sufferings and his austere life. Without feeling the same enthusiasm about him as Dussardier, he experienced nevertheless that admiration which is inspired by every man who sacrifices himself for an idea. He felt that, if he had helped this man, he would not be in his present position; and the two friends anxiously sought to devise some plan whereby they could set him free.

It was impossible for them to get access to him.

Frederick read the newspapers to try to find out what had become of him, and for three weeks he was a constant visitor at the reading-rooms.

One day several numbers of the *Flambard* fell into his hands. The leading article was invariably devoted to cutting up some distinguished man. After that came some society gossip and scandals. Then there were some chaffing observations about the Odéon Carpentras, pisciculture, and prisoners under sentence of death, when there happened to be any. The disappearance of a packet-boat furnished material for a whole year's jokes. In the third column a picture-canvasser, under the form of anecdotes or advice, gave some tailors' announcements, together with accounts of evening parties, advertisements as to auctions, and analysis of artistic productions, writing in the same strain about a volume of verse and a pair of boots. The only serious portion of it was the criticism of the small theatres, in which fierce attacks were made on two or three managers; and the interests of art were invoked on the subjects of the decorations of the Rope-dancers' Gymnasium and of the actress who played the part of the heroine at the Délassements.

Frederick was glancing over all these items when his eyes alighted on an article entitled *A Lass between three Lads*. It was the story of his duel related in a lively Gallic style. He had no difficulty in recognising himself, for he was constantly referred to as: "A young man from the College of Sens who has no sense." He was even represented as a poor devil from the provinces, an obscure booby trying to rub against persons of high rank. As for the Vicomte, he was made to play a fascinating part, first by having forced his way into the supper-room, then by having carried off the lady, and, finally, by having behaved throughout like a perfect gentleman.

Frederick's courage was not denied exactly, but it was pointed out that an intermediary—the *protector* himself—had arrived on the scene just in the nick of time. The article concluded with this phrase, pregnant perhaps with sinister meaning:

"What is the cause of their affection? A problem! and, as Bazile says, who the deuce is it that is deceived here?"

This was, beyond all doubt, Hussonnet's revenge against Frederick for having refused him five thousand francs.

What was he to do? If he demanded an explanation, the Bohemian would protest that he was innocent, and nothing would be gained. The best course was to swallow the affront in silence. Nobody, after all, read the *Flambard*.

As he left the reading-room, he saw some people standing in front of a picture-dealer's shop. They were looking at the portrait of a woman, with this line traced underneath in black letters: "Mademoiselle Rosanette Bron, belonging to Monsieur Frederick Moreau of Nogent."

It was indeed she—or at least, like her—her full face displayed, her bosom uncovered, her hair hanging loose, and a purse of red velvet in her hand, while behind her a peacock leaned his beak over her shoulder, covering the wall with his immense plumage in the shape of a fan.

Pellerin had got up this exhibition in order to compel Frederick to pay, persuaded that he was a celebrity, and that all Paris, roused to take his part, would be interested in this wretched piece of work.

Was this a conspiracy? Had the painter and the journalist maliciously agreed to attack him at the same time?

His duel had not put a stop to anything. He had become an object of ridicule, and everyone had been laughing at him.

Three days afterward, at the end of June, the Northern shares having risen fifteen francs, and he having bought two thousand of them within the past month, he found that he had made thirty thousand francs. This caress of fortune gave him renewed self-confidence. He said to himself that he needed nobody's help, and that all his embarrassments were the result of his timidity and indecision. He ought to have begun his intrigue with the Maréchale with brutal directness and refused Hussonnet the very first day. He should not have compromised himself with Pellerin. And, in order to show that he was not at all embarrassed, he presented himself at one of Madame Dambreuse's ordinary evening parties.

In the middle of the anteroom, Martinon, who had arrived at the same time, turned round:

"What! you are visiting here?" with a look of surprise and displeasure.

"Why not?"

And, while wondering what could be the cause of such a display of hostility on Martinon's part, Frederick made his way into the drawing-room.

The light was dim, in spite of the lamps placed in the corners, for the three windows, which were wide open, made three squares of black shadows parallel with each other. Under the pictures, flower-stands occupied, at a man's height, the spaces on the walls, and a silver teapot with a samovar cast their reflections in a mirror on the background. There was a murmur of hushed voices. Pumps could be heard creaking on the carpet. He could distinguish a number of black coats, then a round table lighted up by a large shaded lamp, seven or eight ladies in summer toilets, and at some little distance Madame Dambreuse in a rocking armchair. Her dress of lilac taffeta had slashed sleeves, from which fell muslin puffs, the charming tint of the material harmonising with the shade of her hair; and she sat slightly back with the tip of her foot on a cushion.

M. Dambreuse and an old gentleman with a white head were walking from one end of the drawing-room to the other. Some of the guests chatted here and there, sitting on the edges of little sofas, while others, standing up, formed a circle in the centre of the apartment.

They were talking about votes, amendments, counter-amendments, M. Grandin's speech, and M. Benoist's reply. The third party had decidedly gone too far. The Left Centre ought to have had a better recollection of its origin. Serious attacks had been made on the ministry. It must be reassuring, however, to see that it had no successor. In short, the situation was completely analogous to that of 1834.

As these things bored Frederick, he drew near the ladies. Martinon was with them, standing up, with his hat under his arm, showing himself in three-quarter profile, and looking so neat that he resembled a piece of Sèvres porcelain. He took up a copy of the *Revue des Deux Mondes* which was lying on the table between an *Imitation* and an *Almanach de Gotha,* and spoke of a distinguished poet in a contemptuous tone, remarked he was going to the "conferences of Saint-Francis," complained of his larynx, swallowed from time to time a pellet of gummatum, and in the meantime kept talking about music, and played the part of the elegant trifler. Mademoiselle Cécile, M. Dambreuse's niece, who happened to be embroidering a pair of ruffles, gazed at him with her pale blue eyes; and

Miss John, the governess, who had a flat nose, laid aside her tapestry on his account. Both of them appeared to be exclaiming internally:

"How handsome he is!"

Madame Dambreuse turned toward him.

"Please give me my fan; it is on that pier-table over there. You are taking the wrong one! the other!"

She rose, and as he came across to her, they met in the middle of the drawing-room face to face. She addressed a few sharp words to him, no doubt of a reproachful character, judging by the haughty expression of her face. Martinon tried to smile; then he joined the circle in which grave men were holding discussions. Madame Dambreuse resumed her seat, and, bending over the arm of her chair, said to Frederick:

"I saw somebody the day before yesterday who was speaking about you—Monsieur de Cisy. You know him, don't you?"

"Yes, slightly."

Suddenly Madame Dambreuse uttered an exclamation:

"Oh! Duchesse, what a pleasure to see you!"

And she advanced toward the door to meet a little old lady in a Carmelite taffeta gown and a cap of guipure with long borders. The daughter of a companion in exile of the Comte d'Artois, and the widow of a marshal of the Empire, who had been created a peer of France in 1830, she adhered to the court of a former generation as well as to the new court, and possessed sufficient influence to procure many things. Those who stood talking stepped aside, and then resumed their conversation.

It had now turned on pauperism, of which, according to these gentlemen, all the descriptions that had been given were grossly exaggerated.

"However," urged Martinon, "let us confess that there is such a thing as poverty! But the remedy depends neither on science nor on power. It is purely an individual question. When the lower classes are willing to give up their vices, they will free themselves from their necessities. Let the people be more moral, and they will be less poor!"

According to M. Dambreuse, nothing could be attained without a superabundance of capital. Therefore, the only practicable method was to intrust, "as the Saint-Simonians, however, proposed (good heavens! there was some merit in their views—let us be just to everybody)—to intrust, I say, the cause of progress to those who can increase the public wealth." By degrees they began to touch on great industrial undertakings—the railways, the coal-mines. And M. Dambreuse, addressing Frederick, said to him in a low whisper:

"You have not called to see me about that business of ours?"

Frederick pleaded illness; but, feeling that this excuse was too absurd, added:

"Besides, I need my ready money."

"Is it to buy a carriage?" asked Madame Dambreuse, who was brushing past him with a cup of tea in her hand, and for a minute she looked him in the face with her head inclined slightly over her shoulder.

She believed that he was Rosanette's lover—the allusion was obvious. It seemed to Frederick that all the ladies were staring at him and whispering to one another.

In order to get a better idea as to what they were thinking, he once more approached them. On the opposite side of the table, Martinon, seated near Mademoiselle Cécile, was turning over the leaves of an album. It contained lithographs representing Spanish costumes. He read the descriptive titles aloud: *A Lady of Seville, A Valencia Gardener, An Andalusian Picador;* and once, when he had reached the bottom of the page, he continued all in one breath:

"Jacques Arnoux, publisher. One of your friends, no doubt?"

"That is so," said Frederick, hurt by the tone he had assumed.

Madame Dambreuse again interposed:

"In fact, you called here one morning—about a house, I believe—a house belonging to his wife." (This meant: "She is your mistress.")

He blushed up to his ears; and M. Dambreuse, who joined them at the same moment, made this additional remark:

"You appear to be deeply interested in them."

These last words had the effect of putting Frederick entirely out of countenance. His confusion, which, he could not help feeling, was evident to them, and was on the point of confirming their suspicions, when M. Dambreuse drew close to him, and, in a tone of great seriousness, said:

"I suppose you don't do business together?"

He protested by repeated shakes of the head, without realising the exact meaning of the capitalist, who wished to give him advice.

He felt a desire to leave; a servant removed the teacups. Madame Dambreuse was talking to a diplomatist in a blue coat. Two young girls, putting their heads close together, showed each other their jewellery. The others, seated in a semicircle on armchairs, kept gently moving their white faces crowned with black or fair hair. Nobody, in fact, minded them. Frederick turned; and, by a succession of long zigzags, had almost reached the door, when, passing close to a bracket, he remarked on the top of it a journal folded in two. He drew it out a little, and read these words—*The Flambard*.

Who had brought it there? Cisy. Obviously no one else. What did it matter, however? They would believe—already, perhaps, everyone believed—in the article. What was the cause of this bitterness? He wrapped himself up in ironical silence. He felt as if lost in a desert. Suddenly he heard Martinon's voice:

"Talking of Arnoux, I saw in the newspapers, amongst the names of those accused of preparing incendiary bombs, that of one of his *employés*, Sénécal. Is that our Sénécal?"

"The very same!"

Martinon repeated several times very loudly:

"What? our Sénécal! our Sénécal!"

Then questions were asked him about the conspiracy. It was assumed that his connection with the prosecutor's office ought to enable him to give some information on the subject.

He declared that he knew nothing. He had seen him only two or three times. He positively regarded him as a very ill-conditioned fellow. Frederick exclaimed indignantly:

"Not at all! he is a very honest fellow."

"All the same, Monsieur," said a landowner, "no conspirator can be an honest man."

Most of the men present had served at least four governments; and they would have sold France or the human race in order to preserve their own incomes, to save themselves from any discomfort or embarrassment, or even through sheer baseness, through worship of force. They all insisted that political crimes were inexcusable. It would be less harmful to pardon those which were provoked by want. And they did not fail to put forward the eternal illustration of the father of a family stealing the eternal loaf of bread from the eternal baker.

A gentleman occupying an administrative office even went so far as to exclaim:

"For my part, Monsieur, if I were told that my own brother were a conspirator I would denounce him!"

Frederick invoked the right of resistance, and recalling some phrases that Deslauriers had used in their conversations, he referred to Deslosmes, Blackstone, the English Bill of Rights, and Article 2 of the Constitution of '91. It was by virtue of this law that the fall of Napoleon had been proclaimed. It had been recognised in 1830, and inscribed at the head of the Charter. Besides, when the sovereign fails to fulfil his contract, justice requires that he should be overthrown.

"Why, this is abominable!" exclaimed a prefect's wife.

The others remained silent, filled with vague terror, as if they had heard the noise of bullets. Madame Dambreuse rocked herself in her chair, and smilingly listened to him.

A manufacturer, who had formerly been a member of the Carbonari, tried to show that the Orléans family possessed good qualities. No doubt there were some abuses.

"Well, what then?"

"But we should not talk about them, my dear Monsieur! If you knew how all these clamourings of the Opposition injure business!"

"What do I care about business?" said Frederick.

Frederick was exasperated by the rottenness of these old men; and, carried away by the recklessness which sometimes takes possession of even the most timid, he attacked the financiers, the deputies, the government, the king, defended the Arabs, and gave vent to a great deal of abusive language. A few of those around him encouraged him in a spirit of irony:

"Go on, pray! continue!" whilst others muttered: "The deuce! what enthusiasm!" At last he thought it was time to retire; and, as he was going away, M. Dambreuse said to him, alluding to the post of secretary:

"No definite arrangement has been yet arrived at; but make haste!"

And Madame Dambreuse:

"You'll call again soon, will you not?"

Frederick considered their parting words a last mockery. He had resolved never to come back to this house, or to visit any of these people again. He imagined that he had offended them, not realising what vast funds of indifference society possesses. These women especially excited his indignation. Not a single one of them had supported him even with a look of sympathy. He felt angry with them for not having been moved by his words. As for Madame Dambreuse, he found in her something at the same time languid and cold, which prevented him from defining her character by a phrase. Had she a lover? and, if so, who was her lover? Was it the diplomatist or some other? Perhaps it was Martinon? Impossible! Nevertheless, he experienced a sort of jealousy against Martinon, and an unaccountable ill-feeling against her.

Dussardier, having called this evening as usual, was awaiting him. Frederick's heart was swelling with bitterness; he unburdened it, and his grievances, though vague and hard to understand, saddened the honest shop-assistant. He even complained of his isolation. Dussardier, after some hesitation, suggested that they might call on Deslauriers.

Frederick, at the mention of the advocate's name, was seized with a longing to see him again. He was now living in the midst of profound intellectual solitude, and found Dussardier's company insufficient. In reply to the latter's question, Frederick told him to arrange matters any way he liked.

Deslauriers had likewise, since their quarrel, felt a void in his life. He yielded without much reluctance to the cordial advances which were made to him. The pair embraced each other, then began chatting about matters of no consequence.

Frederick's heart was touched by Deslauriers' reserve, and in order to make him a sort of reparation, he told the other next day how he had lost the fifteen thousand francs, without mentioning that these fifteen thousand francs had been originally intended for him. The advocate, nevertheless, had a shrewd suspicion of the truth; and this misadventure, which justified, in his own mind, his prejudices against Arnoux, entirely disarmed his rancour; and he did not again refer to the promise made by his friend on a former occasion.

Frederick, misled by his silence, thought he had forgotten all about it. A few days later, he asked Deslauriers whether there was any way in which he could get back his money.

They might raise the point that the prior mortgage was fraudulent, and might take proceedings against the wife personally.

"No! no! not against her!" exclaimed Frederick, and, yielding to the ex-law clerk's questions, he confessed the truth. Deslauriers was convinced that Frederick had not told him everything, no doubt through a feeling of delicacy. He was hurt by this want of confidence.

They were, however, on the same intimate terms as before, and they found so much pleasure in each other's society that Dussardier's presence was an obstacle to their free intercourse. Under the pretence that they had appointments, they gradually got rid of him.

There are some men whose only mission amongst their fellow-men is to serve as go-betweens; people use them as if they were bridges, by stepping over them and going on farther.

Frederick concealed nothing from his old friend. He told him about the coal-mine speculation and M. Dambreuse's proposal. The advocate grew somewhat thoughtful.

"That's queer! For such a post a man with a thorough knowledge of law would be required!"

"But you could assist me," returned Frederick.

"Yes!—hold on! faith, yes! certainly."

During the same week Frederick showed Deslauriers a letter from his mother.

Madame Moreau accused herself of having misjudged M. Roque, who had given a satisfactory explanation of his conduct. Then she spoke of his wealth, and of the possibility, later, of a marriage with Louise.

"That would not be a bad match," said Deslauriers.

Frederick said it was entirely out of the question. Besides, Père Roque was an old trickster. That in no way affected the matter, in the advocate's opinion.

At the end of July, an unaccountable diminution in value made the Northern shares fall. Frederick had not sold his. He lost sixty thousand francs in one day. His income was considerably reduced. He would be forced to curtail his expenditure, or take up some calling, or make a brilliant catch in the matrimonial market.

Then Deslauriers spoke of Mademoiselle Roque. There was nothing to prevent him from judging of things by seeing for himself. Frederick was rather tired of city life. Provincial existence and the maternal roof would be a sort of recreation for him.

The appearance of the streets of Nogent, as he passed through them in the moonlight, brought back old memories to his mind; and he experienced a kind of pang, like persons who have just returned home after a long period of travel.

At his mother's house, all the country visitors had assembled as in former days—MM. Gamblin, Heudras, and Chambrion, the Lebrun family, "those young ladies, the Augers," and, in addition, Père Roque, and, seated opposite Madame Moreau at a card-table, Mademoiselle Louise. She was now a woman. She sprang to her feet with a cry of delight. They were all in a flutter of excitement. She remained standing motionless, and the pallor of her face was intensified by the light issuing from four silver candlesticks.

When she resumed play, her hand was trembling. This emotion was exceedingly flattering to Frederick, whose pride had been sorely wounded of late. He said to himself: "You, at any rate, will love me!" and, as if he were thus taking his revenge for the humiliations he had endured in the capital, he began to affect the Parisian lion, retailed all the theatrical gossip, told anecdotes as to the doings of society, which he had learned from the columns of the cheap newspapers, and, in short, dazzled his fellow-townspeople.

Next morning, Madame Moreau expatiated on Louise's fine qualities; then she enumerated the woods and farms of which she would be the owner. Père Roque's wealth was considerable.

He had acquired it while making investments for M. Dambreuse; for he had lent money to persons who were able to give good security in the shape of mortgages, whereby he was enabled to demand additional sums or commissions. The capital, owing to his energetic vigilance, was in no danger of being lost. Besides, Père Roque never hesitated to make a seizure. He bought up the mortgaged property at a low price, and M. Dambreuse, having got back his money, found his affairs in very good order.

But this manipulation of business matters in a way which was not strictly legal compromised M. Dambreuse with his agent. He could refuse Père Roque nothing, and it was owing to the latter's solicitations that he had received Frederick so cordially.

The truth was that in the depths of his soul Père Roque cherished a deep-rooted ambition. He wished his daughter to be a countess; and for the purpose of gaining this object, without imperilling the happiness of his child, he knew no other young man so suitable as Frederick.

Through the influence of M. Dambreuse, he could obtain the title of his maternal grandfather, Madame Moreau being the daughter of a

Comte de Fouvens, and besides, being connected with the oldest families in Champagne, the Lavernades and the D'Etrignys. As for the Moreaus, a Gothic inscription near the mills of Villeneuve-l'Archevêque referred to one Jacob Moreau, who had rebuilt them in 1596; and the tomb of his own son, Pierre Moreau, first esquire of the King under Louis XIV, was to be seen in the chapel of Saint-Nicholas.

So much family distinction fascinated M. Roque, the son of an old servant. If the coronet of a count could not be had, he would console himself with something else; Frederick might get a deputyship when M. Dambreuse had been raised to the peerage, and would then assist him in his commercial pursuits, and obtain for him supplies and grants. He liked the young man personally. In short, he desired Frederick for a son-in-law, because for a long time past he had been smitten with this notion, which grew stronger day by day. Now he went to religious services, and had won Madame Moreau over to his views, especially by holding before her the prospect of a title.

So, eight days later, without there being any formal engagement, Frederick was regarded as Mademoiselle Roque's "intended," and Père Roque, not being troubled with scruples, often left them together.

CHAPTER XII

LITTLE LOUISE BECOMES A WOMAN

FREDERICK had given Deslauriers the copy of the deed of subrogation, with a power of attorney, giving him full authority to act; but, when he had ascended his own five flights of stairs and sat alone in the midst of his dismal room, in his armchair upholstered in sheep-leather, the very sight of the stamped paper disgusted him.

He was sick of these things, and of restaurants at thirty-two sous, of travelling in omnibuses, of enduring want and making futile efforts. He picked up the papers again; there were others with them. They were prospectuses of the coal-mining company, with a list of the mines and the particulars as to their contents, Frederick having given all these matters to him in order to have his opinion on them.

An idea occurred to him—that of presenting himself at M. Dambreuse's house and applying for the post of secretary. This post, it was perfectly certain, could not be obtained without purchasing a certain number of shares. Recognising the folly of his project, he said to himself:

"Oh! no, that would be a wrong step."

Then he ransacked his brains to think of the best way in which he could set about recovering the fifteen thousand francs. Such an amount was a mere trifle to Frederick. But, if he had it, what a power it would be in his hands! And the ex-law clerk was indignant at the other being so well off.

"He makes a miserable use of it. He is a selfish fellow. Ah! what do I care for his fifteen thousand francs!"

Why had he lent the money? For the sake of Madame Arnoux's bright eyes. She was his mistress! Deslauriers had no doubt about it. "That was another way in which money was useful!"

And he was assailed by malignant thoughts.

Then he allowed his mind to dwell on Frederick's personal appearance. It had always exercised over him an almost feminine charm; and he soon came to admire it for a success which he realised that he was himself incapable of achieving.

"Nevertheless, was not the will the main element in every enterprise? and, since by its means we may triumph over everything—"

"Ha! that would be droll!"

But he felt ashamed of such treachery, and the next moment:

"Pooh! am I afraid?"

Madame Arnoux—from having heard her spoken about so often—was pictured in his imagination as something extraordinary. The persistency of this passion had irritated him like a problem. Her austerity, which seemed a little theatrical, now annoyed him. Besides, the woman of the world—or, rather, his own conception of her—dazzled the advocate as a symbol and the epitome of a thousand pleasures. Poor though he was, he hankered after luxury in its more glittering form.

"After all, if he should get angry, so much the worse! He has behaved too badly to me to call for any anxiety about him on my part! I have no assurance that she is his mistress! He has denied it. Therefore, I am free to act as I please!"

He could no longer abandon the desire of taking this step. He wished to make a trial of his own strength, so that one day, all of a sudden, he polished his boots himself, bought white gloves, and set out, substituting himself for Frederick, and almost imagining that he was the other by a singular intellectual evolution, in which there was, at the same time, vengeance and sympathy, imitation and audacity.

He announced himself as "Doctor Deslauriers."

Madame Arnoux expressed surprise, as she had not sent for any physician.

"Ha! a thousand apologies!—'tis a doctor of law! I have come in Monsieur Moreau's interest."

This name appeared to produce a disquieting effect on her mind.

"So much the better!" thought the ex-law clerk.

"Since she has a fancy for him, she will like me, too!" buoying up his courage with the accepted idea that it is much easier to supplant a lover than a husband.

He referred to the fact that he had the pleasure of meeting her on one occasion at the law-courts; he even mentioned the date. This remarkable memory astonished Madame Arnoux. He went on in a tone of mild affectation:

"You have already found your affairs a little embarrassing?"

She made no reply.

"Then it must be true."

He began to chat about one thing or another, her house, the works; then, noticing some medallions at the sides of the mirror:

"Ha! family portraits, no doubt?"

He indicated that of an old lady, Madame Arnoux's mother.

"She has the appearance of an excellent woman, a southern type."

And, on being met with the objection that she was from Chartres:

"Chartres! pretty town!"

He praised its cathedrals and public buildings, and coming back to the portrait, traced resemblances between it and Madame Arnoux, flattering her indirectly. She did not appear to be offended at this. He took confidence, and said that he had known Arnoux a long time.

"He is a fine fellow, but one who compromises himself. Take this mortgage, for example—one can't imagine such a reckless act—"

"Yes, I know," said she, shrugging her shoulders.

This involuntary evidence of contempt encouraged Deslauriers to continue. "That kaolin business of his was near turning out very badly, a thing you may not be aware of, and even his reputation—"

A contraction of her brows made him pause.

Then, falling back on generalities, he expressed his sympathy for the "poor women whose husbands frittered away their means."

"But in this case, Monsieur, the means belong to him. As for me, I have nothing!"

No matter, one never knows. A woman of experience might be useful. He made offers of devotion, exalted his own merits, while he looked into her face through his shining spectacles.

She was seized with a vague torpor; but suddenly said:

"Let us look into the matter, I beg of you."

He opened a bundle of papers.

"This is Frederick's letter of attorney. With such a document in the hands of a process-server, who would make out an order, nothing could be easier; in twenty-four hours—" (She remained impassive; he changed his manœuvre.)

"As for me, however, I don't understand what causes him to demand this sum, for, in fact, he doesn't need it."

"How is that? Monsieur Moreau has been very kind."

"Oh! granted!"

And Deslauriers began by eulogising him, then in a mild fashion disparaged him, stating that he was a forgetful individual, and over-fond of money.

"I thought he was your friend, Monsieur?"

"That does not prevent me from seeing his defects. Thus, he showed very little recognition of—how shall I put it?—the sympathy—"

Madame Arnoux was turning over the leaves of a large manuscript book. She interrupted him in order to ask him to explain a certain word.

He bent over her shoulder, and his face came so close to hers that he grazed her cheek. She blushed. This heightened colour inflamed Deslauriers; he hungrily kissed her head.

"What do you mean, Monsieur?" And, standing against the wall, she compelled him to remain perfectly quiet under the glance of her large blue eyes, glowing with anger.

"Listen to me! I love you!"

She broke into a laugh, a shrill, contemptuous laugh. Deslauriers felt himself suffocating with anger. He restrained his feelings, and, with the expression of a vanquished person imploring mercy:

"Ha! you are wrong! As for me, I would not leave you as he has left."

"Of whom, pray, are you talking?"

"Of Frederick."

"Ah! Monsieur Moreau troubles me little. I told you that!"

"Oh! forgive me! forgive me!" Then, drawling his words, in a sarcastic tone:

"I even fancied that you were sufficiently interested in him personally to learn with pleasure—"

She grew pale. The ex-law clerk added:

"He is about to be married."

"He!"

"In a month at latest, to Mademoiselle Roque, the daughter of Monsieur Dambreuse's agent. He has gone down to Nogent for that purpose."

She placed her hand over her heart, as if at the shock of a great blow; then immediately rang the bell. Deslauriers did not wait to be ordered out. When she turned round he had disappeared.

Madame Arnoux was gasping a little from the strain of her emotions. She drew near the window to get a breath of air.

On the opposite side of the street, on the foot-path, a packer in his shirt-sleeves was nailing down a trunk. Hackney-coaches passed. She closed the window-blinds and then came and sat down. As the high houses in the vicinity intercepted the sun's rays, the light of day stole coldly into the apartment. Her children had gone out; there was not a stir around her. It seemed as if she were utterly deserted.

"He is going to be married! Is it possible?"

And she was seized with a fit of nervous trembling.

"Why is this? Does it mean that I love him?"

Then all of a sudden:

"Yes; I love him—I love him!"

It seemed to her as if she were sinking into endless depths. The clock struck three. She listened to the vibrations of the sounds as they died away. And she remained on the edge of the armchair, with her eyeballs fixed and an unchanging smile on her face.

The same afternoon, at the same moment, Frederick and Mademoiselle Louise were walking in M. Roque's garden at the end of the island.

Old Catherine was watching them, some distance away. They walked side by side and Frederick said:

"You remember when I brought you into the country?"

"How good you were to me!" she replied. "You helped me in making sand-pies, in filling my watering-pot, and you rocked me in the swing!"

"All your dolls, who had the names of queens and marchionesses—what has become of them?"

"Really, I don't know!"

"And your pug Moricaud?"

"He's drowned, poor darling!"

"And the *Don Quixote* of which we coloured the engravings together?"

"I have it still!"

He recalled to her mind the day of her first communion, and how pretty she had been at vespers, with her white veil and her large wax-taper, whilst the girls were all taking their places in a row around the choir, and the bell was tinkling.

These memories had but little charm for Mademoiselle Roque. She had not a word to say; and, a minute later:

"Naughty fellow! never to have written me a line, even once!"

Frederick urged by way of excuse his numerous occupations.

"What, then, are you doing?"

He was embarrassed by the question; then he said that he was studying politics.

"Ha!"

And without questioning him further:

"That gives you occupation; while as for me—!"

Then she spoke about the barrenness of her existence, as there was nobody she could go to see, and nothing to amuse her or distract her thoughts. She wished to ride on horseback.

"The vicar maintains that this is improper for a young lady! How stupid these proprieties are! Long ago I could do whatever I pleased; now, they won't let me do anything!"

"Your father, however, is fond of you!"

"Yes; but—"

She heaved a sigh, which meant: "That is not sufficient to make me happy."

Then there was silence, except for the noise made by their boots in the sand, and the murmur of falling water; for the Seine, above Nogent, is cut into two arms. That which turns the mills discharges in this place the superabundance of its waves in order to unite further down with the natural course of the stream; and coming from the bridge one could see at the right, on the other bank of the river, a grassy slope overlooked by a white house. At the left, in the meadow, a row of poplar-trees extended, and the horizon in front was bounded by a curve of the river. It was flat, like a mirror. Large insects hovered over the noiseless water. Tufts of reeds and rushes formed an uneven border; all kinds of plants which happened to spring up there bloomed out in buttercups, caused yellow clusters to hang down, raised trees in distaff-shape with amaranth-blossoms, and made green rockets spring up at random. In an inlet of the river white water-lilies displayed themselves; and a row of ancient willows, in which wolf-traps were hidden, constituted, on that side of the island, the sole protection of the garden.

In the interior, on this side, four walls with a slate coping enclosed the kitchen-garden, in which the square patches, recently dug up, looked like brown plates. The bell-glasses of the melons shone in a row on the narrow hotbed. The artichokes, the kidney-beans, the spinach, the carrots and the tomatoes succeeded each other to a background where asparagus grew so profusely that it resembled a little wood of feathers.

This piece of land had been under the Directory what is called "a folly." The trees had, since then, grown enormously. Clematis obstructed the hornbeams, the walks were covered with moss, brambles abounded on every side. Fragments of plaster statues crumbled in the grass. The feet of anyone walking through the place got entangled in iron-wire work. There now remained of the pavilion only two apartments on the ground floor, with some blue paper hanging in shreds. Before the façade extended an arbour in the Italian style, in which a vine-tree was supported on columns of brick by a rail-work of sticks.

Soon they arrived at this spot; and, as the light fell through the irregular gaps on the green herbage, Frederick, turning his head to speak to Louise, noticed the shadow of the leaves on her face.

Louise had in her red hair, stuck in her chignon, a needle, terminated by a glass bell in imitation of emerald, and, despite her mourning, she wore (so artless was her bad taste) straw slippers trimmed with pink satin—a vulgar trifle probably bought at some fair.

He remarked this, and ironically congratulated her.

"Don't laugh at me!" she replied.

Then surveying him altogether, from his grey felt hat to his silk stockings: "What an exquisite you are!"

After this, she asked him to mention some books which she might read. He named several; and she said:

"Oh! how learned you are!"

While yet very young, she had been smitten with one of those childish passions which have, at the same time, the purity of a religion and the violence of a natural instinct. He had been her comrade, her brother, her master, had diverted her mind, made her heart beat more quickly, and, without any desire for such a result, had poured into the very depths of her being a latent and continuous intoxication. Then he had left her at the moment of a tragic crisis in her existence, when her mother had only just died, and these two separations had been mingled together. Absence had idealised him in her memory. He had come back with a sort of halo round his head; and she gave herself up ingenuously to the feelings of bliss she experienced at seeing him again.

For the first time in his life Frederick felt himself beloved; and this new pleasure, which did not transcend the ordinary run of agreeable sensations, made his breast swell with so much emotion that he spread out his two arms and flung back his head.

A large cloud passed across the sky.

"It is going toward Paris," said Louise. "You'd like to follow it—wouldn't you?"

"I? Why?"

"Who knows?"

And giving him a sharp look:

"Perhaps you have there" (she searched her mind for the appropriate phrase) "something to engage your affections."

"Oh! I have nothing to engage my affections there."

"Are you perfectly certain?"

"Why, yes, Mademoiselle, perfectly certain!"

In less than a year there had taken place in the young girl an extraordinary transformation, which astonished Frederick. After a minute's silence he added softly:

"We should 'thee' and 'thou' each other, as we used to do long ago—shall we?"

"No."

"Why?"

"Because—"

He persisted. She answered, with downcast face:

"I dare not!"

They had reached the end of the garden, which was close to the shell-bank. Frederick, in a spirit of boyish fun, sent pebbles skimming over the water. She bade him sit down. He obeyed; then, looking at the waterfall:

"'Tis like Niagara!" He began talking about distant countries and long voyages. The idea of travelling herself exercised a fascination over her mind. She would not have been afraid either of tempests or of lions.

Seated close to each other, they collected in front of them handfuls of sand, then, while they were chatting, they let it slip through their fingers, and the hot wind, which rose from the plains, carried to them in puffs odours of lavender, together with the smell of tar from a boat behind the lock. The sun's rays glittered on the cascade. The greenish blocks of stone in the little wall over which the water slipped looked as if they were covered with a silver gauze that was perpetually unfolding itself. A long strip of foam gushed forth at the foot with a harmonious murmur. Then it bubbled up, forming whirlpools and a thousand opposing currents, which ended by intermingling in a single limpid stream of water.

Louise said in a musing tone that she envied the existence of fishes:

"It must be glorious to tumble about down there at your ease, and to feel yourself caressed on every side."

She shivered with sensuously enticing movements; a voice called:

"Where are you?"

"Your maid is calling you," said Frederick.

"All right! all right!" Louise did not disturb herself.

"She may be angry," he suggested.

"It is all the same to me! and besides—" Mademoiselle Roque gave him to understand by a gesture that the girl was entirely subject to her will.

She arose, however, and complained of a headache. As they were passing in front of a large cart-shed containing some faggots:

"Suppose we sat down there, *under shelter?*"

He pretended not to understand this dialectic expression, and even chaffed her about her accent. Gradually the corners of her mouth were compressed, she bit her lips and stepped aside to sulk.

Frederick came over to her, swore he did not mean to annoy her, and that he was very fond of her.

"Is that true?" she exclaimed, looking at him with a smile which lighted up her entire face, smeared here and there with patches of bran.

He could not resist the sentiment of gallantry which was stirred in him by her fresh youthfulness, and he replied:

"Why should I tell you a lie? Have you any doubt about it, eh?" and, as he spoke, he passed his left hand round her waist.

A cry, soft as the cooing of a dove, leaped up from her throat. Her head fell back, she was going to faint; he held her up. And his virtuous scruples were futile. At the sight of this maiden offering herself to him he was seized with fear. He assisted her to take a few steps slowly. He had ceased to address her in soothing words, and no longer caring to speak of anything save the most trifling subjects, he talked about some of the principal figures in the society of Nogent.

Suddenly she repelled him, and in a bitter tone:

"You would not dare to run away with me!"

He remained motionless, with a look of absolute amazement in his face. She burst into sobs, and hiding her face in his breast:

"Can I live without you?"

He tried to calm her emotion. She placed her two hands on his shoulders in order to get a better view of his face, and fixing her green eyes on his with an almost fierce tearfulness:

"Will you be my husband?"

"But," Frederick began, casting about in his inner consciousness for a reply—"Of course, I ask for nothing better."

At that moment M. Roque's cap appeared from behind a lilac-tree.

He took his young friend on a trip through the district in order to show off his property; and when Frederick returned, after two days' absence, he found three letters awaiting him at his mother's house.

The first was a note from M. Dambreuse, inviting him to dinner for the previous Tuesday. What was the reason of this politeness? So, then, they had forgiven his prank.

The second was from Rosanette. She thanked him for having risked his life in her behalf. Frederick did not at first understand what she meant; finally, after a considerable amount of circumlocution, while appealing to his friendship, relying on his delicacy, as she put it, and going on her knees to him on account of the pressing necessity of the case, as she was in want of bread, she asked him for a loan of five hundred francs. He at once made up his mind to supply her with the amount.

The third letter, which was from Deslauriers, spoke of the letter of attorney, and was long and obscure. The advocate had not yet decided on any definite action. He urged his friend not to disturb himself: "'Tis useless for you to come back!" even laying particular stress on this point.

Frederick got lost in conjectures of every sort, and felt anxious to return to Paris. This assumption of a right to control him excited a feeling of revolt.

Moreover, he experienced that nostalgia of the boulevard; and then, his mother was pressing him so much, M. Roque kept revolving about him so constantly, and Mademoiselle Louise was so affectionate, that it was not possible for him to delay speedily declaring his intentions.

He wanted to think, and he would be better able to exercise a clear judgment of things at a distance.

In order to assign a motive for his journey, Frederick invented a story; and as he left home, he told everyone, and believed himself, that he would soon be back again.

CHAPTER XIII

ROSANETTE IN A NEW RÔLE

HE FELT no pleasure as he entered Paris at the close of an August evening. The boulevards seemed empty. The passers-by looked at each other with scowling faces. Here and there a boiler of asphalt was smoking; several houses had their blinds down. He made his way to his own residence. The hangings were covered with dust; and, while dining all alone, Frederick was seized with a strange feeling of forlornness; then his thoughts reverted to Mademoiselle Roque. The idea of being married no longer appeared to him preposterous. They might travel; they might go to Italy, to the East. And he saw her standing on a hillock, or gazing at a landscape, or leaning on his arm in a Florentine gallery while she looked at the pictures. What a pleasure it would be to him merely to watch this little creature developing under the splendours of Art and Nature! When she had got free from the commonplace atmosphere in which she lived, she would, in a little while, become a charming companion. M. Roque's wealth, moreover, tempted him. And yet he shrank from taking this step, regarding it as a weakness, a degradation.

But he was determined (whatever he might do) on changing his mode of life—that is to say, to waste himself no more in fruitless passions; and he even hesitated about executing the commission with which he had been intrusted by Louise. This was to buy for her at Jacques Arnoux's establishment two large-sized statues of many colours representing negroes, like those which were at the Prefecture at Troyes. She knew the manufacturer's number, and would not have any other. Frederick feared that, if he went back to their house, he might once again fall a victim to his old passion.

These reflections occupied his mind during the entire evening; and he was just about to go to bed when a woman presented herself.

"'Tis I," said Mademoiselle Vatnaz, with a laugh. "I have come in behalf of Rosanette."

So, then, they were reconciled?

"Good heavens, yes! I am not ill-natured, as you are well aware. And besides, the poor girl—it would take too long to tell you all about it."

In short, the Maréchale was anxious to see him; she was waiting for an answer, her letter having travelled from Paris to Nogent. Mademoiselle Vatnaz did not know its contents.

Then Frederick asked how the Maréchale was getting on.

She was now with a very rich man, a Russian, Prince Tzernoukoff, who had seen her at the races in the Champ de Mars last summer.

"He has three carriages, a saddle-horse, livery servants, a groom got up in the English style, a country-house, a box at the Italian opera, and a heap of other things. There you are, my dear friend!"

And the Vatnaz, as if she had profited by this change of fortune, appeared prosperous and happier. She took off her gloves and examined the furniture and the objects of virtù in the room. She guessed their exact prices like a second-hand dealer. He ought to have consulted her in order to get them cheaper. Then she complimented him on his good taste:

"Ha! this is pretty, exceedingly nice! There's nobody like you for these ideas."

The next moment, as her eyes fell on a door close to the pillar of the alcove:

"That's the way you let your friends out, eh?"

And, in a familiar fashion, she laid her finger on his chin. He trembled at the touch of her long hands, at the same time thin and soft. Round her wrists she wore an edging of lace, and on the body of her green dress lace embroidery, like a hussar. Her bonnet of black tulle, with borders hanging down, concealed her forehead a little. Her eyes shone underneath; an odour of patchouli escaped from her head-bands. The carcel-lamp on the round table, shining down on her like the footlights of a theatre, made her jaw protrude.

She said to him, in an unctuous tone, while she drew from her purse three square slips of paper:

"You will take these from me?"

They were three tickets for Delmar's benefit performance.

"What! for him?"

"Certainly."

Mademoiselle Vatnaz, without explanation further, said that she adored him more than ever. If she were to be believed, the comedian was now definitely classed amongst "the leading celebrities of the age." And it was not such or such a personage that he represented, but the very genius of France, the People. He had "the humanitarian spirit; he understood the priesthood of Art." Frederick, in order to put an end to these eulogies, paid her for the three seats.

"You need not mention this over the way. How late it is, good heavens! I must leave. Ah! I was forgetting the address—'tis the Rue Grange-Batelier, number fourteen."

And, at the door:

"Good-bye, beloved man!"

"Beloved by whom?" asked Frederick. "What a strange woman!"

And he remembered that Dussardier had said to him one day:

"Oh, she's not much!" as if alluding to stories of a disparaging character.

Next morning he repaired to the Maréchale's abode. It was a new house, the spring-roller blinds of which projected into the street. At the head of each flight of stairs there was a mirror against the wall; before each window there was a flower-stand, and all over the steps extended a carpet of oilcloth; when one got inside the door, the coolness of the staircase was refreshing.

A man-servant opened the door, a footman in a red waistcoat. On a bench in the anteroom a woman and two men, tradespeople, no doubt, were waiting as if in a minister's vestibule. At the left, the door of the dining-room, slightly ajar, afforded a glimpse of empty bottles on the sideboards, and napkins on the backs of chairs; and parallel with it ran a corridor in which gold-coloured sticks supported an espalier of roses. In the courtyard below, two boys with bare arms were scrubbing a landau. Their voices rose to Frederick's ears, mingled with the intermittent sounds made by a currycomb knocking against a stone.

The man-servant returned. "Madame will receive Monsieur," and he conducted Frederick through a second anteroom, and then into a large drawing-room hung with yellow brocatel with twisted fringes at the corners which were joined at the ceiling, and which seemed to be continued by flowerings of lustre resembling cables. No doubt there had been an entertainment there the night before. Some cigar-ashes still remained on the pier-tables.

At last he found his way into a kind of boudoir with stained-glass windows, through which the sun shed a dim light. Trefoils of carved wood adorned the upper portions of the doors.

Rosanette appeared, attired in a pink satin vest with white cashmere trousers, a necklace of piasters, and a red cap encircled with a branch of jasmine.

Frederick started back in surprise, then said he had brought the thing she had been speaking about, and he handed her the bank-note. She gazed at him in astonishment; and, as he still kept the note in his hand, without knowing where to put it:

"Pray take it!"

She seized it; then, as she flung it on the divan:

"You are very kind."

She wanted it to meet the rent of a piece of ground at Bellevue, which she paid in this way every year. Her unceremoniousness wounded Frederick's sensibility. However, it was as well! this would avenge him for the past.

"Sit down," said she. "There—closer." And in a grave tone: "In the first place, I have to thank you, my dear friend, for having risked your life."

"Oh! that's nothing!"

"What! Why, 'tis a very noble act!"—and the Maréchale showed an embarrassing sense of gratitude; for it must have been impressed upon her mind that the duel was entirely on account of Arnoux, as the latter, who believed this himself, was not likely to have resisted the temptation of telling her so.

"She is probably laughing at me," thought Frederick.

He had nothing further to detain him, and, pleading that he had an appointment, he rose.

"Oh! no, stay!"

He resumed his seat and presently complimented her on her costume. She replied, with an air of dejection:

"The Prince likes me to dress in this fashion! And one must smoke such machines as that, too!" Rosanette added, pointing toward the narghileh. "Suppose we try the taste of it? Have you any objection?"

She procured a light, and finding it hard to set fire to the tobacco, she stamped impatiently with her foot. Then a feeling of languor took possession of her; and she sat motionless on the divan, with a cushion under her arm and her body twisted a little on one side, one knee bent and the other leg straight out.

The long serpent of red morocco, which formed rings on the floor, rolled itself over her arm. She put the amber mouthpiece between her lips, and gazed at Frederick while she blinked her eyes in the midst of the cloud of smoke that enveloped her. A gurgling sound came from her throat as she inhaled the fumes, and from time to time she murmured:

"The poor darling! the poor pet!"

Frederick tried to think of something agreeable to talk about. The thought of Vatnaz recurred to his memory.

He remarked that she appeared to him very lady-like.

"Yes, upon my word," replied the Maréchale. "She is very lucky in having me, that same lady!"—without adding another word, so much reserve was there in their conversation.

Each felt a sense of constraint, something that formed a barrier to confidential relations between them. In fact, Rosanette's vanity had been flattered by the duel, of which she believed herself to be the occasion. Then, she was astonished that he did not hasten to take advantage of his achievement; and, in order to compel him to return to her, she had invented this story that she wanted five hundred francs. How was it that

Frederick did not expect a little love from her in return? This was a piece of refinement that filled her with amazement, and, with a gush of emotion, she said to him:

"Will you come with us to the sea-baths?"

"What does 'us' mean?"

"Myself and my bird. I'll pass you off for a cousin of mine, as in the old comedies."

"A thousand thanks!"

"Well, then, you will take lodgings near ours."

The idea of hiding himself from a rich man humiliated him.

"No! that is impossible."

"Just as you please!"

Rosanette turned away with tears in her eyes. Frederick noticed this, and in order to prove what an interest he took in her, he said that he was delighted to see her at last in a comfortable position.

She shrugged her shoulders. What, then, was troubling her? Was it, perchance, that she was not loved?

"Oh! I have always some one to love me!"

She added:

"It remains to be seen in what way."

Complaining that she was "suffocating with the heat," the Maréchale unfastened her vest; and, without any other garment round her body, save her silk chemise, she leaned her head on his shoulder so as to arouse his tenderness.

A man of less introspective egoism would not have given a thought at such a moment to the possibility of the Vicomte, M. de Comaing, or anyone else appearing on the scene. But Frederick had too often been the dupe of these very glances to subject himself to a fresh humiliation.

She wished to know all about his relationships and his amusements. She even inquired about his financial affairs, and offered to lend him money if he wanted it. Frederick, unable to stand it any longer, took up his hat.

"I'm off, my dear! I hope you'll enjoy yourself thoroughly down there. *Au revoir!*"

She opened her eyes wide; then, in a dry tone:

"*Au revoir!*"

He made his way out through the yellow drawing-room, and through the second anteroom. There was on the table, between a vase full of visiting-cards and an inkstand, a chased silver chest. It was Madame Arnoux's. Then he experienced a feeling of tenderness, and, at the same time, as it were, the scandal of a profanation. He felt a longing to raise his hands toward it, and open it. He was afraid of being seen, and went away.

Frederick was virtuous. He did not go back to the Arnouxs' house.

He sent his man-servant to buy the two negroes, having given him all the necessary directions; and the case containing them started the same evening for Nogent. Next morning, as he was repairing to Deslauriers' lodgings, at the turn where the Rue Vivienne opened out on the boulevard, he met Madame Arnoux face to face.

The first movement of each of them was to draw back; then the same smile came to the lips of both, and they advanced toward each other. For a minute neither uttered a single word.

The sunlight fell round her, and her oval face, her long eyelashes, her black lace shawl, which showed the outline of her shoulders, her gown of shot silk, the bunch of violets at the corner of her bonnet; all seemed to him to possess extraordinary magnificence. An infinite softness poured itself out of her beautiful eyes; and in a faltering voice, uttering at random the first words that came to his lips:

"How is Arnoux?"

"Well, I thank you!"

"And the children?"

"They are very well!"

"Ah! ah! What fine weather we are having, are we not?"

"Splendid, indeed!"

"You are out shopping?"

And, with a slow inclination of the head:

"Good-bye!"

She put out her hand, without having spoken one affectionate word, and did not even invite him to dinner at her house. No matter! He would not have missed this interview for the most delightful of adventures; and he pondered over its sweetness as he proceeded on his way.

Deslauriers, surprised at seeing him, dissembled his spite; for he cherished still some hope with regard to Madame Arnoux; and he had written to Frederick to prolong his stay in the country, that he might be free in his manœuvres.

He informed Frederick, however, that he had presented himself at her house in order to ascertain if their contract stipulated for a community of property between husband and wife: in that case, proceedings might be taken against the wife; "and she looked queer when I told her about your marriage."

"Now, why such an invention?"

"It was necessary in order to show that you must have your own capital! A person who was indifferent would not have been attacked with the species of fainting fit that she had."

"Really?" exclaimed Frederick.

"Ha! my fine fellow, you are betraying yourself! Come! be honest!"

A feeling of nervous weakness stole over Madame Arnoux's lover.

"Why, no! I assure you! upon my word of honour!"

These weak denials ended by convincing Deslauriers. He congratulated his friend, and asked him for details. Frederick gave him none, and even resisted a secret yearning to concoct a few. As for the mortgage, he told the other to do nothing about it, but to wait. Deslauriers thought he was wrong on this point, and remonstrated with him in rather a churlish fashion.

He was more gloomy, malignant, and irascible than ever. In a year, if fortune did not change, he would embark for America or blow out his brains. Indeed, he appeared to be so furious against everything, and so uncompromising in his radicalism, that Frederick could not refrain from saying:

"Here you are going on in the same way as Sénécal!"

Deslauriers, at this remark, informed him that Sénécal had been discharged from Saint-Pélagie, the magisterial investigation having failed to supply sufficient evidence to justify his being sent for trial.

Dussardier was so much overjoyed at his release that he wanted to invite his friends to come and take punch with him, and begged of Frederick to be one of the party, giving the latter, at the same time, to understand that he would be found in the company of Hussonnet, who had proved himself a very good friend to Sénécal.

In fact, the *Flambard* had just become associated with a business establishment whose prospectus contained the following references: "Vineyard Agency. Office of Publicity. Debt Recovery and Intelligence Office, etc." But the Bohemian was afraid that his connection with trade might injure his literary reputation, and he had accordingly taken the mathematician to keep the accounts. Although the situation was a poor one, Sénécal would, but for it, have died of starvation. Not wishing to offend the worthy shopman, Frederick accepted his invitation.

Dussardier, three days beforehand, had himself waxed the red floor of his garret, beaten the armchair, and dusted the chimney-piece, on which might be seen under a globe an alabaster timepiece between a stalactite and a cocoanut. As his two chandeliers and his chamber candlestick were not sufficient, he had borrowed two more candlesticks from the doorkeeper; and these five lights shone on the top of the chest of drawers, which was covered with three napkins in order that it might serve as a stand for some macaroons, biscuits, a fancy cake, and a dozen bottles of beer. At the opposite side, close to the wall, which was hung with yellow paper, there was a little mahogany bookcase containing the *Fables of Lachambeaudie,* the *Mysteries of Paris,* and Norvins' *Napoléon*—and, in the middle of the alcove, the face of Béranger was smiling out of a rosewood frame.

The guests (in addition to Deslauriers and Sénécal) were an apothecary who had just been admitted, but who had not enough capital to start in business for himself, a young man of his own house, a town-traveller in wines, an architect, and a gentleman employed in an insurance office. Regimbart had been unable to come. Regret was expressed at his absence.

They welcomed Frederick with enthusiasm, as they all knew through Dussardier what he had said at M. Dambreuse's house. Sénécal contented himself with putting out his hand in a dignified manner.

He remained standing near the chimney-piece. The others seated, with their pipes in their mouths, listened to him, while he held forth on universal suffrage, from which he predicted the triumph of Democracy and the practical application of the principles of the Gospel. The hour was at hand. The banquets of the reform party were becoming more numerous in the provinces. Piedmont, Naples, Tuscany—

"'Tis true," said Deslauriers, interrupting him abruptly. "This cannot last much longer!"

And he began to draw a picture of the situation. We had sacrificed Holland to obtain from England the recognition of Louis Philippe; and this precious English alliance was lost, owing to the Spanish marriages. In Switzerland, M. Guizot, in tow with the Austrian, maintained the treaties of 1815. Prussia, with her Zollverein, was preparing trouble for us. The Eastern question was still pending.

"The fact that the Grand Duke Constantine sends presents to M. d'Aumale is no reason for placing confidence in Russia. As for home affairs, never have there been so many blunders, such stupidity. The Government no longer even keeps up its majority. Everywhere, indeed, according to the well-known expression, it is naught! naught! naught! And in the teeth of such public scandals," continued the advocate, with his arms akimbo, "they express themselves satisfied!"

The allusion to a notorious vote called forth applause. Dussardier uncorked a bottle of beer; the froth splashed on the curtains. He did not mind it. He filled the pipes, cut the cake, passed it round, and several times went downstairs to see about the punch; and ere long they lashed themselves into a state of excitement, as they all felt equally exasperated against Power. Their rage was of a violent character for no other reason save that they hated injustice, and they mixed up with legitimate griev-ances the most idiotic complaints.

The apothecary groaned over the pitiable condition of our fleet. The insurance agent could not tolerate Marshal Soult's two sentinels. Deslauriers denounced the Jesuits, who had just installed themselves pub-licly at Lille. Sénécal execrated M. Cousin; for eclecticism, by teaching that certitude can be deduced from reason, developed selfishness and destroyed solidarity. The traveller in wines, knowing very little about these matters, remarked loudly that he had forgotten many infamies:

"The royal carriage on the Northern line must have cost eighty thousand francs. Who'll pay it?"

"Aye, who'll pay it?" repeated the clerk, as angrily as if this amount had been drawn out of his own pocket.

Then followed recriminations against the lynxes of the Bourse and the corruption of officials. According to Sénécal they ought to go higher up, and hold responsible, first of all, the princes who had revived the morals of the Regency period.

"Have you not lately seen the Duc de Montpensier's friends coming back from Vincennes, no doubt in a state of intoxication, and disturbing with their songs the workmen of the Faubourg Saint-Antoine?"

"There was even a cry of 'Down with the thieves!'" said the apothecary. "I was there, and I joined in the cry!"

"So much the better! The people are at last waking up."

"For my part, that case caused me some pain," said Dussardier, "because it imputed dishonour to an old soldier!"

"Do you know," Sénécal went on, "what they have discovered at the Duchesse de Praslin's house—?"

Here the door was sent flying open with a kick. Hussonnet entered.

"Hail, Messeigneurs," said he, as he seated himself on the bed.

No allusion was made to his article, which he was sorry for having written, as the Maréchale had sharply reprimanded him on account of it.

He had just seen at the Théâtre de Dumas the *Chevalier de Maison-Rouge,* and said that it seemed to him a stupid play.

Such a criticism surprised the democrats, as this drama by its tendency, or rather by its scenery, flattered their passions. They protested. Sénécal, in order to bring the discussion to a close, asked whether the play served the cause of Democracy.

"Yes, perhaps; but it is written in a style—"

"Well, then, 'tis a good play. What does style matter? 'Tis the idea!"

And, without allowing Frederick to say a word:

"Now, I was pointing out that in the Praslin case—"

Hussonnet interrupted him with his usual brusqueness.

"Ha! here's another played-out trick! I'm disgusted at it!"

"And others as well as you," returned Deslauriers. "It has only got five papers taken. Listen, while I read this paragraph."

Drawing his note-book from his pocket, he read:

"'We have, since the establishment of the best of republics, been subjected to twelve hundred and twenty-nine press prosecutions, from which the results to the writers have been imprisonment extending over a period of three thousand one hundred and forty-one years, and the light sum of seven million one hundred and ten thousand five hundred francs by way of fine.' That's pleasant, eh?"

They all sneered bitterly.

Frederick, incensed against the others, broke in:

"*The Democratic Pacifique* has had proceedings taken against it on account of its feuilleton, a novel entitled *The Woman's Share.*"

"Come! that's good," said Hussonnet. "Suppose they objected to our having our share of the women!"

"But what is it that's not prohibited?" exclaimed Deslauriers. "To smoke in the Luxembourg is prohibited; to sing the Hymn to Pius IX is prohibited!"

"And the typographers' banquet has been interdicted," a voice cried, with a thick articulation.

It was that of an architect, who had sat concealed in the shade of the alcove, and who had remained silent up to that moment. He added that, the week before, a man named Rouget had been convicted of offering insults to the king.

"That gurnet* is fried," said Hussonnet.

This joke appeared so out of place to Sénécal that he reproached Hussonnet for defending the Juggler of the Hôtel de Ville, the friend of the traitor Dumouriez.

"I? quite the contrary!"

Sénécal considered Louis Philippe commonplace, one of the National Guard types of men, all that savoured most of the provision-shop and the cotton night-cap! And laying his hand on his heart, the Bohemian gave utterance to the rhetorical phrases:

"It is always with a new pleasure. . . . Polish nationality will not perish. . . . Our great works will be pursued. . . . Give me some money for my little family. . . ."

They all laughed loudly, declaring that he was a delightful fellow, full of wit. Their joy was redoubled at the sight of the bowl of punch which was brought in from a nearby café.

The flames of the alcohol and those of the wax-candles soon heated the apartment, and the light from the garret, passing across the courtyard, illuminated the side of an opposite roof, where the outlines of the flue of a chimney could be traced through the darkness of night. They talked in very loud tones all at the same time. They had taken off their coats; they gave blows to the furniture; they touched glasses.

Hussonnet exclaimed:

"Send up some great ladies, in order that this may be more Tour de

---

Rouget means a gurnet.—EDITOR.

Nesles, have more local colouring, and be more Rembrandtesque, by Jove!"

And the apothecary, who kept stirring the punch indefinitely, began to sing with expanded chest:

> "I've two big oxen in my stable,
> Two big white oxen—"

Sénécal laid his hand on the apothecary's mouth; he did not like disorderly conduct; and the lodgers pressed their faces against the window-panes, surprised at the unwonted uproar in Dussardier's room. The honest fellow was happy, and said that this recalled to his mind their little parties on the Quai Napoléon in days gone by; however, they missed many who used to be present at these reunions, "Pellerin, for instance."

"We can do without him," observed Frederick.

And Deslauriers inquired about Martinon.

"What has become of that interesting gentleman?"

Frederick immediately giving vent to the ill-will which he bore to Martinon, attacked his mental capacity, his character, his false elegance, his entire personality. He was a perfect specimen of an upstart peasant! The new aristocracy, the mercantile class, was not equal to the old—the nobility. He maintained this, and the democrats expressed their approval, as if he were a member of the one class, and they were on visiting terms with the other. They were charmed with him. The apothecary compared him to M. d'Alton Shée, who, though a peer of France, defended the cause of the people.

At last the time had come for taking their departure. They all separated with great handshakings. Dussardier, in a spirit of affectionate solicitude, saw Frederick and Deslauriers home. As soon as they were in the street, the advocate assumed a thoughtful air, and, after a moment's silence:

"You have a great grudge, then, against Pellerin?"

Frederick did not hide his bitterness.

The painter, in the meantime, had withdrawn the notorious picture from the show-window. A person should not let himself be put out by trifles. What was the good of making an enemy?

"He has given way to a burst of ill-temper, excusable in a man who hasn't a sou. You, of course, can't appreciate that!"

And, when Deslauriers had gone up to his own apartments, the shopman did not part with Frederick. He urged his friend to buy the portrait. In fact, Pellerin, abandoning the hope of being able to intimidate him, had induced them to use their influence to arrange the matter for him.

Deslauriers spoke about it again, and pressed him on the point, urging that the artist's claims were reasonable.

"I am sure that for a sum of, perhaps, five hundred francs—"

"Oh, give it to him! Wait! here it is!" said Frederick.

The picture arrived the same evening. It appeared to him a still more atrocious daub than when he had seen it first. The half-tints and the shades were darkened under the excessive retouchings, and they seemed obscured when brought into relation with the lights, which, having remained very brilliant here and there, destroyed the harmony of the picture.

Frederick revenged himself for having had to pay for it by bitterly disparaging it. Deslauriers believed Frederick's statement on the point, and expressed approval of his conduct, for he had always been ambitious of constituting a phalanx of which he would be the leader. Certain men take delight in persuading their friends to do things which are disagreeable to them.

Meanwhile Frederick did not renew his visits to the Dambreuses. He lacked the capital for the investment. He would have to enter into endless explanations on the subject; he hesitated about coming to a decision. Perhaps he was in the right. Nothing was certain now, the coal-mining speculation any more than other things. He would have to give up society of that sort. The end of the matter was that Deslauriers was dissuaded from having anything further to do with the undertaking.

From sheer force of hatred he had grown virtuous, and again he preferred Frederick in a position of mediocrity. In this way he remained his friend's equal and in more intimate relationship with him.

Mademoiselle Roque's commission had been very badly executed. Her father wrote to him, supplying him with the most precise directions, concluding his letter with this piece of foolery: "At the risk of giving you *nigger on the brain!*"

Frederick could not do otherwise than call upon the Arnouxs', once more. He went to the warehouse, but could find nobody. The firm being in a tottering condition, the clerks were as careless as their master.

He brushed against the shelves laden with earthenware, which filled up the entire space in the centre of the establishment; then, when he reached the lower end, facing the counter, he walked with a more noisy tread in order to make himself heard.

The portières parted, and Madame Arnoux appeared.

"What! you here! you!"

"Yes," she faltered, with some agitation. "I was looking for—"

He saw her handkerchief near the desk, and concluded that she had come down to her husband's warehouse to have an account given her as to the business, in order to clear up some matter that caused her anxiety.

"But perhaps there is something you want?" said she.

"A mere nothing, Madame."

"These shop-assistants are intolerable! they are always out of the way."

They should not be blamed. On the contrary, he congratulated himself on the circumstance.

She looked at him in an ironical fashion.

"Well, and this marriage?"

"What marriage?"

"Your own!"

"Mine? I'll never marry as long as I live!"

She made a gesture as if to contradict his words.

"Though, indeed, such things must be, after all! We take refuge in the commonplace, despairing of ever realising the beautiful existence of which we have dreamed."

"All your dreams, however, are not so—candid!"

"What do you mean?"

"When you drive to races with women!"

He cursed the Maréchale. Then something recurred to his memory.

"But it was you who begged of me yourself to visit her at one time in the interest of Arnoux."

She replied with a shake of her head:

"And you take advantage of it to amuse yourself?"

"Good God! let us forget all these foolish things!"

"'Tis right, since you are about to be married."

And she stifled a sigh, while she bit her lips.

Then he exclaimed:

"But I tell you again I am not! Can you believe that I, with my intellectual requirements, my habits, am going to bury myself in the provinces, playing cards, looking after masons, and walking about in wooden shoes? What object, pray, could I have for taking such a step? You've been told that she was rich, haven't you? Ah! what do I care about money? Could I, after yearning so long for that which is most lovely, tender, enchanting, a sort of Paradise under a human form, and having found this sweet ideal at last, when this vision hides every other from my view—"

And taking her head between his two hands, he kissed her on the eyelids, repeating:

"No! no! no! never will I marry! never! never!"

She submitted to these caresses, her mingled amazement and delight having bereft her of the power of motion.

The door of the storeroom above the staircase fell back, and she remained with outstretched arms, as if to bid him keep silence. Steps drew near. Then some one said from behind the door:

"Is Madame there?"

"Come in!"

Madame Arnoux had her elbow on the counter and was twisting a pen between her fingers quietly when the book-keeper drew aside the portière.

Frederick started up, as if on the point of leaving.

"Madame, I have the honour to salute you. The set will be ready—will it not? I may rely on this?"

She made no reply. But by thus silently becoming his accomplice in the deception, she made his face flush with the crimson glow of adultery.

On the following day he called again. She received him; and, in order to follow up the advantage he had gained, Frederick, without any preamble, attempted to offer some justification for the accidental meeting in the Champ de Mars. It was the merest chance that led to his being in that woman's company. While admitting that she was pretty—which really was not the case—how could she for even a moment absorb his thoughts, seeing that he loved another woman?

"You know it well—I told you it was so!"

Madame Arnoux hung down her head.

"I regret that you said such a thing."

"Why?"

"The most ordinary proprieties now demand that I should see you no more!"

He protested the innocence of his love. The past ought to be a guaranty as to his future conduct. He had of his own accord made it a point of honour with himself not to disturb her existence, not to annoy her with his complaints.

"But yesterday my heart overflowed."

"We ought not to let our thoughts dwell on that moment, my friend!"

And yet, where would be the harm in two unhappy beings mingling their griefs?

"For, indeed, you are not happy any more than I am! Oh! I know you. You have no one who responds to your craving for affection, for devotion. I will do anything you wish! I will not offend you! I swear to you that I will not!"

And he fell on his knees, in spite of himself, giving way beneath the weight of the feelings that oppressed his heart.

"Rise!" she said; "I implore you to do so!"

And she declared in an imperious tone that if he did not comply with her wish, she would never see him again.

"Ha! I defy you to do it!" returned Frederick. "What is there for me in the world? Other men strive for riches, celebrity, power! But I have no profession; you are my exclusive occupation, my whole wealth, the object, the centre of my existence and of my thoughts. I can no more live without you than without the air of heaven! Do you not feel the aspiration of my soul ascending toward yours, and that they must intermingle, and that I am dying on your account?"

Madame Arnoux trembled in every limb.

"Oh! leave me, I beg of you?"

The look of utter confusion in her face made him pause. Then he advanced a step. But she drew back, with her two hands clasped.

"Leave me in the name of Heaven, for mercy's sake!"

And Frederick loved her so much that he went.

Soon afterward he was filled with rage against himself, declared that he must be an idiot, and, after the lapse of twenty-four hours, returned.

Madame was gone. He stood at the head of the stairs, stupefied with anger and indignation. Arnoux appeared, and informed Frederick that his wife had, that very morning, taken up her residence at a little country-house of which he had become tenant at Auteuil, as he had given up the house at Saint-Cloud.

"This is another of her whims. No matter, as she is settled at last; and myself, too, for that matter, so much the better. Let us dine together this evening, will you?"

Frederick pleaded as an excuse some urgent business; then he hurried away to Auteuil.

Madame Arnoux permitted an exclamation of joy to escape her lips. Then all his bitterness vanished.

He did not say one word about his love. In order to inspire her with confidence in him, he even exaggerated his reserve; and on his asking whether he might call again, she replied: "Why, of course!" putting out her hand, which she withdrew the next moment.

From that time forth, Frederick increased his visits. He promised extra fares to the cabman who drove him. But often he grew impatient at the slow pace of the horse, and, alighting, he would make a dash after an omnibus, and climb to the top of it out of breath. Then with what disdain he surveyed the faces of those around him, who were not going to see her!

He could recognise her house at a distance, with an enormous honeysuckle covering, on one side, the planks of the roof. It was a kind of Swiss châlet, painted red, with a balcony. In the garden there were three old chestnut-trees, and on a rising ground in the centre might be seen a parasol made of thatch, held up by the trunk of a tree. Under the slate-work lining the walls, a big vine-tree, badly fastened, hung from one place to another after the fashion of a rotten cable. The gate-bell, which it was rather difficult to pull, was slow in ringing, and a long time always elapsed before it was answered. On each occasion he experienced a pang of suspense, a fear born of irresolution.

Then his ears would be greeted with the pattering of the servant-maid's slippers over the gravel, or else Madame Arnoux herself would come. One day he came up behind her just as she was stooping down to gather violets.

Her daughter's capricious disposition had made it necessary to send the girl to a convent. Her little son was at school every afternoon. Arnoux made a habit of taking prolonged luncheons at the Palais-Royal with Regimbart and their friend Compain. They did not trouble themselves about anything that occurred, no matter how disagreeable it might be.

It was clearly understood between Frederick and her that they should not belong to each other. By this convention they were preserved from danger, and they found it easier to unburden their hearts to each other.

She told him all about her early life at Chartres, which she spent with her mother, her devotion when she had reached her twelfth year, then her passion for music, when she used to sing till nightfall in her little room, from which the ramparts could be seen.

He related to her how melancholy broodings had haunted him at college, and how a woman's face shone brightly in the cloudland of his imagination, so that, when he first laid eyes upon her, he felt that her features were familiar to him.

These conversations, as a rule, covered only the years during which they had been acquainted with each other. He recalled to her insignificant details—the colour of her dress at a certain period, a woman whom they had met on a particular day, what she had said on another occasion; and she replied, quite astonished:

"Yes, I remember!"

Their tastes, their judgments, were the same. Often one of them, when listening to the other, exclaimed:

"That's just the way with me."

And the other replied:

"And with me, too!"

Then there were endless complaints about Providence:

"Why had it not been the will of Heaven? If we had only met—!"

"Ah! if I had been younger!" she sighed.

"No, but if I had been a little older."

And they pictured to themselves a life entirely given up to love, sufficiently rich to fill up the vastest solitudes, surpassing all other joys, defying all forms of wretchedness, in which the hours would glide away in a continual outpouring of their own emotions, and which would be as bright and glorious as the palpitating splendour of the stars.

They often stood at the top of the stairs exposed to the free air of heaven. The tops of trees yellowed by the autumn raised their crests in front of them at unequal heights up to the edge of the pale sky; or else they walked on to the end of the avenue into a summer-house whose only furniture was a couch of grey canvas. Black specks stained the glass; the walls exhaled a mouldy smell; and they remained there chatting freely about all sorts of topics—anything that happened to arise—in a spirit of hilarity. Sometimes the rays of the sun, passing through the Venetian blind, extended from the ceiling down to the flagstones like the strings of a lyre. Particles of dust whirled amid these luminous bars. She amused herself by dividing them with her hand. Frederick gently caught hold of it; and he gazed on the twinings of her veins, the grain of her skin, and the form of her fingers. Each of those fingers of hers was for him more than a thing—almost a person.

She gave him her gloves, and, the week after, her handkerchief. She called him "Frederick;" he called her "Marie," adoring the name, which, he said, was expressly made to be uttered with a sigh of ecstasy, and which seemed to contain clouds of incense and scattered heaps of roses.

They soon came to an understanding as to the days on which he might see her; and, leaving the house as if by mere chance, she would walk along the road to meet him.

She made no effort whatever to excite his love, lost in that listlessness which is characteristic of intense happiness. During the whole season she wore a brown silk dressing-gown with velvet borders of the same colour, a large garment, which harmonised with the indolence of her attitudes and her grave physiognomy. Besides, she had just reached the autumnal period of womanhood, in which reflection is combined with tenderness, in which the beginning of maturity colours the face with a more intense flame, when strength of feeling mingles with experience of life, and when, having completely expanded, the entire being overflows with a richness in unison with its beauty. Never had she possessed more sweetness, more leniency. Secure in the thought that she would not err, she abandoned herself to a sentiment which seemed to her justified by her sorrows. And, moreover, it was so innocent and fresh! What an abyss lay between the coarseness of Arnoux and the adoration of Frederick!

He trembled at the thought that by an imprudent word he might lose all that he had gained, saying to himself that an opportunity might come again, but a foolish step could never be repaired. He wished that she should give herself rather than that he should take her. The assurance of being loved by her delighted him like a foretaste of possession, and then the charm of her person stirred his heart more than his senses. It was an indefinable feeling of bliss, a sort of intoxication that made him lose sight of the possibility of having his happiness completed. When away from her, he was consumed with longing.

Soon the conversations were interrupted by long spells of silence. Sometimes a sort of sexual shame made them blush in each other's presence. All the precautions they took to hide their love only served to unveil it; the stronger it grew, the more constrained they became. The effect of this dissimulation was to intensify their sensibility. They experienced a sensation of delight at the odour of moist leaves; they could not endure the east wind; they got irritated without apparent cause, and had melancholy forebodings. The sound of a footstep, the creaking of the wainscoting, filled them with as much terror as if they had been guilty. They felt as if they were being pushed toward the edge of a chasm. They were surrounded by a tempestuous atmosphere; and when complaints escaped Frederick's lips, she accused herself.

"Yes, I am doing wrong. I am acting as if I were a coquette! Don't come any more!"

Then he would repeat the same oaths, to which on each occasion she listened with renewed pleasure.

His return to Paris, and the fuss occasioned by New Year's Day, interrupted their meetings for a time. When he returned, he had an air of greater self-confidence. Every moment she went out to give orders, and in spite of his entreaties she received all visitors that called during the evening.

After this, they conversed about Léotade, M. Guizot, the Pope, the insurrection at Palermo, and the banquet of the Twelfth Arrondissement, which had caused some disquietude. Frederick eased his mind by railing against Power, for he longed, like Deslauriers, to turn the whole world upside down, so soured had he now become. Madame Arnoux, on her side, had become sad.

Her husband, indulging in displays of wild folly, was flirting with one of the girls in his pottery works, the one who was known as "the girl from Bordeaux." Madame Arnoux was informed of it by Frederick. He wanted to make use of it as an argument, "inasmuch as she was the victim of deception."

"Oh! I'm not much troubled about it," she said.

This admission on her part seemed to him to strengthen the intimacy between them. Would Arnoux be suspicious with regard to them?

"No! not now!"

It seemed that, one evening, he had left them talking together, and had afterward come back and listened behind the door, and as they both were chatting at the time of matters that were of no consequence, he had lived since in a state of complete security.

"With good reason, too—is that not so?" said Frederick bitterly.

"Yes, no doubt!"

It would have been better for him not to have given so risky an answer.

One day she was out at the hour when he usually called. To him there seemed to be a sort of treason in this.

He was next displeased at seeing the flowers which he used to bring her always placed in a glass of fresh water.

"Where, then, would you have me put them?"

"Oh! not there! However, they are not so cold there as they would be near your heart!"

Not long afterward he reproached her for having been at the Italian opera the night before without telling him previously of her intention to go there. Others had seen, admired, fallen in love with her, perhaps; Frederick was fastening on those suspicions of his merely in order to pick a quarrel with her, to torment her; for he was beginning to hate her, and the very least he might expect was that she should share in his sufferings!

One afternoon, toward the middle of February, he found her in a state of great mental excitement. Eugène had been complaining about his sore throat. The doctor had told her that it was a trifling ailment—a bad cold, an attack of influenza. Frederick was astonished at the child's stupefied look. Nevertheless, he reassured the mother, and brought forward the cases of several children of the same age who had been attacked with similar ailments, and had been speedily cured.

"Really?"

"Why, yes, assuredly!"

"Oh! how good you are!"

And she caught his hand. He clasped hers tightly in his.

"Oh! let it go!"

"What does it matter, when it is to one who sympathises with you that you offer it? You place every confidence in me when I speak of these things, but you distrust me when I talk about my love!"

"I don't doubt you on that point, my poor friend!"

"Why this distrust, as if I were a wretch capable of abusing—"

"Oh! no!—"

"If I had only a proof!—"

"What proof?"

"The proof that might be given to the first comer—what you have granted to myself!"

And he recalled to her how, on one occasion, they had gone out together, on a winter's twilight, when there was a fog. This seemed now a long time ago. What, then, was to prevent her from showing herself on his arm before the whole world without any fear on her part, and without any mental reservation on his, not having anyone around them who could importune them?

"Be it so!" she said, with a promptness of decision that at first astonished Frederick.

But he replied, in a lively fashion:

"Would you like me to wait at the corner of the Rue Tronchet and the Rue de la Ferme?"

"Good heavens, my friend!" faltered Madame Arnoux.

Without giving her time to think, he added:

"Next Tuesday, I suppose?"

"Tuesday?"

"Yes, between two and three o'clock."

"I will be there!"

And she turned aside her face with a movement of shame. Frederick placed his lips on the nape of her neck.

"Oh! this is not right," she said. "You will make me repent."

He turned away, dreading the fickleness which is usual with women. Then, on the threshold, he murmured softly, as if it were a thing that was thoroughly understood:

"On Tuesday!"

She lowered her beautiful eyes in a cautious and resigned fashion.

Frederick had a plan in his mind.

He hoped that, owing to the rain or the sun, he might get her to stop under some doorway, and that, once there, she would enter some house. The difficulty was to find one that would suit.

He made a search, and about the middle of the Rue Tronchet he read, on a signboard, "Furnished apartments."

The waiter, divining his object, showed him immediately above the ground-floor a room and a closet with two exits. Frederick took it for a month, and paid in advance. Then he went into three shops to buy the rarest perfumery. He got a piece of imitation guipure, to replace the horrible red cotton coverlet; he selected a pair of blue satin slippers, and only the fear of appearing coarse checked the amount of his purchases. He came back with them; and with more devotion than those show who erect processional altars, he altered the position of the furniture, arranged the curtains himself, put heather in the fireplace, and covered the chest of drawers with violets. He would have liked to pave the entire apartment with gold. "To-morrow is the time," said he to himself. "Yes, to-morrow! I am not dreaming!" and his heart throbbed violently under the delirious excitement begotten by his anticipations. Then, when everything was ready, he carried off the key in his pocket, as if the happiness which slept there might have flown away along with it.

A letter from his mother was awaiting him:

"Why such a long absence? Your conduct is beginning to look ridiculous. I understand your hesitating more or less with regard to this union. However, think well upon it."

And she placed the matter before him with the utmost clearness: an income of forty-five thousand francs. However, "people were talking about it;" and M. Roque was expecting a definite answer. As for the young girl, her position was truly most embarrassing.

"She is deeply attached to you."

Frederick threw aside the letter even before he had finished reading it, and opened an epistle from Deslauriers.

"DEAR OLD BOY—The *pear* is ripe. In accordance with your promise, we may count on you. We meet to-morrow at daybreak in the Place du Panthéon. Drop into the Café Soufflot. It is necessary for me to talk with you before the manifestation takes place."

"Oh! I know them, with their manifestations! A thousand thanks! I have a more agreeable appointment."

And on the following morning, at eleven o'clock, Frederick left the house. He wanted to give one last glance at the preparations. Then, who could tell but that, by some chance or other, she might be at the place of meeting before him? As he emerged from the Rue Tronchet, he heard a great clamour behind the Madeleine. He pressed forward, and saw at the far end of the square, to the left, a number of men in blouses and well-dressed people.

A manifesto published in the newspapers had summoned to this spot all who had subscribed to the banquet of the Reform Party. The Ministry had, almost without a moment's delay, posted up a proclamation prohibiting the meeting. The Parliamentary Opposition had, on the previous evening, disclaimed any connection with it; but the patriots, who were unaware of this resolution on the part of their leaders, had come to the meeting-place, followed by a great crowd of spectators. A deputation from the schools had made its way, a little earlier, to the house of Odillon Barrot. It was now at the residence of the Minister for Foreign Affairs; and nobody could tell whether the banquet would take place, whether the Government would carry out its threat, and whether the National Guards would make their appearance. People were as furious against the deputies as against Power. The crowd was growing bigger and bigger, when suddenly the strains of the *Marseillaise* rang through the air.

It was the students' column which had just arrived on the scene. They marched at an ordinary walking pace, in double file and in good order, with angry faces, bare hands, and all shouting at intervals:

"Long live Reform! Down with Guizot!"

Frederick's friends were there, sure enough. They would have seen him and dragged him along with them. He quickly sought refuge in the Rue de l'Arcade.

When the students had taken two turns round the Madeleine, they went in the direction of the Place de la Concorde. It was full of people; and, at a distance, the crowd pressed close together, had the appearance of a field of dark ears of corn swaying to and fro.

At the same moment, some soldiers of the line ranged themselves in battle-array at the left-hand side of the church.

The groups remained standing there, however. In order to scatter them, some police-officers in civilian dress seized the most riotous in a brutal fashion, and carried them off to the guard-house. Frederick, in spite of his indignation, remained silent; he feared being arrested along with the others, and thus missing Madame Arnoux.

A little while afterward the helmets of the Municipal Guards appeared. They kept striking about them with the flat side of their sabres. A horse fell. The people made a rush forward to save him, and as soon as the rider was in the saddle, they all ran away.

Then there was a great silence. The thin rain, which had moistened the asphalt, was no longer falling. Clouds floated past, gently swept on by the wind.

Frederick began running through the Rue Tronchet, looking before and behind him.

At length it struck two o'clock.

"Ha! now is the time!" said he to himself. "She is leaving her house; she is approaching," and a minute after, "she has had plenty of time to be here."

Up to three he tried to keep quiet. "No, she is not going to be late— a little patience!"

And for want of something to do he examined the most interesting shops that he passed—a bookseller's, a saddler's and a mourning ware-house. Soon he knew the names of the different books, the various kinds of harness, and every sort of material. The persons who were in atten-dance in these establishments, from seeing him continually going to and fro, were at first surprised, and then alarmed, and finally they closed up their shop-fronts.

No doubt she had met with some obstacle, and must be enduring pain at the delay. But what delight would be afforded in a very short time! For she would come—that was certain. "She has given me her promise!" In the meantime an intolerable feeling of anxiety was gradually seizing hold of him. Impelled by an absurd idea, he returned to his hotel, as if he expected to find her there. At the same moment, she might have reached the street in which their meeting was to take place. He rushed out. There was no one. And he resumed his tramp up and down the footpath.

He stared at the gaps in the pavement, the mouths of the gutters, the candelabra, and the numbers above the doors. The most trifling objects became for him companions, or rather, ironical spectators, and the uni-form fronts of the houses seemed to him to have a pitiless aspect. He was suffering from cold feet. He felt as if he were about to succumb to the dejection which was crushing him. The reverberation of his footsteps vibrated through his brain as he tramped to and fro.

When he saw by his watch that it was four o'clock, he experienced, as it were, a sense of vertigo, a feeling of despair. He tried to repeat some verses to himself, to make a calculation, no matter of what sort, to invent some kind of story. Impossible! He was beset by the image of Madame Arnoux; he felt a longing to run in order to meet her. But what road ought he to take so that they might not pass each other?

He went up to a messenger, put five francs into his hand, and told him to go to the Rue de Paradis to Jacques Arnoux's residence and inquire "if Madame were at home." Then he took up his post at the corner of the Rue de la Ferme and of the Rue Tronchet, so as to be able to look down both of them at the same time. On the boulevard, in the background of the scene before him, confused masses of people were gliding past. He could distinguish, every now and then, the aigrette of a dragoon or a woman's hat; and he strained his eyes in an effort to recognise the wearer. A child in rags, exhibiting a jack-in-the-box, asked him, with a smile, for alms.

The man with the velvet vest reappeared. "The porter had not seen her going out." What had kept her in? If she were ill he would have been told about it. Was it a visitor? Nothing was easier than to say that she was not at home. He struck his forehead.

"Ah! I am stupid! Of course, this political outbreak prevented her from coming!"

He was relieved by this apparently natural explanation. Then, suddenly: "But her quarter of the city is quiet." And a horrible doubt seized hold of his mind: "Suppose she never intended coming at all, and merely gave me a promise in order to get rid of me? No, no!" What had prevented her from coming was, no doubt, some extraordinary mischance, one of those occurrences that baffled all one's anticipations. In that case she would have written to him.

He sent the hotel errand-boy to his residence in the Rue Rumfort to find out whether there was a letter waiting for him there.

No letter had been brought. This absence of news reassured him.

He drew omens from the number of coins which he took out of his pocket by chance, from the physiognomies of the passers-by, and from the colour of different horses; and when the augury was unfavourable, he forced himself to disbelieve it. In his sudden outbursts of rage against Madame Arnoux, he abused her in muttering tones. Then came fits of weakness that nearly made him swoon, followed, all of a sudden, by fresh rebounds of hopefulness. She would appear presently! She was there, behind his back! He turned round—there was nobody there! Once he saw, about thirty paces away, a woman of the same height, with a dress of the same kind. He came up to her—it was not she. It struck five—half-past five—six. The gas-lamps were lighted. Madame Arnoux had not come.

The night before, she had dreamed that she had been, for some time, on the footpath in the Rue Tronchet. She was waiting for something the nature of which she was not quite clear about, but which, nevertheless, was of great importance; and, without knowing why, she was afraid of being seen. But a pestiferous little dog kept barking at her furiously and biting at the hem of her dress. Every time she shook him off he returned stubbornly to the attack, always barking more violently than before. Madame Arnoux woke up. The dog's barking continued. She strained her ears to listen. It came from her son's room. She rushed to the spot in her bare feet. It was the child himself who was coughing. His hands were burning, his face flushed, and his voice singularly hoarse. Every minute he found it more difficult to breathe. She remained there till daybreak, bent over the coverlet watching him.

At eight o'clock the drum of the National Guard reminded M. Arnoux that his comrades were expecting his arrival. He dressed himself quickly and went out, promising that he would immediately send their doctor, M. Colot, whose house he would be passing.

At ten o'clock, when M. Colot did not make his appearance, Madame Arnoux despatched her chamber-maid for him. The doctor was away in the country; and the young man who was taking his place had gone out on some business.

Eugène kept his head on one side on the bolster with contracted eyebrows and dilated nostrils. His pale little face was whiter than the sheets; and there escaped from his larynx a wheezing caused by his oppressed breathing, which gradually grew shorter, dryer, and more metallic. His cough resembled the noise made by those barbarous mechanical inventions known as barking toy-dogs.

Madame Arnoux was seized with terror. She rang the bell violently, calling out for help, and exclaiming:

"A doctor! a doctor!"

Ten minutes later came an elderly gentleman in a white tie, and with grey whiskers well trimmed. He put several questions as to the habits, the age, and the constitution of the young patient, and studied the case with his head thrown back. Then he wrote out a prescription.

The calm manner of this old man was intolerable. He smelt of aromatics. She would have liked to beat him. He said he would return in the evening.

The horrible coughing soon began again. Sometimes the child sat up suddenly. Convulsive movements shook the muscles of his breast; and in his efforts to breathe his stomach shrank in as if he were suffocating after running too hard. Then he sank down, with his head thrown back and his mouth wide open. With infinite pains, Madame Arnoux tried to make him swallow the contents of the phials, hippo wine, and a potion containing trisulphate of antimony. But he pushed away the spoon, groaning in a feeble panting voice. He seemed to be blowing out his words.

At intervals she re-read the prescription. The observations of the formulary frightened her. Perhaps the apothecary had made some mistake. Her powerlessness filled her with despair. M. Colot's pupil arrived.

He was a young man of modest demeanour, new to medical work, and he made no attempt to disguise his opinion about the case. He was at first undecided as to what should be done, for fear of compromising himself, and finally he ordered pieces of ice to be applied to the sick child. It took a long time to get ice. The bladder containing it burst. It was necessary to change the little boy's shirt. This disturbance brought on an attack of even a more dreadful character than any of the previous ones.

The child began tearing off the linen round his neck, as if he were trying to remove the obstacle that was choking him; and he scratched the walls and seized the curtains of his bedstead, trying to get a point of support to assist him in breathing.

His face was now of a bluish hue, and his entire body, bathed in a cold perspiration, appeared to be growing lean. His haggard eyes were fixed with terror on his mother. He threw his arms round her neck, and hung there desperately; and repressing her rising sobs, she gave utterance in a broken voice to loving words:

"Yes, my pet, my angel, my treasure!"

Then came intervals of calm.

She went to look for playthings—a punchinello, a collection of images, and spread them out on the bed in an effort to amuse him. She even attempted to sing.

She began a little ballad which she used to sing years before, when she was nursing him, wrapped up in swaddling-clothes in this same little upholstered chair. But a shiver ran all over his frame, just as when a wave is agitated by the wind. The balls of his eyes protruded. She thought he was about to die, and turned away her eyes to avoid seeing him.

The next moment she felt strength enough in her to look at him. He was still living. The hours succeeded each other—dull, mournful, interminable, hopeless, and she no longer counted the minutes, save by the progress of this mental anguish. The shakings of his chest threw him forward as if to shatter his body. Finally, he vomited something strange, which was like a parchment tube. What could it be? She fancied that he had evacuated one end of his entrails. But he now began to breathe freely and regularly. This improved appearance alarmed her more than anything else that had happened. She was sitting like one petrified, her arms hanging by her sides, her eyes fixed, when M. Colot suddenly entered. The child, in his opinion, was saved.

She did not realise what he meant at first, and made him repeat the words. Was not this one of those consoling phrases which were customary with medical men? The doctor departed with an air of tranquillity. Then it seemed as if the cords that pressed round her heart were loosened.

"Saved! Is it possible?"

Suddenly the thought of Frederick presented itself to her mind in a clear and inexorable fashion. This was a warning sent to her by Providence. But the Lord in His mercy had not completed her chastisement. What expiation could she offer at another time if she were to persevere in this love-affair? No doubt insults would be cast at her son on her account; and Madame Arnoux saw him a young man, wounded in a combat, carried off on a litter, dying. At one spring she threw herself on the little chair, and, letting her soul escape toward the heights of heaven, she vowed to God that she would sacrifice, as a holocaust, her first real passion, her only weakness as a woman.

Frederick had returned home. He remained in his armchair, without energy enough to curse her. A sort of slumber fell upon him, and, in the midst of his nightmare, he could hear the rain falling, still under the impression that he was there outside on the footpath.

Next morning, unable to resist the temptation which assailed him, he again sent a messenger to Madame Arnoux's house.

Whether the true explanation happened to be that the fellow did not deliver his message or that she had too many things to say to explain herself in a word or two, the same answer was brought back. This insolence was too great! A feeling of angry pride took possession of him. He swore to himself that he would never again cherish even a desire; and, like a group of leaves swept away by a hurricane, his love disappeared. He experienced a sense of relief, a feeling of stoical joy, then a need of violent action; and he walked at random through the streets.

Men from the faubourgs were marching past armed with guns and old swords, some of them wearing red caps, and all singing the *Marseillaise* or the *Girondins*. Here and there a National Guard was hurrying to join his mayoral department. Drums could be heard rolling in the distance. A conflict was going on at Porte Saint-Martin. There was something lively and warlike in the air. Frederick kept continuously walking on. The excitement of the great city made him gay.

On the Frascati hill he got a glimpse of the Maréchale's windows: a wild idea occurred to him, a reaction of youthfulness. He crossed the boulevard.

The yard-gate was just being closed; and Delphine, who was in the act of writing on it with a piece of charcoal, "Arms given," said to Frederick in an eager tone:

"Ah! Madame is in a nice state! She discharged a groom who insulted her this morning. She thinks there's going to be pillage everywhere. She is frightened to death! and the more so as Monsieur has gone!"

"What Monsieur?"

"The Prince!"

Frederick entered the boudoir. The Maréchale was there, in her petticoat, her hair hanging down her back in disorder.

"Ah! thanks! You are going to save me! 'tis the second time! You are one of those who never count the cost!"

"A thousand pardons!" said Frederick, catching her round the waist with both hands.

"How now? What are you doing?" stammered the Maréchale, at the same time surprised and cheered by his manner.

He replied:

"I am in the fashion! I'm reformed!"

She let herself fall back on the divan, and continued laughing under his kisses.

They spent the afternoon looking out of the window at the people in the street. Then he took her to dine at the Trois Frères Provençaux. The meal was a long and dainty one. They returned on foot for want of a vehicle.

At the announcement of a new Ministry, Paris had changed. Everyone was in a state of delight. People promenaded about the streets, and every floor was illuminated with lamps, so that it seemed as if it were broad daylight. The soldiers returned to their barracks, worn out and looking quite depressed. The people saluted them with exclamations of "Long live the Line!"

They continued on their way without making any response. Among the National Guard, on the contrary, the officers, flushed with enthusiasm, brandished their sabres, vociferating:

"Long live Reform!"

And every time the two lovers heard this word they laughed.

Frederick told droll stories, and was quite gay.

Passing through the Rue Duphot, they reached the boulevards. Venetian lanterns hanging from the houses formed wreaths of flame. Underneath, a confused swarm of people kept in constant motion. In the midst of those moving shadows could be seen, here and there, the steely glitter of bayonets. There was a great uproar. The crowd was so compact that it was impossible to make one's way back in a straight line. They were entering the Rue Caumartin, when suddenly behind them burst forth a noise like the crackling of an immense piece of silk being torn across. It was the discharge of musketry on the Boulevard des Capucines.

"Ha! a few of the citizens are getting a crack," said Frederick calmly; for there are situations in which a man of the least cruel disposition is so much detached from his fellow-men that he would see the entire human race exterminated without a single throb of the heart.

The Maréchale was clinging to his arm with her teeth chattering. She declared that she could not walk twenty steps farther. Then, by a refinement of hatred, in order the better to offer an outrage in his own soul to Madame Arnoux, he took Rosanette to the hotel in the Rue Tronchet, and brought her up to the room which he had got ready for the other.

The flowers were still fresh. The guipure was spread out on the bed. He drew out from the cupboard the little slippers. Rosanette considered this forethought on his part a great proof of his delicacy of sentiment. About one o'clock she was awakened by distant rolling sounds, and she found that he was sobbing bitterly with his head buried in the pillow.

"What is troubling you, darling?"

"'Tis the extreme joy," said Frederick. "I have been too long waiting for you!"

BOOK II

CHAPTER XIV

REVOLUTIONARY DAYS

A DISCHARGE of musketry aroused Frederick from sleep; and, in spite of Rosanette's entreaties, he determined to go and see what was happening. He hurried down to the Champs-Elysées, where shots were being fired. At the corner of the Rue Saint-Honoré some men in blouses ran past him, exclaiming:

"No! not that way! to the Palais-Royal!"

Frederick followed them. The grating of the Convent of the Assumption had been torn away. A little farther on there were three paving-stones in the middle of the street, the beginning of a barricade, no doubt; then fragments of bottles and bundles of iron-wire, to obstruct the cavalry; and there rushed suddenly out of a lane a tall young man of pale complexion, with his black hair flowing over his shoulders, and with an odd sort of pea-coloured swaddling-cloth thrown round him. In his hand he held a long military musket, and he dashed along on the tips of his slippers with the air of a somnambulist and the nimbleness of a tiger. At intervals a detonation could be heard.

On the evening of the day before, the sight of a waggon containing five corpses picked up from amongst those that were lying on the Boulevard des Capucines had changed the disposition of the people; and, while at the Tuileries the aides-de-camp succeeded each other, and M. Molé, having set about the composition of a new Cabinet, did not come back, and M. Thiers was making efforts to constitute another, and while the King was cavilling and hesitating, and finally assigned the post of commander-in-chief to Bugeaud in order to prevent him from making use of it, the insurrection was organising itself in a formidable manner, as if it were directed by a single arm.

Men inspired with a kind of frantic eloquence were engaged in haranguing the populace at the street-corners, others were in the churches ringing the tocsin as loudly as ever they could. Lead was cast for bullets, cartridges were rolled about. The trees on the boulevards, the urinals, the benches, the gratings, the gas-burners, everything was torn off and thrown about. Paris, that morning, was covered with barricades. The resistance which was offered was of short duration, so that at eight o'clock the people, by voluntary surrender or by force, had got possession of five barracks, nearly all the municipal buildings, the most favourable strategic points. Of its own accord, without any effort, the monarchy was rapidly dissolving, and now an attack was made on the guard-house of the Château d'Eau, in order to liberate fifty prisoners, who were not there.

Frederick was forced to stop at the entrance to the square. It was filled with groups of armed men. The Rue Saint-Thomas and the Rue Fromanteau were occupied by companies of the Line. The Rue de Valois was choked up by an enormous barricade. The smoke which fluttered about at the top of it partly opened. Men kept running overhead, making violent gestures; they vanished from sight; then the firing was again renewed. It was answered from the guard-house without anyone being visible. Its windows, protected by oaken window-shutters, were pierced with loopholes; and the monument with its two stories, its two wings, its fountain on the first floor and its little door in the centre, was beginning to be speckled with white spots under the shock of the bullets. The three steps in front of it remained unoccupied.

At his side a man in a Greek cap, with a cartridge-box over his knitted vest, was disputing with a woman with a Madras neckerchief round her shoulders. She said to him:

"Come back now! Come back!"

"Leave me alone!" replied the husband. "You can easily mind the porter's lodge by yourself. I ask, citizen, is this fair? I have on every occasion done my duty—in 1830, in '32, in '34, and in '39! Now they're fighting again. I must fight! Go away!"

And the porter's wife ended by yielding to his remonstrances and to those of a National Guard near them—a man of forty, whose simple face was adorned with a circle of white beard. He loaded his gun and fired while talking to Frederick, as calm in the midst of the outbreak as a horticulturist in his garden. A young lad with a packing-cloth thrown over him was trying to coax this man to give him a few caps, so that he might make use of a gun he had, a fine fowling-piece which a "gentleman" had made him a present of.

"Catch on behind my back," said the good man, "and keep yourself from being seen, or you'll get yourself killed!"

The drums sounded for the charge. Sharp cries, hurrahs of triumph burst forth. A continual ebbing to and fro made the multitude sway backward and forward. Frederick, caught between two thick masses of people, did not move an inch, all the time fascinated and entertained by the scene around him. The wounded who sank to the ground, the dead lying at his feet, did not seem like persons really wounded or really dead. The impression left on him was that he was looking on at a show.

In the midst of the surging throng, above the sea of heads, could be seen an old man in a black coat, mounted on a white horse with a velvet saddle. He held in one hand a green bough, in the other a paper, and he kept shaking them continuously; but at length, abandoning all hope of obtaining a hearing, he withdrew from the scene.

The soldiers of the Line had gone, and only the municipal troops were left to defend the guard-house. A wave of dauntless spirits dashed up the steps; they were flung down; others came on to replace them, and the gate resounded under blows from iron bars. The municipal guards did not give way. A waggon, stuffed full of hay, and burning like a gigantic torch, was dragged against the walls. Faggots were speedily brought, then straw, and a barrel of spirits of wine. The fire mounted up to the stones along the wall; the building began to send forth smoke on all sides like the crater of a volcano; and at its summit, between the balustrades of the terrace, huge flames escaped with a harsh noise. The first story of the Palais-Royal was occupied by National Guards. Shots were fired through every window in the square; the bullets whizzed, the water of the fountain, which had burst, mingled with the blood, forming little pools on the ground. People slipped in the mud over clothes, shakos, and weapons. Frederick felt something soft under his foot. It was the hand of a sergeant in a grey great-coat, stretched on his face in the stream that ran along the street. Fresh bands of people continually came up, pushing on the combatants at the guard-house. The firing became quicker. The wine-shops were open; people went into them from time to time to smoke a pipe and drink a glass of beer, and then came back again to fight. A lost dog began to howl. This made the people laugh.

Frederick was shaken by the impact of a man falling on his shoulder with a bullet through his back; he could hear the death-rattle in his throat. At this shot, perhaps directed against himself, he felt stirred up to rage; and he was plunging forward when a National Guard stopped him.

"'Tis useless! the King has just gone! If you don't believe me, go and see for yourself!"

This assurance calmed Frederick. The Place du Carrousel had a tranquil aspect. The Hôtel de Nantes stood there as firm as ever; and the houses in the rear; the dome of the Louvre in front, the long gallery of wood at the right, and the waste plot of ground that ran unevenly as far as the sheds of the stall-keepers were, so to speak, steeped in the grey hues of the atmosphere, where indistinct murmurs seemed to mingle with the fog; while, at the other side of the square, a stiff light, falling through the parting of the clouds on the façade of the Tuileries, outlined all its windows in white patches. Near the Arc de Triomphe a dead horse lay on the ground. Behind the gratings groups consisting of five or six persons were chatting. The doors leading into the château were open, and the servants at the entrances allowed the people to enter.

Below stairs, in a kind of little parlour, bowls of *café au lait* were passed round. A few sat down to the table and made merry; others remained standing, and amongst the latter was a hackney-coachman. He snatched up with both hands a glass vessel full of powdered sugar, cast a restless glance right and left, and then began to eat voraciously, with his nose stuck into the mouth of the vessel.

At the foot of the great staircase a man was writing his name in a register.

Frederick recognised him by his back.

"Hallo, Hussonnet!"

"Yes, 'tis I," replied the Bohemian. "I am introducing myself at court. This is a nice joke, isn't it?"

"Suppose we go upstairs?"

And they reached presently the Salle des Maréchaux. The portraits of those illustrious generals, save that of Bugeaud, which had been pierced through the stomach, were all intact. They were represented leaning on their sabres with a gun-carriage behind each of them, and in formidable attitudes in contrast with the occasion. A large timepiece indicated that it was twenty minutes past one.

Suddenly the *Marseillaise* resounded. Hussonnet and Frederick looked over the balusters. It was the people. They rushed up the stairs, shaking with a dizzying, wave-like motion bare heads, or helmets, or red caps, or else bayonets or human shoulders with such impetuosity that somebody disappeared every now and then in the swarming mass, which was mounting up without a moment's pause, like a river compressed by an equinoctial tide, with a continuous roar under an irresistible impulse. When they reached the top of the stairs, they were scattered, and their chant died away. Nothing could any longer be heard but the tramp of feet intermingled with the chopping sound of many voices. The crowd not being in a mischievous mood, contented themselves with looking about them. But, from time to time, an elbow, pressing too hard, broke through a pane of glass, or else a vase or a statue fell from a bracket down on the floor. The wainscotings cracked under the pressure of people against them. Every face was flushed; the perspiration was rolling down their features in large beads. Hussonnet remarked:

"Heroes have not a good smell."

"Ah! you are provoking," returned Frederick.

And, pushed forward in spite of themselves, they entered an apartment in which a daïs of red velvet rose as far as the ceiling. On the throne below sat a representative of the proletariat in effigy with a black beard, his shirt gaping open, a jolly air, and the stupid look of a baboon. Some climbed up the platform to sit in his place.

"What a myth!" said Hussonnet. "There you see the sovereign people!"

The armchair was raised up on the hands of a number of persons and passed across the hall, swaying from side to side.

"By Jove, 'tis like a boat! The Ship of State is tossing about in a stormy sea! Let it dance the cancan! Let it dance the cancan!"

They had drawn it toward a window, and in the midst of hisses, they launched it out.

"Poor old chap!" said Hussonnet, as he saw the effigy falling into the garden, where it was speedily picked up, in order to be afterward carried to the Bastile to be burned.

Then a mad joy burst forth, as if, in place of the throne, a future of boundless happiness had arrived; and the people, less through a spirit of vindictiveness than to enjoy their right of possession, broke or tore the glasses, the curtains, the lustres, the tapers, the tables, the chairs, the stools, the entire furniture, including the very albums and engravings, and the corbels of the tapestry. Since they were the victors, they must needs amuse themselves! The common herd ironically wrapped themselves up in laces and cashmeres. Gold fringes were rolled round the sleeves of blouses. Hats with ostriches' feathers adorned blacksmiths' heads, and ribbons of the Legion of Honour supplied waistbands for prostitutes. Each person satisfied his or her caprice; some danced, others drank. In the queen's apartment a woman glossed her hair with pomatum. Behind a folding-screen two lovers played cards. Hussonnet drew Frederick's attention to an individual who was smoking a dirty pipe with his elbows resting on a balcony; and the popular frenzy redoubled with the continuous crash of broken porcelain and pieces of crystal, which, as they rebounded, made sounds resembling those produced by the plates of musical glasses.

Then their fury was overshadowed. A vulgar curiosity made them rummage all the dressing-rooms, all the recesses. Liberated convicts thrust their arms into the beds of princesses, and rolled themselves on the top of them, to console themselves for not being able to embrace their owners. Others, with sinister faces, wandered about silently, looking for something to steal, but too great a multitude was there. Through the bays of the doors could be seen in the suite of apartments only the dark mass of people between the gilding of the walls under a cloud of dust. Every breast was beating. The heat became more and more suffocating; and the two friends, afraid of being stifled, seized opportunity of escaping, making their way out.

In the antechamber, standing on a heap of garments, appeared a girl of the town as a statue of Liberty, motionless, her grey eyes wide open—a fearful sight.

They had taken about three steps outside the château when a company of the National Guards, in great-coats, advanced toward them, and, removing their foraging-caps from their slightly bald heads, they bowed very low to the people. At this testimony of respect, the ragged victors bridled up. Hussonnet and Frederick experienced a certain pleasure from it as well as the rest.

They were filled with ardour. They went back to the Palais-Royal. In front of the Rue Fromanteau, soldiers' corpses were heaped up on the straw. They passed close to the dead without a single quiver of emotion, feeling a certain pride in being able to control themselves.

The Palais overflowed with people. In the inner courtyard seven piles of wood were burning. Pianos, chests of drawers, and clocks were hurled out through the windows. Fire-engines sent streams of water up to the roofs. Some vagabonds tried to cut the hose with their sabres. Frederick urged a pupil of the Polytechnic School to interfere. The latter did not understand him, and, moreover, appeared to be idiotic. All around, in the two galleries, the populace, having got possession of the cellars, gave themselves up to a horrible carouse. Wine flowed in streams around people's feet; the mudlarks drank out of the tail-ends of the bottles, and shouted songs and oaths as they staggered along.

"Come out of this," said Hussonnet; "I am disgusted with the people."

All over the Orléans Gallery the wounded lay on mattresses on the ground, with purple curtains over them as coverlets; and the small shop-keepers' wives and daughters from the quarter brought them broth and linen.

"No matter!" said Frederick; "after all, the people are sublime."

The great vestibule was filled with a whirlwind of furious individuals. Men tried to ascend to the upper stories in order to continue the work of wholesale destruction. National Guards, on the steps, strove to keep them back. The most intrepid was a chasseur, who stood with bare head, his hair bristling, and his straps in pieces. His shirt caused a swelling between his trousers and his coat, and he struggled desperately in the midst of the others. Hussonnet, who had a sharp sight, recognised Arnoux.

Then they went into the Tuileries garden, so as to be able to breathe more freely. They sat down on a bench and remained for some minutes with their eyes closed, so stunned that they had not the energy to say a word. The people who were passing stopped to inform them that the Duchesse d'Orléans had been appointed Regent, and that it was all over. They were feeling that species of comfort which follows rapid *dénoue-*

ments, when at the windows of the attics in the château appeared men-servants tearing their liveries to pieces. They flung their torn clothes into the garden, as a token of renunciation. The people hooted at them, and then they retired.

The attention of Frederick and Hussonnet was distracted by a tall fellow who was walking quickly between the trees with a musket on his shoulder. A cartridge-box was pressed against his pea-jacket; a handkerchief was wound round his forehead under his cap. He turned his head to one side. It was Dussardier; and casting himself into their arms:

"Ah! what good fortune, my dear old friends!" without being able to say another word, so breathless was he from fatigue.

He had been on his feet for the last twenty-four hours. He had been engaged at the barricades of the Latin Quarter, had fought in the Rue Rabuteau, had saved three dragoons' lives, had entered the Tuileries with Colonel Dunoyer, and, after that, had repaired to the Chamber, and then had gone to the Hôtel de Ville.

"I have come right from it! all goes well! the people are victorious! the workmen and the employers are embracing one another! Ha! if you knew what I have seen! what brave fellows! what a fine sight it was!"

And without noticing that they had no arms:

"I was quite certain of finding you there! This has been a bit rough—no matter!"

A drop of blood ran down his cheek, and in answer to the questions put to him by the two others:

"Oh! 'tis nothing! a slight scratch from a bayonet!"

"Still, you ought to take care of yourself."

"Pooh! I am substantial! What does this matter? The Republic is proclaimed! We'll be happy henceforth! Some journalists, who were talking near me just now, said they were going to liberate Poland and Italy! No more kings! You understand? The entire land free! the entire land free!"

And with one comprehensive glance at the horizon, he spread out his arms triumphantly. Just then a long file of men rushed over the terrace on the water's edge.

"Ah, deuce take it! I was forgetting. I must be off. Good-bye!"

He went off shouting with them, while brandishing his musket:

"Long live the Republic!"

From the chimneys of the château escaped enormous whirlwinds of black smoke which bore sparks along with them. The ringing of the bells sent out over the city a wild and startling alarm. Right and left, in every direction, the conquerors discharged their weapons.

Frederick, though he was not a warrior, felt the Gallic blood bounding in his veins. The magnetism of the public enthusiasm had seized hold of him. He inhaled with a voluptuous delight the stormy atmosphere filled with the odour of gunpowder; and he quivered under the effluvium of an immense love, a supreme and universal tenderness, as if the heart of all humanity were throbbing in his breast.

Hussonnet said, with a yawn:

"It might be time, perhaps, to go and instruct the populace."

Frederick accompanied him to his correspondence-office in the Place de la Bourse; and he began to compose for the Troyes newspaper an account of recent events in a lyric style—a veritable tit-bit—to which he attached his signature. Then they dined together at a tavern. Hussonnet was pensive; the eccentricities of the Revolution surpassed his own.

After leaving the café, they repaired to the Hôtel de Ville to learn the news, and the boyish impulses which were natural to him had got the upper hand once more. He scaled the barricades like a chamois, and answered the sentinels with broad jokes of a patriotic flavour.

They heard the Provisional Government proclaimed by torchlight. At last, Frederick got back to his house at midnight, overcome with fatigue.

"Well," said he to his man-servant, while the latter was undressing him, "are you satisfied?"

"Yes, no doubt, Monsieur; but I don't like to see the people dancing to music."

Next morning, when he awoke, Frederick thought of Deslauriers. He hastened to his friend's lodgings. He ascertained that the advocate had just left Paris, having been appointed a provincial commissioner. At the *soirée* given the night before, he had come into contact with Ledru-Rollin, and laying siege to him in the name of the Law Schools, had snatched from him a post, a mission. However, the doorkeeper explained, he had promised to write giving his address the following week.

After this, Frederick went to see the Maréchale. She received him. She resented his desertion of her. Her bitterness disappeared when he repeatedly assured her that peace was restored.

All was quiet now. There was no reason to be alarmed. He kissed her, and she declared herself in favour of the Republic, as his lordship the Archbishop of Paris had already done, and as the magistracy, the Council of State, the Institute, the marshals of France, Changarnier, M. de Falloux, all the Bonapartists, all the Legitimists, and a considerable number of Orléanists were about to do with a swiftness indicative of marvellous zeal.

The overthrow of the monarchy had been so rapid that, as soon as the first stupefaction that succeeded it had passed away, there was amongst the middle class a feeling of astonishment at the fact that they were still alive. The summary execution of some thieves, who were shot without a trial, was regarded as an act of signal justice. For a month Lamartine's phrase was repeated with reference to the red flag, "which had only gone the round of the Champ de Mars, while the tricoloured flag," etc.; and all placed themselves under its shade, each party seeing amongst the three colours only its own, and firmly determined, as soon as it gained the most power, to tear away the two others.

As business was suspended, anxiety and love of gaping drove everyone into the open air. The careless style of costume generally adopted lessened differences of social position. Hatred disguised itself; expectations were openly indulged in; the multitude seemed full of good-nature. The pride of having maintained their rights shone in the people's faces. They displayed the gaiety of a carnival, the manners of a bivouac. Nothing could be more amusing than the aspect of Paris during the first days that followed the Revolution.

Frederick gave the Maréchale his arm, and they strolled along through the streets. She was highly diverted by the display of rosettes in every buttonhole, by the banners hung from every window, and the bills of various colours that were posted upon the walls; she threw some money here and there into the collection-boxes for the wounded, which were placed on chairs in the middle of the pathway. Then she stopped before some caricatures representing Louis Philippe as a pastry-cook, as a mountebank, as a dog, or as a leech. But she was a little frightened at the sight of Caussidière's men with their sabres and scarfs. At other times it was a tree of Liberty that was being planted. The clergy vied with each other in blessing the Republic; they were escorted by servants in gold lace; and the populace thought this very fine. The most frequent sight was that of deputations from no matter what, going to demand something at the Hôtel de Ville—every trade, every industry, was looking to the Government to put a complete end to its miseries. Some, it is true, went to offer advice or congratulate, or merely to pay a little visit, and to see the Government machine performing its functions.

One day, about the middle of the month of March, as they were passing the Pont d'Arcole, doing some commission for Rosanette in the Latin Quarter, Frederick saw approaching a column of individuals with oddly-shaped hats and long beards. At its head, beating a drum, walked a negro who had formerly been an artist's model; and the man who bore the banner, on which this inscription floated in the wind, "Artist-Painters," was no other than Pellerin.

He signed to Frederick to wait for him, and then reappeared five minutes afterward, having some time before him; for the Government was, at that moment, receiving a deputation from the stone-cutters. He was going with his colleagues to ask for the creation of a Forum of Art, a kind of Exchange where the interests of Æsthetics would be discussed. Sublime masterpieces would be produced, as a result of the workers amalgamating their talents. Ere long Paris would be covered with gigan-

tic monuments. He would decorate them. He had even begun a figure of
the Republic. One of his comrades had come to take it, for they were
closely followed by the deputation from the poulterers.

"What stupidity!" growled a voice in the crowd. "Always some humbug, nothing strong!"

It was Regimbart. He did not salute Frederick, but took advantage of
the occasion to give vent to his own bitterness.

The Citizen spent his days wandering about the streets, pulling his
moustache, rolling his eyes about, accepting and spreading any dismal
news that was communicated to him; and he had only two phrases: "Take
care! we're going to be run over!" or else, "Why, confound it! they're jug-
gling with the Republic!" He was dissatisfied with everything, and especially with the fact that we had not regained our natural frontiers.

The very name of Lamartine made him shrug his shoulders. He did
not consider Ledru-Rollin "sufficient for the problem," referred to
Dupont (of the Eure) as an old numbskull, Albert as an idiot, Louis Blanc
as an Utopist, and Blanqui as an exceedingly dangerous man; and when
Frederick asked him what he would advise as the best thing to do, he
replied, pressing his arm till he nearly bruised it:

"To take the Rhine, I tell you! to take the Rhine, damn it!"

Then he blamed the Reactionaries. They were taking off the mask. The
sack of the Château of Neuilly and Suresne, the fire at Batignolles, the
troubles at Lyons, all the excesses and all the grievances, were just now
being exaggerated by having superadded to them Ledru-Rollin's circular,
the forced currency of bank-notes, the fall of the funds to sixty francs, and,
to crown all, as the supreme wrong, a final blow, a culminating horror, the
duty of forty-five centimes! And over and above all these things, there was
Socialism! Although these theories, as new as the game of goose, had been
discussed sufficiently for forty years to fill a number of libraries, they terrified the wealthier citizens, as if they had been a hailstorm of aërolites; and
they expressed indignation at them by reason of that hatred which the
advent of every idea provokes, simply because it is an idea—an odium from
which it derives subsequently its glory, and which causes its enemies to be
always beneath it, however lowly it may be.

Then Property attained in the public regard the level of Religion, and
was confounded with God. The attacks made on it appeared to them a
sacrilege; almost a species of cannibalism. In spite of the most humane
legislation that ever existed, the spectre of '93 reappeared, and the chopper of the guillotine vibrated in every syllable of the word "Republic,"
which did not prevent them from despising it for its weakness. France,
no longer feeling herself in command of the situation, was beginning to
shriek with terror, like a blind man without his stick or an infant that has
lost its nurse.

Of all Frenchmen, M. Dambreuse was the most alarmed. The new condition of things threatened his fortune, but, more than anything else, it deceived his experience. A system so good! a king so wise! was it possible? The ground was tottering beneath their feet! Next morning he dismissed three of his servants, sold his horses, bought a soft hat to go out into the streets, considered even letting his beard grow; and he remained at home, prostrated, reading over and over again newspapers most hostile to his own ideas; he was plunged into such gloomy reflections that even the jokes about the pipe of Flocon had not the power to make him smile.

As a supporter of the late reign, he was dreading the vengeance of the people on his estates in Champagne, when Frederick's lucubration fell into his hands. Then it occurred to his mind that his young friend was a very useful personage, and that he might be able, if not to serve him, at least to protect him; so, one morning, M. Dambreuse presented himself at Frederick's residence, accompanied by Martinon.

This visit, he said, had no purpose save that of seeing him for a little while, and having a chat. He rejoiced at the events that had happened, and with his whole heart adopted "our sublime motto, *Liberty, Equality and Fraternity,*" having always been at heart a Republican. If he voted under the other *régime* with the Ministry, it was simply in order to accelerate an inevitable downfall. He even inveighed against M. Guizot, "who has got us into a nice hobble, we must admit!" By way of retaliation, he spoke enthusiastically about Lamartine, who had shown himself "magnificent, upon my word of honour, when, with reference to the red flag—"

"Yes, I know," said Frederick. After which he declared that his sympathies were on the side of the working-men.

"For, in fact, more or less, we are all working-men!" And he carried his impartiality so far as to admit that Proudhon had a certain amount of logic in his views. "Oh, a great deal of logic, deuce take it!"

Then, with the disinterestedness of a superior mind, he chatted about the exhibition of pictures, at which he had seen Pellerin's work. He considered it original and well-painted.

Martinon supported all he said with expressions of approval; and likewise was of his opinion that it was necessary to rally boldly to the side of the Republic. And he talked about the husbandman, his father, and assumed the part of the peasant, the man of the people. They soon came to the question of the elections for the National Assembly, and the candidates in the arrondissement of La Fortelle. The Opposition candidate had no chance.

"You should take his place!" said M. Dambreuse.

Frederick protested.

"But why not?" For he would obtain the suffrages of the Extremists

owing to his personal opinions, and that of the Conservatives on account
of his family; "And perhaps also," added the banker, with a smile, "thanks
to my influence, in some measure."

Frederick urged as an obstacle that he did not know how to set about
the matter.

Nothing was easier if he only got himself recommended to the patriots of the Aube by one of the clubs of the capital. All he had to do was
to read out, not a profession of faith such as might be seen every day, but
a serious statement of principles.

"Bring it to me; I am familiar with what goes down in the locality;
and you can, I say again, render great services to the country—to us all—
to myself."

In such times people ought to assist each other, and, if Frederick had
need of anything, he or his friends—

"Oh, a thousand thanks, my dear Monsieur!"

"You'll do as much for me in return, mind!"

Decidedly, the banker was a decent man.

Frederick could not refrain from pondering over his advice; and soon
he was dazzled by a kind of dizziness.

The great figures of the Convention passed before his mental vision.
It seemed to him that a splendid dawn was about to rise. Rome, Vienna
and Berlin were in a state of insurrection, and the Austrians had been
driven out of Venice. All Europe was agitated. Now was the time to
make a plunge into the movement, and perhaps to accelerate it; and then
he was fascinated by the costume which it was said the deputies would
wear. Already he could see himself in a waistcoat with lapels and a tricoloured sash; and this itching, this hallucination, became so violent that
he talked the matter over with Dambreuse.

The honest fellow's enthusiasm had not abated.

"Certainly—sure enough. Offer yourself."

Frederick, nevertheless, consulted Deslauriers.

The idiotic opposition which trammelled the commissioner in his
province had augmented his Liberalism. He at once replied, exhorting
Frederick with the utmost vehemence to present himself as a candidate.
However, as the latter was desirous of having the approval of a great
number of persons, he confided the thing to Rosanette one day, when
Mademoiselle Vatnaz happened to be present.

She was one of those Parisian spinsters who, every evening, when they
have given their lessons or tried to sell little sketches, or to dispose of
poor manuscripts, return to their own homes with mud on their petticoats, prepare their own dinner, which they eat by themselves, and then,
with their soles resting on a foot-warmer, by the light of a filthy lamp,
dream of love, a family, a hearth, wealth—all that they lack. So it was that,

like many others, she had hailed in the Revolution the advent of vengeance, and she delivered herself up to a Socialistic propaganda of the most extreme description.

The enfranchisement of the proletariat, according to the Vatnaz, was only possible by the enfranchisement of woman. She wished to have her own sex admitted to every kind of employment, to have strict inquiry made into the paternity of children, a different code, the abolition, or at least a more intelligent regulation, of marriage. In that case every Frenchwoman would be bound to marry a Frenchman, or to adopt an old man. Nurses and midwives should be State paid officials.

There should be a jury to examine the works of women, special editors for women, a polytechnic school for women, a National Guard for women, everything for women! And since the Government ignored their rights, they ought to overcome force by force. Ten thousand citizenesses with good guns could make the Hôtel de Ville quake!

Frederick's candidature appeared to her favourable to the carrying out of her ideas. She encouraged him, pointing out the glory that shone on the horizon. Rosanette was delighted at the notion of having a lover who would make speeches at the Chamber.

"And then, perhaps, they'll give you a good place?"

Frederick, a man prone to every kind of weakness, was infected by the universal mania. He wrote an address and took it to M. Dambreuse.

At the sound made by the great door falling back, a curtain gaped open a little behind a casement, and a woman appeared at it. He had not time to find out who she was; but, in the anteroom, a picture arrested his attention—Pellerin's picture—which lay on a chair, no doubt provisionally.

It represented the Republic, or Progress, or Civilisation, under the form of Jesus Christ driving a locomotive, which was passing through a virgin forest. Frederick, after a minute's contemplation, exclaimed:

"What a vile thing!"

"Is it not, eh?" said M. Dambreuse, entering unexpectedly just at the moment when the other was giving utterance to this opinion, and fancying that it had reference, not so much to the picture as to the doctrine it glorified. Martinon presented himself at the same time. They made their way into the study, and Frederick was drawing a paper out of his pocket, when Mademoiselle Cécile, entering suddenly, said, articulating her words in an ingenuous fashion:

"Is my aunt here?"

"You know perfectly well she is not," replied the banker. "No matter! act as if you were at home, Mademoiselle."

"Oh, thanks! I am going away!"

Scarcely had she left when Martinon seemed to be searching for his handkerchief.

"I forgot to take it out of my coat—excuse me!"

"All right!" said M. Dambreuse.

Evidently he was not deceived by this manœuvre, and even seemed to regard it with favour. Why? But Martinon soon reappeared, and Frederick began reading his address.

At the second page, which pointed toward the preponderance of financial interests as a disgraceful fact, the banker made a grimace. Then, touching on reforms, Frederick demanded free trade.

"What? Allow me, now!"

The other paid no attention, and continued. He favoured a tax on yearly incomes, a progressive tax, a European federation, and the education of the people, the encouragement of the fine arts on a liberal scale.

"When the country could provide men like Delacroix or Hugo with incomes of a hundred thousand francs, where would be the harm?"

At the close of the address advice was given to the upper classes.

"Spare nothing, ye rich; but give! give!"

He stopped, and remained standing. His two listeners did not utter a word. Martinon opened his eyes wide; M. Dambreuse was quite pale. At last, concealing his emotion under a bitter smile:

"That address of yours is simply perfect!" And he praised the style highly in order to avoid giving his opinion as to the matter of the address.

This virulence on the part of an inoffensive young man frightened him, especially as a dangerous sign of the times.

Martinon tried to reassure him. The Conservative party, in a little while, would certainly be in a position to take its revenge. In several cities the commissioners of the provisional government had been driven away; the elections were not due till the twenty-third of April; there was plenty of time. In short, it was necessary for M. Dambreuse to present himself personally in the Aube; and from that time forth, Martinon remained by his side, became his secretary, and was as attentive to him as a son.

Frederick arrived at Rosanette's house in a very self-complacent mood. Delmar happened to be there, and told him of his intention to stand as a candidate at the Seine elections. In a placard to the people, in which he addressed them in the familiar manner which one adopts toward an individual, the actor boasted of being able to understand them, and of having, in order to save them, got himself "crucified for the sake of art," so that he was the incarnation, the ideal of the popular spirit, believing that he had, in fact, such enormous power over the masses that he proposed by-and-by, when he occupied a ministerial office, to quell any outbreak alone; and, when asked what means he would employ, he gave this answer: "Never fear! I'll show them my head!"

Frederick, in order to mortify him, gave him to understand that he was himself a candidate. The mummer, from the moment that his future colleague aspired to represent the province, pronounced himself his servant, and offered to be his guide to the various clubs.

They visited them, or nearly all, the red and the blue, the furious and the tranquil, the puritanical and the licentious, the mystical and the intemperate, those that had voted for the death of kings, and those in which the frauds in the grocery trade had been denounced; and everywhere the tenants cursed the landlords; the blouse was full of spite against broadcloth; and the rich conspired against the poor. Many wanted indemnities on the ground that they had formerly been martyrs of the police; others appealed for money to carry out certain inventions, or else there were plans of phalansteria, projects for cantonal bazaars, systems of public felicity; then, here and there a flash of genius amid these clouds of folly, sudden as splashes, the law formulated by an oath, and flowers of eloquence on the lips of some soldier-boy, with a shoulder-belt strapped over his bare, shirtless chest. Sometimes, too, a gentleman made his appearance—an aristocrat of humble demeanour, talking in a plebeian strain, and with his hands unwashed, so as to make them look hard. A patriot would recognise him; the most virtuous would mob him; and he would go off with rage in his soul. On the pretext of good sense, it was desirable to be always disparaging the advocates, and to reiterate as often as possible these expressions: "To carry his stone to the building," "social problem," "workshop."

Delmar did not miss any opportunity for getting in a word; and when he no longer found anything to say, he would plant himself in some conspicuous position with one of his arms akimbo and the other in his waistcoat, turning himself round abruptly in profile, so as to give a good view of his head. Then there were outbursts of applause, led by Mademoiselle Vatnaz at the lower end of the hall.

Frederick, in spite of the weakness of orators, did not dare to try the experiment of speaking. All the people around seemed to him too unpolished or too hostile.

Dussardier made inquiries, and informed him that there existed in the Rue Saint-Jacques a club which bore the name of the "Club of Intellect." Such a name sounded hopeful. Besides, he would bring some friends of his own there.

He brought those whom he had invited to take punch with him—the bookkeeper, the traveller in wines, and the architect; even Pellerin had agreed to come, and Hussonnet would probably form one of the party, and on the footpath before the door stood Regimbart, with two men, the first of whom was his faithful Compain, a rather thick-set man marked with smallpox and with bloodshot eyes; and the second, an apelike negro, exceedingly hairy, and whom he knew only in the character of "a patriot from Barcelona."

They passed through a passage, leading into a large room, probably used by a joiner, with walls still fresh and smelling of plaster. Four argand lamps hung parallel to each other, and shed an unpleasant light. On a platform, at the end of the room, there was a desk on which was a bell; underneath it a table, representing the rostrum, and on each side two others, somewhat lower, for the secretaries. The audience that occupied the benches consisted of old painters of daubs, ushers, and literary men who could not get their works published.

In the midst of those lines of paletôts with greasy collars might be seen here and there a woman's cap or a workman's linen smock. The end of the apartment was full of workmen, who had in all likelihood come there to pass away an idle hour, and who had been invited by some of the speakers in order that they might applaud.

Frederick took care to place himself between Dussardier and Regimbart, who was scarcely seated before he leaned both hands on his walking-stick and his chin on his hands and shut his eyes, whilst at the other end of the room Delmar stood looking down at the crowd. Sénécal appeared at the president's desk.

The worthy bookkeeper thought Frederick would be pleased at this. It only annoyed him.

The meeting manifested great respect for the president. He was one who, on the twenty-fifth of February, had advised an immediate organisation of labour. On the following day, at the Prado, he had declared himself in favour of attacking the Hôtel de Ville; and, as every person at that period took some model for imitation, one copied Saint-Just, another Danton, another Marat; he tried to be like Blanqui, who imitated Robespierre. His black gloves, and his straight hair brushed back, gave him a rigid aspect exceedingly becoming.

He opened the proceedings with the declaration of the Rights of Man and of the Citizen—a customary act of faith. Then, a vigorous voice struck up Béranger's *Souvenirs du Peuple*.

Other voices were raised: "No! no! not that!"

"*La Casquette!*" the patriots at the end of the apartment began to howl. And they sang in chorus the favourite lines of the period:

> "Doff your hat before my cap—
> Kneel before the working-man!"

At a word from the president the audience became silent.

One of the secretaries proceeded to inspect the letters.

Some young men announced that they burned a number of copies of the *Assemblée Nationale* every evening in front of the Panthéon, and they urged on all patriots to follow their example.

"Bravo! adopted!" responded the audience.

The Citizen Jean Jacques Langreneux, a printer in the Rue Dauphin, suggested that a monument should be raised to the memory of the martyrs of Thermidor.

Michel Evariste Népomucène, ex-professor, gave expression to the wish that the European democracy should adopt unity of language. A dead language might be used for that purpose—as, for example, improved Latin.

"No; no Latin!" exclaimed the architect.

"Why?" said the college-usher.

And these two gentlemen engaged in a discussion, in which the others joined, each putting in a word of his own for effect; and the conversation on this topic soon became so tedious that many left. A little old man, who wore at the top of his prodigiously high forehead a pair of green spectacles, asked permission to speak in order to make an important communication.

It was a memorandum on the assessment of taxes. The figures flowed on in a continuous stream, as if they were never going to end. The impatience of the audience was shown at first in murmurs, in whispered talk. He allowed nothing to stop him. Then they began hissing; they catcalled him. Sénécal called the persons who were interrupting to order. The speaker went on like a machine. It was necessary to catch him by the shoulder in order to make him cease. The old fellow looked as if he were waking out of a dream, and, placidly lifting his spectacles, said:

"Pardon me, citizens! pardon me! I am going—a thousand excuses!"

Frederick was disconcerted with the failure of the old man's attempts to read this written statement. He had his own address in his pocket, but an extemporaneous speech would have been preferable.

Finally the president announced that they were about to pass on to the important matter, the electoral question. They would not discuss the big Republican lists. However, the "Club of Intellect" had every right, like every other, to form one, "with all respect for the pachas of the Hôtel de Ville, and the citizens who solicited the popular mandate might now set forth their claims.

"Go on, now!" said Dussardier.

A man in a cassock, with woolly hair and a petulant expression on his face, had raised his hand. He said, with a stutter, that his name was Ducretot, priest and agriculturist, and that he was the author of a work entitled *Manures.* He was advised to send it to a horticultural club.

Then a patriot in a blouse climbed to the rostrum. He was a plebeian, with broad shoulders, a big face, very mild-looking, with long black hair. He cast on the assembly an almost voluptuous glance, flung back his head, and, finally, spreading out his arms:

"You have repelled Ducretot, O my brothers! and you have done right; but it was not through irreligion, for we are all religious."

Many of those present listened open-mouthed, with the air of catechumens and in ecstatic attitudes.

"It is not either because he is a priest, for we, too, are priests! The workman is a priest, just as the founder of Socialism was—the Master of us all, Jesus Christ!"

The time had arrived to inaugurate the Kingdom of God. The Gospel led directly to '89. After the abolition of slavery, the abolition of the proletariat. They had had the age of hate—the age of love was about to begin.

"Christianity is the keystone and the foundation of the new edifice—"

"You are making game of us!" exclaimed the traveller in wines. "Who has given me a priest's cap?"

This interruption gave great offence. Nearly all the audience got on benches, and, shaking their fists, shouted: "Atheist! aristocrat! low rascal!" whilst the president's bell kept ringing continuously, and the cries of "Order! order!" redoubled. But, aimless, and, moreover, fortified by three cups of coffee which he had swallowed before coming to the meeting, he struggled in the midst of the others:

"What? I an aristocrat? Come, now!"

When, at length, he was permitted to explain, he declared that he would never be at peace with the priests; and, since something had just been said about economical measures, it would be a splendid beginning to put an end to the churches, the sacred pyxes, and finally all creeds.

Somebody raised the objection that he was going very far.

"Yes! I am going very far! But, when a vessel is caught suddenly in a storm—"

Without waiting for the conclusion of this simile, another said:

"Granted! But this is to demolish at a single stroke, like a mason devoid of judgment—"

"You are insulting the masons!" yelled a citizen covered with plaster. And persisting in the belief that provocation had been offered to him, he poured forth insults, and wished to fight, clinging tightly to the bench whereon he sat. It took no less than three men to put him out.

Meanwhile the workman still remained on the rostrum. The two secretaries gave him an intimation that he should descend. He protested against the injustice done to him.

"You shall not prevent me from crying out, 'Eternal love to our dear France! eternal love to the Republic!'"

"Citizens!" said Compain, after this—"Citizens!"

And, by dint of repeating "Citizens," having obtained a little silence, he leaned on the rostrum with his two red hands, which looked like stumps, bent forward his body, and blinking his eyes:

"I believe that it would be necessary to give a larger extension to the calf's head."

All who heard him kept silent, fancying that they had misunderstood his words.

"Yes! the calf's head!"

Three hundred laughs burst forth at the same moment. The ceiling shook.

At the sight of all these faces convulsed with mirth, Compain shrank back. He continued in an angry tone:

"What! you don't know what the calf's head is!"

It was a paroxysm, a delirium. They held their sides. Some of them even tumbled off the benches to the ground in convulsions of laughter. Compain, not being able to bear it any longer, took refuge beside Regimbart, and wanted to drag him away.

"No! I shall remain till 'tis all over!" said the Citizen.

This reply caused Frederick to come to a decision; and, as he looked about to the right and the left to see whether his friends were prepared to support him, he saw Pellerin standing on the rostrum in front of him.

The artist assumed a haughty tone in addressing the meeting.

"I would like to get some notion as to who is the candidate amongst all these that represent art. For my part, I have painted a picture."

"We have nothing to do with painting pictures!" was the churlish remark of a thin man with red spots on his cheek-bones.

Pellerin protested against this interruption.

But the other, in a tragic tone:

"Ought not the Government to make an ordinance abolishing prostitution and want?"

And this phrase having at once won the popular favour, he thundered against the corruption of great cities.

"Shame and infamy! We ought to catch hold of wealthy citizens on their way out of the Maison d'Or and spit in their faces—unless it be that the Government justifies debauchery! The collectors of the city dues exhibit toward our daughters and our sisters an amount of indecency—"

A voice exclaimed, some distance away:

"This is blackguard language! Turn him out!"

"They extract taxes from us to pay for licentiousness! Thus, the high salaries paid to actors—"

"Help!" cried Pellerin.

He leaped from the rostrum, pushed everybody aside, and declaring that he regarded such stupid accusations with disgust, expatiated on the civilising mission of the player. Inasmuch as the theatre was the focus of national education, he would record his vote for the reform of the theatre; and to begin with, no more managements, no more privileges!

"Yes; of any sort!"

The actor's manner excited the audience, and people moved backward and forward knocking each other down.

"No more academies! No more institutes!"

"No missions!"

"No more bachelorships! Down with the University degrees!"

"Let us preserve them," said Sénécal; "but let them be conferred by universal suffrage, by the people, the only true judge!"

Besides, these things were not the most important. It was necessary to find a level which would be above the heads of the wealthy. And he represented them as gorging themselves with crimes under their gilded ceilings; while the starving poor, writhing in their garrets, cultivated every virtue. The applause became so vehement that it interrupted his discourse. For several minutes he remained with his eyes closed, his head thrown back, and, as it were, lulling himself to sleep over the fury which he had aroused.

Then he began to talk in a dogmatic way, in phrases as imperious as laws. The State should take possession of the banks and the insurance offices. Inheritances should be abolished. A social fund should be established for the workers. Many other measures were desirable in the future. For the time being, these would suffice, and, returning to the question of the elections: "We need pure citizens, men entirely fresh. Let some one offer himself."

Frederick arose. There was a buzz of approval made by his friends. Sénécal, assuming the attitude of a Fouquier-Tinville, began to ask questions as to his first name and surname, his antecedents, life, and morals.

Frederick answered succinctly, and bit his lips. Sénécal asked whether anyone saw any impediment to this candidature.

"No! no!"

But, for his part, he saw some. All around him bent forward and strained their ears to listen. The citizen who was seeking for their support had not delivered a certain sum promised by him for the founding of a democratic journal. Moreover, on the twenty-second of February, though he had had due notice, he had failed to be at the meeting-place in the Place de Panthéon.

"I swear that he was at the Tuileries!" exclaimed Dussardier.

"Can you swear to having seen him at the Panthéon?"

Dussardier hung down his head. Frederick was silent. His friends, scandalised, regarded him anxiously.

"In any case," Sénécal went on, "do you know any patriot who will answer to us for your principles?"

"I will!" said Dussardier.

"Oh! that is not enough; another!"

Frederick turned round to Pellerin. The artist replied to him with a number of gestures, which meant:

"Ah! my dear boy, they have rejected myself! The deuce! What would you have?"

Thereupon Frederick gave Regimbart a nudge.

"Yes, all right; 'tis time! I'm going."

And Regimbart stepped upon the platform; then, pointing toward the Spaniard, who had followed him:

"Allow me, citizens, to present to you a patriot from Barcelona!"

The patriot made a low bow, rolled his gleaming eyes about, and with his hand on his heart:

"*Ciudadanos! mucho aprecio el* honour that you have bestowed on me! however, great may be *vuestra bondad, mayor vuestra atención!*"

"I claim the right to speak!" cried Frederick.

"*Desde que se proclamo la constitución de Cadiz, ese pacto fundamental de las libertades Españolas, hasta la ultima revolución, nuestra patria cuenta numeros y heroicos mártires.*"

Frederick once more endeavoured to obtain a hearing:

"But, citizens!—"

The Spaniard continued: "*El martes proximo tendra lugar en la iglesia de la Magdelena un servicio fúnebre.*"

"This is ridiculous! Nobody understands him!"

This observation exasperated the audience.

"Turn him out! Turn him out!"

"Who? I?" asked Frederick.

"Yourself!" said Sénécal, majestically. "Out with you!"

He rose to leave, and the voice of the Iberian pursued him:

"*Y todos los Españoles descarien ver alli reunidas las disputaciónes de los clubs y de la milicia nacional. An oración fúnebre en* honour of the *libertad Española y del mundo entero* will be *prononciado por un miembro del clero* of Paris *en la sala Bonne Nouvelle.* Honour *al pueblo frances que llamaria yo el primero pueblo del mundo, sino fuese ciudadano de otra nación!*"

"*Aristo!*" screamed one blackguard, shaking his fist at Frederick, as the latter, boiling with indignation, rushed out into the yard adjoining the place where the meeting was held.

He blamed himself for his devotedness, without reflecting that, after all, the accusations brought against him were just.

What fatal idea was this candidature! But what asses! what idiots! He drew comparisons between himself and these men, and soothed his wounded pride with the thought of their stupidity.

Then he sought Rosanette. After such an exhibition of ugly traits, and so much magniloquence, her dainty person would be a relaxation. She was aware that he had intended to present himself at a club that evening.

However, she did not ask a single question when he came in. She was seated near the fire, ripping open the lining of a dress. He was surprised to find her thus occupied.

"Hallo! what are you doing?"

"You can see for yourself," said she, dryly. "I am mending my clothes! So much for this Republic of yours!"

"Why do you call it mine?"

"Perhaps you want to make out that it's mine!"

And she began to reproach him for everything that had happened in France for the last two months, accusing him of having brought about the Revolution and with having ruined her prospects by making everybody with money leave Paris, and that she would by-and-by be dying in a hospital.

"It is easy for you to talk lightly about it, with your yearly income! However, at the rate at which things are happening, you won't have your yearly income long."

"That may be," said Frederick. "The most devoted are always misunderstood, and if one were not sustained by one's conscience, the brutes that you mix yourself up with would disgust you with your own self-denial!"

Rosanette gazed at him with knitted brows.

"Eh? What? What self-denial? Monsieur has not been successful, it would seem? So much the better! It will teach you to make patriotic donations. Oh, don't lie! I know you have given them three hundred francs, for this Republic of yours has to be kept. Well, amuse yourself with it, my good man!"

Under this avalanche of abuse, Frederick passed from his former disappointment to a more painful disillusion.

He withdrew to the lower end of the apartment. She came after him.

"Listen to me! Think it out a bit! In a country as in a house, there must be a master, otherwise, everyone pockets something out of the money spent. Everybody knows that Ledru-Rollin is head over ears in debt. As for Lamartine, how can you expect a poet to understand politics? Ah! 'tis all very well for you to shake your head and to think that you have more brains than others; all the same, what I say is true! But you are always cavilling; one can't get in a word with you! For instance, there's Fournier-Fontaine, who had stores at Saint-Roch! do you know how much he failed for? Eight hundred thousand francs! And Gomer, the packer opposite to him—another Republican, that one—he smashed the tongs on his wife's head, and he drank so much absinthe that he is going to be put into a private asylum. That's the way with the lot of them—the Republicans! A Republic at twenty-five per cent. Ah! plume yourself upon it!"

Frederick took himself off. He was disgusted at the foolishness of this girl, which revealed itself all at once in the language of the populace. He felt himself becoming a little patriotic once more.

The ill-temper of Rosanette only increased. Mademoiselle Vatnaz irritated him with her enthusiasm. Believing that she had a mission, she felt a furious desire to make speeches, to carry on discussions, and—sharper than Rosanette in matters of this sort—overwhelmed her with arguments.

One day she made her appearance burning with indignation against Hussonnet, who had just indulged in some blackguard remarks at the Woman's Club. Rosanette approved of his conduct, declaring that she would take to men's clothes herself to go and "give them a bit of her mind, the entire lot of them, and to whip them."

Frederick entered at the same moment.

"You'll accompany me—won't you?"

And, in spite of his presence, there was a bickering match, one of them playing the part of a citizen's wife and the other of a female philosopher.

According to Rosanette, women were born exclusively for love, or in order to bring up children, to be housekeepers.

According to Mademoiselle Vatnaz, women were entitled to a position in the Government. In former times, the Gaulish women, and also the Anglo-Saxon women, took part in the legislation; the squaws of the Hurons formed a portion of the Council. The work of civilisation was common to both. It was necessary that all should contribute toward it, and that fraternity should be substituted for egoism, association for individualism, and cultivation on a large scale for minute subdivision of land.

"Come, that is good! you know a great deal about culture just now!"

"Why not? Besides, it is a question of the future of humanity!"

"Attend to our own business!"

"This is my business!"

They got into a passion. Frederick interposed. The Vatnaz became very heated, and went so far as to uphold Communism.

"What nonsense!" said Rosanette. "How could such a thing ever come to pass?"

The other brought forward in support of her theory the examples of the Essenes, the Moravian Brethren, the Jesuits of Paraguay, the family of the Pingons near Thiers in Auvergne; and, as she gesticulated wildly, her gold chain became entangled in her bundle of trinkets, to which was attached a gold ornament in the form of a sheep.

Suddenly, Rosanette turned exceedingly pale.

Madame Vatnaz continued extricating her trinkets.

"Don't give yourself so much trouble," said Rosanette. "Now, I know your political opinions."

"What?" replied the Vatnaz, with a blush on her face, like that of a virgin.

"Oh! oh! you understand me."

Frederick did not understand. Something had evidently taken place between them of a more important and intimate character than Socialism.

"And even though it should be so," said the Vatnaz in reply, rising up unflinchingly. "'Tis a loan, my dear—set off one debt against the other."

"Faith, I never deny my own debts. I owe some thousands of francs— a nice sum. I borrow, at least; I don't rob anyone."

Mademoiselle Vatnaz made an effort to laugh.

"Oh! I would put my hand in the fire for him."

"Take care! it is dry enough to burn."

The spinster extended her right hand, and keeping it raised in front of her:

"But there are friends of yours who find it convenient to use."

"Andalusians, I suppose? as castanets?"

"You beggar!"

The Maréchale made her a low bow.

"There's nobody so charming!"

Mademoiselle Vatnaz did not reply. Beads of perspiration stood on her temples. Her eyes fixed themselves on the carpet. She panted for breath. At last she reached the door, and slamming it vigorously: "Good night! You'll hear from me!"

"Much I care!" said Rosanette. The effort of self-control had shattered her nerves. She sank down on the divan, shaking all over, stammering forth words of abuse, shedding tears. Was it this threat on the part of the Vatnaz that had agitated her mind? Oh, no! what did she care, indeed, about that one? It was the golden sheep, a present, and in the midst of her tears the name of Delmar escaped her lips. So, then, she was still in love with the mummer?

"In that case, why did she take on with me?" Frederick asked himself. "How is it that he has returned again? Who compels her to keep me? Where is the sense of this sort of thing?"

Rosanette was still sobbing. She lay all the time on the edge of the divan, with her right cheek resting on her two hands, and she seemed a being so dainty, so free from self-consciousness, and so sorely troubled, that he drew closer to her and softly kissed her on the forehead.

Thereupon she gave him assurances of her affection for him; the Prince had just left her, they would be free. But she was for the time being short of money. "You saw yourself that this was so, the other day, when I was trying to turn my old linings to use." No more equipages now! And this was not all; the upholsterer was threatening to take possession of the bedroom and the large drawing-room furniture. She did not know what to do.

Frederick felt disposed to answer:

"Don't annoy yourself about it. I will pay."

But the lady knew how to lie. Experience had enlightened him. He confined himself to mere expressions of sympathy.

Rosanette's fears were not unfounded. It was necessary to give up the furniture and to quit the handsome apartment in the Rue Drouot. She took another on the Boulevard Poissonnière, on the fourth floor.

The curiosities of her old boudoir were quite sufficient to give to the three rooms a coquettish air. There were Chinese blinds, a tent on the terrace, and in the drawing-room a second-hand carpet still perfectly new, with ottomans covered with pink silk. Frederick had contributed largely to these purchases. He had felt the joy of a newly-married man who possesses at last a house of his own, a wife of his own—and, being much pleased with the place, he slept there nearly every evening.

One morning, as he was passing out through the ante-room, he saw, on the third floor, on the staircase, the shako of a National Guard who was ascending it. Where in the world was he going?

Frederick waited. The man continued his progress up the stairs, with his head slightly bent. He raised his eyes. It was my lord Arnoux!

The situation was obvious. They both reddened simultaneously, overcome by a feeling of embarrassment common to both.

Arnoux was the first to find a way out of the difficulty.

"She is better—is she not?" as if Rosanette were ill, and he had come to inquire how she was.

Frederick took advantage of this opening.

"Yes, certainly! at least, so I was told by her maid," wishing to convey that he had not been allowed to see her.

Then they stood facing each other, both undecided as to what to do next, and eyeing each other intently. The question now was, which of the two would remain. Arnoux once more solved the problem.

"Pshaw! I'll come back later. Where are you going? I will go with you!"

And, when they were in the street, he chatted as naturally as usual. Unquestionably he was not a man of jealous disposition, or else he was too good-natured to get angry. Besides, his time was devoted to serving his country. He was never out of his uniform now. On the twenty-ninth of March he had defended the offices of the *Presse*. When the Chamber was invaded, he distinguished himself by his courage, and he was at the banquet given to the National Guard at Amiens.

Hussonnet, who was still on duty with him, availed himself of his flask and his cigars; but, irreverent by nature, he delighted in contradicting him, disparaging the somewhat inaccurate style of the decrees; and decrying the conferences at the Luxembourg, the women known as the

"Vésuviennes," the political section bearing the name of "Tyroliens;" everything, in fact, down to the Car of Agriculture, drawn by horses to the ox-market, and escorted by ill-favoured young girls. Arnoux, on the other hand, upheld authority, and dreamed of uniting the different parties. However, his own affairs had taken an unfavourable turn, and he was more or less troubled about them.

He was not disturbed about Frederick's relations with the Maréchale; for this discovery made him feel justified (in his conscience) in withdrawing the allowance which he had renewed since the Prince had left her. He pleaded by way of excuse for this step the embarrassed condition in which he found himself, uttered many lamentations—and Rosanette was generous. The result was that M. Arnoux regarded himself as the lover who appealed entirely to the heart, an idea that raised him in his own estimation and made him feel young again. Having no doubt that Frederick was paying the Maréchale, he flattered himself that he was "playing a nice trick" on the young man. He called at the house in such a stealthy fashion as to keep the other in ignorance of the fact, and when they happened to meet, left the coast clear for him.

Frederick was not pleased with this partnership, and his rival's politeness seemed only an elaborate piece of sarcasm. But by taking offence at it, he would have removed every opportunity of ever finding his way back to Madame Arnoux; and then, this was the only means whereby he could hear about her movements. The earthenware-dealer, in accordance with his usual practice, or perhaps with some cunning design, mentioned her readily in the course of conversation, and asked him why he no longer came to see her.

Frederick, having exhausted every excuse he could think of, assured him that he had called several times to see Madame Arnoux, but without success. Arnoux believed this, for he had often referred in an eager tone at home to the absence of their friend, and she had invariably replied that she was out when he called, so that these two lies, in place of contradicting, corroborated each other.

The young man's gentle ways and the pleasure of finding a dupe in him made Arnoux like him all the better. He carried familiarity to its extreme limits, not through disdain, but through assurance. One day he wrote saying that urgent business compelled him to be away in the country for twenty-four hours. He begged of the young man to mount guard in his stead. Frederick dared not refuse, so he repaired to the guard-house in the Place du Carrousel.

He had to put up with the society of the National Guards, and, with the exception of a sugar-refiner, a witty fellow who drank to an inordinate extent, they all appeared to him more stupid than their cartridge-boxes. The principal subject of conversation amongst them was the substitution of sashes for belts. Others declaimed against the national workshops.

One man said:

"What is this leading to?"

The man to whom the words had been addressed opened his eyes as if he were on the verge of an abyss.

"Where are we going?"

Then, one who was more daring than the rest exclaimed:

"It cannot last! It must come to an end!"

And as similar talk went on till night, Frederick was bored to death.

Great was his surprise when, at eleven o'clock, he suddenly beheld Arnoux, who explained that he had hurried back to set him at liberty, having disposed of his business.

The fact was that he had no business to transact. The whole thing was made up to enable him to spend twenty-four hours alone with Rosanette. But the worthy Arnoux had placed too much confidence in his own powers, so that, now in the state of lassitude which was the result, he was seized with remorse. He had come to thank Frederick, and to invite him to supper.

"A thousand thanks! I'm not hungry. All I want is to go to bed."

"A reason the more for having a snack together. How flabby you are! One does not go home at such an hour as this. It is too late! It would be dangerous!"

Frederick once more yielded. Arnoux was quite a favourite with his brethren-in-arms, who had not expected to see him—and he was a particular crony of the refiner. They all liked him, and he was such a good fellow that he was sorry Hussonnet was not there. But he wanted to shut his eyes for one minute, no longer.

"Sit down beside me!" said he to Frederick, stretching himself on the camp-bed without removing his belt and straps. Through fear of an alarm, in spite of the regulation, he even kept his gun in his hand. He stammered out some words:

"My darling! my little angel!" and ere long was fast asleep.

Those who had been conversing became silent; and gradually there was a deep silence in the guard-house. Frederick, tormented by the fleas, kept staring about him. The wall, painted yellow, had, half-way up, a long shelf, on which the knapsacks formed a succession of little humps, while underneath, the lead-coloured muskets rose up side by side; and there could be heard a succession of snores, produced by the National Guards, whose stomachs were outlined through the darkness in a confused fashion. On the top of the stove stood an empty bottle and some plates. Three straw chairs were ranged around the table, on which a pack of cards was displayed. A drum, in the middle of the bench, had its strap hanging down.

A warm breath of air making its way through the door caused the lamp to smoke. Arnoux slept with his two arms wide apart; and, as his gun was in a slightly crooked position, with the butt-end downward, the mouth of the barrel came up right under his arm. Frederick noticed this, and was alarmed.

"But, no, it's impossible, there's nothing to be afraid of! And yet, suppose he met his death!"

And immediately pictures unrolled themselves before his mind in endless succession.

He saw himself with her at night in a post-chaise, then on a river's bank on a summer's evening, and again, under the reflection of a lamp at home in their own house. He even thought of household expenses and domestic arrangements, contemplating, feeling already his happiness between his hands; and in order to realise it, all that was needed was that the cock of the gun should rise. The end of it could be pushed with one's toe, the gun would go off—it would be a mere accident—nothing more!

Frederick brooded over this idea like a playwright in the agonies of composition. Suddenly it seemed to him that it was about to be carried into practical operation, and that he was going to contribute to that result—that, in fact, he was yearning for it; and then a feeling of absolute terror took possession of him. In the midst of this mental distress he experienced a sense of pleasure, and he allowed himself to sink deeper and deeper into it, with a dreadful consciousness all the time that his scruples were weakening. In the wildness of his reverie the rest of the world become effaced, and he only realised that he was still alive by the intolerable oppression on his chest.

"Let us take a drop of white wine!" said the refiner, as he awoke.

Arnoux sprang to his feet, and, as soon as the white wine was swallowed, he offered to relieve Frederick of his sentry duty.

Then he took him to breakfast in the Rue de Chartres, at Parly's, and as he required to recuperate his energies, he ordered two dishes of meat, a lobster, an omelet with rum, a salad, etc., and finished this off with a brand of Sauterne of 1819 and one of '42 Romanée, not to speak of the champagne at dessert and the liqueurs.

Frederick did not in any way gainsay him. He was disturbed in mind as if by the thought that the other might somehow detect on his countenance the idea that had lately flitted before his imagination. With both elbows on the table and his head bent forward, so that Frederick felt annoyed by his fixed stare, he confided some of his hobbies to the young man.

He wanted to obtain for farming purposes all the embankments on the Northern line, in order to plant potatoes there, or else to organise on the boulevards a monster cavalcade in which the celebrities of the period would figure. He would let all the windows, which would, at the rate of three francs for each person, produce a handsome profit. In short, he dreamed of making a great fortune by means of a monopoly. He assumed a moral tone, nevertheless, found fault with excesses and all sorts of misconduct, spoke about his "poor father," and every evening, as he said, made an examination of his conscience before offering his soul to God.

"A little curaçao, eh?"

"Just as you please."

As for the Republic, things would adjust themselves; in fact, he considered himself the happiest man on earth; and forgetting himself, he exalted Rosanette's attractive qualities, and even compared her with his wife. It was quite a different thing, of course. You could not imagine a lovelier person!

"Your health!"

Frederick touched glasses with him. He had, out of complaisance, drunk a little too much. Besides, the strong sunlight dazzled him; and when they walked up the Rue Vivienne together again, their shoulders touched in a fraternal fashion.

When he got home, Frederick slept till seven o'clock. Then he called on the Maréchale. She was out with somebody—with Arnoux, perhaps! Not knowing what to do with himself, he continued his promenade along the boulevard, but could not pass the Porte Saint-Martin, owing to the immense crowd that blocked the way.

Want had abandoned to their own resources a considerable number of workmen, and they came there every evening, no doubt for the purpose of holding a review and awaiting a signal.

In spite of the law against riotous assemblies, these clubs of despair increased to a frightful extent. Many citizens repaired every day to the spot through bravado, and because it was the fashion.

All of a sudden Frederick caught a glimpse, three paces away, of M. Dambreuse along with Martinon. He turned his head away, for on account of M. Dambreuse having got himself nominated as a representative of the people, he cherished a secret spite against him. But the capitalist stopped him.

"One word, my dear Monsieur! I have some explanations to make to you."

"I am not asking for any."

"Pray listen to me!"

It was not his fault in any way. Appeals had been made to him; pressure had, to a certain extent, been placed on him. Martinon immediately endorsed all that he said. Some of the electors of Nogent had presented themselves in a deputation at his house.

"Besides, I expected to be free as soon as—"

A crush of people on the footpath forced M. Dambreuse to get out of the way. A minute after he regained his place, saying to Martinon:

"This is a genuine service, really, and you won't have any reason to regret—"

All three stood with their backs against a shop in order to be able to chat more at their ease.

From time to time there was a cry of, "Long live Napoléon! Long live Barbès! Down with Marié!"

The countless throng kept talking very loudly; and all these voices, echoing through the houses, made so to speak, the continuous ripple of waves in a harbour. At intervals they ceased; and then could be heard voices singing the *Marseillaise*.

Under the court-gates, men of mysterious appearance offered sword-sticks to those who passed. Sometimes two individuals, one of whom preceded the other, would wink, and then quickly hurry away. The foot-paths were filled with groups of staring idlers. A dense crowd swayed to and fro on the pavement. Entire bands of police-officers, emerging from the alleys, had scarcely made their way into the midst of the multitude when they were swallowed up in the mass of people. Little red flags here and there looked like flames. Coachmen, from their high seats, gesticulated energetically, and then turned to go back. It was a scene of perpetual movement—one of the strangest sights that could be conceived.

"How all this," said Martinon, "would have amused Mademoiselle Cécile!"

"My wife, as you know, does not like my niece to come with us," returned M. Dambreuse with a smile.

One could scarcely recognise in him the same man. For the past three months he had been crying, "Long live the Republic!" and he had even voted in favour of the banishment of Orleans. But there should be an end of concessions. He exhibited his indignation so far as to carry a tom-ahawk in his pocket.

Martinon had one, too. The magistracy not being any longer irre-movable, he had withdrawn from Parquet, so that he surpassed M. Dambreuse in his display of violence.

The banker had a special antipathy to Lamartine (for having supported Ledru-Rollin) and, at the same time, to Pierre Leroux, Proudhon, Considérant, Lamennais, and all the cranks, all the Socialists.

"For, in fact, what is it they want? The duty on meat and arrest for debt have been abolished. Now the project of a bank for mortgages is under consideration; the other day it was a national bank; and there are five millions in the Budget for the working-men! But luckily, it is over, thanks to Monsieur de Falloux! Good-bye to them! let them go!"

Not knowing how to maintain the three hundred thousand men in the national workshops, the Minister of Public Works had that very day signed an order inviting all citizens between the ages of eighteen and twenty to take service as soldiers, or else to go to the provinces and cultivate the ground there.

They were indignant at the alternative thus put before them, convinced that the object was to destroy the Republic. They were aggrieved at having to live at a distance from the capital, as if it were a kind of exile. They pictured themselves dying of fevers in desolate parts of the country. To many of them, moreover, who had been accustomed to work of a refined description, agriculture seemed a degradation; it was, in short, a mockery, a decisive breach of all the promises which had been made to them. If they offered any resistance, force would be employed against them. They had no doubt of this, and made preparations to anticipate it.

About nine o'clock the riotous assemblies which had gathered at the Bastille and at the Châtelet ebbed back toward the boulevard. From the Porte Saint-Denis to the Porte Saint-Martin nothing could be discerned save an enormous swarm of people, a single mass of a dark blue shade, nearly black. The men of whom one caught a glimpse all had glowing eyes, pale complexions, faces emaciated with hunger and excited with a sense of injustice.

Meanwhile clouds had gathered. The tempestuous sky roused the electricity that was in the people, and they kept whirling about of their own accord with the great swaying movements of a swelling sea, and one felt that there was an incalculable force in the depths of this excited throng, and as it were, the energy of an element. Then they all began shouting: "Lamps! lamps!" Many windows had no illumination, and stones were flung at the panes. M. Dambreuse deemed it prudent to withdraw from the scene. The two young men accompanied him home. He predicted great disasters. The people might once more invade the Chamber, and he told them how he should have been killed on the fifteenth of May had it not been for the devotion of a National Guard.

"But I had forgotten! he is a friend of yours—the earthenware manufacturer—Jacques Arnoux!" The rioters had been actually throttling him, when that brave citizen caught him in his arms and dragged him out of their reach.

Since then, there had been a kind of intimacy between them.

"One of these days they would dine together, and, since you often see him, give him the assurance that I like him very much. He is an excellent man, and has, in my opinion, been slandered; and he has his wits about him in the morning. My compliments once more! A very good evening!"

Frederick, after he had left M. Dambreuse, went back to the Maréchale, and in a very gloomy fashion, said that she could choose between him and

Arnoux. She replied that she did not understand "dumps of this sort," that she did not care about Arnoux, and had no desire to be with him. Frederick was thirsting to fly from Paris. She offered no opposition to this whim; and next morning they set out for Fontainebleau.

The hotel at which they stayed could be distinguished from others by a fountain that rippled in the middle of the courtyard attached to it. The doors of the various apartments opened out on a corridor, as in monasteries. The room assigned to them was large, well-furnished, hung with print, and noiseless, owing to the scarcity of tourists. Alongside the houses, people who had nothing to do passed up and down; then, under their windows, at the close of the day, children in the street would engage in a game of base. This tranquillity, following so soon the tumult they had witnessed in Paris, filled them with astonishment and exercised over them a soothing influence.

Every morning at an early hour, they paid a visit to the Château. As they passed in through the gate, they had a view of its entire front, with the five pavilions covered with sharp-pointed roofs, and its staircase of horseshoe-shape opening into the end of the courtyard, which is hemmed in, to right and left, by two main portions of the building further down. On the paved ground lichens blended their colours here and there with the tawny hue of bricks, and the entire appearance of the palace, rust-coloured like old armour, had about it something of the impassiveness of royalty—a sort of warlike, melancholy grandeur.

At last, a man-servant would make his appearance with a bunch of keys. He first showed them the apartments of the queens, the Pope's oratory, the gallery of Francis I, the mahogany table on which the Emperor signed his abdication, and in one of the rooms cut in two the old Galérie des Cerfs, the place where Christine got Monaldeschi assassinated. Rosanette listened to this narrative attentively, then, turning toward Frederick:

"No doubt it was through jealousy! Mind yourself!" After this they passed through the Council Chamber, the Guards' Room, the Throne Room, and the drawing-room of Louis XIII. The uncurtained windows admitted a white light. The handles of the window-fastenings and the copper feet of the pier-tables were slightly tarnished with dust. The arm-chairs were covered with coarse linen covers. Above the doors could be seen reliquaries of Louis XIV, and here and there hangings representing the gods of Olympus, Psyche, or the battles of Alexander.

As she was passing in front of the mirrors, Rosanette stopped for a moment to smooth her head-bands.

After going through the donjon-court and the Saint-Saturnin Chapel, they reached the Festal Hall.

They were dazzled by the magnificence of the ceiling, which was divided into octagonal sections set off with gold and silver, more finely chiselled than a jewel, and by the vast number of paintings covering the walls, from the immense chimney-piece, where the arms of France were surrounded by crescents and quivers, down to the musicians' gallery, which had been erected at the other end along the entire width of the hall. The ten arched windows were wide open; the sun threw its lustre on the pictures, so that they glowed beneath its rays; the blue sky continued in an endless curve the ultramarine of the arches; and from the depths of the woods, where the lofty summits of the trees filled up the horizon, there seemed to come an echo of flourishes from ivory trumpets, and mythological ballets, together under the foliage princesses and nobles disguised as nymphs or fauns—an epoch of ingenuous science, of violent passions, and sumptuous art, when the ideal was to eliminate the world in a vision of the Hesperides, and when the mistresses of kings mingled their glory with the stars. There was a portrait of one of the most beautiful of these celebrated women in the form of Diana the huntress, and even as the Infernal Diana, on doubt in order to indicate the power which she wielded even beyond the limits of the tomb. All these symbols confirmed her glory, and there hovered about the spot something of her, an indistinct voice, a radiation that stretched out indefinitely. A feeling of mysterious retrospective voluptuousness took possession of Frederick.

In order to divert these passionate longings into another channel, he gazed tenderly on Rosanette, and asked her would she not like to have been this woman?

"What woman?"

"Diane de Poitiers!"

He repeated:

"Diane de Poitiers, mistress of Henry the Second."

She gave utterance to a little "Ah!" that was all.

Her silence demonstrated that she knew nothing about the matter, and did not comprehend his meaning, so that out of complaisance he said to her:

"Perhaps you are getting tired of this?"

"No, no—quite the reverse." And lifting up her chin, and casting around her a vague glance, Rosanette said:

"It recalls some memories to me!"

Meanwhile, it was easy to trace on her countenance a strained expression, a certain sense of awe; and, as this air of gravity made her look all the prettier, Frederick enjoyed it.

The carps' pond amused her more. For a quarter of an hour she kept flinging pieces of bread into the water in order to see the fishes jumping about.

Frederick had seated himself by her side under the linden-trees. He saw in imagination all the personages who had haunted these walls—Charles V, the Valois kings, Henry IV, Peter the Great, Jean Jacques Rousseau, and "the fair mourners of the stage-boxes," Voltaire, Napoléon, Pius VII, and Louis Philippe; and he felt himself surrounded, elbowed, by these tumultuous dead people. He was stunned by such a confusion of historic figures, even though he found a certain fascination in contemplating them, nevertheless.

Presently they descended into the flower-garden.

It is a vast rectangle, which presents to the spectator, at the first glance, its wide yellow walks, its square grass-plots, its ribbons of box-wood, its yew-trees shaped like pyramids, its low-lying greenswards, and its narrow borders, in which thinly-sown flowers edge the grey soil. At the end of the garden may be seen a park through whose entire length a canal makes its way.

Royal residences have connected with them a peculiar kind of melancholy, due, no doubt, to their dimensions being much too large for the limited number of guests entertained within them, to the silence which one feels astonished to find in them after so many flourishes of trumpets, to the immobility of their luxurious furniture, which symbolises by its age and decay the transitory character of dynasties, the eternal wretchedness of all things; and this exhalation of the centuries, enervating and funereal, like the perfume of a mummy, impresses even untutored brains. Rosanette yawned immoderately. They went back to the hotel.

After breakfast an open carriage came round for them. They set out from Fontainebleau at a point where several roads diverged, then ascended at a walking pace a gravelly road leading toward a little pine-wood. The trees became larger, and, from time to time, the driver would say, "This is the Frères Siamois, the Pharamond, the Bouquet de Roi," not forgetting a single one of these notable sites, sometimes even drawing up to enable them to admire the view.

They entered the forest of Franchard. The carriage glided over the grass like a sledge; pigeons which were not in sight began cooing. Suddenly, the waiter of a café made his appearance, and they alighted before the railing of a garden in which a number of round tables were placed. Then, passing on the left by the walls of a ruined abbey, they made their way over big boulders of stone and soon reached the lower part of the gorge.

It is covered on one side with sandstones and juniper-trees tangled together, while on the other side the ground, almost bare, inclines toward the hollow of the valley, where a foot-track makes a pale line through the brown heather; and far above could be distinguished a flat cone-shaped summit with a telegraph-tower behind it.

Half an hour later they stepped out of the vehicle once more, to climb the heights of Aspremont.

The roads form zigzags between the thick-set pine-trees under rocks with angular faces. All this corner of the forest has a sort of choked-up look—a wild and solitary aspect. One is reminded of hermits—companions of huge stags with fiery crosses between their horns, who were wont to welcome with paternal smiles the good kings of France when they knelt before their grottoes. The warm air was filled with a resinous odour, and roots of trees crossed one another like veins close to the soil. Rosanette stumbled over them, grew dejected, and felt inclined to shed tears.

But, at the very top, she became joyous once more on finding, under a roof made of branches, a sort of tavern where carved wood was sold. She drank a bottle of lemonade, and bought a holly-stick; and, without one glance toward the landscape which disclosed itself from the plateau, she entered the Brigands' Cave, with a waiter carrying a torch in front of her. Their carriage awaited them in the Bas Breau.

A painter in a blue blouse was working at the foot of an oak-tree with his box of colours on his knees. He raised his head and watched them as they passed.

In the middle of the hill of Chailly, the sudden breaking of a cloud necessitated the turning up of the hoods of their cloaks. Almost immediately the rain stopped, and the paving-stones of the street glistened under the sun as they reëntered the town.

Some travellers, who had recently arrived, informed them that a terrible battle had stained Paris with blood. Rosanette and her lover were not surprised. Then everybody left; the hotel became quiet, the gas was put out, and they were lulled to sleep by the murmur of the fountain in the courtyard.

On the following day they went to see the Wolf's Gorge, the Fairies' Pool, the Long Rock, and the *Marlotte*. Two days later, they began driving again at random, just where their coachman thought fit to take them, without asking where they were, and often even neglecting the famous sites.

They felt so comfortable in their old landau, low as a sofa, and covered with a rug made of a striped material which was quite faded. The moats, filled with brushwood, stretched out under their eyes with a gentle, continuous movement. White rays gleamed like arrows through the tall ferns. Sometimes a road no longer in use presented itself before them, in a straight line, and here and there might be seen a feeble growth of weeds. In the centre between four cross-roads, a crucifix extended its four arms. In other places, stakes were bending down like dead trees, and little curved paths, which were hidden under the leaves, made them feel a longing to pursue them. At the same moment the horse turned round; they entered there; they plunged into the mire. Further down moss had sprouted out at the sides of the deep ruts.

They believed that they were far away from everybody, quite alone. But suddenly a game-keeper with his gun, or a band of ragged women, with big bundles of faggots strapped on their backs, would hurry past them.

When the carriage stopped, there was a universal silence. The only sounds were the blowing of the horse in the shafts or the faint cry of a bird more than once repeated.

The light at certain points illuminating the outskirts of the wood, left the interior in deep shadow, or else, attenuated in the foreground by a sort of twilight, it exhibited in the background violet vapours, a white radiance. The midday sun, falling directly on wide tracts of greenery, made splashes of light over them, hung gleaming drops of silver from the ends of the branches, streaked the grass with long lines of emeralds, and flung golden spots on the beds of the dead leaves. Looking upward, they could distinguish the sky through the tops of the trees. Some of them, which were enormously high, looked like patriarchs or emperors, or, touching one another at their extremities formed with their long shafts, as it were, triumphal arches; others springing forth obliquely from below, seemed like falling columns. This heap of big vertical lines gaped open. Then, enormous green billows unrolled themselves in unequal emboss-ments as far as the surface of the valleys, toward which advanced the brows of other hills looking down on white plains, which finally lost themselves in an undefined pale tinge.

Standing side by side, on some rising ground, they felt, as they drank in the air, the pride of a fuller life penetrating into the depths of their souls, with a superabundance of energy, a joy which they could not explain.

The variety of trees furnished a spectacle of the most diversified char-acter. The smooth, white-barked beeches twisted their tops together. Ash trees softly curved their bluish branches. In the tufts of the hornbeams rose up holly stiff as bronze. Then came a row of thin birches, bent into elegiac attitudes; and the pine-trees, symmetrical as organ pipes, seemed to be singing as they swayed to and fro. There were gigantic oaks with knotted forms, which had been violently shaken, stretched out from the soil and pressed close against each other, and with firm trunks resembling torsos, launched forth to heaven despairing appeals with their bare arms and furious threats, like a group of Titans struck rigid in the midst of their rage. An atmosphere of gloom, a feverish languor, brooded over the pools, whose sheets of water were cut into flakes by the overshadowing thorn-trees. The lichens on their banks, where the wolves come to drink, are of the colour of sulphur, burnt, as it were, by the footprints of witches, and the incessant croaking of the frogs responds to the cawing of the crows as they wheel through the air. Then they passed through the monotonous glades planted here and there with a staddle. The sound of iron falling with a succession of rapid blows could be heard. On the side of the hill a group of quarrymen were breaking the rocks. These rocks became more and more numerous and finally filled up the entire landscape, cube-shaped like houses, flat like flag-stones, propping up, overhanging, and becoming intermingled with each other, as if they were the ruins, unrecognisable and monstrous, of some vanished city. But this wild chaos reminded one rather of volcanoes, of deluges, of great unknown cataclysms. Frederick said they had been there since the beginning of the world, and would remain so till the end. Rosanette turned aside her head, declaring that it would drive her out of her mind, and went off to collect sweet heather. The little violet blossoms, heaped up near one another, formed unequal surfaces, and the soil, which was giving way underneath, formed soft dark fringes on the sand spangled with mica.

One day they reached a point half-way up a hill, where the soil was full of sand. Its surface, untrodden till now, was streaked, and resembled symmetrical waves. Here and there, like promontories on the dry bed of an ocean, rose up rocks with the vague outlines of animals, tortoises thrusting forward their heads, crawling seals, hippopotami, and bears. Not a soul near them. Not a single sound. The shingle glowed under the dazzling rays of the sun, and all at once in this vibration of light these specimens of the brute creation began to move before their eyes. They returned home quickly, flying from the dizziness that had seized hold of them, almost dismayed at their own fancies.

The gravity of the forest influenced them, and hours passed in silence, during which, allowing themselves to yield to the lulling effects of springs, they remained as it were sunk in the torpor of a calm intoxication. With his arm around her waist, he listened to her talking while the birds were warbling, noticed with the same glance the black grapes on her bonnet and the juniper-berries, the draperies of her veil, and the spiral forms assumed by the clouds, and when he bent toward her the freshness of her skin blended with the strong perfume of the woods. Everything amused them. They showed one another, as a curiosity, gossamer threads of the Virgin hanging from bushes, holes full of water in the middle of stones, a squirrel on the branches, the way in which two butterflies kept following them; or else, at twenty paces from them, under the trees, a hind strode on peacefully, with an air of nobility and gentleness, its doe walking by its side.

Rosanette would have liked to run after it to embrace it.

She got very much alarmed once, when a man, suddenly presenting himself, showed her three vipers in a box. She wildly flung herself on Frederick's breast. He felt happy at the thought that she was weak and that he was strong enough to protect her.

One evening they dined at an inn on the banks of the Seine. The table was near the window; Rosanette sat opposite him, and he contemplated her little well-shaped white nose, her turned-up lips, her bright eyes, the swelling bands of her nut-brown hair, and her pretty oval face. Her dress of raw silk clung to her somewhat drooping shoulders, and her two hands, emerging from their sleeves, joined close together as if they were one—carved, poured out wine, moved over the table-cloth. The waiter placed before them a chicken with its four limbs stretched out, a stew of eels in a dish of pipe-clay, wine that had got spoiled, bread that was too hard, and knives with notches in them. All these things made the repast more enjoyable and heightened the illusion. They fancied themselves in the middle of a journey in Italy on their honeymoon. Before starting again they went for a walk along the bank of the river.

The soft blue dome-like sky, touched at the horizon on the indentations of the woods. On the opposite side, at the end of the meadow, was a village steeple; and further away, to the left, the roof of a house made a red splash on the river, which wound its way without any apparent motion. Some rushes bent over it, and the water lightly shook some poles fixed at its edge in order to hold nets. An osier bow-net and two or three old fishing-boats were to be seen. Near the inn a girl in a straw hat was drawing buckets out of a well. Every time they came up, Frederick heard the grating sound of the chain with a feeling of inexpressible delight.

He had no doubt that he would be happy till the end of his days, so natural did his felicity appear to him, so much a part of his life, and so intimately associated with this woman's being. He was irresistibly impelled to address her with words of endearment. She answered with pretty little speeches, gentle taps on the shoulder, displays of tenderness that charmed him by their unexpectedness. He discovered in her quite a new sort of beauty, which, perhaps, was only the reflection of surrounding things, unless indeed it happened to bud forth from hidden potentialities.

Sometimes they lay down in the middle of the field, and he would stretch himself out with his head on her lap, under the shelter of her parasol; or else with their faces turned toward the greensward, in the centre of which they rested, they gazed, toward each other till their pupils seemed to intermingle, thirsting for each other and ever satiating their thirst, and then with half-closed eyelids they lay side by side without uttering a single word.

Now and then the distant rolling of a drum reached their ears. It was the signal-drum which was being beaten in the different villages calling on people to go to the defence of Paris.

"Oh! 'tis the rising!" said Frederick, with a disdainful pity, all this excitement now presenting to his mind a pitiful aspect by comparison with their love and eternal nature.

And they talked about whatever happened to come into their heads, things that were perfectly familiar to them, persons in whom they took no interest, a thousand trifles. She chatted about her chambermaid and her hairdresser. One day she was so self-forgetful that she told him her age—twenty-nine years. She was becoming quite an old woman.

Several times, almost unconsciously, she gave him some particulars with reference to her own life. She had been a "shop girl," had taken a trip to England, and had begun studying for the stage; all this she told without any explanation of how these changes had come about; and he found it impossible to reconstruct her entire history.

She related still more about herself one day when they were seated side by side under a plane-tree at the back of a meadow. At the road-side, further down, a little barefooted girl, standing amid a heap of dust, was driving a cow to pasture. As soon as she caught sight of them she came up to beg, and while with one hand she held up her tattered petticoat, she kept scratching with the other her black hair, which, like a wig of Louis XIV's time, curled round her dark face, lighted by a magnificent pair of eyes.

"She will be very pretty later," said Frederick.

"How lucky she is if she has no mother!" remarked Rosanette.

"Eh? How is that?"

"Certainly. I, if it were not for mine—"

She sighed, and began to talk about her childhood. Her parents were weavers in the Croix Rousse. She acted as an apprentice to her father. In vain did the poor man wear himself out with hard work; his wife was continually abusing him, and sold everything for drink. Rosanette could see, as if it were yesterday, the room they occupied, with the looms ranged length-wise against the windows, the pot boiling on the stove, the bed painted to represent mahogany, a cupboard facing it, and the obscure loft where she used to sleep up to the time when she was fifteen years old. At length a gentleman made his appearance on the scene—a fat man with a face the colour of boxwood, the manners of a devotee, and a suit of black clothes. Her mother and this man had a conversation together, with the result that three days afterward—Rosanette stopped, and with a look in which there was as much bitterness as shamelessness:

"It was done!"

Then, in response to a gesture of Frederick:

"As he was married (he would have been afraid of compromising himself in his own house), I was brought to a private room in a restaurant, and told that I would be very happy, and would get a handsome present.

"At the door, the first thing that struck me was a candelabrum of vermilion on a table, on which there were two covers. A mirror on the ceiling reflected them, and the blue silk hangings on the walls made the entire apartment resemble an alcove; I was overcome with astonishment. You understand—a poor creature who had never seen anything before. In spite of my dazed condition of mind, I got frightened. I wanted to go away. However, I remained.

"The only seat in the room was a sofa close beside the table. It was so soft that it yielded under me. The mouth of the hot-air stove in the middle of the carpet emitted toward me a warm breath, and there I sat without taking anything. The waiter, who was standing near me, urged me to eat. He poured out for me a large glass of wine. My head began to swim, I wanted to open the window. He said to me:

"'No, Mademoiselle! that is forbidden.'

"And he left me.

"The table was laden with a heap of things that I had no knowledge of. Nothing there seemed to me good. Then I fell back on a pot of jam, and patiently waited. I did not know what prevented him from coming. It was very late—midnight at last—I couldn't bear the fatigue any longer. While pushing aside one of the pillows, in order to hear better, I found under my hand a kind of album—a book of engravings, they were vulgar pictures. I was asleep on top of it when he entered the room."

She hung down her head and remained pensive.

The leaves rustled around them. Amid the tangled grass a great foxglove swayed to and fro. The sunlight swept like a wave over the green expanse, and the silence was interrupted at intervals only by the browsing of the cow, which they could no longer see.

Rosanette kept her eyes fixed on a particular spot, three paces away from her, her nostrils heaving, and her mind absorbed in thought. Frederick caught hold of her hand.

"How you suffered, poor darling!"

"Yes," said she, "more than you imagine! So much so that I tried to make an end of it—they had to fish me up!"

"What?"

"Ah! think no more about it! I love you, I am happy! kiss me!"

And she picked off, one by one, the sprigs of the thistles which clung to her gown.

Frederick was thinking more than all on what she had not told him. By what means had she gradually emerged from wretchedness? To what lover did she owe her education? What had occurred in her life down to the day when he first came to her house? Her latest avowal was a bar to these questions. All he asked her was how she had made Arnoux's acquaintance.

"Through the Vatnaz."

"Wasn't it you that I once saw with both of them at the Palais-Royal?"

He mentioned the exact date. Rosanette made a movement which showed a sense of deep pain.

"Yes, it is true! I was not gay at that time!"

But Arnoux had proved himself a very good fellow. Frederick had no doubt of it. However, their friend was a queer character, full of faults. He took care to recall them all. She quite agreed with him on this point.

"Never mind! One likes him, all the same, this camel!"

"Still—even now?" said Frederick.

She reddened, half smiling, half angry.

"Oh, no! that's an old story. I don't keep anything hidden from you. Even though it might be so, with him it is different. Besides, I don't think you are nice toward your victim!"

"My victim!"

Rosanette caught hold of his chin.

"No doubt!"

And in the lisping fashion in which nurses talk to babies:

"Having always been so good! Never went a-by-by with his wife?"

"I! never at any time!"

Rosanette smiled. He felt hurt by that smile of hers, which seemed to him an evidence of indifference.

But she went on gently, and with one of those looks which seem to appeal for a denial of the truth:

"Are you perfectly certain?"

"Not a doubt about it!"

Frederick solemnly declared on his word of honour that he had never bestowed a thought on Madame Arnoux, as he was far too much in love with another woman.

"With whom, pray?"

"Why, with you, my beautiful one!"

"Ah! don't laugh at me! You only annoy me!"

He thought it a prudent course to invent a story—to pretend that he was swayed by a passion. He made up some circumstantial details. This woman, however, had rendered him very unhappy.

"Decidedly, you have not been lucky," said Rosanette.

"Oh! oh! I may have been!" wishing to convey that he had been often fortunate in his love-affairs, so that she might have a better opinion of him, just as Rosanette did not confess how many lovers she had had, in order that he might have more respect for her—for there will always be found in the midst of the most intimate confidences restrictions, false shame, delicacy, and pity. You divine either in the other or in yourself precipices or miry paths which deter you from penetrating any farther; moreover, you feel that you will not be understood. It is difficult to express accurately the thing you mean, whatever it may be: and this is the reason why perfect unions are rare.

The poor Maréchale had never known one better than this. Often, when she gazed at Frederick, tears came into her eyes; then she would raise them or cast a glance toward the horizon, as if she saw there some bright dawn, perspectives of boundless felicity. At last, she confessed one day to him that she would like to have a mass said, "so that it might bring a blessing on our love."

How was it, then, that she had resisted him so long? She could not tell herself. He repeated his question a great many times; and she replied, as she clasped him in her arms:

"It was because I was afraid, my darling, of loving you too well!"

On Sunday morning, Frederick read, amongst the list of the wounded in the newspaper, the name of Dussardier. He uttered a cry, and showing the paper to Rosanette, declared that he would start at once for Paris.

"For what purpose?"

"In order to see him, to nurse him!"

"You are not going, I'm sure, to leave me by myself?"

"Come with me!"

"Ha! to poke my nose in a squabble of that sort? Oh, no, thanks!"

"However, I cannot—"

"Ta! ta! ta! as if they had need of nurses in the hospitals! And then, what concern is he of yours now? Everyone for himself!"

He was roused to indignation by this egoism on her part, and he reproached himself for not being in Paris with the others. Such indifference to the misfortunes of the nation had in it something shabby, and only worthy of a small shopkeeper. And now, all of a sudden, his intrigue with Rosanette weighed on his mind as if it were a crime. For an hour they were quite cool toward each other.

Then she implored him to wait, and not expose himself to danger.

"Suppose you happen to be killed?"

"Well, I should only have done my duty!"

Rosanette gave a jump. His first duty was to love her; but perhaps he did not care about her any longer. There was no common sense in what he was going to do. Good heavens! what an idea!

Frederick rang for his bill. But to return to Paris was no easy matter. The Leloir stage-coach had just left; the Lecomte berlins would not be starting; the diligence from Bourbonnais would not be passing till a late hour that night, and perhaps it might be full, one could never tell. When he had lost a great deal of time in making inquiries about the various modes of conveyance, the idea occurred to him to travel post. The master of the post-house refused to supply him with horses, as Frederick had no passport. Finally, he hired an open carriage—the same one in which they had driven about the country—and at about five o'clock they reached the Hôtel du Commerce at Melun.

The market-place was covered with piles of arms. The prefect had forbidden the National Guards to proceed toward Paris. Those who did not belong to his department wished to go on. There was a great deal of shouting, and the inn was packed with a noisy crowd.

Rosanette, terrified, said she would not go a step further, and once more begged of him to stay. The innkeeper and his wife joined in her entreaties. A decent sort of man who happened to be dining there interposed, and said that the fighting would be over in a very short time. Besides, each man ought to do his duty. Thereupon the Maréchale redoubled her sobs. Frederick got exasperated. He handed her his purse, kissed her quickly, and disappeared.

On reaching Corbeil, he learned at the station that the insurgents had cut the rails at regular distances, and the coachman refused to drive him any farther; he said that his horses were "overspent."

Frederick managed to procure an indifferent cabriolet, which, for the sum of sixty francs, without taking into account the price of a drink for the driver, was to convey him as far as the Italian barrier. But at a hundred paces from the barrier his coachman made him descend and turn back. Frederick was walking along the pathway, when suddenly a sentinel thrust out his bayonet. Four men seized him, exclaiming:

"This is one of them! Look out! Search him! Brigand! scoundrel!"

And he was so thoroughly stunned that he let himself be dragged to the guard-house of the barrier, at the very point where the Boulevards des Gobelins and de l'Hôpital and Rues Godefroy and Mauffetard converge.

Four barricades formed at the ends of four different ways enormous sloping ramparts of paving-stones. Torches glimmered here and there. In spite of the rising clouds of dust he could distinguish foot-soldiers of the Line and National Guards, all with their faces blackened, their chests uncovered, and an appearance of wild excitement. They had just captured the square, and had shot down a number of men. Their rage had not yet cooled. Frederick said he had come from Fontainebleau to the relief of a wounded comrade who lodged in the Rue Bellefond. Not one of them would believe him at first. They examined his hands; they even put their noses to his ear to make sure that he did not smell of powder.

However, by dint of repeating the same thing, he finally convinced a captain, who directed two fusiliers to conduct him to the guard-house of the Jardin des Plantes. They descended the Boulevard de l'Hôpital. A strong breeze was blowing. It restored him to animation.

After this they turned up the Rue du Marché aux Chevaux. The Jardin des Plantes at the right formed a long black mass, whilst at the left the entire front of the Pitié, illuminated at every window, blazed like a conflagration, and shadows passed rapidly across the window-panes.

Two of the men in charge of Frederick left him. Another accompanied him to the Polytechnic School. The Rue Saint-Victor was quite dark, without a gas-lamp or a light at any window to relieve the gloom. Every ten minutes could be heard the words:

"Sentinels! mind yourselves!"

And this exclamation, cast into the midst of the silence, was prolonged like the repeated striking of a stone against the side of a chasm as it falls through space.

Every now and then the stamp of heavy footsteps could be heard coming nearer. This was nothing less than a patrol consisting of about a hundred men. From this confused mass escaped whisperings and the dull clanking of iron; and, moving along with a rhythmic swing, it melted into the darkness.

In the middle of the crossing, where several streets met, a dragoon sat motionless on his horse. Occasionally an express rider passed at a rapid gallop; then the silence was renewed. Cannons, which were being drawn along the streets, made, on the pavement, a heavy rolling sound that seemed full of menace—a sound different from every ordinary sound—which oppressed the heart. These interruptions served to intensify the silence, which was profound, unlimited—a black abyss. Men in white blouses accosted the soldiers, spoke one or two words to them, and then vanished like phantoms.

The guard-house of the Polytechnic School was crowded. The threshold was blocked up with women, who had come to see their sons or their husbands. They were sent on to the Panthéon, which was being utilised as a dead-house; and no attention was paid to Frederick. He pressed forward resolutely, solemnly declaring that his friend Dussardier was waiting for him, that he was at death's door. At last they sent a corporal to accompany him to the top of the Rue Saint-Jacques, to the Mayor's office in the twelfth arrondissement.

The Place du Panthéon was filled with soldiers lying asleep on straw. The day was breaking; the bivouac-fires were extinguished.

The insurrection had left terrible traces in this quarter. The soil of the streets, from end to end, was covered with piles of various sizes. On the wrecked barricades had been piled up omnibuses, gas-pipes, and cartwheels. In certain places there were little dark pools, which must have been blood. The houses were riddled with projectiles, and their framework could be seen under the plaster that was peeled off. Window-blinds, attached by a single nail, hung like rags. The staircases having fallen in, doors opened on vacancy. The interiors of rooms could be seen with their papers in strips. In some instances dainty objects had remained quite intact. Frederick noticed a timepiece, a parrot-stick, and some engravings.

When he entered the Mayor's office, the National Guards were chattering without a moment's pause about the deaths of Bréa and Négrier, about the Deputy Charbonnel, and about the Archbishop of Paris. He heard them saying that the Duc d'Aumale had landed at Boulogne, that Barbès had fled from Vincennes, that the artillery were due from Bourges, and that abundant aid was arriving from the provinces. About three o'clock some one brought good news.

Truce-bearers from the insurgents were in conference with the President of the Assembly.

Thereupon they all made merry; and as he had a dozen francs left, Frederick sent for a dozen bottles of wine, hoping in this way to hasten his deliverance. Suddenly a discharge of musketry was heard. The drinking stopped. The men peered with distrustful eyes into the unknown— it might be Henry V.

In order to shift responsibility, they took Frederick to the Mayor's office in the eleventh arrondissement, which he was not permitted to leave till nine o'clock in the morning.

He started at a running pace from the Quai Voltaire. At an open window an old man in his shirt-sleeves was crying, with his eyes raised. The Seine glided peacefully along. The sky was of a clear blue; and in the trees round the Tuileries birds were singing.

Frederick was just crossing the Place du Carrousel when a litter happened to pass by. The soldiers at the guard-house immediately presented arms; and the officer, putting his hand to his shako, said: "Honour to unfortunate bravery!" This phrase seemed to have almost become a matter of duty. He who pronounced it appeared to be, on each occasion, filled with profound emotion. A group of people in a state of fierce excitement followed the litter, exclaiming:

"We will avenge you! we will avenge you!"

The vehicles kept moving about on the boulevard, and women were making lint before the doors. Meanwhile, the outbreak had been quelled, or very nearly so. A proclamation from Cavaignac, just posted up, announced the fact. At the top of the Rue Vivienne, a company of the Garde Mobile appeared. Then the citizens uttered enthusiastic shouts. They raised their hats, applauded, danced, wished to embrace them, and to invite them to drink; and flowers, flung by ladies, fell from the balconies.

At last, at ten o'clock, just at the moment when the booming of the cannon announced that an attack was being made on the Faubourg Saint-Antoine, Frederick reached the abode of Dussardier. He found the bookkeeper in his garret, lying asleep on his back. From the adjoining apartment a woman came forth with silent tread—Mademoiselle Vatnaz.

She led Frederick aside and told him how Dussardier had got wounded.

On Saturday, on the top of a barricade in the Rue Lafayette, a young fellow wrapped in a tricoloured flag cried out to the National Guards: "Are you going to shoot your brothers?" As they advanced Dussardier flung down his gun, pushed away the others, sprang over the barricade, and, with a blow of an old shoe, knocked down the insurgent, from whom he tore the flag. He had afterward been found under a heap of rubbish with a slug of copper in his thigh. It was found necessary to make an incision in order to extract the projectile. Mademoiselle Vatnaz arrived the same evening, and since then had not left his side.

She prepared intelligently everything that was needed for the dressings, assisted him in taking his medicine or other liquids, attended to his slightest wishes, left and returned again with footsteps lighter than those of a fly, and gazed at him with eyes full of tenderness.

Frederick, during the two following weeks, did not fail to call every morning. One day, while he was speaking about the devotion of the Vatnaz, Dussardier shrugged his shoulders:

"Oh, no! she does this through interested motives."

"Do you think so?"

He replied. "I am sure of it!" without attempting to give any further explanation.

She had loaded him with kindnesses, carrying her attentions so far as to bring him the newspapers in which his gallant action was extolled. He confessed to Frederick that he felt uneasy in his conscience.

Perhaps he ought to have put himself on the other side with the men in blouses; for, indeed, a heap of promises had been made to them which had not been fulfilled. Those who had vanquished them hated the Republic; and, in the next place, they had treated them very harshly. No doubt they were in the wrong—not quite, however; and the honest fellow was tormented by the thought that he might have fought against the righteous cause. Sénécal, who was imprisoned in the Tuileries, under the terrace at the water's edge, suffered none of this mental anguish.

There were nine hundred men in the place, huddled together in the midst of filth, with no attempt at order, their faces blackened with powder and clotted blood, shivering with ague and breaking out into cries of rage; those who were brought there to die were not separated from the rest. Sometimes, on hearing the sound of a detonation, they believed that they were all going to be shot. Then they dashed themselves against the walls, and after that fell back again into their places, so much stupefied by suffering that it seemed to them that they were living in a nightmare, an awful hallucination. The lamp, suspended from the arched roof, looked like a stain of blood, and little green and yellow flames fluttered about, caused by the emanations from the vault. Through fear of epidemics, a commission was appointed. When he had advanced a few steps, the President recoiled, frightened by the stench from the excrements and from the corpses.

As soon as the prisoners drew near a vent-hole, the National Guards who were on sentry, in order to prevent them from shaking the bars of the grating, prodded them indiscriminately with their bayonets.

As a rule they showed no pity. Those who were not beaten wished to signalise themselves. There was a regular panic of fear. They avenged themselves at the same time on newspapers, clubs, mobs, speech-making —everything that had exasperated them during the last three months, and in spite of the victory that had been gained, equality (as if for the punishment of its defenders and the exposure of its enemies to ridicule) manifested itself in a triumphal fashion—an equality of brute beasts, a dead level of sanguinary vileness; for the fascination of self-interest equalled the madness of want, aristocracy had the same fits of fury as low debauchery, and the cotton cap did not show itself less hideous than the red cap. The public mind was agitated just as it would be after great convulsions of nature. Sensible men were rendered imbeciles by it for the rest of their lives.

Père Roque had become very courageous, almost foolhardy. Having arrived on the 26th at Paris with some of the inhabitants of Nogent, instead of returning with them, he had offered his assistance to the National Guard encamped at the Tuileries; and he was quite satisfied to be placed on sentry in front of the terrace at the water's side. There, at any rate, he had these brigands under his feet! He was delighted to see them beaten and humiliated, and he could not refrain from uttering invectives against them.

One, a young lad with long fair hair, pressed his face to the bars, and asked for bread. M. Roque ordered him to hold his tongue. But the young man repeated in a mournful tone:

"Bread!"

"Have I any to give you?"

Other prisoners presented themselves at the vent-hole, with their bristling beards, their burning eyeballs, all pushing forward, and yelling:

"Bread!"

Père Roque was indignant at seeing his authority slighted. In order to frighten them he took aim at them; and, borne backward into the vault by the crush that nearly smothered him, the young man, with his eyes staring upward, once more exclaimed:

"Bread!"

"Hold on! here it is!" said Père Roque, firing a shot from his gun. There was a fearful howl—then, silence. At the side of the trough something white could be seen lying.

After this, M. Roque returned to his abode, for he had a house in the Rue Saint-Martin, which he used as a temporary residence; and the injury done to the front of the building during the riots had in no slight degree contributed to his rage. It seemed to him, when he next looked at it, that he had exaggerated the amount of damage. His recent act had a soothing effect on him, as if it indemnified him for his loss.

His daughter opened the door for him. She immediately made the remark that she had felt uneasy at his excessively prolonged absence. She was afraid that he had met with some misfortune.

This manifestation of filial love softened Père Roque. He was astonished that she should have set out on a journey without Catherine.

"I sent her out on a message," was Louise's reply.

And she inquired about his health, about one thing or another; then, with an air of indifference, she asked him whether he had come across Frederick:

"No; I have not seen him!"

It was on his account alone that she had come up from the country.

Some one was heard walking in the lobby.

"Oh! excuse me—"

And she disappeared.

Catherine had not found Frederick. He had been several days away, and his intimate friend, M. Deslauriers, was now living in the provinces.

Louise once more presented herself, trembling all over, unable to speak. She leaned against the furniture.

"What's the matter with you? Tell me—what's the matter with you?" exclaimed her father.

She indicated by a wave of her hand that it was nothing, and with a great effort she regained her composure.

The keeper of the restaurant at the opposite side of the street brought them soup. But Père Roque had passed through too exciting an ordeal to be able to control his emotions. "He is not likely to die;" and at dessert he had a sort of fainting fit. A doctor came, and he prescribed a potion. Then, when M. Roque was in bed, he was well wrapped up in order to bring on perspiration. He gasped; he moaned.

"Thanks, my good Catherine! Kiss your poor father, my dear! Ah! those revolutions!"

And, when his daughter scolded him for making himself ill by worrying over her, he replied:

"Yes! perhaps so! But I couldn't help it. I am very sensitive!"

CHAPTER XV

LOUISE IS DISILLUSIONED

M. ROQUE described the severe military duties he had performed to Madame Dambreuse, in her boudoir, as she sat between her niece and Miss John.

She was biting her lips, as if in pain.

"Oh! 'tis nothing! it will pass away!"

And, with a gracious air:

"We are going to have an acquaintance of yours to dine with us—Monsieur Moreau."

Louise gave a start.

"Oh! we'll just have a few intimate friends there—amongst others, Alfred de Cisy."

And she spoke in terms of high praise about his manners, his personal appearance, and especially his moral character.

Madame Dambreuse was nearer to a correct estimate of the state of affairs than she imagined; the Vicomte was contemplating marriage. He said so to Martinon, adding that Mademoiselle Cécile would surely like him, and that her parents would be agreeable.

To justify him in going so far as to confide to another his intentions on the point, he required satisfactory information with regard to her dowry. Now Martinon suspected that Cécile was M. Dambreuse's natural daughter; and it is probable that it would have been a very daring step on his part to ask for her hand at any risk. Such audacity, of course, was not unaccompanied by danger; and for this reason Martinon had, so far, acted in a way that could not compromise him. Besides, he did not see how he could well get rid of the aunt. Cisy's confidence induced him to make up his mind; and he had formally made his proposal to the banker, who, seeing no objection to it, had just informed Madame Dambreuse about the matter.

Cisy presently made his appearance. She arose and said:

"You have been forgetting us. Cécile, shake hands!"

At the same moment Frederick entered the room.

"Ha! at last we have found you again!" exclaimed Père Roque. "I called with Cécile on you three times this week!"

Frederick had carefully avoided them. He pleaded by way of excuse that he had been spending all his days beside a wounded comrade.

For a long time, however, a heap of misfortunes had happened to him, and he tried to invent stories to explain his conduct. Luckily the guests arrived in the midst of his explanation. First of all M. Paul de Grémonville, the diplomatist whom he met at the ball; then Fumichon, that manufacturer whose conservative zeal had scandalised him one evening. After them came the old Duchesse de Montreuil Nantua.

Two loud voices in the anteroom reached his ears. They were that of M. de Nonancourt, an old beau with the air of a mummy preserved in cold cream, and that of Madame de Larsillois, the wife of a prefect of Louis Philippe. She was terribly frightened, for she had just heard an organ playing a polka which was known to be a signal amongst the insurgents. Many of the wealthy class of citizens had similar apprehensions;

they thought that men in the catacombs were going to blow up the Faubourg Saint-Germain. Noises escaped from cellars, and suspicious looking things were passed up to windows.

Everyone in the meantime made an effort to calm Madame de Larsillois. Order was reëstablished. There was no longer cause for fear.

"Cavaignac has saved us!"

As if the horrors of the insurrection had not been sufficiently numerous, they exaggerated them. There had been twenty-three thousand convicts on the side of the Socialists—no less!

They were certain that food had been poisoned, that Gardes Mobiles had been sawn between two planks, and that there had been inscriptions on flags inciting the people to pillage and incendiarism.

"Aye, and more than that!" added the ex-prefect.

"Oh, dear!" said Madame Dambreuse, whose modesty was shocked, while she indicated the three young girls with a glance.

M. Dambreuse came forth from his study accompanied by Martinon. She turned her head and responded to a bow from Pellerin, who was advancing toward her. The artist gazed in a restless fashion toward the walls. The banker took him aside, and told him that it was desirable for the present to conceal his revolutionary picture.

"No doubt," said Pellerin, the rebuff which he received at the Club of Intellect having modified his opinions.

M. Dambreuse hinted very politely that he would give him orders for other works.

"But excuse me. Ah! my dear friend, what a pleasure!"

Arnoux and Madame Arnoux stood before Frederick.

He had a sort of vertigo. Rosanette had been irritating him all the afternoon with her display of admiration for soldiers, and the old passion was reawakened.

The steward announced that dinner was on the table. With a look she directed the Vicomte to take in Cécile, while she said in a low tone to Martinon, "You wretch!" And then they passed into the dining-room.

Under the green leaves of a pineapple, in the centre of the table-cloth, a dorado stood, with its snout reaching toward a quarter of roebuck and its tail just grazing a bushy dish of crayfish. Figs, huge cherries, pears, and grapes (the first fruits of Parisian cultivation) rose like pyramids in baskets of old Saxe. Here and there a bunch of flowers mingled with the shining silver plate. The white silk blinds, in front of the windows, filled the apartment with a mellow light. It was cooled by two fountains, in which there were pieces of ice; and tall men-servants, in short breeches, waited on them. All these luxuries seemed the more precious for the emotion of the past few days. There was a fresh delight at possessing things which they had been afraid of losing; and Nonancourt voiced the general sentiment when he said:

"Ah! let us hope that these Republican gentlemen will allow us to dine!"

"In spite of their fraternity!" Père Roque added, with an attempt at wit.

These two personages were placed respectively at the right and at the left of Madame Dambreuse, her husband being exactly opposite her, between Madame Larsillois, at whose side was the diplomatist and the old Duchesse, whom Fumichon elbowed. Then came the painter, the dealer in faïence, and Mademoiselle Louise; and, thanks to Martinon, who had carried her chair to enable her to take a seat near Louise, Frederick found himself beside Madame Arnoux.

She wore a black barège gown, a gold hoop encircled her wrist, and, as on the first day that he dined at her house, there was something red in her hair, a branch of fuchsia twisted round her chignon. He could not help saying:

"It is a long time since we saw each other."

"Ah!" she returned coldly.

He continued, in a mild tone, which mitigated the impertinence of his question:

"Have you thought of me now and then?"

"Why should I think of you?"

Frederick was hurt by these words.

"You are right, perhaps, after all."

But very soon, regretting what he had said, he swore that he had not lived a single day without being ravaged by the remembrance of her.

"I don't believe a single word you are saying, Monsieur."

"However, you know that I love you!"

Madame Arnoux made no reply.

"You know that I love you!"

She still remained silent.

"Well, then, go be hanged!" said Frederick to himself.

And, as he raised his eyes, he perceived Mademoiselle Roque at the other side of Madame Arnoux.

She imagined it gave her a coquettish look to dress entirely in green, a colour which contrasted horribly with her red hair. The buckle of her belt was too large and her collar cramped her neck. This lack of elegance had, no doubt, contributed to the coldness which Frederick at first displayed toward her. She watched him from where she sat, some distance away, with curious glances; and Arnoux, by her side, in vain lavished his gallantries—he could not get her to utter three words, so that, finally abandoning all hope of making himself agreeable to her, he listened to the conversation. She now began rolling about a slice of Luxembourg pine-apple in her pea-soup.

Louis Blanc, according to Fumichon, owned a large house in the Rue Saint-Dominique, which he refused to let to the workmen.

"I think it rather a funny thing," said Nonancourt, "to see Ledru-Rollin hunting over the Crown lands."

"He owes twenty thousand francs to a goldsmith!" Cisy interposed, "and 'tis maintained—"

Madame Dambreuse interrupted him.

"Ah! how nasty it is to be getting hot about politics! and for such a young man, too! fie, fie! Pay attention rather to your fair neighbour!"

After this, those who were of a grave turn of mind attacked the newspapers. Arnoux took it on himself to defend them. Frederick mixed himself up in the discussion, describing them as commercial establishments just like any other house of business. Those who wrote for them were, as a rule, imbeciles or humbugs; he led his listeners to believe that he was acquainted with journalists, and he combated with sarcasms his friend's generous sentiments.

Madame Arnoux did not realise that this was said through a feeling of spite against her.

Meanwhile the Vicomte was torturing his brain in the effort to make a conquest of Mademoiselle Cécile. He commenced by criticising the shape of the decanters and the graving of the knives, in order to show his artistic tastes. Then he talked about his stable, his tailor and his shirt-maker. Finally, he took up the subject of religion, and seized the opportunity of conveying to her that he fulfilled all his duties.

Martinon set to work in a better fashion. With his eyes fixed on her continually, he praised, in a monotonous fashion, her birdlike profile, her dull fair hair, and her hands, which were unusually short. The plain-looking young girl was charmed at this shower of flatteries.

It was impossible to hear anything, as all present were talking at the tops of their voices. M. Roque wanted "an iron hand" to govern France. Nonancourt regretted that the political scaffold was abolished. All these scoundrels should be put to death together.

"Now that I think of it, what about Dussardier?" said M. Dambreuse, turning toward Frederick.

The worthy shopman was now a hero, like Sallesse, the brothers Jeanson, the wife of Pequillet, etc.

Frederick, without waiting to be asked, related his friend's history; it threw around him a kind of halo.

This naturally led to a discussion on different traits of courage.

According to the diplomatist, it was not hard to face death, witness the case of men who fight duels.

"We might take the Vicomte's testimony on that point," said Martinon. The Vicomte's face got very red.

The guests stared at him, and Louise, more astonished than the rest, murmured:

"What is it, pray?"

"He *sank* before Frederick," returned Arnoux, in a very low tone.

"Do you know anything of it, Mademoiselle?" said Nonancourt presently, and he repeated her answer to Madame Dambreuse, who, bending forward a little, fixed her gaze on Frederick.

Martinon did not wait for Cécile's questions. He informed her that the affair had reference to a woman of improper character. The young girl drew back slightly in her chair, as if to escape from contact with such a libertine.

The conversation was renewed. The great wines of Bordeaux were passed round, and the guests became animated. Pellerin had a dislike to the Revolution, because he attributed to it the loss of the Spanish Museum.

This is what grieved him most as a painter.

As he made the latter remark, M. Roque asked:

"Are you not yourself the painter of a very notable picture?"

"Perhaps! What is it?"

"It depicts a lady in a costume—faith!—a little light, with a purse, and a peacock in the background."

Frederick, in his turn, reddened. Pellerin pretended that he did not understand.

"Nevertheless, it is certainly by you! For your name is written at the bottom of it, and there is also a line on it stating that it is Monsieur Moreau's property."

One day, when Père Roque and his daughter were waiting for him at his residence, they saw the Maréchale's portrait. The old gentleman had taken it for "a Gothic painting."

"No," said Pellerin rudely, "'tis a woman's portrait."

Martinon added:

"And a living woman's, too, and no mistake! Isn't that so, Cisy?"

"Oh! I know nothing about it."

"I thought you were acquainted with her. But, since it causes you pain, I must beg a thousand pardons!"

Cisy lowered his eyes, proving by his embarrassment that he must have played a discreditable part in connection with this portrait. As for Frederick, the model could only be his mistress. It was one of those convictions which are immediately formed, and the faces of the assembly revealed it with the utmost clearness.

"How he lied to me!" said Madame Arnoux to herself.

"It is for that woman, then, that he left me," thought Louise.

Frederick had an idea that these two stories might compromise him; and when they were in the garden, he reproached Martinon. Mademoiselle Cécile's wooer laughed in his face.

"Oh, not at all! 'twill benefit you! Go ahead!"

What did he mean? Besides, what was the cause of this good nature, so contrary to his usual conduct? Without giving any explanation, he proceeded toward the lower end, where the ladies were seated. The men were standing round them, and, in their midst, Pellerin was giving vent to his ideas. The form of government most favourable for the arts was an enlightened monarchy. He was disgusted with modern times, "if it were only on account of the National Guard"—he regretted the Middle Ages and the days of Louis XIV. M. Roque congratulated him on his opinions, acknowledging that they overcame all his prejudices against artists. But almost without a moment's delay he went off when he heard the voice of Fumichon.

Arnoux tried to prove that there were two Socialisms—a good and a bad. The manufacturer saw no difference whatever between them, his head becoming dizzy with rage at the utterance of the word "property."

"'Tis a law written on the face of Nature! Children cling to their toys. All peoples, all animals have the same instinct. The lion even, if he were able to speak, would declare himself a proprietor! I myself, messieurs, began with a capital of fifteen thousand francs. Would you be surprised to hear that for thirty years I used to get up at four o'clock every morning? I've had as much pain as five hundred devils in making my fortune! And people want to tell me I'm not the master, that my money is not my money; in short, that property is theft!"

"But Proudhon—"

"Don't bother me with your Proudhon! if he were here I think I'd strangle him!"

He would have strangled him. After the intoxicating drink he had swallowed Fumichon did not know what he was talking about any longer, and his apoplectic face was on the point of bursting like a bombshell.

"Good morrow, Arnoux," said Hussonnet, who was walking briskly over the grass.

He brought M. Dambreuse the first leaf of a pamphlet, entitled *The Hydra,* the Bohemian defending the interests of a reactionary club, and in that capacity he was presently introduced by the banker to his guests.

Hussonnet amused them by relating how the dealers in tallow hired three hundred and ninety-two street boys to bawl out every evening "Lamps,"* and then turning into ridicule the principles of '89, the eman-

---

*The word may also be translated "grease-pots."—TRANSLATOR.

cipation of the negroes, and the orators of the Left; he even went so far as to do *Prudhomme on a Barricade,* perhaps under the influence of a kind of jealousy of these rich people who had enjoyed a good dinner. The caricature did not appeal to them. Their faces grew long.

This was no time for joking, so Nonancourt observed, as he recalled the death of Monseigneur Affre and that of General de Bréa. These events were being constantly alluded to, and arguments were constructed out of them. M. Roque described the archbishop's end as "everything that one could call sublime." Fumichon gave the palm to the military personage, and instead of simply expressing regret for these two murders, they disputed with a view to determining which ought to excite the greatest indignation. A second comparison was next instituted, namely, between Lamoricière and Cavaignac, M. Dambreuse glorifying Cavaignac, and Nonancourt, Lamoricière.

Not one of those present, with the exception of Arnoux, had ever seen either of them engaged in the exercise of his profession. None the less everyone spoke decisively with reference to their operations.

Frederick, however, declined to express an opinion on the matter, confessing that he had not served as a soldier. The diplomatist and M. Dambreuse gave him an approving nod of the head. In fact, to have fought against the insurrection was to have defended the Republic. The result, although favourable, consolidated it; and now they had rid themselves of the vanquished, they wanted to be conquerors.

As soon as they got out into the garden, Madame Dambreuse, taking Cisy aside, chided him for his awkwardness. When she caught sight of Martinon, she sent him away, and then tried to find out from her future nephew the cause of his witticisms at the Vicomte's expense.

"There's nothing of the kind."

"And all this, as it were, for the glory of Monsieur Moreau. What is the object of it?"

"There's no object. Frederick is a delightful fellow. I am very fond of him."

"And so am I, too. Let him come here. Go and bring him!"

After a few commonplace phrases, she began by lightly disparaging her guests, and in this way she placed him on a higher level than the others. He did not omit to sneer at the ladies more or less, which was an ingenious way of paying her compliments. She left his side from time to time, as it was a reception-night, and ladies were every moment arriving; then she returned to her seat, and the entirely accidental arrangement of the chairs prevented their being overheard.

She was playful and yet grave, melancholy and yet quite rational. Her daily occupations interested her very little—there were depths of sentiments of a less transitory kind. She complained of the poets, who misrepresent the facts of life, then she raised her eyes toward heaven, asking him what was the name of a certain star.

Two or three Chinese lanterns had been suspended from the trees; the wind shook them, and lines of coloured light quivered on her white dress. She sat after her usual style, a little back in her armchair, with a footstool in front of her. The tip of a black satin shoe could be seen; and at intervals Madame Dambreuse allowed a louder word than usual, and sometimes even a laugh, to escape her.

These coquetries did not disturb Martinon, who was occupied with Cécile; but they were bound to make an impression on M. Roque's daughter, who was chatting with Madame Arnoux. She was the only member of her own sex present whose manners were not disdainful. Louise came and sat beside her; then, yielding to the desire to give an immediate vent to her emotions:

"Does he not talk well—Frederick Moreau, I mean?"

"Do you know him?"

"Oh! very well! We are neighbours; he used to amuse himself with me when I was quite a little girl."

Madame Arnoux cast at her a sidelong glance, which meant:

"I suppose you are not in love with him?"

The young girl's face replied with an untroubled look:

"Yes."

"You see him quite often, then?"

"Oh, no! only when he comes to his mother's house. 'Tis ten months now since he was there. He promised, however, to be more particular."

"The promises of men are not to be too much relied on, my child."

"But he has never deceived me!"

"As he has others!"

Louise shivered: "Could it be by any chance that he promised something to her;" and her features became distracted with distrust and hate.

Madame Arnoux felt almost afraid of her; she would have gladly withdrawn what she had said. Then both became silent.

As Frederick was seated opposite them on a folding-stool, they kept looking at him, the one with propriety out of the corner of her eye, the other boldly, with parted lips, so that Madame Dambreuse said to him:

"Come, now, turn round, and let her have a good look at you!"

"Whom do you mean?"

"Why, Monsieur Roque's daughter!"

And she chaffed him on having won the heart of this young girl from the provinces. He denied that it was so, and tried to make a laugh of it.

"Is it likely, I ask you? Such an ugly creature as that!"

However, he experienced an intense feeling of gratified vanity. He recalled to mind the reunion from which he had returned one night, some time before, his heart filled with bitter humiliation, and he drew a long breath, for it seemed to him that he was now in the environment that really suited him; he felt as if all these things, including the Dambreuse mansion, belonged to himself. The ladies formed a semicircle around him while they listened to what he was saying, and in order to create an effect, he declared that he was in favor of the reëstablishment of divorce, which he maintained should be easily procurable, so as to enable people to leave one another and come back to one another without any limit and as often as they liked. They uttered loud protests; a few of them began to talk in whispers. Little exclamations every now and then burst forth from the place where the wall was overshadowed with aristolochia. It sounded like a mirthful cackling of hens; and he developed his theory with that self-complacency which is generated by the consciousness of success. A man-servant brought into the arbour a tray laden with ices. The gentlemen drew close together and began to chat about the recent arrests.

Thereupon Frederick revenged himself on the Vicomte by making him believe that he might be prosecuted as a Legitimist. The other urged by way of reply that he had not stirred outside his own room. His adversary enumerated in a heap the possible mischances. MM. Dambreuse and Grémonville were much amused at the discussion. Then they paid Frederick compliments, expressing regret at the same time that he did not employ his abilities in the defence of order. They grasped his hand with the utmost warmth; he might for the future count on their support. At last, just as everyone was leaving, the Vicomte made a low bow to Cécile:

"Mademoiselle, I have the honour of wishing you a very good evening."

She replied coldly:

"Good evening." But she gave Martinon a parting smile.

Père Roque, desiring to continue his conversation with Arnoux, offered to see him home, "as well as Madame"—they were going the same way. Louise and Frederick walked in front of them. She had taken his arm; and, when she was some distance away from the others she said:

"Ah! at last! at last! I've had enough to bear all the evening! How nasty those women were! What haughty airs they had!"

He made an effort to defend them.

"First of all, you might certainly have spoken to me the moment you came in, after being away a whole year!"

"It was not a year," said Frederick, glad to be able to make some sort of rejoinder on this point in order to avoid the other questions.

"Be it so; the time appeared very long to me, that's all. But, during this horrid dinner, one would think you were ashamed of me. Ah! I understand—I don't possess what is necessary to please as they do."

"You are mistaken," said Frederick.

"Really! Swear to me that you don't love anyone else!"

He did swear.

"You love nobody but me alone?"

"I assure you, I do not."

This assurance filled her with delight. She would have liked to lose her way in the streets, so that they might walk about together the whole night.

"I have been so much tormented down there! Nothing was talked about but barricades. I imagined I saw you lying on your back covered with blood! Your mother was confined to her bed with rheumatism. She knew nothing about what was happening. I had to hold my tongue. I could bear it no longer, so I came with Catherine."

And she related to him all about her departure, her journey, and the lie she told her father.

"He's taking me back in two days. Come to-morrow evening, as if you were merely paying a casual visit, and take advantage of the opportunity to ask for my hand in marriage."

Never had Frederick been further from the idea of marriage. Besides, Mademoiselle Roque appeared to him a rather absurd young person. How unlike she was to a woman like Madame Dambreuse! A very different future was in store for him. He had found reason to-day to feel perfectly certain on that point; and, therefore, this was not the time to involve himself, from mere sentimental motives, in a step of such momentous importance. It was necessary now to be decisive—and then he had seen Madame Arnoux again. Nevertheless he was rather embarrassed by Louise's candour.

He said in reply to her last words:

"Have you thoroughly considered this matter?"

"How is that?" she exclaimed, frozen with astonishment and indignation.

He said that to marry at such a time as this would be absolute folly.

"So you don't want to have me?"

"Nay, you don't understand me!"

And he plunged into a confused mass of verbiage in order to impress upon her that he was kept back by serious considerations; that he had business on hand which it would take a long time to dispose of; that even his inheritance had been placed in jeopardy (Louise cut all this explanation short with one plain word); that, last of all, the present political situation made the thing undesirable. So, then, the most reasonable course was to wait patiently. Matters would, no doubt, right themselves—at least, he hoped so; and, as he could think of no further excuses to offer just at that moment, he pretended to have suddenly remembered that he should have been with Dussardier two hours ago.

Then, bowing to the others, he darted down the Rue Hauteville, took a turn round the Gymnase, returned to the boulevard, and quickly rushed up Rosanette's four flights of stairs.

M. and Madame Arnoux left Père Roque and his daughter at the entrance of the Rue Saint-Denis. Husband and wife returned home without exchanging a word, as he was worn out and unable to continue chattering any longer. She even leaned against his shoulder. He was the only man who had displayed any honourable sentiments during the evening. She entertained toward him feelings of the utmost indulgence. Meanwhile, he cherished a certain degree of spite against Frederick.

"Did you notice his face when a question was asked about the portrait? When I told you that he was her lover, you would not believe what I said!"

"Oh! yes, I was wrong!"

Arnoux, gratified with his triumph, pressed the matter even further.

"I'd even make a bet that when he left us, a little while ago, he went straight to see her. He's with her at this moment, you may be sure! He's finishing the evening with her!"

Madame Arnoux had pulled down her hat very low.

"Why, you're trembling all over!"

"I feel cold!" was her reply.

As soon as her father was asleep, Louise made her way into Catherine's room, and catching her by the shoulders, shook her.

"Get up—quick, as quick as ever you can! and go and fetch a cab for me!"

Catherine replied that there was not one to be had at such an hour.

"Will you come with me yourself there, then?"

"Where, might I ask?"

"To Frederick's house!"

"Impossible! Why do you want to go there?"

It was in order to have a talk with him. She could not wait. She must see him at once.

"Just think of what you're about to do! To present yourself this way at a house in the middle of the night! Besides, he's asleep by this time!"

"I'll wake him up!"

"But this is not a proper thing for a young girl to do!"

"I am not a young girl—I'm his wife! I love him! Come—put on your shawl!"

Catherine, standing at the side of the bed, was trying to decide how to act. She said at last:

"No! I won't go!"

"Well, stay behind then! I'll go by myself!"

Louise glided like an adder toward the staircase. Catherine rushed after her, and came up with her on the footpath outside the house. Her remonstrances were fruitless; so she followed the girl, fastening her undervest as she hurried along in the rear. The walk appeared to her exceedingly tedious. She complained that her legs were getting weak from age.

"I'll go on after you—faith, I haven't the same thing to drive me on that you have!"

Then she softened.

"Poor soul! You haven't anyone now but your Catau, don't you see?"

From time to time scruples took hold of her mind.

"Ah, this is a nice thing you're making me do! Suppose your father happened to miss you! Lord God, let us hope no misfortune will happen!"

In front of the Théâtre des Variétés, a patrol of National Guards stopped them.

Louise immediately explained that she was going with her servant to look for a doctor in the Rue Rumfort. The patrol allowed them to pass.

At the corner of the Madeleine they met a second patrol, and, Louise having given the same explanation, one of the National Guards asked:

"Is it for a nine months' ailment, ducky?"

"Oh, damn it!" exclaimed the captain, "no black-guardisms in the ranks! Pass on, ladies!"

Despite the captain's orders, they still kept cracking jokes.

"I wish you much joy!"

"My respects to the doctor!"

"Mind the wolf!"

"They like laughing," Catherine remarked in a loud tone. "That's what it is to be young."

At length they reached Frederick's house.

Louise gave the bell a vigorous pull, which she repeated several times. The door opened a little, and, in answer to her inquiry, the porter said:

"No!"

"But he must be in bed!"

"I tell you he's not. Why, for nearly three months he has not slept at home!"

And the little pane of the lodge fell down sharply, like the blade of a guillotine.

They stood in the darkness under the archway.

An angry voice cried out to them:

"Be off!"

The door was again opened; they went away.

Louise sat down on a boundary-stone; and clasping her face with her hands, she wept copious tears welling up from her full heart. The day was breaking, and market carts were making their way into the city.

Catherine led her back home, holding her up, kissing her, and offering every sort of consolation that she could extract from her own experience. Why trouble so much about one lover? There were plenty more.

CHAPTER XVI

THREE CHARMING WOMEN

ROSANETTE became more charming than ever when her enthusiasm for the Gardes Mobiles had died down, and Frederick gradually fell into the habit of living with her.

The best part of the day was the morning on the terrace. In a light cambric dress, and with her stockingless feet thrust into slippers, she kept moving about him—cleaned her canaries' cage, gave her gold-fishes some water, and, with a fire-shovel did a little amateur gardening in the box filled with clay, from which arose a trellis of nasturtiums, brightening the wall. Then, resting, with their elbows on the balcony, they stood side by side, gazing at the vehicles and the passers-by; and they basked in the sunlight, and made plans for spending the evening. He absented himself only for two hours at most, and, after that, they would go to some theatre, where they would get seats near the stage; and Rosanette, with a large bouquet of flowers in her hand, would listen to the instruments, while Frederick, leaning close to her ear, would tell her comic or amatory stories. At other times they would drive in an open carriage to the Bois de Boulogne. They walked about slowly until the middle of the night. At last they made their way home through the Arc de Triomphe and the grand avenue, inhaling the breeze, with the stars above their heads, and with all the gas-lamps ranged in the background of the perspective like a double string of luminous pearls.

Frederick always waited for her when they were going out together. She took a very long time fastening the two ribbons of her bonnet; and she smiled at herself in the mirror set in the wardrobe; then she would draw her arm through his, and, making him look at himself in the glass beside her:

"We look well this way, the two of us side by side. Ah! my darling, I could eat you!"

He was now her chattel, her property. She wore on her face a continuous radiance, while at the same time she appeared more languishing in manner, more rounded in figure; and, without being able to explain the difference, he found her altered.

One day she informed him, as if it were a very important bit of news, that my lord Arnoux had lately set up a linen-draper's shop for a woman who was formerly employed in his pottery-works. He used to go there every evening—"he spent a lot on it no later than a week ago; he had even given her a set of rosewood furniture."

"How do you know that?" said Frederick.

"Oh! I'm sure of it."

Delphine, while carrying out some orders for her, had made enquiries about the matter. She must, then, be much attached to Arnoux to take such a deep interest in his movements. He contented himself with saying to her in reply:

"What does this signify to you?"

Rosanette looked surprised at the question.

"Why, the rascal owes me money. Isn't it atrocious to see him supporting beggars?"

Then, with a look of triumphant hate in her face:

"Besides, she is only laughing at him. She has three others on hand. So much the better; and I'll be glad if she eats him up, even to the last farthing!"

Arnoux had, in fact, let himself be used by the girl from Bordeaux with the indulgence which characterises senile attachments. His manufactory no longer existed. The entire state of his affairs was pitiable; so that, in order to set them afloat again, he projected the establishment of a *café chantant,* at which only patriotic pieces would be sung. With a grant from the Minister, this establishment would become at the same time a focus for the purpose of propagandism and a source of profit. Now that power had been directed into a different channel, the thing was impossible.

His next idea was a big military hat-making business. He lacked capital, however, to open it.

He was not more fortunate in his domestic life. Madame Arnoux was less agreeable in manner toward him, sometimes even a little rude. Berthe always took her father's part. This increased the discord, and the house was becoming intolerable. He often set forth in the morning, passed his day in making long excursions out of the city, in order to divert his thoughts, then dined at a rustic tavern, abandoning himself to his reflections.

The prolonged absence of Frederick disturbed his habits. He presented himself one afternoon, begged of him to come and see him as in former days, and obtained from him a promise to do so.

Frederick did not feel sufficient courage within him to go back to Madame Arnoux's house. He felt as if he had betrayed her. But this conduct was very pusillanimous. There was no excuse for it. There was only one way of ending the matter, and so, one evening, he set out for her house.

As the rain was falling, he had just turned up the Passage Jouffroy, when, under the light shed from the shop-windows, a fat little man accosted him. Frederick had no difficulty in recognising Compain, that orator whose motion had excited so much laughter at the club. He was leaning on the arm of an individual whose head was muffled in a zouave's red cap, with a very long upper lip, a complexion as yellow as an orange, a tuft of beard under his jaw, and big staring eyes glistening with wonder.

Compain seemed to be proud of him, for he said:

"Let me introduce you to this jolly dog! He is a bootmaker whom I include amongst my friends. Come and let us take something!"

Frederick having thanked him, he immediately thundered against Rateau's motion, which he described as a manœuvre of the aristocrats. In order to put an end to it, it would be necessary to begin '93 over again! Then he inquired about Regimbart and some others, who were also well known, such as Masselin, Sonson, Lecornu, Maréchale, and a certain Deslauriers, who had been implicated in the case of the carbines lately intercepted at Troyes.

All this was new to Frederick. Compain knew nothing further about the subject. He left the young man with these words:

"You'll come soon, will you not? for you belong to it."

"To what?"

"The calf's head!"

"What calf's head?"

"Ha, you rogue!" returned Compain, giving him a nudge in the ribs.

And the two terrorists plunged into a café.

Ten minutes later Frederick had forgotten Deslauriers. He was on the footpath of the Rue de Paradis in front of a house; and he was staring at the light which came from a lamp in the second floor behind a curtain.

At length he ascended the stairs.

"Is Arnoux in?"

The chambermaid answered:

"No; but come in all the same."

And, abruptly opening a door:

"Madame, it is Monsieur Moreau!"

She arose, whiter than the collar round her neck.

"To what do I owe the honour—of a visit—so unexpected?"

"Merely the pleasure of seeing old friends once more."

And as he took a seat:

"How is the worthy Arnoux?"

"Very well. He has gone out."

"Ah, I understand! still following his old nightly practices. A little distraction!"

"And why not? After a day spent in making calculations, the head needs a rest."

She even praised her husband as a hard-working man. Frederick was irritated at this eulogy; and pointing toward a piece of black cloth with a narrow blue braid which lay on her lap:

"What is it you are doing there?"

"A jacket which I am trimming for my daughter."

"Now that you remind me of it, I have not seen her. Where is she, pray?"

"At a boarding-school," was the reply.

Tears came into her eyes. She held them back, while she rapidly plied her needle. To compose himself, he took up a number of *L'Illustration* which had been lying on the table close to where she sat.

"These caricatures of Cham are very funny, are they not?"

"Yes."

Then they relapsed into silence once more.

All of a sudden a fierce gust of wind shook the window-panes.

"What weather!" said Frederick.

"It was very good of you, indeed, to come here in the midst of this dreadful rain."

"Oh! what do I care about that? I'm not like some, whom it prevents, no doubt, from keeping their appointments."

"What appointments?" she asked ingenuously.

"Don't you remember?"

A shudder ran through her frame and she hung down her head.

He gently laid his hand on her arm.

"You have given me great pain."

She replied, with a sort of wail in her voice:

"But I was frightened about my child."

She told him about Eugène's illness, and all the tortures which she had suffered on that day.

"Thanks! thanks! I doubt you no longer. I love you as much as ever."

"Ah! no; that is not true!"

"Why so?"

She glanced at him coldly.

"You forget the other! the one you took with you to the races! the woman whose portrait you have—your mistress!"

"Well, yes!" exclaimed Frederick, "I don't deny anything! I am a wretch! Just listen to me!"

He had done this through despair, as one commits suicide. However, he had made her very unhappy in order to avenge himself on her with his own shame.

"What mental anguish! Do you not realise what it means?"

Madame Arnoux turned away her beautiful face while she held out her hand to him; and they closed their eyes, absorbed in an intoxication that was like a sweet, ceaseless rocking. Then they stood face to face, gazing at each other.

"Could you believe it possible that I no longer loved you?"

She replied in a low voice, full of caressing tenderness:

. "No! in spite of everything, I felt at the bottom of my heart that it was impossible, and that some day the obstacle between us two would be removed!"

"So did I; and I was dying to see you again."

"I once passed close to you in the Palais-Royal!"

"Did you really?"

And he spoke to her of the happiness he experienced at meeting her again at the Dambreuses' house.

"But how I hated you that evening as I was leaving the place!"

"Poor boy!"

"My life is so sad!"

"And mine, too. If it were only the vexations, the anxieties, the humiliations, all that I endure as wife and as mother, seeing that one must die, I would not complain; the frightful part of it is my solitude, without anyone."

"But you have me here with you!"

"Oh! yes!"

A sob of deep emotion made her bosom swell. She opened her arms, and they strained each other, while their lips met in a long kiss.

A creaking sound on the floor not far from them reached their ears. There was a woman standing close to them; it was Rosanette. Madame Arnoux recognised her. Her eyes, opened to their widest, scanned this woman, full of astonishment and indignation. At length Rosanette said to her:

"I have come to see Monsieur Arnoux about a matter of business."

"You see he is not here."

"Ah! that's true," returned the Maréchale. "Your nurse was right! A thousand apologies!"

And turning toward Frederick:

"So here you are—you?"

The familiar tone in which she addressed him, and in her own presence, too, made Madame Arnoux flush as if she had received a slap right across the face.

"I tell you once more, he is not here!"

Then the Maréchale, who was looking around, said quietly:

"Let us go back together! I have a cab waiting below."

He pretended not to hear.

"Come! let us go!"

"Ah! yes! this is a good opportunity! Go! go!" said Madame Arnoux.

They left together, and she stooped over the head of the stairs in order to see them once more, and a laugh—piercing, heart-rending, reached them from the place where she stood. Frederick pushed Rosanette into the cab, sat down opposite her, and during the entire drive did not utter a word.

The infamy, which it outraged him to see once more flowing back on him, had been occasioned by himself alone. He experienced at the same time the dishonour of a crushing humiliation and the remorse caused by the loss of his new-found happiness. Just when, at last, he had it in his grasp, it had for ever more become impossible, and that through the fault of this girl of the town, this harlot. He would have liked to strangle her. He was choking with rage. When they got into the house he flung his hat on a piece of furniture and tore off his cravat.

"Ha! you have just done a nice thing—confess it!"

She planted herself boldly in front of him.

"Well, what of that? Where's the harm?"

"What! You are playing the spy on me?"

"Is that my fault? Why do you go to amuse yourself with virtuous women?"

"Never mind! I don't wish you to insult them."

"How have I insulted them?"

He could not answer this, and in a more spiteful tone:

"But on the other occasion, at the Champ de Mars—"

"Ah! you bore me to death with your old women!"

"Wretch!"

He raised his fist.

"Don't kill me! I'm pregnant!"

Frederick staggered back.

"You are lying!"

"Why, just look at me!"

She seized a candlestick, and pointing at her face:

"Don't you recognise the fact there?"

Little yellow spots dotted her skin, which was strangely swollen. Frederick could not deny the evidence. He opened the window, took a few steps up and down the room, and then sank into an armchair.

This event was a calamity which, in the first place, put off their rupture, and, in the next place, upset all his plans. The notion of being a father, moreover, appeared to him grotesque, inadmissible. But why? If, in place of the Maréchale— And his reverie became so deep that he had a kind of hallucination. He could see, on the carpet, in front of the chimney-piece, a little girl. She resembled Madame Arnoux and himself a little—dark, and yet fair, with black eyes, very thick eyebrows, and a red ribbon in her curling hair. (Oh, how he would have loved her!) And he seemed to hear her voice saying: "Papa! papa!"

Rosanette, who had just undressed herself, came across to him, and seeing a tear in his eyelids, kissed him gravely on the forehead.

He arose, saying:

"By Jove, we mustn't kill this little one!"

Then she talked a lot of nonsense. To be sure, it would be a boy, and its name would be Frederick. She must begin making its clothes; and, seeing her so happy, a feeling of pity took possession of him. As he no longer cherished any anger against her, he desired to know the reason of the step she had recently taken. She said it was because Mademoiselle Vatnaz had sent her that day a bill which had been protested for some time past; and so she hastened to Arnoux to get the money from him.

"I'd have given it to you!" said Frederick.

"It is a simpler course for me to get over there what belongs to me, and to pay back to the other one her thousand francs."

"Is that really all you owe her?"

She answered:

"Certainly!"

On the following day, at nine o'clock in the evening (the hour specified by the doorkeeper), Frederick repaired to Mademoiselle Vatnaz's residence.

In the anteroom, he jostled against the furniture, which was heaped together. But the sound of voices and of music guided him. He opened a door, and found himself in the middle of a rout. Standing up before a piano, which a young lady in spectacles was playing, Delmar, as serious as a pontiff, was declaiming a humanitarian poem on prostitution; and his hollow voice rolled to the accompaniment of the metallic chords. A row of women sat close to the wall, attired, as a rule, in dark colours without neckbands or cuffs. Five or six men, all people of culture, occupied seats here and there. In an armchair was seated a former writer of fables, a mere wreck now; and the pungent odour of the two lamps was intermingled with the aroma of the chocolate which filled a number of bowls placed on the card-table.

Mademoiselle Vatnaz, with an Oriental shawl thrown over her shoulders, was seated at one side of the chimney-piece. Dussardier faced her at the other side. He seemed to feel himself in an embarrassing position. Besides, he was rather intimidated by his artistic surroundings. Had the Vatnaz, then, broken off with Delmar? Perhaps not. However, she seemed jealous of the worthy shopman; and Frederick, having asked permission to exchange a word with her, she made a sign to him to go with them into her own apartment. When the thousand francs were paid, she asked, in addition, for interest.

"'Tisn't worth while," said Dussardier.

"Pray hold your tongue!"

This want of moral courage on the part of so brave a man was agreeable to Frederick as a justification of his own conduct. He took away the bill with him, and never again referred to the scandal at Madame Arnoux's house. But from that time forth he observed clearly all the defects in the Maréchale's character.

She had incurable bad taste, incomprehensible laziness, the ignorance of a savage, so much so that she regarded Dr. Derogis as a person of great celebrity, and she felt proud of entertaining himself and his wife, because they were "married people." She lectured with a pedantic air on the affairs of daily life to Mademoiselle Irma, a helpless little creature endowed with a weak voice, who had as a protector a gentleman "very well off," an ex-clerk in the Custom-house, who had a rare talent for card tricks. Rosanette used to call him "My big Loulou." Frederick could no longer endure the repetition of her stupid words, such as "Some custard," "To Chaillot," "One could never know," etc.; and she insisted on wiping off the dust in the morning from her trinkets with a pair of old white gloves. He was above all disgusted by her treatment of her servant, whose wages were constantly in arrears, and from whom she even borrowed money. On the days when they settled their accounts, they used to wrangle like two fish-women; and then, on becoming reconciled, used to embrace each other. It was a relief to him when Madame Dambreuse's evening parties began again.

There, at any rate, he found something to amuse him. She was well versed in the intrigues of society, the changes of ambassadors, the personal character of dressmakers; and, if commonplaces escaped her lips, they did so in such a becoming fashion, that her language might be regarded as the expression of respect for propriety or of polite irony. It was interesting to watch the way in which, in the midst of twenty persons chatting around her, she would, without neglecting any of them, bring about the answers she desired and avoid those that were dangerous. Things of a very simple nature, when related by her, assumed the aspect of confidences. Her slightest smile gave rise to dreams; in short, her charm, like the exquisite scent which she usually carried about with her, was complex and indefinable.

While he was in her presence, Frederick experienced on each occasion the pleasure of a new discovery, nevertheless, he always found her equally serene the next time they met, like the reflection of limpid waters.

But why was there such coldness in her manner toward her niece? At times she even darted strange looks at her.

As soon as the question of marriage was started, she had urged as an objection to it, when discussing the matter with M. Dambreuse, the condition of "the dear child's" health, and had at once taken her off to the baths of Balaruc. On her return fresh obstacles were raised by her—that the young man was not in a good position, that this ardent passion did not appear to be a very serious attachment, and that no risk would be run by waiting. Martinon had replied, when the suggestion was made to him, that he would wait. His conduct was sublime. He lectured Frederick. He did more. He enlightened him as to the best method of pleasing Madame Dambreuse, even giving him to understand that he had ascertained from the niece the sentiments of her aunt.

As for M. Dambreuse, far from exhibiting jealousy, he treated his young friend with the utmost attention, consulted him about different things, and even expressed anxiety about his future, so that one day, when they were talking about Père Roque, he whispered with a sly air:

"You have done well."

Cécile, Miss John, the servants and the porter, every one of them exercised a fascination over him in this house. He came there every evening, leaving Rosanette for that purpose. Her approaching maternity rendered her graver in manner, and even a little melancholy, as if she were troubled by anxieties. To every question put to her she replied:

"You are mistaken; I am quite well."

She had, as a matter of fact, signed five notes in her previous transactions, and not having the courage to tell Frederick after the first had been paid, she had returned to the abode of Arnoux, who had promised her, in writing, the third part of his profits in the lighting of the towns of Languedoc by gas (a marvellous undertaking!), while requesting her not to make use of this letter at the meeting of shareholders. The meeting was postponed from week to week.

Meanwhile the Maréchale wanted money. She would have died sooner than ask Frederick for any. She did not wish to get it from him; it would have spoiled their love. He contributed a great deal to the household expenses; but a little carriage, which he hired by the month, and other sacrifices, which were indispensable since he had begun to visit the Dambreuses, prevented him from doing more for his mistress. On two or three occasions, when he got back to the house at a different hour from his usual time, he fancied he could see men's backs disappearing behind the door, and she often went out without saying where she was going. Frederick did not attempt to inquire minutely into these matters. One of these days he would make up his mind as to his future course of action. He dreamed of another life which would be more amusing and more noble. It was having such an ideal before his mind that rendered him indulgent toward the Dambreuse mansion.

It was an establishment in the neighbourhood of the Rue de Poitiers. There he met the great M. A., the illustrious B., the profound C., the eloquent Z., the immense Y., the old terrors of the Left Centre, the paladins of the Right, the burgraves of the golden mean; the eternal good old men of the comedy. He was astonished at their abominable style of talking, their meannesses, their rancours, their dishonesty—all these personages, after voting for the Constitution, were now striving to destroy it; and they got into a state of great agitation, and launched forth manifestoes, pamphlets, and biographies. Hussonnet's biography of Fumichon was a masterpiece. Nonancourt confined himself to the work of propagandism in the country districts; M. de Grémonville worked up the clergy; and Martinon brought together the young men of the wealthy class. Each exerted himself according to his resources, including Cisy. With his thoughts now all day long absorbed in matters of grave moment, he kept making excursions here and there in a cab in the interests of the party.

M. Dambreuse, like a barometer, constantly gave expression to its latest variation. Lamartine could not be mentioned without eliciting from this gentleman the quotation of a famous phrase of the man of the people: "Enough of poetry!" Cavaignac was, from this time forth, nothing better in his eyes than a traitor. The President, whom he had admired for a period of three months, was beginning to fall off in his esteem (as he did not appear to exhibit the "necessary energy"); and, as he always wanted a saviour, his gratitude, since the affair of the Conservatoire, belonged to Changarnier: "Thank God for Changarnier . . . Let us place our hope on Changarnier. . . . Oh, there's nothing to fear as long as Changarnier—"

M. Thiers was lauded, above all, for his book against Socialism, in which he showed that he was quite as much of a thinker as a writer. There was an immense laugh at Pierre Leroux, who had quoted passages from the philosophers in the Chamber. Jokes were made about the phalansterian tail. The "Market of Ideas" came in for a measure of applause, and its authors were compared to Aristophanes. Frederick patronised the work as well as the rest.

Political verbiage and good living had an enervating effect on his morality. Mediocre in capacity as these persons appeared to him, he felt proud of knowing them, and internally longed for the respectability that attached to a wealthy citizen. A mistress like Madame Dambreuse would assure him a position.

He set about taking the necessary steps for achieving that object.

He made it his business to cross her path, never failed to greet her with a bow in her box at the theatre, and, knowing the hours she went to church, he would plant himself behind a pillar in a melancholy attitude. There was a continual interchange of little notes between them with regard to items to which they drew each other's attention, preparations for a concert, or the borrowing of books or reviews. In addition to his visit each evening, he sometimes made a call just as the day was closing; and he experienced a progressive succession of pleasures in passing through the large front entrance, through the courtyard, through the anteroom, and through the two reception-rooms. Finally, he reached her boudoir, which was as still as a tomb, as warm as an alcove, and in which one jostled against the upholstered edging of furniture in the midst of numerous objects placed here and there—chiffoniers, screens, bowls, and trays made of lacquer, or shell, or ivory, or malachite, expensive trifles, to which fresh additions were frequently made. Amongst single specimens of these rarities might be noticed three Etretat rollers which were used as paper-presses, and a Frisian cap hung from a Chinese folding-screen. Nevertheless, all these things harmonised, and one was impressed by the noble aspect of the entire place, due, no doubt, to the loftiness of the ceiling, the richness of the portières, and the long fringes that floated over the gold legs of the stools.

She invariably sat on a little sofa, close to the flower-stand, which garnished the recess of the window. Frederick, seating himself on the edge of a large wheeled ottoman, addressed to her compliments of the most appropriate kind that he could conceive; and she looked at him, with her head a little on one side, and a smile playing round her mouth.

He read aloud to her poetry, into which he threw his whole soul in order to move her and excite her admiration. She would now and then interrupt him with a disparaging remark or a practical comment; and their conversation relapsed incessantly into the eternal question of Love. They discussed the circumstances that produced it, whether women felt it more than men, and what was the difference of feeling between them. Frederick tried to express his opinion, and, at the same time, avoid anything like coarseness or insipidity. This became at length a species of contest between them, sometimes agreeable and at other times tedious.

While at her side, he did not experience that ravishment of his entire being which drew him toward Madame Arnoux, nor the feeling of voluptuous delight with which Rosanette had, at first, inspired him. But he felt a passion for her as a thing that was abnormal and difficult of attainment, because she was of aristocratic rank, because she was wealthy, because she was a devotee—imagining that she had a delicacy of sentiment as rare as the lace and the amulets she wore, and instincts of modesty even in her depravity.

He made some use of his old passion for Madame Arnoux, uttering in his new flame's hearing all those amorous sentiments which the other had caused him to feel earnestly, and pretending that it was Madame Dambreuse herself who had occasioned them. She received these avowals like one accustomed to such things, and, without giving him a formal repulse, did not yield in the slightest degree; and he came no nearer to seducing her than Martinon did to being married. In order to end matters with her niece's suitor, she accused him of having money for his object, and even begged of her husband to put the young man to the test. M. Dambreuse then declared to him that Cécile, being the orphan child of poor parents, had neither expectations nor a dowry.

Martinon, not believing this, or feeling that he had gone too far to draw back, or through one of those outbursts of idiotic infatuation which may be described as acts of genius, replied that his patrimony, amounting to fifteen thousand francs a year, would be sufficient for both of them. The banker was touched by this unexpected display of disinterestedness. He promised the young man a tax-collectorship, undertaking to obtain the post for him; and in the month of May, 1850, Martinon married Mademoiselle Cécile. There was no ball to celebrate the event. The young people left the same evening for Italy. Frederick came next day to visit Madame Dambreuse. She appeared to him paler than usual. She sharply contradicted him about several matters of no importance. However, she observed, all men were egoists.

There were, however, some devoted men, though he might happen himself to be the only one.

"Pooh, pooh! you're just like the rest of them!"

Her eyelids were red; she had been weeping.

Then, forcing a smile:

"Pardon me; I am in the wrong. Sad thoughts have taken possession of my mind."

He could not understand what she meant to convey by the last words.

"No matter! she is not so difficult to overcome as I imagined," he thought.

She rang for a glass of water, drank a mouthful, sent it away again, and then began to complain of the wretched way in which her servant attended on her. In order to amuse her, he offered to become her servant himself, pretending that he knew how to hand round plates, dust furniture, and announce visitors—in fact, to do the duties of a *valet-de-chambre,* or, rather, of a running-footman, although the latter was now out of fashion. He would be charmed to cling on behind her carriage wearing a hat adorned with cock's feathers.

"And how I would follow you with majestic stride, carrying your pug on my arm!"

"You are facetious," said Madame Dambreuse.

Was it not folly, he returned, to take everything seriously? There were enough miseries in the world without creating fresh ones. Nothing was worth the cost of a single pang. Madame Dambreuse raised her eyes with a sort of vague approval.

This agreement in their views of life encouraged Frederick to take a bolder course. His former miscalculations now gave him insight. He went on:

"Our grandsires lived better. Why not obey the impulse that urges us onward? After all, love is not of such importance in itself."

"But that is immoral!"

She had resumed her seat on the little sofa. He sat at the side of it, near her feet.

"Don't you see that I am lying? For in order to please women, one must exhibit the thoughtlessness of a buffoon or all the wild passion of tragedy! They only laugh at us when we simply tell them that we love them! For my part, I consider those hyperbolical phrases which tickle their fancy a profanation of true love, so that it is no longer possible to thus express oneself, especially when addressing women who possess more than ordinary intelligence."

She gazed at him from under her drooping eyelids. He lowered his voice, while he bent his head closer to her face.

"Yes! you frighten me! Perhaps I am offending you? Forgive me! I did not intend to say all that I have said! 'Tis not my fault! You are so beautiful!"

Madame Dambreuse closed her eyes, and he was astonished at his easy victory. The tall trees in the garden ceased their gentle quivering. Motionless clouds streaked the sky with long strips of red, and on every side there seemed to be a suspension of vital movements. Then he recalled to mind, in a confused sort of way, evenings like this, filled with the same unbroken silence. Where was it that he had known them?

He sank upon his knees, seized her hand, and swore that he would love her for ever. Then, as he was leaving, she beckoned to him to come back, and said to him in a low tone:

"Come by-and-by and dine with us! We shall be all alone."

It seemed to Frederick, as he descended the stairs, that he had become a different man, that he was surrounded by the balmy temperature of hot-houses, and that he was now entering into the higher sphere of patrician adulteries and lofty intrigues. In order to occupy the first rank there all he required was a woman of this stamp. Greedy, no doubt, of power and of success, and married to a man of inferior calibre, for whom she had done prodigious services, she longed for some one of ability to guide. Nothing was impossible now. He felt himself capable of riding two hundred leagues on horseback, of travelling for several nights in succession without fatigue. His heart overflowed with pride.

Just in front of him, on the footpath, a man wrapped in a seedy overcoat was walking with downcast eyes, and with such an air of dejection that Frederick, as he passed, turned to have a better look at him. The other raised his head. It was Deslauriers. He hesitated. Frederick fell upon his neck.

"Ah! my poor old friend! 'Tis you!"

And he dragged Deslauriers into his house, at the same time asking him a heap of questions.

Ledru-Rollin's ex-commissioner began by describing the tortures to which he had been subjected. As he preached fraternity to the Conservatives, and respect for the laws to the Socialists, the former tried to shoot him, and the latter brought cords to hang him with. After June he had been brutally dismissed. He found himself involved in a charge of conspiracy—that which was connected with the seizure of arms at Troyes. He had subsequently been released for want of evidence to sustain the charge. Then the acting committee had sent him to London, where his ears had been boxed during a banquet at which he and his colleagues were being entertained. On his return to Paris—

"Why did you not call here, then, to see me?"

"You were always out! Your porter had mysterious airs—I did not know what to think; and, then, I had no desire to reappear before you in the character of a defeated man."

He had knocked at the portals of Democracy, offering to serve it with his pen, with his tongue, with all his energies. He had been everywhere repelled. They had mistrusted him. He had sold his watch, his bookcase, and even his linen.

"It would be better to be breaking one's back on the pontoons of Belle Isle with Sénécal!"

Frederick, who had been fastening his cravat, did not appear to be much affected by this news.

"Ha! so he is transported, this good Sénécal?"

Deslauriers replied, while he surveyed the walls with an envious air:

"Not everybody has your luck!"

"Excuse me," said Frederick, without noticing the allusion to his own circumstances, "but I am dining in the city. You must have something to eat; order whatever you like. Take even my bed!"

This cordial reception dissipated Deslauriers' bitterness.

"Your bed? But that might inconvenience you!"

"Oh, no! I have others!"

"Oh, all right!" returned the advocate, with a laugh. "Pray, where are you dining?"

"At Madame Dambreuse's."

"Can it be that you are—perhaps—?"

"You are too inquisitive," said Frederick, with a smile, which confirmed this hypothesis.

Then, after a glance at the clock, he resumed his seat.

"So that's how it is! but we mustn't despair, my ex-defender of the people!"

"Pardon me; let others bother themselves about the people henceforth!"

The advocate detested the working-men, because he had suffered so much on their account in his province, a coal-mining district. Every pit had appointed a provisional government, from which he received orders.

"Besides, their conduct has been everywhere charming—at Lyons, at Lille, at Havre, at Paris! For, in imitation of the manufacturers, who would fain exclude the products of the foreigner, these gentlemen call on us to banish the English, German, Belgian, and Savoyard workmen. As for their intelligence, what was the use of that precious trades' union of theirs which they established under the Restoration? In 1830 they joined the National Guard, without having the common sense to get in control of it. Was it not a fact that, since the morning when 1848 dawned, the various trade-bodies had not reappeared with their banners? They have even demanded popular representatives for themselves, who are not to speak except in their own behalf. All this is the same as if the deputies who represent beetroot were to concern themselves about nothing save beetroot. Ah! I've had enough of these dodgers who in turn prostrate themselves before the scaffold of Robespierre, the boots of the Emperor, and the umbrella of Louis Philippe—a rabble yielding allegiance to the person that flings bread into their mouths. They cry out against the venality of Talleyrand and Mirabeau; but the messenger down below there would sell his country for fifty centimes if they'd only promise to fix a tariff of three francs on his walk. Ah! what a wretched state of affairs! We ought to set the four corners of Europe on fire!"

Frederick said in reply to the bitter tirade of his friend:

"The spark is what you lack! You were simply a lot of shopboys, and even the best of you were nothing better than penniless students. As for the workmen, no wonder they complain; for, with the exception of a million taken out of the civil list, and of which you made a grant to them with the meanest expressions of flattery, you have done nothing for them, save to talk in stilted phrases! The workman's certificate remains in the hands of the employer, and the person who is paid wages remains (even in the eye of the law), the inferior of his master, because his word is not credited. In short, the Republic seems to me a worn-out institution. Who knows? Perhaps Progress can be realised only through an aristocracy or through a single man? The initiative always comes from the top, and whatever may be the people's pretensions, they are always lower than those placed over them!"

According to Frederick, the vast majority of citizens aimed only at a life of peace (he had been improved by his visits to the Dambreuses), and the chances were all on the side of the Conservatives. That party, however, needed new men.

"If you came forward, I am sure—"

He did not complete the sentence. Deslauriers saw what Frederick meant, and passed his two hands over his head; then, all of a sudden:

"But what about yourself? Is there anything to prevent you presenting yourself? Why would you not be a deputy?"

In consequence of a double election there was in the Aube a vacancy for a candidate. M. Dambreuse, who had been reëlected as a member of the Legislative Assembly, lived in and belonged to a different arrondissement.

"Would you like me to interest myself on your behalf?" He was acquainted with many publicans, schoolmasters, doctors, notaries' clerks and their masters. "Besides, you can make the peasants believe anything you like!"

Frederick felt his ambition rekindling.

Deslauriers added:

"You would have no difficulty in getting a situation for me in Paris."

"Oh! I could manage that through Monsieur Dambreuse."

"Talking of coal-mines," the advocate went on, "what has become of his big company? This is the sort of employment that would suit me, and I could make myself useful to them while preserving my own independence."

Frederick promised that he would introduce him to the banker before three days had passed.

The dinner, which he enjoyed alone with Madame Dambreuse, was a delightful affair. She sat opposite him with a smile on her countenance. On the table was a basket of flowers, while a lamp suspended above their heads shed its light on the scene; and, as the window was open, they could see the stars. They talked very little, distrusting themselves, no doubt; but, the moment the servants had turned their backs, they sent a kiss across to each other from the tips of their lips. He told her about his idea of becoming a candidate. She approved of the project, promising even to get M. Dambreuse to use every effort in his behalf.

As the evening advanced, some of her friends called to congratulate her, at the same time expressing sympathy with her; she must be so much pained at the loss of her niece. It was all very well for newly-married people to go on a trip; by-and-by would come incumbrances, children. But really, Italy did not realise one's expectations. They had not as yet passed the age of illusions; and, of course, the honeymoon made everything look beautiful. The last two who remained behind were M. de Grémonville and Frederick. The diplomatist was not inclined to leave. At last he departed at midnight. Madame Dambreuse signed to Frederick to go with him, and thanked him for this compliance with her wishes by giving him a gentle pressure with her hand more delightful than anything that had gone before.

The Maréchale uttered an exclamation of joy on seeing him again. She had been expecting him for the last five hours. He gave as an excuse for the delay an indispensable step which he had to take in the interests of Deslauriers. His face wore a look of triumph, and was surrounded by an aureole which dazzled Rosanette.

"It is perhaps because of your black coat, which fits you well; but I never have seen you look so handsome! How handsome you are!"

In a transport of tenderness, she vowed internally never again to belong to any other man, no matter what might be the consequence, even if she were to die of starvation.

Her pretty eyes sparkled with such intense passion that Frederick taking her upon his knees thought to himself that he was playing a very rascally part. All the same, he admired his own perversity.

CHAPTER XVII

FREDERICK'S BETROTHAL

DESLAURIERS presented himself to M. Dambreuse, who was thinking of reviving his coal-mining speculation. But this fusion of all the companies into one was looked upon unfavourably; there was prejudice against monopolies, as if immense capital were not necessary for carrying out enterprises of this kind!

Deslauriers, who had studied for the purpose the work of Gobet and the articles of M. Chappe in the *Journal des Mines,* understood the question perfectly. He demonstrated that the law of 1810 established for the benefit of the guarantee a privilege which could not be transferred. Besides, a democratic colour might be given to the transaction. To interfere with the formation of coal-mining companies was against the principle even of association.

M. Dambreuse intrusted to him some notes for the purpose of drawing up a memorandum. As for the way in which he meant to pay for the work, he was all the more profuse in his promises from the fact that they were not very definite.

Deslauriers called again at Frederick's house, and gave him an account of the interview. Moreover, he had caught a glimpse of Madame Dambreuse at the foot of the stairs, just as he was going out.

"I wish you joy—upon my soul, I do!"

Then they had a chat about the election. They would have to plan how to carry it.

Three days later Deslauriers reappeared with a sheet of paper covered with handwriting, intended for the Paris newspapers, which was nothing less than a friendly letter from M. Dambreuse, expressing approval of their friend's candidature. Supported by a Conservative and praised by a Red, he ought to succeed. How had the capitalist come to put his signature to such a lucubration? The advocate had, of his own motion, and without the least appearance of embarrassment, gone and shown it to Madame Dambreuse, who, thinking it quite appropriate, had taken the rest of the business on her own shoulders.

Frederick was astonished at this proceeding. Nevertheless, he approved of it; then, as Deslauriers was to have an interview with M. Roque, his friend explained to him his delicate position with regard to Louise.

"Tell them anything you like; that my affairs are in an unsettled state, that I am putting them in order. She is young enough to wait!"

Deslauriers set forth, and Frederick looked upon himself as a very able man. He experienced, moreover, a feeling of gratification, a profound satisfaction. His delight at being the possessor of a rich woman was not spoiled by any contrast. The sentiment harmonised with the surroundings. His life now would be full of happiness in every sense.

Perhaps the most delicious sensation of all was to gaze at Madame Dambreuse in the midst of a number of other ladies in her drawing-room. The propriety of her manners made him dream of other situations. While she was talking in a tone of coldness, he would recall the loving words which she had murmured in his ear. All the respect which he felt for her virtue gave him a thrill of pleasure, as if it were a homage which was reflected back on himself; and at times he felt a longing to exclaim:

"But I know her better than you! She is mine!"

It was not long ere their relations came to be socially recognised as an established fact. Madame Dambreuse, during the whole winter, had Frederick accompany her into fashionable society.

He nearly always arrived before her; and he watched her as she entered with her arms uncovered, a fan in her hand, and pearls in her hair. She would pause on the threshold (the lintel of the door formed a framework round her head), and she would open and close her eyes with a certain air of indecision, in order to see whether he was there.

She drove him back in her carriage; the rain lashed the carriage-blinds. The passers-by seemed merely shadows wavering in the mire of the street; and, pressed close to each other, they observed all these things vaguely with a calm disdain. Under various pretexts, he would linger in her room for an additional hour.

It was chiefly through a feeling of ennui that Madame Dambreuse had yielded. But this latest experience was not to be wasted. She desired to give herself up to an absorbing passion; and so she began to heap on his head adulations and caresses.

She sent him flowers; she had an upholstered chair made for him. She presented him with a cigar-holder, an inkstand, a thousand little things for daily use, so that every act of his life should recall her to his memory. These kind attentions charmed him at first, and in a little while appeared to him quite natural.

She would step into a cab, discharge it at the opening into a by-way, and come out at the other end; and then, gliding along by the walls, with a double veil on her face, she would reach the street where Frederick, who had been keeping watch, would take her arm quickly and lead her toward his house. His two men-servants would have gone out for a walk, and the door-keeper been sent on some errand. She would throw a glance around her—nothing to fear!—and she would breathe forth the sigh of an exile who beholds his country once more. Their good fortune emboldened them. Their appointments became more frequent. One evening, she presented herself, suddenly, in full ball-dress. These surprises might have perilous consequences. He reproached her for her imprudence. He was not taken with her appearance. The low-cut waist of her dress exposed her thinness too much.

It was then that he discovered what had hitherto been hidden from him—the disillusion of his senses. None the less did he make professions of ardent love; but in order to call up the necessary emotions he had to evoke the images of Rosanette and Madame Arnoux.

This sentimental atrophy left his intellect entirely untrammelled; and he was more ambitious than ever of attaining a high position in society. Inasmuch as he had such a stepping-stone, the very least he could do was to make use of it.

One morning, about the middle of January, Sénécal entered his study, and in response to his exclamation of astonishment, announced that he was Deslauriers' secretary. He brought Frederick a letter. It contained good news, and yet it took him to task for his negligence; he would have to appear on the scene of action at once. The future deputy said he would set out on his way there in two days' time.

Sénécal gave no opinion on the other's merits as a candidate. He spoke about his own concerns and the affairs of the country.

Miserable as the state of things was, it gave him pleasure to see that they were advancing in the direction of Communism. In the first place, the Administration led toward it of its own accord, since every day a greater number of things were under Government control. As for Property, the Constitution of '48, in spite of its weaknesses, had not spared it. The State might, in the name of public utility, henceforth take whatever it thought suitable. Sénécal declared himself in favour of authority; and Frederick noticed in his remarks the exaggeration which characterised what he had said himself to Deslauriers. The Republican even inveighed against the masses for their inadequacy.

"Robespierre, by upholding the right of the minority had brought Louis XVI to acknowledge the National Convention, and saved the people. Things were rendered legitimate by the end toward which they were directed. A dictatorship is sometimes indispensable. Long live tyranny, provided that the tyrant promotes the public welfare!"

Their discussion lasted a long time; and, as he took his departure, Sénécal confessed (perhaps it was the real object of his visit) that Deslauriers was getting very impatient at the silence of M. Dambreuse.

But M. Dambreuse was ill. Frederick saw him every day, his character of an intimate friend enabling him to obtain admission to the invalid's bedside.

General Changarnier's recall had strongly affected the capitalist's mind. He was, on the evening of the occurrence, seized with a burning sensation in his chest, together with an oppression that prevented him from lying down. The application of leeches gave him immediate relief. The dry cough disappeared; the respiration became easier; and, eight days later, he said, while swallowing some broth:

"Ah! I'm better now—but I was near going on the last long journey!"

"Not without me!" exclaimed Madame Dambreuse, intending by this remark to convey that she would not be able to outlive him.

Instead of replying, he cast upon her and upon her lover a singular smile, indicating at the same time, resignation, indulgence, irony, and even, as it were, a touch of humour, a sort of secret satisfaction almost amounting to actual joy.

Frederick wished to start for Nogent. Madame Dambreuse objected to this; and he unpacked and repacked his luggage by turns according to the variations in the invalid's condition.

One day M. Dambreuse spat forth considerable blood. The "princes of medical science," on being consulted, could not think of any fresh remedy. His legs swelled, and his weakness increased. He had several times expressed a desire to see Cécile, who was at the other end of France with her husband, now a collector of taxes, a position to which he had been appointed a month ago. M. Dambreuse gave orders to send for her. Madame Dambreuse wrote three letters, which she showed him.

Without trusting him even to the care of the nun, she did not leave him for one second, and no longer went to bed. The ladies who had their names entered at the door-lodge made inquiries about her with feelings of admiration, and the passers-by were filled with respect on seeing the quantity of straw which was placed on the street under the windows.

On the 12th of February, at five o'clock, a frightful hæmoptysis came on. The doctor who had charge of the case pointed out that it had assumed a dangerous aspect. They sent in hot haste for a priest.

While M. Dambreuse was making his confession, Madame gazed curiously at him from some distance. After this, the young doctor applied a blister, and awaited the result.

The flame of the lamps, obscured by some of the furniture, lighted up the apartment irregularly. Frederick and Madame Dambreuse, at the foot of the bed, watched the dying man. In the recess of a window the priest and the doctor chatted in low tones. The good sister on her knees kept mumbling prayers.

At last came a rattling in the throat. The hands grew cold; the face began to turn white. Now and then he drew a deep breath; but gradually this became rarer and rarer. Two or three confused words escaped him. He turned his eyes upward, and at the same moment his respiration became so feeble that it was almost imperceptible. Then his head sank on one side on the pillow.

For a minute, all present remained motionless.

Madame Dambreuse advanced toward the dead body of her husband, and, without an effort—with the unaffectedness of one discharging a duty—she drew down the eyelids. Then she spread out her two arms, her figure writhing as if in a spasm of repressed despair, and left the room, supported by the physician and the nun.

A quarter of an hour afterward, Frederick entered her apartment.

There was in it an indefinable odour, emanating from some delicate substances with which it was filled. In the middle of the bed lay a black dress, which formed a glaring contrast with the pink coverlet.

Madame Dambreuse was standing at the corner of the mantelpiece. Without attributing to her any passionate regret, he thought she looked a little sad; and, in a mournful voice, he said:

"You are suffering pain?"

"I? No—not at all."

As she turned, her eyes fell on the dress, which she inspected. Then she told him not to stand on ceremony.

"Smoke, if you like! You can make yourself at home here!"

And, with a great sigh:

"Ah! Blessed Virgin!—what a riddance!"

Frederick was astonished at this exclamation. He replied, as he kissed her hand:

"All the same, you were free!"

This allusion to the ease with which the intrigue between them had been carried on hurt Madame Dambreuse.

"Ah! you don't know all I did for him, or the misery in which I lived!"

"What!"

"Why, certainly! Was it a safe thing to have always near him that bastard, a daughter, whom he brought into the house at the end of five years of married life, and who, were it not for me, might have led him into some act of folly?"

Then she explained how her affairs stood. The arrangement on the occasion of her marriage was that the property of each party should be separate and under his and her own control. The amount of her inheritance was three hundred thousand francs. M. Dambreuse had guaranteed by the marriage contract that in the event of her surviving him, she should have an income of fifteen thousand francs a year, together with the ownership of the mansion. But later he had made a will by which he gave her all he possessed, and this she estimated, so far as it was possible to ascertain just at present, at over three millions of francs.

Frederick's eyes opened widely.

"It was worth the trouble, wasn't it? However, I contributed to it! It was my own property I was protecting; Cécile would have unjustly robbed me of it."

"Why did she not come to see her father?"

As he asked her this question Madame Dambreuse eyed him attentively; then, in a dry tone:

"I haven't the least idea! Want of affection, probably! Oh! I know what she is! And for that reason she won't get a farthing from me!"

She had not been very troublesome, he pointed out; at any rate, since her marriage.

"Ha! her marriage!" said Madame Dambreuse, with a sneer. And she repented having treated only too well this stupid creature, who was jealous, self-interested, and hypocritical. "All the faults of her father!" She disparaged him more and more. There was never a person with such profound duplicity, and with such a merciless disposition into the bargain, as hard as a stone—"a bad man, a bad man!"

Even the wisest people fall into errors. Madame Dambreuse had just made a serious one by this overflow of hatred. Frederick, sitting opposite her in an easy chair, was reflecting deeply, scandalised by the language she had used.

She arose and knelt down beside him.

"To be with you is my only real pleasure! You are the only one I love!"

While she gazed at him her heart softened, a nervous reaction brought tears into her eyes, and she murmured:

"Will you marry me?"

For a moment he thought he had not understood what she said. He was stunned by this wealth.

She repeated in a louder tone:

"Will you marry me?"

He answered with a smile:

"Have you any doubt about it?"

Then the thought forced itself on his mind that his conduct was infamous, and in order to make some kind of reparation to the dead man, he offered to watch by his side himself. But, feeling ashamed of this pious sentiment, he added, in a flippant tone:

"It would be perhaps more seemly."

"Perhaps so, indeed," she said, "on account of the servants."

The bed had been drawn completely out of the alcove. The nun was near the foot of it, and at the head of it sat a priest, a different one, a tall, spare man, with the look of a fanatical Spaniard. On the night-table, covered with a white cloth, three wax-tapers were burning.

Frederick seated himself, and gazed at the corpse.

The face was as yellow as straw. At the corners of the mouth there were traces of blood-stained foam. A silk handkerchief was tied around the head, and on the breast, covered with a knitted waistcoat, lay a silver crucifix between the two crossed hands.

It was over, this life of anxieties. How many journeys had he not made? How many rows of figures had he not added together? How many speculations had he not hatched? How many reports had he not heard read? What quackeries, what smiles and curvets! For he had acclaimed Napoleon, the Cossacks, Louis XVIII, 1830, the working-men, every *régime,* loving power so dearly that he would have paid, if necessary, to have the opportunity of selling himself.

He had left behind him the estate of La Fortelle, three factories in Picardy, the woods of Crancé in the Yonne, a farm near Orleans, and much personal property in the form of bills and papers.

Frederick thus estimated her fortune; and it would soon belong to him! First of all, he thought of "what people would say;" then he asked himself what present he ought to make to his mother, and he was concerned about his future equipages, and about employing an old coachman belonging to his own family as the doorkeeper. Of course, the livery would not remain the same. He would convert the large reception-room into his own study. There was nothing to prevent him, by knocking down three walls, from making a picture-gallery on the second-floor. Perhaps there might be an opportunity for introducing into the lower portion of the house a hall for Turkish baths. As for M. Dambreuse's office, a disagreeable place, what use could he make of it?

These reflections were from time to time rudely interrupted by the sounds made by the priest in blowing his nose, or by the good sister in settling the fire.

But the actual facts showed that his thoughts rested on a solid foundation. The corpse was there. The eyelids had reopened, and the pupils, although steeped in clammy gloom, had an enigmatic, intolerable expression.

Frederick fancied that he saw there a judgment directed against himself, and he experienced a sort of remorse, for he had never any grievance against this man, who, on the contrary—

"Come, now! an old wretch!" and he looked at the dead man more closely in order to strengthen his mind, mentally addressing him thus:

"Well, what? Have I killed you?"

The priest still read his breviary; the nun, who sat motionless, had fallen asleep. The wicks of the three wax-tapers had grown longer.

For two hours nothing could be heard but the heavy rolling of carts making their way to the markets. The window-panes began to admit streaks of white. A cab passed; then a group of donkeys trotted over the pavement. Then came strokes of hammers, cries of itinerant vendors of wood and blasts of horns. Already every other sound was blended with the great voice of awakening Paris.

Frederick went out to perform the duties assigned to him. He first repaired to the Mayor's office to make the necessary declaration; then, when the medical officer had given him a certificate of death, he called a second time at the municipal buildings in order to name the cemetery which the family had selected, and to make the final arrangements for the funeral ceremonies.

The clerk in the office showed him a plan which indicated the mode of interment adopted for the various classes, and a programme giving full particulars respecting the spectacular portion of the funeral. Would he like to have an open funeral-car or a hearse with plumes, plaits on the horses, and aigrettes on the footmen, initials or a coat-of-arms, funeral-lamps, a man to display the family distinctions? and what number of carriages would he require?

Frederick did not economise in the slightest detail. Madame Dambreuse was determined to spare no expense.

After this he made his way to the church.

The curate who had charge of burials criticised the waste of money on funeral pomps. For instance, the officer for the display of armorial distinctions was really useless. It would be far more satisfactory to have a goodly display of wax-tapers. A low mass accompanied by music would be appropriate.

Frederick gave written directions on everything agreed upon, with a joint undertaking to defray all the expenses.

He went next to the Hôtel de Ville to purchase a piece of ground. A grant of a piece two metres in length and one in breadth cost five hundred francs. Did he want a grant for fifty years or forever?

"Oh, forever!" said Frederick.

He took the whole thing seriously and got into a state of intense anxiety about it. In the courtyard of the mansion a marble-cutter was waiting to show him estimates and plans of Greek, Egyptian, and Moorish tombs; but the family architect had already been in consultation with Madame; and on the table in the vestibule there were all sorts of prospectuses with reference to the cleaning of mattresses, the disinfection of rooms, and the various processes of embalming.

After dining, he went to the tailor's shop to order mourning for the servants; and he had still to discharge another function, for the gloves that he had ordered were of beaver, whereas the right kind for a funeral were floss-silk.

When he arrived next morning, at ten o'clock, the large reception-room was crowded with people, and nearly everyone said, on encountering the others, in a melancholy tone:

"It is only a month ago since I saw him! Good heavens! it will be the same way with us all!"

"Yes; but let us try to keep it as far away from us as possible!"

Then there were little smiles of satisfaction; and they even engaged in conversations entirely unsuited to the occasion. At length, the master of the ceremonies, in a black coat and short breeches, with a cloak, cambric mourning-bands, a long sword by his side, and a three-cornered hat under his arm, gave utterance, with a bow, to the customary words:

"Messieurs, when it shall be your pleasure."

The funeral procession started. It was the market-day for flowers on the Place de la Madeleine. It was a fine day with brilliant sunshine; and the breeze, which shook the canvas tents, swelled out at the edges the enormous black cloth which was hung over the church-gate. The escutcheon of M. Dambreuse, which covered a square piece of velvet, was repeated there three times. It was: *Sable, with an arm sinister or and a clenched hand with a glove argent;* with the coronet of a count, and this device: *By every path.*

The bearers lifted the heavy coffin to the top of the staircase, and they entered the church. The six chapels, the hemicycles, and the seats were hung with black. The catafalque at the end of the choir formed, with its large wax-tapers, a single point of yellow lights. At the two corners, over the candelabra, flames of spirits of wine were burning.

The persons of highest rank occupied places in the sanctuary, and the rest in the nave; and then the Office for the Dead began.

With a few exceptions, the religious ignorance of all was so profound that the master of the ceremonies had, from time to time, to make signs to them to rise, to kneel, or to resume their seats. The organ and the two double-basses could be heard alternately with the voices. In the intervals of silence, the only sounds that reached the ear were the mumblings of the priest at the altar; then the music and the chanting began again.

The light of day shone dimly through the three cupolas, but the open door let in, as it were, a stream of white radiance, which, entering in a horizontal direction, fell on every uncovered head; and in the air, half-way toward the ceiling of the church, floated a shadow, which was penetrated by the reflection of the gildings that decorated the ribbing of the pendentives and the foliage of the capitals.

Frederick, in an effort to distract his attention, listened to the *Dies iræ*. He gazed at those around him, or tried to catch a glimpse of the pictures hanging far above his head, wherein the life of the Magdalen was represented. Luckily, Pellerin came to sit down beside him, and immediately plunged into a long dissertation on the subject of frescoes. The bell began to toll. They left the church.

The hearse, adorned with hanging draperies and tall plumes, set out for Père-Lachaise drawn by four black horses, with their manes plaited, their heads decked with tufts of feathers, and with large trappings embroidered with silver flowing down to their shoes. The driver of the vehicle, in Hessian boots, wore a three-cornered hat with a long piece of crape hanging down from it. The cords were held by four personages: a questor of the Chamber of Deputies, a member of the General Council of the Aube, a delegate from the coal-mining company, and Fumichon, as a friend. The carriage of the deceased and a dozen mourning-coaches followed. The persons attending at the funeral followed in the rear, filling up the middle of the boulevard.

The passers-by stopped to look at the mournful procession. Women, with their children in their arms, got up on chairs, and people who had been drinking beer in the cafés, presented themselves at the windows with billiard-cues in their hands.

The way was long, and, as at formal meals at which people are at first reserved and then expansive, the general deportment speedily relaxed. They all talked of the refusal of an allowance by the Chamber to the President. M. Piscatory had shown himself harsh; Montalembert had been "magnificent, as usual," and MM. Chamballe, Pidoux, Creton, in short, the entire committee would probably be compelled to follow the advice of MM. Quentin-Bauchard and Dufour.

This conversation was continued as they passed through the Rue de la Roquette, with shops on each side, in which could be seen only chains of coloured glass and black circular tablets covered with drawings and letters of gold—making them resemble grottoes full of stalactites and crockery-ware shops. When they had reached the cemetery-gate, everyone ceased speaking.

The tombs stood among the trees: broken columns, pyramids, temples, dolmens, obelisks, and Etruscan vaults with doors of bronze. In some of them might be seen funereal boudoirs, so to speak, with rustic arm-chairs

and folding-stools. Spiders' webs hung like rags from the little chains of
the urns; and the bouquets of satin ribbons and the crucifixes were covered with dust. Everywhere, between the balusters on the tombstones,
were crowns of immortelles and chandeliers, vases, flowers, black discs set
off with gold letters, and plaster statuettes—little boys or little girls or
angels suspended in the air by brass wires; several of them having even a
roof of zinc overhead. Huge cables made of glass strung together, black,
white, or azure, descended from the tops of the monuments to the ends
of the flagstones with long folds, like boas. The rays of the sun, striking
on them, made them scintillate in the midst of the black wooden crosses.
The hearse advanced along the broad paths, paved like the streets of a
city. From time to time the axletrees cracked. Women, kneeling down,
with their dresses trailing in the grass, addressed the dead in tones of tenderness. Little white fumes arose from the green leaves of the yew trees.
These came from offerings that had been left behind, waste material that
had been burnt.

M. Dambreuse's grave was close to the graves of Manuel and Benjamin
Constant. The soil in this part slopes with an abrupt decline. Beneath
one are the tops of green trees, further down the chimneys of steam-
pumps, then the entire great city.

Frederick found an opportunity of admiring the scene while the various addresses were being delivered.

The first was in the name of the Chamber of Deputies, the second
in the name of the General Council of the Aube, the third in the name of
the coal-mining company of Saone-et-Loire, the fourth in the name of
the Agricultural Society of the Yonne, and there was another in the name
of a Philanthropic Society. Finally, just as everyone was departing, a
stranger began reading a sixth address, in the name of the Amiens Society
of Antiquaries.

They all took advantage of the occasion to denounce Socialism, of
which M. Dambreuse had died a victim. It was the effect produced on
his mind by the exhibitions of anarchic violence, together with his devotion to order, that had shortened his days. They praised his intellectual
powers, his integrity, his generosity, and even his silence as a representative of the people, "for, if he was not an orator, he possessed instead those
solid qualities a thousand times more useful," etc., with all the requisite
phrases—"Premature end; eternal regrets; the better land; farewell, or
rather no, *au revoir!*"

The clay, mingled with stones, fell on the coffin, and he would never
again be a subject for discussion in society.

However, there were a few allusions to him as the persons who had followed his remains left the cemetery. Hussonnet, who would have to give
an account of the interment in the newspapers, spoke of all the addresses

in a chaffing style, for, in truth, the worthy Dambreuse had been one of the most notable *pots-de-vin* of the last reign. Then the mourners were driven in the coaches to their various places of business; the ceremony had not lasted very long; they congratulated themselves on the circumstance.

Frederick returned to his own abode quite worn out.

When he presented himself next day at Madame Dambreuse's residence, he was informed that she was below stairs in the room where M. Dambreuse had kept his papers.

The cardboard receptacles and the different drawers had been hurriedly opened, and the account-books had been flung about right and left. A roll of papers on which were endorsed the words "Repayment hopeless" lay on the ground. He was near falling over it, and picked it up. Madame Dambreuse had sunk back in the armchair, so that he did not see her.

"Well? where are you? What is the matter?"

She jumped to her feet with a bound.

"What is the matter? I am ruined, ruined! do you understand?"

M. Adolphe Langlois, the notary, had sent her a message to call at his office, and had informed her of the contents of a will made by her husband before their marriage. He had bequeathed everything to Cécile; and the other will could not be found. Frederick turned very pale. No doubt she had not made sufficient search.

"Well, then, look for yourself!" said Madame Dambreuse, pointing at the various objects in the room.

The two strong-boxes were gaping wide, having been broken open with blows of a cleaver, and she had turned up the desk, rummaged in the cupboards, and shaken the straw-mattings. All of a sudden, uttering a piercing cry, she dashed into a corner where she had just noticed a little box with a brass lock. She opened it—nothing!

"Ah! the wretch! I, who took such devoted care of him!"

Then she burst into tears.

"Perhaps it is somewhere else?" said Frederick.

"Oh! no! it was there! in that strong-box. I saw it there recently. It is burned! I'm certain of it!"

One day, in the early stage of his illness, M. Dambreuse had gone down to this room to sign some documents.

"It was then he must have done the trick!"

And she fell back on a chair, crushed. A mother grieving beside an empty cradle could not be more woeful than Madame Dambreuse at the sight of the open strong-boxes. Indeed, her sorrow, in spite of the baseness of the motive which inspired it, appeared so deep that he tried to console her by reminding her that, after all, she was not reduced to sheer poverty.

"It is poverty, when I am not in a position to offer you a large fortune!"

She had not more than thirty thousand lires a year, without taking into account the mansion, which was worth from eighteen to twenty thousand, perhaps.

Although to Frederick, this would have been opulence, he felt, none the less, a certain amount of disappointment. Farewell to his dreams and to the splendid life on which he had intended to enter! Honour compelled him to marry Madame Dambreuse. For a minute he reflected; then, in a tone of tenderness:

"I shall always have yourself!"

She threw herself into his arms, and he clasped her to his breast with an emotion in which there was a certain element of admiration for himself.

Madame Dambreuse, whose tears had ceased to flow, raised her face, beaming all over with happiness, and seizing his hand:

"Ah! I never doubted you! I knew I could rely on you!"

The young man did not like this tone of anticipated certainty with regard to what he was pluming himself on as a noble action.

Then she brought him into her own apartment, and they began to arrange their plans for the future. Frederick should now consider the best way of advancing himself in life. She even gave him excellent advice with reference to his candidature.

The first step was to be familiar with two or three phrases borrowed from political economy. It was necessary to take up a specialty, such as the stud system, for example; to write a number of notes on questions of local interest, to have always at his disposal post-offices or tobacconists' shops, and to do numerous little services. In this respect M. Dambreuse had shown himself a true model. Thus, on one occasion, in the country, he had drawn up his waggonette, full of friends of his, in front of a cobbler's stall, and had bought a dozen pairs of shoes for his guests, and for himself a dreadful pair of boots, which he had not the courage to wear even for a fortnight. This anecdote restored their good humour. She related others, and that with a renewal of grace, youthfulness, and wit.

She approved of his idea of taking a trip immediately to Nogent. Their parting was an affectionate one; then, on the threshold, she murmured once more:

"You love me—do you not?"

"Eternally," was his reply.

A messenger was waiting for him at his own house with a line written in lead-pencil informing him that Rosanette was about to be confined. He had been so much preoccupied for the past few days that he had not given a thought to the matter.

She had been placed in a special establishment at Chaillot.

Frederick took a cab and set out for this institution.

At the corner of the Rue de Marbeuf he read on a board in big letters: "Private Lying-in-Hospital, kept by Madame Alessandri, first-class midwife, ex-pupil of the Maternity, author of various works, etc." Then, in the centre of the street, over the door—a little side-door—there was another sign-board: "Private Hospital of Madame Alessandri," with all her titles.

Frederick knocked. A chambermaid, with the figure of an Abigail led him into the reception-room, which was adorned with a mahogany table and armchairs of garnet velvet, and with a clock under a globe.

Almost immediately Madame appeared. She was a tall brunette of forty, with a slender waist, fine eyes, and the manners of good society. She apprised Frederick of the mother's happy delivery, and brought him up to her apartment.

Rosanette gave him a smile of unutterable bliss, and, as if drowned in the floods of love that were suffocating her, she said in a low tone:

"A boy—there, there!" pointing toward a cradle close to her bed.

He opened the curtains, and saw, wrapped up in linen, a yellowish-red object, exceedingly shrivelled-looking, which had a bad smell, and was bawling lustily.

"Embrace him!"

He replied, in order to hide his repugnance:

"But I am afraid of hurting him."

"No! no!"

Then, with the tips of his lips, he kissed his child.

"How like you he is!"

And with her two weak arms, she clung to his neck with an outburst of feeling which he had never witnessed on her part before.

The remembrance of Madame Dambreuse came back to him. He reproached himself as a brute for having deceived this poor creature, who loved and suffered with all the sincerity of her nature. For several days he remained with her till night.

She was happy in this quiet place; the window-shutters in front of it remained always closed. Her room, hung with bright chintz, looked out on a large garden. Madame Alessandri, whose only weakness was that she liked to talk about her intimate acquaintanceship with eminent physicians, showed her the utmost attention. Her associates, nearly all provincial young ladies, were exceedingly bored, as nobody came to see them. Rosanette saw that they regarded her with envy, and told this proudly to Frederick. It was desirable to speak low, nevertheless. The partitions were thin, and everyone was listening at hiding-places, in spite of the constant thrumming of the pianos.

At last, he was about to take his departure for Nogent, when he got a letter from Deslauriers. Two new candidates had offered themselves, the one a Conservative, the other a Red; a third, whoever he might be, would have no chance. It was all Frederick's fault; he had let the lucky moment pass by; he should have come sooner and stirred himself.

"You have not even been seen at the agricultural assembly!" The advocate blamed him for not having any newspaper connection.

"Ah! if you had only followed my advice long ago! If we had only a public print of our own!"

He laid special stress on this point. However, many who would have voted for him out of consideration for M. Dambreuse, abandoned him now. Deslauriers was one of the number. Not having anything more to expect from the capitalist, he had deserted his *protégé*.

Frederick showed the letter to Madame Dambreuse.

"You have not been to Nogent, then?" said she.

"Why do you ask?"

"Because I saw Deslauriers three days ago."

Having learned that her husband was dead, the advocate had come to make a report about the coal-mines, and to offer his services to her as a man of business. This seemed strange to Frederick; and what was his friend doing down there?

Madame Dambreuse wanted to know what he had been doing since they parted.

"I have been ill," he replied.

"You ought at least to have told me about it."

"Oh! it wasn't worth while;" besides, he had to settle a heap of things, to keep appointments, and to pay visits.

From that time forth he led a double life, sleeping religiously at the Maréchale's abode and spending the afternoon with Madame Dambreuse, so that there was scarcely a single hour of freedom left to him in the middle of the day.

The infant was in the country at Andilly. They went to see it once a week.

The wet-nurse's house was on rising ground in the village, at the end of a little yard as dark as a pit, with straw on the ground, hens here and there, and a vegetable-cart under the shed.

Rosanette would frantically kiss her baby, and, seized with a kind of delirium, would keep moving to and fro, trying to milk the goat, eating big pieces of bread, and inhaling the odour of manure; she even wanted to put a little of it into her handkerchief.

Then they took long walks, in the course of which she went into the nurseries, tore off branches from the lilac-trees which hung down over the walls, and exclaimed, "Gee ho, donkey!" to the asses that were drawing cars along, and stopped to gaze through the gate into the interior of one of the lovely gardens; or else the wet-nurse would take the child and place it under the shade of a walnut-tree; and for hours the two women would talk the most tiresome nonsense.

Frederick, not far away, gazed at the beds of vines on the slopes, with here and there a clump of trees; at the dusty paths resembling strips of grey ribbon; at the houses, which showed white and red spots in the midst of the greenery; and sometimes the smoke of a locomotive stretched out horizontally to the bases of the hills, covered with foliage, like a gigantic ostrich's feather, the thin end of which was disappearing from view.

Frederick's eyes would rest on his son. He imagined the child grown into a young man; he would make a companion of him; but perhaps he would be a blockhead, a wretched creature, in any event. He felt oppressed by the illegality of the infant's birth; it would have been better if he never had been born! And Frederick would murmur, "Poor child!" his heart throbbing with feelings of unutterable sadness.

They often missed the last train. Then Madame Dambreuse would scold him for his want of punctuality. He would invent some falsehood.

It was necessary to make explanations, too, to satisfy Rosanette. She could not understand where he spent all his evenings; and when she sent a messenger to his house, he was never there! One day, when he chanced to be at home, the two women made their appearance almost at the same time. He persuaded the Maréchale to go away, and concealed Madame Dambreuse, pretending that his mother was coming up to Paris.

Ere long, he found these lies amusing. He would repeat to one the oath which he had just uttered to the other, send them bouquets of the same sort, write to them at the same time, and then would institute a comparison between them. There was a third always present in his thoughts. The impossibility of possessing her seemed to him a justification of his perfidies, which were intensified by the fact that he had to practise them alternately; and the more he deceived, no matter which of the two, the fonder of him she grew, as if the love of one of them added heat to that of the other, and, as if by a sort of emulation, each was seeking to make him forget the other.

"Admire my confidence in you!" said Madame Dambreuse one day to him, opening a sheet of paper, in which she was informed that M. Moreau and a certain Rose Bron were living together as husband and wife.

"Can it be that this is the lady of the races?"

"How absurd!" he returned. "Let me have a look at it!"

The letter, written in Roman characters, had no signature. Madame Dambreuse, in the beginning, had tolerated this mistress, who furnished a cloak for their adultery. But, as her passion became stronger, she had insisted on a rupture—a thing which had been effected long since, according to Frederick's account; and when he had ceased to protest, she said, half closing her eyes, in which shone a look like the point of a stiletto under a muslin robe:

"Well—and the other?"

"What other?"

"The earthenware-dealer's wife!"

He shrugged his shoulders disdainfully. She did not press the matter.

But, a month later, while they were talking about honour and loyalty, and he was boasting about his own (in a casual sort of way, for the sake of precaution), she said to him:

"It is true—you are acting uprightly—you don't go there any more?"

Frederick, who was at the moment thinking of the Maréchale, stammered:

"Where, pray?"

"To Madame Arnoux's."

He implored her to tell him from whom she got the information. It was through her second dress-maker, Madame Regimbart.

So, she knew all about his life, and he knew nothing about hers!

He had found in her dressing-room the miniature of a gentleman with long moustaches—was this the same person about whose suicide a vague story had been told him at one time? But there was no way of learning any more about it! However, what did it matter? The hearts of women are like little pieces of furniture wherein things are secreted, full of drawers fitted into each other; one hurts himself, breaks his nails in opening them, and then finds within only some withered flower, a few grains of dust—or emptiness! And perhaps he feared to learn too much about the matter.

She made him refuse invitations where she was unable to accompany him, stuck to his side, was afraid of losing him; and, in spite of this union which was every day becoming stronger, all of a sudden, abysses would disclose themselves between the pair about the most trifling questions—an estimate of an individual or a work of art.

She had a style of playing on the piano which was correct but hard. Her spiritualism (Madame Dambreuse believed in the transmigration of souls into the stars) did not prevent her from taking the utmost care of her cash-box. She was haughty toward her servants; her eyes remained dry at the sight of the rags of the poor. Amongst her habitual expressions were: "What concern is that of mine? I should be very silly! What need have I?" and a thousand little acts incapable of analysis revealed hateful qualities in her. She would have listened behind doors; she could not help lying to her confessor. Through a spirit of despotism, she made Frederick accompany her to church on Sunday. He obeyed, and carried her prayer-book.

The loss of the property she had expected to inherit had changed her considerably. These marks of grief, which people attributed to the death of M. Dambreuse, rendered her interesting, and, as in former times, she had a great number of visitors. Since Frederick's defeat at the election, she was ambitious of obtaining for both of them an embassy in Germany; therefore, it was important that they should submit to the reigning ideas.

Some persons favoured the Empire, others the Orléans family, and others the Comte de Chambord; but they were all of one opinion as to the importance of decentralisation, and several expedients were proposed with that view, such as to cut up Paris into many large streets in order to establish villages there, to transfer the seat of government to Versailles, to have the schools set up at Bourges, to suppress the libraries, and to entrust everything to the generals of division; and they glorified a rustic existence on the assumption that the uneducated man had naturally more sense than other men! Hatreds increased—hatred of primary teachers and wine-merchants, of the classes of philosophy, of the courses of lectures on history, of novels, red waistcoats, long beards, of independence in any shape, or any manifestation of individuality, for it was necessary "to restore the principle of authority"—let it be exercised in the name of no matter whom; let it come from no matter where, as long as it was Force, Authority! The Conservatives now talked on the very same lines as Sénécal. Frederick was no longer able to understand their drift, and once more he found at the house of his former mistress the same remarks uttered by the same men.

The salons of the unmarried women (it was from this period that their importance dates) were a sort of neutral ground where reactionaries of all kinds met. Hussonnet, who depreciated contemporary glories (a good thing for the restoration of Order), inspired Rosanette with a longing to have evening parties like the others. He undertook to publish accounts of them, and first of all he brought a man of grave deportment, Fumichon; then came Nonancourt, M. de Grémonville, the Sieur de Larsilloix, ex-prefect, and Cisy, who was now an agriculturist in Lower Brittany, and more Christian than ever.

In addition, men who had at one time been the Maréchale's lovers, such as the Baron de Comaing, the Comte de Jumillac, and others, presented themselves; and Frederick was resentful of their free-and-easy behaviour.

In order that he might assume the attitude of master in the house, he increased the rate of expenditure there. Then he went in for keeping a groom, took a new habitation, and got a fresh supply of furniture. These displays of extravagance were for the purpose of making his alliance appear less out of proportion with his pecuniary position. As a result his means were soon terribly reduced—and Rosanette was entirely ignorant of the fact!

One of the lower middle-class, who had lost caste, she adored a domestic life, a quiet little home. However, it gave her pleasure to have an "at home day." In speaking of persons of her own class, she called them "Those women!" She wished to be a society lady, and believed herself to be one. She requested him not to smoke in the drawing-room any more, and for the sake of good form she tried to make herself look thin.

She played her part badly, after all; for she grew serious, and even before going to bed always exhibited a little melancholy, just as there are cypress trees at the door of a tavern.

He found out the cause of it; she was dreaming of marriage—she, too! Frederick was exasperated at this. Besides, he had not forgotten her appearance at Madame Arnoux's house, and then he cherished a certain spite against her for having held out against him so long.

He inquired none the less as to who her lovers had been. She denied having had any relations with any of the persons he mentioned. A sort of jealous feeling took possession of him. He irritated her by asking questions about presents that had been made to her, and were still being made to her; and in proportion to the exciting effect which the lower portion of her nature produced upon him, he was drawn toward her by momentary illusions which ended in hate.

Her words, her voice, her smile, all had an antagonistic effect on him, and especially her glances with that woman's eye forever limpid and foolish. Sometimes he felt so tired of her that he would have willingly seen her die. But how could he get into a passion with her? She was so mild that there was no hope of quarrelling.

Deslauriers reappeared, and explained his sojourn at Nogent by saying that he was making arrangements to buy a lawyer's office. Frederick was glad to see him again. It was somebody! and as a third person in the house, he helped to break the monotony.

The advocate dined with them occasionally, and whenever any little disputes arose, always took Rosanette's part, so that Frederick, on one occasion, said to him:

"Ah! you may have her, if it amuses you!" so much did he desire some chance of getting rid of her.

About the middle of the month of June, she was served with an order made by the law courts by which Maître Athanase Gautherot, sheriff's officer, called on her to pay him four thousand francs due to Mademoiselle Clémence Vatnaz; if not, he would make a seizure on her.

Of the four bills which she had at various times signed, only one had been paid; the money which she happened to get since then having been spent on other things that she required.

She rushed off at once to see Arnoux. He lived now in the Faubourg Saint-Germain, and the porter was unable to tell her the name of the street. She went next to the houses of several friends of hers, but did not find one of them at home, and came back in a state of utter despair.

She did not wish to tell Frederick anything about it, fearing lest this new trouble might prejudice the chance of a marriage between them.

On the following morning, M. Athanase Gautherot presented himself with two assistants close behind him, one of them sallow with a mean-looking face and an expression of devouring envy in his glance, the other wearing a collar and straps drawn very tightly, with a sort of thimble of black taffeta on his index-finger—and both ignobly dirty, with greasy necks, and the sleeves of their coats too short.

Their employer, a very good-looking man, on the contrary, began by apologising for the disagreeable duty he had to perform, while at the same time he glanced round the room, "full of pretty things, upon my word of honour!" he added, "Not to speak of the things that can't be seized." At a gesture the two bailiff's men disappeared.

Then he redoubled his politeness. Could anyone believe that a lady so charming would not have a genuine friend! A sale of her goods under an order of the courts would be a real misfortune. One does not get over a thing like that. He tried to excite her fears; then, seeing that she was very much agitated, suddenly assumed a paternal tone. He knew the world. He had been brought into business relations with all these ladies—and as he mentioned their names, he examined the frames of the pictures on the walls. They were old pictures of the worthy Arnoux, sketches by Sombary, water-colours by Burieu, and three landscapes by Dittmer. It was evident that Rosanette knew nothing of their value. Maître Gautherot turned round to her:

"Look here! to show that I am a decent fellow; give me up those Dittmers here—and I am ready to pay all. Do you agree?"

At that moment Frederick, who had been informed about the matter by Delphine in the anteroom, and who had just seen the two assistants, came in with his hat on his head, in a rude fashion. Maître Gautherot resumed his dignity; and, as the door had been left open:

"Come on, gentlemen—write down! In the second room, let us say—an oak table with its two leaves, two sideboards—"

Frederick here stopped him, asking whether there was not some way of preventing the seizure.

"Oh! certainly! Who paid for the furniture?"

"I did."

"Well, draw up a claim—there is still time for you to do it."

Maître Gautherot did not take long in writing out his official report, wherein he directed that Mademoiselle Bron should attend at an inquiry in chambers with reference to the ownership of the furniture, and having done this he withdrew.

Frederick uttered no reproach. He gazed at the traces of mud left on the floor by the bailiff's shoes, and, speaking to himself:

"It will soon be necessary to make some money!"

"Ah! my God, how stupid I am!" said the Maréchale.

She ransacked a drawer, took out a letter, and made her way rapidly to the Languedoc Gas Lighting Company, in order to get the transfer of her shares of stock.

She returned an hour later. The interest in the shares had been sold to another. The clerk had said, in answer to her demand, while examining the sheet of paper containing Arnoux's written promise to her: "This document in no way constitutes you the proprietor of the shares. The company has no cognisance of the matter." In short, he dismissed her unceremoniously, while she choked with rage; and Frederick must go to Arnoux's house at once to have the matter cleared up.

But Arnoux would perhaps imagine that he had come to recover in an indirect fashion the fifteen thousand francs due on the mortgage which he had lost; and then this claim on a man who had been his mistress's lover seemed to him a piece of baseness.

Selecting a middle course, he went to the Dambreuse mansion to get Madame Regimbart's address, sent a messenger to her residence, and in this way ascertained the name of the café which the Citizen now haunted.

It was the little café on the Place de la Bastille, where he sat all day in the corner to the right at the lower end of the establishment, as motionless as if he were a portion of the building.

After having gone successively through the half-cup of coffee, the glass of grog, the "bishop," the glass of mulled wine, and even the red wine and water, he fell back on beer, and every half hour he called out, "Bock!" having reduced his language to what was actually indispensable. Frederick asked him if he ever saw Arnoux.

"No!"

"Look here—why?"

"An imbecile!"

Politics, perhaps, kept them apart, and so Frederick thought it a judicious thing to inquire about Compain.

"What a brute!" said Regimbart.

"How is that?"

"His calf's head!"

"Ha! explain to me what the calf's head is!"

Regimbart's face took on a contemptuous smile.

"Some tomfoolery!"

After a long interval of silence, Frederick said:

"So, then, he has changed his address?"

"Who?"

"Arnoux!"

"Yes—Rue de Fleurus!"

"What number?"

"Do I associate with the Jesuits?"

"What, Jesuits!"

The Citizen replied angrily:

"With the money of a patriot whom I introduced to him, this pig has set up as a dealer in beads!"

"It isn't possible!"

"Go there, and find out for yourself!"

It was perfectly true; Arnoux, enfeebled by a fit of sickness, had become religious; besides, he had always had a stock of religion in his composition, and (with that mixture of commercialism and ingenuity which was natural to him), in order to obtain salvation and fortune at the same time, he had begun to traffic in religious objects.

Frederick had no difficulty in discovering his establishment, on whose signboard appeared these words: *"Emporium of Gothic Art*—Restoration of articles used in ecclesiastical ceremonies—Church ornaments—Polychromatic sculpture—Frankincense of the Magi, Kings, &c., &c."

At the two corners of the shop-window were two wooden statues, streaked with gold, cinnabar, and azure, a Saint John the Baptist with his sheepskin, and a Saint Geneviève with roses in her apron and a distaff under her arm; next, groups in plaster, a sister teaching a little girl, a mother on her knees beside a little bed, and three collegians before the holy table. The prettiest object there was a kind of châlet representing the interior of a crib with the ass, the ox, and the child Jesus stretched on straw—real straw. From the top to the bottom of the shelves were medals by the dozen, every variety of beads, holy-water basins in the form of shells, and portraits of ecclesiastical dignitaries, amongst whom Monsignor Affre and our Holy Father appeared with smiling faces.

Arnoux sat at his counter asleep, with his head bent. He had aged terribly. He had round his temples a wreath of rosebuds, and the reflection of the gold crosses touched by the rays of the sun fell over him.

Frederick was filled with sadness at this spectacle of decay. Through devotion to the Maréchale he, however, submitted to the ordeal, and stepped forward. At the end of the shop Madame Arnoux suddenly stepped forward; thereupon, he turned on his heel.

"I couldn't see him," he said, when he came back to Rosanette.

And in vain he promised that he would write at once to his notary at Havre for some money—she flew into a rage. She had never seen a man so weak, so flabby. While she was enduring a thousand privations, other people were enjoying themselves.

Frederick was thinking about poor Madame Arnoux, and picturing to himself the heart-rending impoverishment of her surroundings. He had seated himself before the writing-desk; and, as Rosanette's voice still kept up its bitter railing:

"Ah! in the name of Heaven, hold your tongue!"

"Perhaps you are going to defend them?"

"Well, yes!" he exclaimed; "for what's the cause of this fury?"

"But why is it that you don't want to make them pay up? 'Tis for fear of vexing your old flame—confess it!"

He felt an inclination to smash her head with the timepiece. Words failed him. He lapsed into silence.

Rosanette, as she walked up and down the room, continued:

"I am going to hurl a writ at this Arnoux of yours. Oh! I shall not need your assistance. I'll get legal advice."

Three days later, Delphine rushed abruptly into the room where her mistress sat.

"Madame! Madame! there's a man here with a pot of paste who has given me such a fright!"

Rosanette went down to the kitchen, and saw there a vagabond whose face was pitted with smallpox. Moreover, one of his arms was paralysed, and he was three fourths drunk, and hiccoughed every time he attempted to speak.

This was Maître Gautherot's bill-sticker. The objections raised against the seizure having been overruled, the sale followed as a matter of course.

For his trouble in getting up the stairs he demanded, in the first place, a half-glass of brandy; then he wanted another favour, namely, tickets for the theatre, assuming that the lady of the house was an actress. After this he indulged for some minutes in winks, whose import was perfectly incomprehensible. Finally, he declared that for forty sous he would tear off the corners of the poster which he had already affixed to the door below stairs. Rosanette found herself referred to by name in it—a piece of harshness which showed the spite of the Vatnaz.

She had at one time exhibited sensibility, and had even, while suffering from the effects of a heartache, written to Béranger for his advice. But under the ravage of life's storms, her spirit had soured, for she had been forced, in turn, to give lessons on the piano, to act as manageress of a *table d'hôte,* to assist others in writing for the fashion journals, to sublet apartments, and to traffic in lace in the world of light women, her relations with whom enabled her to make herself useful to many persons, and amongst others to Arnoux. She had at one time been employed in a commercial establishment.

There it was one of her duties to pay the workwomen; and for each of them there were two livres, one of which always remained in her hands. Dussardier, who, through kindness, kept the amount payable to a girl named Hortense Baslin, presented himself one day at the cash-office at the moment when Mademoiselle Vatnaz was presenting this girl's account, 1,682 francs, which the cashier paid her. Now, on the same evening, Dussardier had entered down the sum as 1,082 in the girl Baslin's book. He made some pretext for having it given back to him; then, anxious to bury out of sight the story of this theft, he stated that he had lost it. The workgirl ingenuously repeated this falsehood to Mademoiselle Vatnaz, and the latter, to satisfy her mind about the matter, came with a show of indifference to talk to the shopman on the subject. He contented himself with the answer: "I have burned it!"—that was all. She left the house, without believing that the book had been really destroyed, and filled with the idea that Dussardier had kept it.

On hearing that he had been wounded, she rushed to his abode, with the object of getting the book. Then, having discovered nothing, in spite of the closest search, she was seized with respect, and presently with love, for his youth, so loyal, so gentle, so heroic and so strong! At her age such good fortune in an affair of the heart was unusual. She threw herself into it with the appetite of an ogress; and she had given up literature, Socialism, "the consoling doctrines and the generous Utopias," the course of lectures which she had organised on the "Desubalternisation of Woman"—everything, even Delmar himself; finally she offered to unite herself to Dussardier in marriage.

Although she was his mistress, he was not at all in love with her. Besides, he had not forgotten her theft. Then she was too wealthy for him. He refused her offer. Thereupon, with tears in her eyes, she told him what she had hoped—it was to have for both of them a confectioner's shop. She possessed the capital that was required for the purpose, and next week this would be increased to the extent of four thousand francs. By way of explanation, she referred to the proceedings she had taken against the Maréchale.

Dussardier was annoyed at this on account of his friend. He remembered the cigar-holder that had been presented to him at the guard-house, the evenings spent in the Quai Napoléon, the many pleasant chats, the books lent to him, the thousand acts of kindness which Frederick had done in his behalf. He begged of Mademoiselle Vatnaz to abandon the proceedings.

She rallied him on his good nature, while exhibiting an antipathy against Rosanette which he could not understand. She longed for wealth, in order to crush her, by-and-by, with her four-wheeled carriage.

Dussardier was terrified by these black abysses of hate, and when he had ascertained the exact day fixed for the sale, he hurried out. On the following morning he made his appearance at Frederick's house with an embarrassed countenance.

"I owe you an apology."

"For what, pray?"

"You must take me for an ingrate, I, whom she is the——" He faltered.

"Oh! I'll see no more of her. I am not going to be her accomplice!" And as the other gazed at him in astonishment:

"Isn't your mistress's furniture to be sold in three days' time?"

"Who told you that?"

"Herself—the Vatnaz! But I am afraid of offending you——"

"Impossible, my dear friend!"

"Ah! that is true—you are so good!"

And he held out to him, nervously, a hand in which he clasped a little pocket-book made of sheep-leather.

It contained four thousand francs—all his savings.

"What! Oh! no! no!——"

"I knew well I should wound your feelings," returned Dussardier, with a tear in the corner of his eye.

Frederick pressed his hand, and the honest fellow went on in a piteous tone:

"Take the money! Give me that much happiness! I am in such a state of despair. Can it be that all is over? I thought we should be happy when the Revolution had come. Do you remember what a beautiful thing it was? how freely we breathed! But here we are flung back into a worse condition of things than ever.

"Now, they are destroying our Republic, just as they destroyed the other one—the Roman! ay, and poor Venice! poor Poland! poor Hungary! What abominable deeds! First of all, they knocked down the trees of Liberty, then they restricted the right to vote, shut up the clubs, reëstablished the censorship and surrendered to the priests the power of teaching, so that we might look out for the inquisition. Why not? The Conservatives want to give us a taste of the stick. The newspapers are fined merely for printing an opinion in favour of abolishing the death-penalty. Paris is overflowing with bayonets; sixteen departments are in a state of siege; and then the demand for amnesty is again rejected!"

He placed both hands on his forehead, then, spread out his arms as if his mind were in a distracted state:

"If, however, we only made the effort! if we were only sincere, we might understand each other. But no! The workmen are as bad as the capitalists, you see! At Elbœuf recently they refused to help at a fire! There are wretches who profess to regard Barbès as an aristocrat! In order to make the people ridiculous, they want Nadaud nominated for the presidency, a mason—just imagine! And there is no way out of it—no remedy! Everybody is against us! I have never done any harm; and yet this is like a weight pressing down on my stomach. If this state of things continues, I'll go mad. I have a mind to do away with myself. I tell you I want no money for myself! You'll pay it back to me, deuce take it! I am lending it to you."

Frederick, who felt himself constrained by necessity, ended by taking the four thousand francs from him. And so they had no more disquietude so far as the Vatnaz was concerned.

But it was not long ere Rosanette was defeated in her action against Arnoux; and through sheer obstinacy she wished to appeal.

Deslauriers exhausted his energies in trying to convince her that Arnoux's promise constituted neither a gift nor a regular transfer. She did not pay the slightest attention to him, her notion being that the law was unjust—it was because she was a woman; men supported one another among themselves. In the end, however, she followed his advice.

He made himself so much at home in the house, that on several occasions he brought Sénécal to dine there. Frederick, who had advanced him money, and even got his own tailor to supply him with clothes, did not like this unceremoniousness; and the advocate gave his old clothes to the Socialist, whose means of existence were now of an exceedingly precarious character.

He was, however, anxious to be of service to Rosanette. One day, when she showed him a dozen shares in the Kaolin Company (that enterprise which led to Arnoux being cast in damages to the extent of thirty thousand francs), he said to her:

"But this is a shady transaction, and you have now a grand chance!"

She would be justified in calling on him to pay her debts. In the first place, she could prove that he was jointly bound to pay all the company's liabilities, since he had certified personal debts as collective debts—in short, he had embezzled sums which were payable only to the company.

"All this renders him guilty of fraudulent bankruptcy under articles 586 and 587 of the Commercial Code, and you may be sure, my pet, we'll send him packing."

Rosanette threw herself on his neck. He entrusted her case next day to his former master, not having time to devote to it himself, as he had business at Nogent. In case of any urgency, Sénécal could write to him.

His negotiations for the purchase of an office were a mere pretext. He spent his time at M. Roque's house, where he had begun not only by sounding the praises of Frederick, but by imitating his manners and language as much as possible; and in this way he had gained Louise's confidence, while he won over her father by attacking Ledru-Rollin.

If Frederick did not return, it was because he mingled in aristocratic society, and gradually Deslauriers gave them to understand that he was in love, that he had a child, and that he was keeping a fallen creature.

Louise's despair was intense. The indignation of Madame Moreau was not less strong. She saw her son whirling toward the bottom of a gulf the depth of which could not be determined, was wounded in her religious ideas as to propriety, and as it were, experienced a sense of personal dishonour; then all of a sudden her attitude underwent a change. To the questions which people put to her with regard to Frederick, she replied in a sly fashion:

"He is well, quite well."

She was aware that he was about to be married to Madame Dambreuse.

The date of the event had been fixed, and he was trying to think of some way of making Rosanette swallow the thing.

About the middle of autumn she won her action with reference to the kaolin shares. Frederick was told about it by Sénécal, whom he met at his own door, on his way back from the courts.

It had been held that M. Arnoux was privy to all the frauds, and the ex-tutor had such an air of making merry over it that Frederick stopped him from coming further, informing Sénécal that he would convey the intelligence to Rosanette. He presented himself before her with a look of irritation on his face.

"Well, now you are satisfied!"

But, without minding what he had said:

"Look there!"

And she pointed toward her child, which was lying in a cradle close to the fire. She had found it so ill at the house of the wet-nurse that morning that she had brought it back with her to Paris.

The infant's limbs were exceedingly thin, and the lips were covered with white specks, which in the interior of the mouth became, so to speak, clots of blood-stained milk.

"What did the doctor say?"

"Oh! the doctor! He pretends that the journey has increased his—I don't know what it is, some name in 'ite'—in short, that he has the thrush. Do you know what it is?"

Frederick replied without hesitation: "Certainly," adding that it was not serious.

But in the evening he was alarmed by the child's debilitated look and by the progress of these whitish spots, resembling mould, as if life, already abandoning the little frame, had left nothing but matter from which vegetation was sprouting. His hands were cold; he was no longer able to drink; and the nurse, another woman, whom the porter had taken on chance from an office, kept repeating:

"It seems to me he's very low, very low!"

Rosanette was up all night with the child.

In the morning she went for Frederick.

"Just come and look at him. He doesn't move any longer."

He was dead. She took him up, shook him, clasped him in her arms, calling him most tender names, covered him with kisses, broke into sobs, rocked from side to side in a state of distraction, tore her hair, uttered a number of shrieks, and then sank on the edge of the divan, where she lay with her mouth open and a flood of tears rushing from her wildly-glaring eyes.

Then a torpor fell upon her, and all became still in the apartment. The furniture was overturned. Two or three napkins were lying on the floor. It struck six. The night-light had gone out.

Frederick, as he gazed at the scene, could almost believe that he was dreaming. His heart was oppressed with anguish. It seemed to him that this death was only a beginning, and that behind it was a worse calamity, which was just about to overwhelm him.

Suddenly, Rosanette said in an appealing tone:

"We'll preserve the body—shall we not?"

She wished to have the dead child embalmed. There were many objections to this. The principal one, in Frederick's opinion, was that the thing was impracticable in the case of children so young. A portrait would be better. She adopted this idea. He wrote a line to Pellerin, and Delphine hastened to deliver it.

Pellerin arrived at once, anxious by this display of zeal to efface all recollection of his former conduct. The first thing he said was:

"Poor little angel! Ah, my God, what a misfortune!"

But gradually (the artist in him getting the upper hand) he declared that nothing could be made out of those yellowish eyes, that livid face, that it was a real case of still-life, and would, therefore, require very great talent to treat it effectively; and so he murmured:

"Oh, it isn't easy—it isn't easy!"

"No matter, as long as it is life-like," urged Rosanette.

"Pooh! what do I care about a picture being life-like? Down with Realism! 'Tis the spirit that must be portrayed by the painter! Let me alone! I am going to try to conjure up what it ought to be!"

He reflected, with his left hand clasping his brow, and his right hand clutching his elbow; then, all of a sudden:

"Ha, I have an idea! a pastel! With coloured mezzotints, almost spread out flat, a lovely model could be obtained with the outer surface alone!"

He sent the chambermaid for his box of colours; then, having a chair under his feet and another by his side, he began to make great touches with as much complacency as if he had drawn them in accordance with the bust. He praised the little Saint John of Correggio, the Infanta Rosa of Velasquez, the milk-white flesh-tints of Reynolds, the distinction of Lawrence, and especially the child with long hair that sits in Lady Gower's lap.

"Besides, could you find anything more charming than these little toads? The type of the sublime (Raphael has proved it by his Madonnas) is probably a mother and her child!"

Rosanette, who felt herself stifling, went away; and presently Pellerin said:

"Well, about Arnoux; you know what has happened?"

"No! What?"

"It was bound to end that way!"

"What has happened, might I ask?"

"Perhaps by this time he is— Excuse me!"

The artist got up in order to raise the head of the little corpse higher.

"You were saying—" Frederick resumed.

And Pellerin, half-closing his eyes, in order to take his dimensions better: "I was saying that our friend Arnoux is probably by this time locked up!"

Then, in a tone of satisfaction:

"Just give a glance at it. Is that the thing?"

"Yes, 'tis quite right. But about Arnoux?"

Pellerin laid down his pencil.

"As far as I could understand, he was sued by one Mignot, an intimate friend of Regimbart—a long-headed fellow that, eh? What an idiot! Just imagine! one day—"

"What! it's not Regimbart that's in question, is it?"

"It is, indeed! Well, yesterday evening, Arnoux had to produce twelve thousand francs; if not, he was a ruined man."

"Oh! that must be exaggerated," said Frederick.

"Not a bit. It looked to me a very serious business."

At that moment Rosanette reappeared, with red spots under her eyes, which glowed like dabs of paint. She seated herself near the drawing and gazed at it. Pellerin made a sign to the other to hold his tongue on account of her. But Frederick said:

"Nevertheless, I can't believe—"

"I tell you I met him yesterday," said the artist, "at seven o'clock in the evening, in the Rue Jacob. He had even taken the precaution to have his passport with him; and he spoke about embarking from Havre, he and his whole camp."

"What! with his wife?"

"No doubt. He is too much of a family man to live by himself."

"And are you certain of this?"

"Certain, faith! Where do you suppose he would find twelve thousand francs?"

Frederick took two or three turns round the room. He panted for breath, bit his lips, and then snatched up his hat.

"Where are you off to now?" said Rosanette.

He made no reply as he left the room.

CHAPTER XVIII

UNDER THE HAMMER

BETWEEN Frederick and Madame Arnoux stood twelve thousand francs. Without that amount he would see her no more—and there yet lingered in his heart an unconquerable hope. Did she not, as it were, constitute the very substance of his heart, the very foundation of his life? For some minutes he went staggering along the footpath, his mind tortured with anxiety, and nevertheless gladdened by the thought that he was away from the other.

Where was he to get the money? Frederick was well aware from his own experience how hard it was to obtain it immediately, no matter at what cost. There was only one person who could help him in the matter—Madame Dambreuse. She always kept a good supply of bank-notes in her escritoire. He called at her house; and in an unblushing fashion:

"Have you twelve thousand francs to lend me?"

"What for?"

That was another person's secret. She asked who this person was. He would not give way on this point. They were equally determined not to yield. Finally, she declared that she would give nothing until she knew the purpose for which it was intended.

Frederick's face became very flushed; and he stated that one of his comrades had committed a theft. It was necessary to replace the sum this very day.

"Let me know his name? His name? Come! what's his name?"

"Dussardier!"

And he threw himself on his knees, imploring of her not to say a word about it.

"What idea have you got into your head about me?" Madame Dambreuse replied. "One would imagine that you were the guilty party yourself. Pray, have done with your tragic airs! Hold on! here's the money! and much good may it do him!"

He hurried off to see Arnoux. That worthy merchant was not in his shop. But he was still residing in the Rue de Paradis, for he had two domiciles.

In the Rue de Paradis, the porter said that M. Arnoux had been away since the evening before. As for Madame, he could say nothing; and Frederick, having rushed like an arrow up the stairs, laid his ear against the keyhole. At length, the door was opened. Madame had gone out with Monsieur. The servant did not know when they would be back; her wages had been paid, and she was leaving herself.

Suddenly he heard the door creaking.

"But is anyone in the room?"

"Oh, no, Monsieur! it is the wind."

Thereupon he withdrew. There was something inexplicable in such a rapid disappearance.

Regimbart, being Mignot's intimate friend, could perhaps enlighten him? And Frederick got himself driven to that gentleman's house at Montmartre in the Rue l'Empereur.

In front of the house there was a small garden shut in by a grating which was stopped up with iron plates. Three steps before the hall-door set off the white front; and a person passing along the foot-path could see the two rooms on the ground-floor, the first of which was a parlour with ladies' dresses lying on the furniture, and the second the workshop in which Madame Regimbart's female assistants were accustomed to sit.

They were all convinced that Monsieur had important occupations, distinguished connections, that he was a man altogether beyond comparison. When he passed through the lobby with his hat cocked up at the sides, his long grave face, and his green frock-coat, the girls stopped in the midst of their work. He never failed to address to them a few words of encouragement, some observation which showed his ceremonious courtesy; and afterward in their own homes they felt unhappy at not having been able to preserve him as their ideal.

No one, however, was so devoted to him as Madame Regimbart, an intelligent little woman, who maintained him by her handicraft.

As soon as M. Moreau had sent in his name, she came out quickly to meet him, knowing through the servants what his relations were with Madame Dambreuse. Her husband would be back in a moment; and Frederick, while he followed her, admired the appearance of the house and the profusion of oil-cloth that was displayed in it. Then he waited a few minutes in a kind of office, into which the Citizen was in the habit of retiring, in order to be alone with his thoughts.

When they met Regimbart's manner was less eccentric than usual.

He related Arnoux's recent history. The ex-manufacturer of earthenware had excited the vanity of Mignot, a patriot who owned a hundred shares in the *Siècle,* by professing to show that it would be necessary from the democratic standpoint to change the management and the editorship of the newspaper. Under the pretext of making his views prevail in the next meeting of shareholders, he had given the other fifty shares, telling him that he could pass them on to reliable friends who would back up his vote. Mignot would have no personal responsibility, and need not worry himself about anyone; then, when he had achieved success, he would be able to secure a good place in the administration of at least from five to six thousand francs. The shares had been delivered. But Arnoux had at once sold them, and with the money had entered into partnership with a dealer in religious articles. Thereupon came complaints from Mignot, to which Arnoux sent evasive answers. At last the patriot had threatened to bring against him a charge of cheating if he did not restore his share-certificates or pay an equivalent sum—fifty thousand francs.

Frederick's expression was despondent.

"That is not all," said the Citizen. "Mignot, who is an honest fellow, has reduced his claim to one fourth. New promises on the part of the other, and, of course, new evasions. In short, on the morning of the day before yesterday Mignot sent him a written application to pay up, within twenty-four hours, twelve thousand francs, without prejudice to the balance."

"I have the amount!" said Frederick.

The Citizen slowly turned round:

"Humbug!"

"Excuse me! I have the money in my pocket. I brought it with me."

"How you do go at it! By Jove, you do! However, 'tis too late now—the complaint has been lodged, and Arnoux is gone."

"Alone?"

"No, with his wife. They were seen at the Havre terminus."

Frederick grew exceedingly pale. Madame Regimbart thought he was going to faint. He regained his composure with an effort, and had even sufficient presence of mind to ask two or three questions about the matter. Regimbart was grieved at the affair, considering that it would injure the cause of Democracy. Arnoux had always been lax in his conduct and disorderly in his life.

"A regular hare-brained fellow! He burned the cradle at both ends. The petticoat has ruined him! 'Tis not himself that I pity, but his poor wife!" For the Citizen admired virtuous women, and held Madame Arnoux in high esteem.

"She must have suffered much!"

Frederick felt grateful to him for his sympathy; and, as if Regimbart had done him a service, pressed his hand effusively.

"Have you done all that's necessary in the matter?" was Rosanette's greeting to him when he returned.

He replied that he had not been able to pluck up courage to do it, and he walked about the streets at random to divert his thoughts.

At eight o'clock, they went into the dining-room; but they remained seated face to face in silence, giving vent each to a deep sigh every now and then, and finally pushed away their plates.

Frederick drank some brandy. He felt quite shattered, crushed, annihilated, no longer conscious of anything save a sensation of extreme fatigue.

She went to look at the portrait. The red, the yellow, the green, and the indigo made glaring stains that jarred with each other, so that it looked a hideous thing—almost ridiculous.

The dead child was now unrecognisable. The purple hue of his lips made the whiteness of his skin more remarkable. His nostrils were drawn, his eyes hollow; and his head rested on a pillow of blue taffeta, surrounded by petals of camelias, autumn roses, and violets. This was an idea suggested by the chambermaid, and both of them had thus with pious care decorated the little corpse. The mantelpiece, covered with a cloth of guipure, supported silver-gilt candlesticks with bunches of consecrated box in the spaces between them. At the corners were a pair of vases in which pastilles were burning. All these things, viewed in conjunction with the candle, presented the aspect of an altar; and Frederick recalled to mind the night when he had watched beside M. Dambreuse's death-bed.

Nearly every quarter of an hour Rosanette drew aside the curtains to take a look at her child. She saw him in imagination, a few months hence, beginning to walk; then at college, in the middle of the recreation-ground, playing a game of base; then at twenty years a full-grown young man; and all these pictures conjured up by her brain created for her, as it were, the son she would have had, if only he had lived, the excess of her grief intensifying in her maternal instinct.

Frederick, sitting silent in another armchair, was thinking of Madame Arnoux.

Probably, at that moment, she was in a train, with her face leaning against a carriage window, while she watched the country disappearing behind her in the direction of Paris; or else on the deck of a steamboat, as on the occasion when they first met; but this vessel was carrying her away into distant countries, from which she would never return. He next saw her in a room at an inn, with trunks covering the floor, the wallpaper hanging in shreds, and the door shaking in the wind. And after that—to what would she be compelled to turn? Would she have to become a school-mistress or a lady's companion, or perhaps a chambermaid? She was exposed to all the vicissitudes of poverty. His utter ignorance as to what might become of her tortured his mind. He ought either to have prevented her departure or to have followed her. Was he not her real husband? And as the thought impressed itself on his consciousness that he would never meet her again, that it was all over forever, that she was lost to him beyond recall, he felt a rending of his entire being, and the tears that had been gathering since morning in his heart overflowed.

Rosanette noticed this.

"Ah! you are crying just like me! You are grieving, too?"

"Yes! yes! I am—"

He pressed her to his heart, and they both sobbed, locked in each other's arms.

Madame Dambreuse was weeping too, as she lay, face downward, on her bed, with her hands clasped over her head.

Olympe Regimbart having come that evening to try on her first coloured gown after mourning, had told her about Frederick's visit, and about the twelve thousand francs which he had with him ready to transfer to M. Arnoux.

So, then, this money, the very money which he had got from her, was intended to be used simply for the purpose of keeping the other in Paris—for the purpose, in fact, of preserving a mistress!

At first, she broke into a violent rage, and determined to drive him from her door, as she would have driven a lackey. A copious flow of tears had a soothing effect upon her. It was better to keep it all to herself, and say nothing about it.

Frederick brought her back the twelve thousand francs on the following day.

She begged of him to keep the money lest he might require it for his friend, and she asked a number of questions about this gentleman. Who, then, had tempted him to such a breach of trust? A woman, no doubt! Women drag men into every kind of crime.

This bantering tone discomposed Frederick. He felt deep remorse for the calumny he had invented. He was reassured by the reflection that Madame Dambreuse could not be aware of the facts. All the same, she was very persistent about the subject; for, two days later, she again made inquiries about his young friend, and, after that, about another—Deslauriers.

"Is this young man trustworthy and intelligent?"

Frederick spoke highly of him.

"Ask him to call on me one of these mornings; I want to consult him about a matter of business."

She had found a roll of old papers in which there were some bills of Arnoux, which had been duly protested, and which had been signed by Madame Arnoux. It was relative to these very bills Frederick had called on M. Dambreuse on one occasion while the latter was at breakfast; and, although the capitalist had not enforced repayment of this outstanding debt, he had not only got judgment on foot of them from the Tribunal of Commerce against Arnoux, but also against his wife, who knew nothing about the matter, as her husband had not given her any information on the point.

Here was a weapon placed in Madame Dambreuse's hands—she had no doubt about it. But her notary advised her to take no step in the affair. She would have preferred to act through some obscure person, and she thought of that big fellow with such an impudent expression of face, who had offered her his services.

Frederick ingenuously performed this commission for her.

The advocate was enchanted at the idea of having business relations with such an aristocratic lady.

He hurried to Madame Dambreuse's house.

She informed him that the inheritance belonged to her niece, a further reason for liquidating those debts which she should repay, her object being to overwhelm Martinon's wife by a display of greater attention to the deceased's affairs.

Deslauriers surmised that there was some hidden design underlying all this. He reflected while he was examining the bills. Madame Arnoux's name, written by her own hand, brought once more before his eyes her entire person, and the insult which he had received from her. Since vengeance was offered to him, why should he not snatch at it?

He accordingly advised Madame Dambreuse to have the bad debts which went with the inheritance sold by auction. A man of straw, whose name would not be divulged, would buy them up, and would exercise the legal rights thus given him to realise them. He would undertake to provide a man to discharge this function.

Toward the end of the month of November, Frederick, happening to pass through the street in which Madame Arnoux had lived, raised his eyes toward the windows of her house, and saw posted on the door a placard on which was printed in large letters:

"Sale of valuable furniture, consisting of kitchen utensils, body and table linen, shirts and chemises, lace, petticoats, trousers, French and Indian cashmeres, an Erard piano, two Renaissance oak chests, Venetian mirrors, Chinese and Japanese pottery."

"'Tis their furniture!" said Frederick to himself, and his suspicions were confirmed by the door-keeper.

As for who had given instructions for the sale, he could get no information on that matter. But perhaps the auctioneer, Maître Berthelmot, might be able to throw light on the subject.

The functionary did not at first want to tell what creditor was having the sale carried out. Frederick pressed him on the point. It was a gentleman named Sénécal, an agent; and Maître Berthelmot even carried his politeness so far as to lend his newspaper—the *Petites Affiches*—to Frederick.

The latter, on reaching Rosanette's house, flung down this paper wide open on the table.

"Read that!"

"Well, what?" said she with a face so calm that it roused up in him a feeling of revolt.

"Ah! keep up that air of innocence!"

"I don't understand what you are talking about."

"It is you who are selling out Madame Arnoux yourself!"

She re-read the announcement.

"Where is her name?"

"Oh! 'tis her furniture. You know that as well as I do."

"What does that signify to me?" said Rosanette, shrugging her shoulders.

"What does it signify to you? You are taking your revenge, that's all. This is the consequence of your persecutions. Haven't you outraged her sufficiently by calling at her house?—you, a worthless creature! and this the most saintly, the most charming, the best woman that ever lived! Why do you set your heart on ruining her?"

"I assure you, you are mistaken!"

"Come now! As if you had not incited Sénécal to do this!"

"What nonsense!"

Then he was carried away with rage.

"You lie! you lie! you wretch! You are jealous of her! You have got a judgment against her husband! Sénécal is already mixed up in your affairs. He detests Arnoux; and your two hatreds have combined. I saw how delighted he was when you won that action of yours about the kaolin shares. Are you going to deny this?"

"I give you my word—"

"Oh, I know what that's worth—your word!"

And Frederick reminded her of her lovers, giving their names and circumstantial details. Rosanette drew back, all the colour fading from her face.

"You are astonished at this. You thought I was blind because I kept my eyes shut. Now I have had enough of it. We do not die through the treacheries of a woman of your sort. When they become too monstrous we get out of the way. To inflict punishment on account of them would be only to degrade oneself."

She twisted her arms about.

"My God, who can it be that has changed him?"

"Nobody but yourself."

"And all this for Madame Arnoux!" exclaimed Rosanette, weeping.

He replied coldly:

"I have never loved any other woman!"

At this insult her tears ceased to flow.

"That shows your good taste! A woman of mature years, with a complexion like liquorice, a thick waist, big eyes like the ventholes of a cellar, and just as empty! As you think so much of her, go and join her!"

"This is just what I expected. Thank you!"

Rosanette remained motionless, stupefied by this extraordinary behaviour.

She even allowed the door to be shut; then, with a bound, she pulled him back into the anteroom, and flinging her arms around him:

"Why, you are mad! you are mad! this is absurd! I love you!" Then she changed her tone to one of entreaty:

"Good heavens! for the sake of our dead infant!"

"Acknowledge that it was you who did this trick!" said Frederick.

She still protested that she was innocent.

"You will not acknowledge it?"

"No!"

"Well, then, farewell! and forever!"

"Listen to me!"

Frederick turned round:

"If you understood me better, you would know that my decision is irrevocable!"

"Oh! oh! you will come back to me again!"

"Never as long as I live!"

And he slammed the door behind him violently.

Rosanette wrote to Deslauriers saying that she wished to see him at once.

He called one evening, about five days later; and, when she told him about the rupture:

"That's all! A nice piece of bad luck!"

She thought at first that he would have been able to bring back Frederick; but now all was lost. She learned through the doorkeeper that he was about to be married to Madame Dambreuse.

Deslauriers gave her a lecture, and showed himself an exceedingly gay fellow, quite a jolly dog; and, as it was very late, asked permission to pass the night in an armchair.

Then, next morning, he set out again for Nogent, telling her that he was unable to say when they would meet again. In a little while, there would perhaps be a great change in his life.

Two hours after his return, the town was in a state of revolution. The news went round that M. Frederick was going to marry Madame Dambreuse. At length the three Mesdemoiselles Auger, unable to stand it any longer, made their way to the house of Madame Moreau, who with an air of pride confirmed this intelligence. Père Roque became quite ill when he heard it. Louise locked herself up; it was even rumoured that she had gone mad.

Meanwhile, Frederick was unable to hide his dejection. Madame Dambreuse, in order to divert his mind from gloomy thoughts, redoubled her attentions. Every afternoon they went driving in her carriage; and, on one occasion, as they were passing along the Place de la Bourse, she took the idea into her head to pay a visit to the public auction-rooms for the sake of amusement.

It was the first day of December, the very day on which the sale of Madame Arnoux's furniture was to take place. He remembered the date, and expressed repugnance, declaring that this place was intolerable on account of the crush and the noise. She only wanted to get a peep at it. The brougham drew up. He had no alternative but to accompany her.

In the open space could be seen washhand-stands without basins, the wooden portions of armchairs, old hampers, pieces of porcelain, empty bottles, mattresses; and men in blouses or in dirty frock-coats, all grey with dust, and mean-looking faces, some with canvas sacks over their shoulders, were chatting in separate groups or hailing each other in a disorderly fashion.

Frederick urged that they had better not go any further.

"Pooh!"

They ascended the stairs. In the first room, at the right, gentlemen, with catalogues in their hands, were examining pictures; in another, a collection of Chinese weapons were being sold. Madame Dambreuse wanted to go down again. She looked at the numbers over the doors, and led him to the end of the corridor toward an apartment which was blocked up with people.

Frederick immediately noticed the two whatnots belonging to the office of *L'Art Industriel,* her worktable, all her furniture. Heaped up at the end of the room according to their respective heights, they formed a long slope from the floor to the windows, and at the other sides of the apartment, the carpets and the curtains hung straight along the walls. There were, underneath, steps occupied by old men who had fallen asleep. At the left rose a sort of counter at which the auctioneer, in a white cravat, was lightly swinging a little hammer. By his side a young man was writing, and below him stood a sturdy fellow, between a commercial traveller and a vendor of countermarks, crying out: "Furniture for sale." Three attendants placed the articles on a table, at the sides of which sat in a row second-hand dealers and old-clothes women. The general public at the auction kept walking in a circle behind them.

As Frederick entered, the petticoats, the neckerchiefs, and even the chemises were being passed on from hand to hand, and then given back. Sometimes they were flung some distance, and strips of whiteness went flying through the air. After that her gowns were sold, and then one of her hats, the broken feather of which was hanging down, then her furs, and then three pairs of boots; and the selling of these relics, wherein he could trace in a confused sort of way the very outlines of her form, appeared to him an atrocity, as if he had seen carrion crows mangling her corpse. The atmosphere of the room, heavy with so many breaths, made him feel sick. Madame Dambreuse offered him her smelling-bottle. She said that she found the sale of this strange collection highly amusing.

The bedroom furniture was now exhibited. Maître Berthelmot named a price. The crier immediately repeated it in a louder voice, and the three auctioneer's assistants quietly waited for the stroke of the hammer, and then removed the article sold to an adjoining apartment. In this way disappeared, one after the other, the large blue carpet spangled with camel-

lias, which her dainty feet used to touch so lightly as she advanced to
meet him, the little upholstered easy-chair, in which he used to sit facing her when they were alone together, the two screens belonging to the
mantelpiece, the ivory of which had been rendered smoother by the
touch of her hands, and a velvet pin-cushion, which was still bristling
with pins. It was as if portions of his heart had been carried away with
these things; and the monotony of the same voices and the same gestures
benumbed him with fatigue, and caused within him a mournful torpor,
a sensation like that of death itself.

There was a rustle of silk near by. Rosanette touched him.

It was through Frederick himself that she had learned about this auction. When her first feelings of vexation were over, the idea of profiting
by it occurred to her mind. She had come to see it in a white satin vest
with pearl buttons, a furbelowed gown, tight-fitting gloves on her hands,
and a look of triumph on her face.

He grew pale with anger. She stared at the woman who was by his side.

Madame Dambreuse had recognised her, and for a minute each examined the other from head to foot minutely, in order to discover the
defect, the blemish—the one perhaps envying the other's youth, and the
other filled with spite at the extreme good form, the aristocratic simplicity of her rival.

At last Madame Dambreuse turned her head away with a smile of
inexpressible insolence.

The crier had opened a piano—her piano! While he remained standing before it he ran the fingers of his right hand over the keys, and put up
the instrument at twelve hundred francs; then he brought down the figures
to one thousand, then to eight hundred, and finally to seven hundred.

Madame Dambreuse laughed at the appearance of some socket that
was out of gear.

The next thing placed before the second-hand dealers was a little chest
with medallions and silver corners and clasps, the same one which he had
seen at the first dinner in the Rue de Choiseul, which had subsequently
been in Rosanette's house, and again transferred to Madame Arnoux's
residence. Often during their conversations his eyes had wandered
toward it. He was bound to it by the dearest memories, and his soul was
melting with tender emotions about it, when suddenly Madame
Dambreuse said:

"I am going to buy that!"

"But it is not a very rare article," he returned.

She considered it, on the contrary, very pretty, and the appraiser com-
mended its delicacy.

"A gem of the Renaissance! Eight hundred francs, Messieurs! Almost
entirely of silver! With a little whiting it can be made to shine brilliantly."

And, as she was pushed forward through the crush of people:

"What an odd idea!" said Frederick.

"Does it annoy you?"

"No! But what use can be made of a fancy article of that sort?"

"Who knows? Love-letters might be kept in it, perhaps!"

She gave him a look which made the significance very clear.

"A reason the more for not robbing the dead of their secrets."

"I did not imagine she was dead." And then in a loud voice she went on to bid:

"Eight hundred and eighty francs!"

"What you're doing is not right," murmured Frederick.

She began to laugh.

"But this is the first favour, dear, that I have ever asked from you."

"Come, now! doesn't it strike you that at this rate you won't be a very considerate husband?"

Some one had just at that moment made a higher bid.

"Nine hundred francs!"

"Nine hundred francs!" repeated Maître Berthelmot.

"Nine hundred and ten—fifteen—twenty—thirty!" squeaked the auctioneer's crier, with jerks of his head as he cast a sweeping glance at those assembled around him.

"Show me that I am to have a wife who is amenable to reason," said Frederick.

And he gently drew her toward the door.

The auctioneer proceeded:

"Come, come, Messieurs; nine hundred and thirty. Is there any bidder at nine hundred and thirty?"

Madame Dambreuse, who had just reached the door, stopped, and raising her voice to a high pitch:

"One thousand francs!"

There was a murmur of astonishment, and then a dead silence.

"A thousand francs, Messieurs, a thousand francs! Is nobody advancing on this bid? Is that clear? Very well, then—one thousand francs! going!—gone!"

And down came the ivory hammer. She passed in her card, and the little chest was handed to her. She thrust it into her muff.

Frederick felt a great chill penetrating his heart.

Madame Dambreuse was still holding his arm; and she had not the courage to look up at his face in the street, where her carriage was awaiting her.

She flung herself into it, like a thief flying away after a robbery, and then turned toward Frederick. He had his hat in his hand.

"Are you not coming?"

"No, Madame!"

And, bowing to her frigidly, he shut the carriage-door, and signed to the coachman to drive away.

The first feeling that he experienced was one of joy at having regained his independence. He was filled with pride at the thought that he had avenged Madame Arnoux by sacrificing a fortune to her; then, he was astounded at his own act, and he felt doubled up with extreme physical exhaustion.

Next morning his man-servant brought him the news.

The city had been declared to be in a state of siege; the Assembly had been dissolved; and a number of the representatives of the people had been imprisoned at Mazas. Public affairs had become utterly unimportant to him, so deeply preoccupied was he by his private troubles.

He wrote to several tradesmen countermanding various orders which he had given for the purchase of articles in connection with his projected marriage, which now appeared to him in the light of a rather mean speculation; and he execrated Madame Dambreuse, because, on her account, he had been very near perpetrating a vile action. He had forgotten the Maréchale, and did not even bother himself about Madame Arnoux— absorbed only in one thought—lost amid the wreck of his dreams, sick at heart, full of grief and disappointment, and in his abhorrence of the artificial atmosphere wherein he had suffered so much, he longed for the freshness of green fields, the repose of provincial life, a sleeping existence spent beneath his natal roof in the midst of ingenuous hearts. When Wednesday evening arrived, he made his way out into the open air.

On the boulevard numerous groups had gathered. From time to time a patrol came and dispersed them; they got together again in regular order behind it. They talked freely and in loud tones, made chaffing remarks about the soldiers, without anything further happening.

"What! are they not going to fight?" said Frederick to a workman.

"They're not such fools as to get themselves killed for the well-off people! Let them look after themselves!"

And a gentleman muttered, as he glanced across at the inhabitants of the faubourgs:

"Socialist rascals! If it were only possible, this time, to exterminate them!"

Frederick could not, for the life of him, understand the necessity of so much rancour and vituperative language. His feeling of disgust against Paris was intensified by these occurrences. Two days later he set out for Nogent by the first train.

The houses were soon lost to view; the country stretched out before his gaze. Alone in his carriage, with his feet on the seat in front of him, he pondered over the events of the last few days, and then on his entire past. The recollection of Louise came back to his mind.

"She, indeed, loved me truly! I was wrong not to grasp at that chance of happiness. Pooh! let us not think any more about it!"

Then, five minutes afterward: "Who knows, after all? Why not, later?"

His reverie, like his eyes, wandered afar toward vague horizons.

"She was artless, a peasant girl, almost a savage; but so good!"

As he drew nearer to Nogent, her image seemed closer to him. As they were passing through the meadows of Sourdun, he saw her once more in imagination under the poplar-trees, as in the old days, cutting rushes on the edges of the pools. He reached his destination and stepped out of the train.

Then he leaned with his elbows on the bridge, to gaze again at the isle and the garden where they had walked together one sunshiny day, and the dizzy sensation caused by travelling, together with the weakness engendered by his recent emotions, arousing in his breast a sort of exaltation, he said to himself:

"She has gone out, perhaps; suppose I were to go and meet her!"

The bell of Saint-Laurent was ringing, and in the square in front of the church there was a crowd of poor people around an open carriage, the only one in the district—the one which was always hired for weddings. All of a sudden, under the church-gate, accompanied by a number of well-dressed persons in white cravats, a newly-married couple appeared.

He thought he must be labouring under some delusion. But no! It was, indeed, Louise! covered with a white veil which flowed from her red hair down to her heels; and with her was no other than Deslauriers, attired in a blue coat embroidered with silver—the costume of a prefect.

How was this?

Frederick concealed himself behind the corner of a house to let the procession pass.

Shamefaced, vanquished, crushed, he retraced his steps to the railway-station, and returned to Paris.

The cabman who drove him assured him that the barricades were erected from the Château d'Eau to the Gymnase, and turned down the Faubourg Saint-Martin. At the corner of the Rue de Provence, Frederick stepped out in order to reach the boulevards.

It was five o'clock. A thin shower was falling. A number of citizens blocked up the footpath close to the Opera House. The houses opposite were closed. Not a face at any of the windows. All along the boulevard, dragoons were galloping behind a row of waggons, leaning with drawn swords over their horses; and the plumes of their helmets, and their large white cloaks, rising up behind them, could be seen under the glare of the gas-lamps, which shook in the wind in the midst of a haze. The crowd, mute with fear, gazed at them.

In the intervals between the cavalry-charges, squads of policemen arrived to keep back the people in the streets.

But on the steps of Tortoni's, a man—Dussardier—who could be recognised at a distance by his great height, remained standing as motionless as a caryatide.

One of the police-officers, marching at the head of his men, with his three-cornered hat drawn over his eyes, threatened him with his sword.

The other thereupon advancing one step, shouted:

"Long live the Republic!"

The next instant he fell on his back with his arms crossed.

A yell of horror arose from the crowd. The police-officer, with a look of command, made a circle around him; and Frederick, gazing up at him in open-mouthed astonishment, recognised Sénécal.

CHAPTER XIX

AFTER MANY YEARS

FREDERICK travelled a long time.

He experienced the melancholy associated with packet-boats, the chill feeling on waking up under tents, the dizzy effect of mountains and ruins, and the bitterness of broken sympathies.

He returned home.

He mingled in society, and he conceived attachments to many women. But the constant recollection of his first love made them all appear insipid; and besides, the vehemence of desire, the bloom of the sensation had gone. In like manner, his intellectual ambitions had grown weaker. Years passed; and he was merely supporting the burthen of a life in which his mind was unoccupied and his heart bereft of energy.

Toward the end of March, 1867, just as the day was drawing to a close, he was sitting all alone in his study, when a woman suddenly entered.

"Madame Arnoux!"

"Frederick!"

She caught hold of his hands, and drew him gently toward the window. As she gazed into his face, she kept repeating:

"'Tis he! Yes, indeed—'tis he!"

In the lengthening shadows of the twilight, only her eyes were visible under the black lace veil that hid her face.

She laid down on the edge of the mantelpiece a little pocket-book bound in garnet velvet; she seated herself in front of him, and they both remained silent, unable to utter a word, smiling at each other.

At last he asked her a number of questions about herself and her husband.

They were living in a remote part of Brittany for the sake of economy, so as to be able to pay their debts. Arnoux, now almost a chronic invalid, had become quite an old man. Her daughter had been married and was living at Bordeaux, and her son was in garrison at Mostaganem.

Then she raised her head to look at him again:

"But I see you once more! I am happy!"

He did not fail to let her know that, as soon as he heard of their misfortune, he had hastened to their house.

"I knew it!"

"How?"

She had seen him in the street outside the house, and had hidden herself.

"Why did you do that?"

Then, in a trembling voice, and with long pauses between her words:

"I was afraid! Yes—afraid of you and of myself!"

This confession gave him a shock of voluptuous joy. His heart began to throb wildly. She went on:

"Forgive me for not having come sooner." And, pointing toward the little pocket-book covered with golden palm-branches:

"I embroidered it on your account expressly. It contains the amount for which the Belleville property was given as security."

Frederick thanked her, while chiding her at the same time for having given herself any trouble about it.

"No! 'tis not for this I came! I was determined to pay you this visit—then I would go back there again."

And she spoke about the place where they had taken up their abode.

It was a low-built house of only one story; and there was a garden full of huge box-trees, and a double avenue of chestnut-trees, reaching up to the top of the hill, from which there was a view of the sea.

"I go there and sit on a bench, which I have called 'Frederick's bench.'"

Then she gazed at the furniture, the objects of virtu, the pictures, with eager intentness, so that she might be able to carry away the impressions of them in her memory. The Maréchale's portrait was almost hidden behind a curtain. But the gilding and the white spaces of the picture, which showed their outlines through the midst of the surrounding darkness, attracted her attention.

"It seems to me I knew that woman?"

"Impossible!" said Frederick. "It is an old Italian painting."

She said that she would like to take a walk through the streets on his arm.

They went out.

The light from the shop-windows fell, now and then, on her pale pro-file; then once more she was wrapped in shadow, and in the midst of the carriages, the crowd, and the din, they walked on heedless to what was happening around them, hearing nothing, like those who walk across the fields over beds of dead leaves.

They talked about the days which they had formerly spent in each other's society, the dinners at the time when *L'Art Industriel* flourished, Arnoux's fads, his habit of drawing up the ends of his collar and of using cosmetic on his moustache, and other matters of a more intimate and serious character. What delight he experienced when he first heard her singing! How lovely she looked on her feast-day at Saint-Cloud! He recalled to her memory the little garden at Auteuil, evenings at the the-atre, a chance meeting on the boulevard, and some of her old servants, including the negress.

She was astonished at his vivid recollection of these things.

"Sometimes your words come back to me like a distant echo, like the sound of a bell carried by the wind, and when I read love passages in books, it seems to me that it is you about whom I am reading."

"All that people have criticised as exaggerated in fiction you have made me feel," said Frederick. "I can understand Werther, who felt no disgust at his Charlotte for eating bread and butter."

"Poor, dear friend!"

She heaved a sigh; and, after a prolonged silence:

"No matter; we shall have loved each other truly!"

"And still without having ever belonged to each other!"

"That perhaps is all the better," she replied.

"No, no! What happiness we might have enjoyed!"

And it must have been very strong to endure after so long a separation. Frederick wished to know how she first discovered that he loved her.

"It was when you kissed my wrist one evening between the glove and the cuff. I said to myself, 'Ah! yes, he loves me—he loves me;' neverthe-less, I was afraid of being assured of it. So charming was your reserve, that I felt myself the object, as it were, of an involuntary and continuous homage."

He regretted nothing now. He was compensated for all he had suffered in the past.

When they returned to the house, Madame Arnoux removed her bonnet. The lamp, placed on a bracket, threw its light on her white hair. Frederick felt as if some one had struck him in the middle of the chest.

In order to conceal from her his sense of disillusion, he flung himself on the floor at her feet, and seizing her hands, whispered in her ear words of tenderness:

"Your person, your slightest movements, seemed to me to have a more than human importance in the world. My heart was like dust under your feet. You produced on me the effect of moonlight on a summer's night, when around us we find nothing but perfumes, soft shadows, gleams of whiteness, infinity; and all the delights of the flesh and of the spirit were for me embodied in your name, which I kept repeating to myself while I tried to kiss it with my lips. I thought of nothing else. It was Madame Arnoux such as you were with your two children, tender, grave, dazzlingly beautiful, and yet so good! This image effaced every other. Did I not dream of it alone? for always, in the very depths of my soul, were the music of your voice and the brightness of your eyes!"

She accepted with transports of joy these tributes of adoration to the woman whom she could no longer claim to be. Frederick, becoming intoxicated with his own words, came to believe himself in the reality of what he said. Madame Arnoux, with her back to the light of the lamp, stooped toward him. He felt the caress of her breath on his forehead, and the undefined touch of her entire body through the garments that kept them apart. Their hands were clasped; the tip of her shoe peeped out from beneath her gown, and he said to her, as if ready to faint:

"The sight of your foot makes me lose my self possession."

An impulse of modesty caused her to rise. Then, without any further movement, she said, with the strange intonation of a somnambulist:

"At my age!—he—Frederick! Ah! no woman has ever been loved as I have been. No! Where is the use in being young? What do I care about them, indeed? I despise them—all those women who come here!"

"Oh! very few women come to this place," he returned, in a complaisant fashion.

Her face brightened, and then she asked him whether he ever meant to marry.

He swore that he never would.

"Are you perfectly sure? Why should you not?"

"'Tis on your account!" said Frederick, clasping her in his arms.

She remained thus pressed to his heart, with her head thrown back, her lips parted, and her eyes raised. Suddenly she pushed him away from her with a look of despair, and when he implored of her to say something to him in reply, she whispered:

"I would have liked to make you happy!"

Frederick had a suspicion that Madame Arnoux had come to offer herself to him, and once more he was seized with a desire to possess her—stronger, fiercer, more desperate than he had ever experienced before. And yet he felt, the next moment, an unaccountable repugnance to the thought of such a thing, and, as it were, a dread of incurring the guilt of incest. Another fear, too, affected him—lest disgust might afterward take possession of him. Besides, how embarrassing it would be!—

and, abandoning the idea, partly through prudence, and partly through a resolve not to degrade his ideal, he walked away and proceeded to roll a cigarette between his fingers.

She watched him with admiration.

"How dainty you are! There is no one like you! No one!"

It struck eleven.

"Already!" she exclaimed; "at a quarter-past I must go."

She sat down again, but she kept looking at the clock, and he walked up and down the room, puffing at his cigarette. Neither could think of anything further to say. There is a moment at the hour of parting when the person that we love is with us no longer.

At last, when the hands of the clock passed the twenty-five minutes, she slowly took up her bonnet, holding it by the strings.

"Good-bye, my friend—my dear friend! I shall never see you again! This is the last page in my life as a woman. My soul shall remain with you even when you see me no more. May all the blessings of Heaven be yours!"

And she kissed him on the forehead, like a mother.

But she appeared to be looking for something, and presently she asked him for a pair of scissors.

She unfastened her comb, and all her white hair fell down.

With a quick movement of the scissors, she cut off a long lock from the roots.

"Keep it! Good-bye!"

When she was gone, Frederick rushed to the window and threw it open. On the footpath he saw Madame Arnoux beckoning a passing cab. She stepped into it. The vehicle was soon out of sight.

And all was over.

CHAPTER XX

WHEN A MAN'S FORTY

FREDERICK and Deslauriers were talking by the fireside one evening about the beginning of winter. They were once more reconciled by the fatality of their nature, which seemed to force them to reunite and be friends again.

Frederick briefly explained his quarrel with Madame Dambreuse, who had married again, her second husband being an Englishman.

Deslauriers, without telling how he had come to marry Mademoiselle Roque, related how his wife had one day eloped with a singer. In order to expunge to some extent the ridicule that this brought upon him, he had compromised himself by an excess of governmental zeal in the exercise of his functions as prefect. He had been dismissed. After that, he had been an agent for colonisation in Algeria, secretary to a pasha, editor of a newspaper, and canvasser for advertisements, his latest employment being the settling of disputed cases for a manufacturing company.

Frederick, having squandered two thirds of his means, was now living like a citizen of comparatively humble rank.

Then they questioned each other about their mutual friends.

Martinon was now a member of the Senate.

Hussonnet occupied a high position, in which he was fortunate enough to have all the theatres and entire press dependent upon him.

Cisy, given up to religion, and the father of eight children, was living in the château of his ancestors.

Pellerin, after turning his hand to Fourierism, homœopathy, table-turning, Gothic art, and humanitarian painting, had become a photographer; and he might be seen on every dead wall in Paris, where he was represented in a black coat with a very small body and a big head.

"And what about your chum, Sénécal?" asked Frederick.

"Disappeared—I don't know where! And yourself—what about the woman you were so passionately attached to, Madame Arnoux?"

"She is probably at Rome with her son, a lieutenant of chasseurs."

"And her husband?"

"He died a year ago."

"You don't say so?" exclaimed the advocate. Then, striking his forehead:

"Now that I think of it, the other day, in a shop, I met that worthy Maréchale, holding by the hand a little boy whom she has adopted. She is the widow of a certain Monsieur Oudry, and is now very stout. What a change!—she who formerly had such a slender waist!"

Deslauriers acknowledged that he had taken advantage of the other's despair to satisfy himself of that fact by personal experience.

"As you gave me permission, however."

This avowal was a compensation for the silence he had maintained with reference to his attempt with Madame Arnoux.

Frederick would have forgiven him, inasmuch as he had not succeeded.

Although a little annoyed at the discovery, he pretended to laugh at it; and the allusion to the Maréchale recalled the Vatnaz.

Deslauriers had not seen her, nor any of the others who used to come to the Arnoux's house; but he remembered Regimbart perfectly.

"Is he still living?"

"He is barely alive. Every evening regularly he drags himself from the Rue de Grammont to the Rue Montmartre, to the cafés, enfeebled, bent in two, emaciated, a spectre!"

"Well, and what about Compain?"

Frederick uttered a cry of joy, and begged of the ex-delegate of the provisional government to explain to him the mystery of the calf's head.

"'Tis an English importation. In order to parody the ceremony which the Royalists celebrated on the thirtieth of January, some Independents founded an annual banquet, at which they have been accustomed to eat calves' head, and at which they drank red wine out of calves' skulls while giving toasts in favour of the extermination of the Stuarts. After Thermidor, the Terrorists organised a brotherhood of a similar description, which proves how universally prolific folly is."

"You appear to be dispassionate about politics?"

"Effects of age," said the advocate.

Then they each proceeded to summarise their lives.

They had both failed in their objects—the one who dreamed only of love, and the other of power.

What was the reason of this?

"'Tis perhaps on account of not having taken up the proper line," said Frederick.

"In your case that may be so. I, on the contrary, have sinned through excess of rectitude, without giving due weight to a thousand secondary things more important than any. I had too much logic, and you too much sentiment."

Then they blamed luck, circumstances, the epoch at which they were born.

Frederick went on:

"We have never done what we thought of doing long ago at Sens, when you wished to write a critical history of Philosophy and I a great mediæval romance about Nogent, the subject of which I had found in Froissart: 'How Messire Brokars de Fenestranges and the Archbishop of Troyes attacked Messire Eustache d'Ambrecicourt.' Do you remember?"

And, exhuming their youth with every sentence, they continually said to each other:

"Do you remember?"

They saw once more the college playground, the chapel, the parlour, the fencing-school at the bottom of the staircase, the faces of the ushers and of the pupils—one named Angelmare, from Versailles, who used to cut off trousers-straps from old boots, M. Mirbal and his red whiskers, the two professors of linear drawing and large drawing, who were always wrangling, and the Pole, the fellow-countryman of Copernicus, with his planetary system on pasteboard, an itinerant astronomer whose lecture had been paid for by a dinner in the refectory, then a terrible debauch while they were out on a walking excursion, the first pipes they had smoked, the distribution of prizes, and the delightful sensation of going home for the holidays.

It was during the vacation of 1837 that they had called at the house of the Turkish woman.

This was a phrase used to designate a woman whose real name was Zoraide Turc; and many persons believed her to be a Mohammedan, a Turk; this added to the poetic character of her establishment, situated at the water's edge behind the rampart. Even in the middle of summer there was a shadow around her house, which was distinguished by a glass bowl of goldfish near a pot of mignonette at a window. Women in white negligées, with painted cheeks and long earrings, used to tap at the panes as the students passed; and as it grew dark, their custom was to hum softly in their hoarse voices as they stood on the doorsteps.

This home of perdition spread its fantastic notoriety over all the arrondissement. References were made to it in a circumlocutory style: "The place you know—a certain street—at the bottom of the Bridges." It made the farmers' wives of the district tremble for their husbands, and the ladies grow apprehensive as to their servants' virtue, inasmuch as the sub-prefect's cook had been found there; and, of course, it exercised a fascination over the minds of all the young lads of the place.

One Sunday, during vesper-time, Frederick and Deslauriers, having previously curled their hair, gathered some flowers in Madame Moreau's garden, then went out through the gate leading into the fields, and, after taking a wide circuit round the vineyards, came back through the Fishery, and stole into the Turkish woman's house with their big bouquets in their hands.

Frederick presented his as a lover does to his betrothed. But the heat, the fear of the unknown, and even the very pleasure of seeing at one glance so many women at his disposal, excited him so strangely that he turned exceedingly pale, and stood there without advancing a single step or uttering a word. All the girls burst out laughing, amused at his embarrassment. Fancying that they were ridiculing him, he ran away; and, as Frederick had the money, Deslauriers was obliged to follow him.

They were observed leaving the house; and the episode furnished material for a bit of local gossip which was remembered three years later.

They related the story to each other in a prolix fashion, each supplementing the narrative where the other's memory failed; and, when they had finished the tale:

"I believe that was the best time we ever had!" said Frederick.

"Well, perhaps! Yes, I, too, believe that was the best time we ever had," said Deslauriers.